# THE OUTCASTS

## PETER HUTTON

SilverWood

Published in 2016 by SilverWood Books

SilverWood Books Ltd
14 Small Street, Bristol, BS1 1DE, United Kingdom
www.silverwoodbooks.co.uk

Copyright © Peter Hutton 2016
Map design by SilverWood Books 2016

ISBN 978-1-78132-519-3 (paperback)
ISBN 978-1-78132-520-9 (ebook)

British Library Cataloguing in Publication Data
A CIP catalogue record for this book is available from
the British Library

Page design and typesetting by SilverWood Books
Printed on responsibly sourced paper

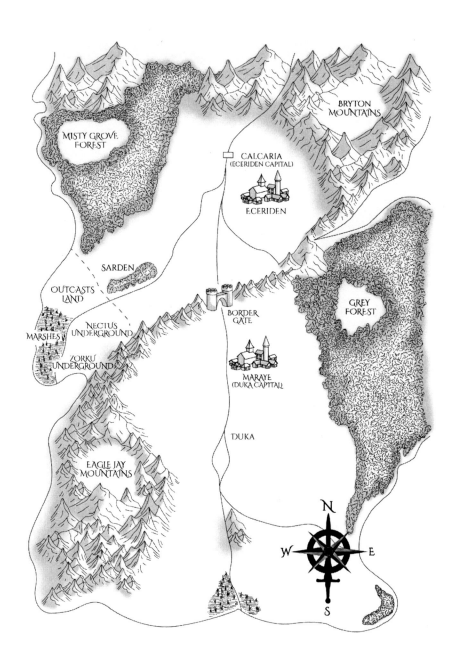

*To all those who have supported me*
*in the creation of this book*

# 1

# THIEF

The wall was high, certainly higher than it looked from a distance. But then again, everything looked smaller from a distance.

Dorren sighed as he gazed up at the daunting obstacle. This was going to make things harder for him. It had to be at least thirty feet high. However, due to the age of the stone, it had eroded a little and this left places he could use as hand holds to climb. At least that made the job easier.

Dorren stuck one hand into a hole in the wall that had been slowly created by the elements and used his other hand to feel around for another grip. Once he found one he began to climb. It was a slow process but at least it was possible. A new wall, or a repaired one, would have made this job impossible.

After a couple of feet, he looked up. A while to go yet, he thought as he made out the top. Why did there have to be a wall? he asked himself with frustration. Why not an open plain, or even just a small fence that could easily be vaulted over? These people had to make things harder for him. However, he did know the reason for it. The wall was there to keep intruders such as him out of the town which lay beyond, and to protect it from any invaders. After all, the town of Sarden was right next to the Outcasts' Land and was prone to the occasional theft. A robber was going to steal from them right now – him!

Dorren was nearly at the top now. It was a shame there was no possibility of using the front entrance, he mused to himself. But the idea was to avoid being noticed, and for a thief he was not very good at it. He would reach the gates and either overact or not even attempt to pretend that his motives were sincere. Lying was not something Dorren was good at, and acting was just another form of lying.

He looked down at the drop below. For some reason heights never bothered him, although he knew his fair share of people for whom they did. As he glanced down he looked at what he was wearing. His trousers and shirt were made from a very tough material, though it was worn away a little at the knees and elbows, which confused him because he couldn't remember ever falling on his elbows. Well, once he was safely back home he could change into something that was not wearing away.

Apart from those items, and leather shoes, he also had a katana strapped to his back and a bag which would soon be filled with stolen food for the journey back home, and whatever else he could find. The only items held within the bag were two syringes with sufficient doses of potions to knock out the toughest man for at least a day. He also had a knife strapped to his leg in case he lost his trusty katana. The sword had managed to keep him out of many unsavoury situations and he had not lost it yet, but it was always important to be prepared for these situations, just in case. Besides, his ideal fighting stance usually had him holding both weapons.

Finally! Dorren reached the top of the wall and looked over. Standing barely a few inches away was a guard looking as surprised as Dorren was to see the man before him. There was a second of silence as they stared at each other, although to Dorren, this second felt a lot longer. The only sound was that of the wind moving past their ears. The guard was dressed in armour with the red phoenix emblem of Eceriden on his chest. Judging by his face he looked about mid-forties, while Dorren was only his mid-twenties. So he did have stamina on his side, but the soldier obviously had strength.

The guard went for his sword and was about to yell, but Dorren was quicker. Going for his knife and drawing it from the scabbard he slashed at the guard's exposed throat. Instead of yelling the guard gurgled as blood gushed from his throat to the floor, his hand frozen on the hilt of his sword.

Dorren cursed. Someone was going to see the blood and body if they passed here. If that happened the alarm would be raised, and then the real problems would start. Quickly, he jumped onto the wall and pushed the guard over the edge. After hearing a thud, he peered over. The guard was lying still on the ground below.

Dorren took a moment to lean on the merlon, breathing a sigh of relief. The outcome could have been a lot worse as his mission might have been over a lot sooner than he intended. He felt relieved that the situation was resolved, but also sick inside, as he did every time he took a life. Dorren didn't like killing but accepted it was necessary for his survival when away from home. This soldier could have had family, but that was something Dorren tried not to think about. The syringe containing a potion to knock someone out was in the bag and he would never have been able to get it out in time.

The first time he killed someone was a couple of years ago, and afterwards he had felt so sick inside that he was surprised that he didn't throw up. However, after a time the sickness he felt when taking a life began to slowly dissipate and now all that was left in his stomach was the bitterness.

Ignoring the sour feeling, he turned round and looked down at the town of Sarden. From this height he could make out most of the town before him. Houses were dotted all over the place, from one end where the slums for the poor and weak stood, to the other which held the more extravagant properties. At the centre of town was the market, which was buzzing with commotion. It was midday so it would be at the peak of life.

Behind the market was the church where the people of Eceriden worshipped their great god Abodem; something that did not sit well with Dorren. All his life he had been taught to hate the gods of both Eceriden and Duka. They were false gods, he thought, and were the reason for his mess. Most Outcasts were thrown from their homes and the land because they would not follow the ways of the gods in Eceriden. People could enjoy each other's company for years. But the moment they find out that the people they had known their entire lives just happen to not believe something they do, they are sent into exile, into the void of the Outcasts' Land where they were expected to die.

Even though it was a terrible thing to do, it was not as bad as what happened in Duka if an individual did not follow their god. A much more barbaric land, if the things Dorren had heard were true.

At the far side of Sarden was the keep where the lord of the town stayed. From the information Dorren had learned, the lord was called Nerida. His wife had died years ago in childbirth and he currently had a son and a daughter. The first heir was the son, called Nok. He would get the town and the surrounding land if his father died. The lord's son was apparently a very skilled fighter and hunter.

The second heir was the daughter, Sileena, and there was little information on her. Apparently she had never been seen by any of the spies keeping an eye on the nearby lord. All they knew was that she existed. This information was important for Dorren as it helped him understand the opposition he was facing. It would be a little unfair if he didn't know whose town he was stealing from, Dorren thought to himself as he observed the keep in the distance.

He looked back to the town and the people moving through the streets. The clothing varied depending on how wealthy the person was. Rags were worn by the very poor, while the rich wore more precious materials. It was easy to tell what class each individual was in. A very typical village.

Dorren looked back down at his own clothing and decided that he would be fine and won't stand out...too much. People would probably suspect he was from the poorer district. Some citizens wore weaponry for protection or just for show, so he didn't need to hide his katana. It was a very fine piece of steel, but was sheathed so the guards would not be able to see its quality. Otherwise he might have been accused of stealing it, considering the clothing he wore. A poor man with a high quality blade. The handle was of a finer construction too, but Dorren had owned the katana his entire life and the handle's inscriptions had faded to the point of being barely legible.

He walked down the staircase and into the village, avoiding anyone's attention until he had finally made his way to the centre. As he entered the market Dorren took careful note of the guards moving around. At the centre of the square stood the flag of Eceriden, with its great red phoenix poised for a fight on a gold background. The flag indicated that any people who did not come from Eceriden wanting to sell their property and goods would have to pay a tax, but this did not stop them. There were stalls all over the place, set in rows so people could easily walk through them and see what each one sold. The foreign traders were still making more money than the amount they paid in tax, so they were happy to sell. Dorren was aware that Eceriden was a very rich land.

There were clothing stalls from all over the land selling silk, leather and even animal skins and rugs. The men from Bryton Mountains had stalls selling the best armour and weaponry ever manufactured in all the land. The people from the Misty Grove Forest were selling the best-crafted furniture and ornaments, which had many people in awe – some even had hidden magical abilities. This was because the forests had access to the finest woods and the Bryton Mountains had the best stone. Both of these kingdoms held close friendships with Eceriden, and the perks of this could clearly be seen through trade.

Mages and wizards were also selling some of their products such as books and staffs. Although some people had absolutely no magical talent, they still managed to make use of the staffs that were sold. Some were infused with magical potential so even the least talented user of magic could still achieve results. Staffs were originally used to enhance the magical abilities of wizards and mages, but over time they had been used for other purposes like helping with everyday life. However, only the wealthy could afford to get one. The making of staffs fell to the most powerful of wizards, so there was a limited number of them to go around and this made them expensive. Dorren didn't really care much about getting his own staff. He had no magical potential and he had done well for himself without it. The tools that he used had served him well so far and so there was no point in fixing his methods if they didn't need fixing.

Dorren passed a magician's stall which sold fake magic items like gas bombs, and other products such as potions to heal wounds quicker, enhance senses and even allow you to see through walls. These items were produced by the weaker magic users and their effects were usually temporary. Some of them even had a few nasty side effects that would dissuade many people from trying them again.

Traders from Duka also came with rich fragrances and perfumes that had managed to grab the attention of a lot of the ladies. Again, very typical, Dorren thought. But there were as few Dukan stalls as there were wizards' ones. This was probably due to the tensions between the kingdoms, mostly over religious beliefs. Dorren sighed at the thought. Perhaps he was being brainwashed by those at home, but he never dwelled on that thought for long. The two kingdoms were at war many years ago over their religious differences; however, that was before Dorren's time. Peace was made and it was a bitter peace as neither side actually admitted whether they lost or not.

Right then, there were three things he had to do in the town, not including getting in and out. First he had to steal food from one of the stalls. Although the Outcasts managed to grow plenty of food for their own, Dorren had none for the return journey and home was about two days' travel away, so it would be ideal if he could manage to get something. The last thing he needed was to achieve his goals only to collapse on the return journey. Unfortunately, he could not just buy the food. Outcasts left their old homes with nothing when they were exiled, and they couldn't make any currency of their own, so stealing was the only way. A couple of pieces of fruit and a loaf of bread ought to do it. There was a river further south so he could get all the fresh water he needed from there.

Task two was to steal whatever jewels he could from the town without being noticed. But his timing was a bit off. The massive number of people around him made stealing from the stalls rather difficult, especially those with precious items as the guards seemed to be paying closer attention to them, for obvious reasons.

The third and final task was to kidnap either the lord's daughter or his son. Of the two Nok would certainly put up more of a fight, but the ransom the lord would pay would be a lot more than for Sileena as Nok was the rightful heir to the land. Most of the money made from the ransom would go to the Outcasts' cause, which was to be granted full independence. The rest of the wealth would go to drying up and turning the marshes next to the ocean into decent land to live on. This would greatly expand their borders.

Eceriden and Duka did not see the land of the Outcasts as a great threat to them. They were too busy bickering amongst themselves. They also believed that the Outcasts' Land was too small to be a threat, and that the inhabitants were preoccupied with fighting amongst each other. It was true that the land was home to different groups, but there was no fighting. On the contrary, they were working together to achieve the same goals. Dorren laughed quietly to himself at the thought. The Outcasts were more of a threat to Eceriden and Duka than they realised.

After a bit of walking around he eventually found the bakery stall. As he approached Dorren saw that the baker was a fairly broad-shouldered man who looked like he was in his mid-thirties and wore neat leather trousers, a white shirt and an apron. He gave Dorren a quick smile and nod as he neared and then went to serve another costumer. Dorren looked back and fore and saw no guards. This would probably be the best time, with everything clear to get the food he needed. He grabbed the loaf of bread nearest him and put it in his bag before quickly turning to move away. However, within a few steps a hand caught him on the shoulder. Dorren turned to see the baker staring back, and he was clearly very angry. There was even a vein sticking out on the man's forehead. This was probably a clear indication that the baker had caught him in the act. How on earth did thieves manage it without getting caught? He always got caught. This was bad.

Dorren instinctively kicked the baker into one of his stands, grabbed another loaf of bread and made a run for it.

"Guards!" The voice – probably the baker's – sounded and faded as Dorren ran. He turned a corner into a side street where a guard was waiting for him. As the guard swung his sword Dorren ducked underneath it, took out his knife and jammed it into the soldier's leg, causing the man to collapse. He then ran past the man and managed to get round the corner before the guard hit the ground. As Dorren ran he could hear footsteps from behind that obviously belonged to other guards giving chase. He weaved round another corner, and then another and another, avoiding guards here and there while trying to avoid detection. The footsteps from behind gradually diminished until it was clear that he had lost them. However, after many corners and alleyways he was now hopelessly lost.

Forget the three plans now – the alarm was sounded and there was absolutely no chance of succeeding. It wouldn't be long until an armed force would be out and looking for him. A new plan was needed, and this plan was simply to find a way out of the town. This was going to prove difficult because for one there was a brick wall surrounding the town with guards stationed all over, and Dorren was lost so would likely blunder into the nobles' hall where he would not be greeted so kindly. From this point on he would never try something like this again. It was clear this was not his greatest strength. This could be the only chance he got, as he might not see past today. So instead of going round corners, he would have to try and maintain a straight path until he could reach the edge of the town.

Eventually after another minute of walking Dorren could finally see a wall at the end of a street. If he could run for it, climb the steps and head back down the other side without being noticed he would be completely free, and with enough food to get home. He would be a failure but he would be safe. No doubt Severa and Pagar would not let this go. Pagar especially was going to have a fit. Not because Dorren had failed, but because he had left his home when he was not supposed to. Dorren at least wanted to say he was successful, but apparently this was not going to be the case. He could not help but feel despair. Whichever way this played out he was not going to be happy.

When Dorren reached the clearing at the end of the street the wall expanded and suddenly stopped. This confused him for a moment before he realised that it was not the wall at all, but the keep. He cursed. Getting out of the town was going to be that much more difficult...or was it? He looked again. This place held a lot of resources. Wine, food, clothing and weapons. He could sneak in and steal a guard's uniform and the rest would be easy. This was his chance.

Dorren sneaked past two guards and into the keep. Their attention was attracted to the commotion taking place not far away – his escape had created quite a stir amongst the people. He then moved through the corridors without too much difficulty – the place was deserted. This was the lord's house, so why were there so few people here? Perhaps they were all at the market. It was brilliant that all the soldiers were out looking for him in the town and not in the keep. Dorren had also studied the keep's map before he arrived, so finding the storeroom was easy. He just had to stay away from the lord's rooms, as the family were no doubt being protected by fighting odds that even Dorren would not willingly face. He peered round the corner and saw another guard at the entrance, and held his dagger out at the ready. News spread fast. The whole town must know now that a thief was in their midst. He'd thought that there would be the occasional thief stealing bread within the town, but apparently not. The people here seemed to be pure-hearted. Or were they just too scared to break the rules?

Dorren peered round the side to the guard, who had clearly not noticed the head sticking round the corner. The quickest man will win, Dorren thought to himself. He dashed round the corner and headed straight for the man. The guard noticed and raised his sword in response, but was too slow as Dorren hit him on the head with the hilt of the dagger. The man fell to the floor with a thud, out cold. It would be a while before he could recover.

Dorren took a step over him and entered the room beyond. He closed the door behind him and looked round. The room was filled with all kinds of fruit and vegetables, a lot of which seemed to be rotting a bit. Obviously the people of Sarden were well fed to be able to leave some food to rot. On the other side was armour of many different sizes, and weapon racks carrying different varieties of swords, spears, bows and arrows, pikes, maces and daggers. At the far end of the room were some wine shelves and a huge assortment of wines and mead. Clearly the lord liked his drink. They took up more room than the weapons and food did, and it was a rather large storeroom, all of which was devoted to the keep itself. There were other stores in town that were intended for the public. This was the lord's private stash.

Looking, Dorren noticed that beside the wines was a young woman, about early twenties, holding what looked like a bottle of red wine in her hands. She had long brown hair that was tied back neatly, and was wearing a blue dress that covered her from shoulders to feet. He couldn't even see her feet. This was not important to Dorren as he gazed upon the one trinket that was on her finger. It was the ring of nobility. The girl was of nobility, so this must be Sileena. Ah, hope at last.

She had a confused expression on her face, but recoiled when Dorren smiled. Perhaps he smiled too harshly. It was an evil smile, but the point was made. She made a run for the weapon rack and drew out a broadsword that was clearly too heavy for her as she tried to lift it off the ground and point it towards him. Well, at least he now knew how much difficulty she was going to be. The girl clearly had no fighting capabilities, and the fact that he had not been blasted into the wall indicated she had no magical potential either. This should be easy, he thought.

He moved casually towards her and put his knife back into its holster. As he approached he had noticed the look of panic in her face and could not help but wonder what she planned to do next. Gazing at her expression as he approached, he caught her eyes. Their colour was unlike that of any eyes he had seen before. They were golden. You couldn't help but notice something that you don't usually see – not a mere hint of gold, but really noticeable. But his attention soon shifted back to her efforts to wield the broadsword. She didn't say much, he thought to himself. Not even to say 'stop' or 'don't come closer'. Did she know these would have been futile efforts? Or was it because she was spending all her energy trying to handle that sword?

"Get out or I'll stab you!"

Hmm, thought Dorren. Apparently I speculated too soon. The high-pitched way she said it didn't make the threat very…well…threatening.

Once he neared her, she made a lunge for him. Dorren took a step to the side and drew the needle from his bag. But when she attacked she couldn't bring the sword round for a second attempt in time before Dorren moved to the side and plunged the needle into her neck. It was a knockout potion for the purpose of kidnapping one of Lord Nerida's children, but she didn't know that. She probably thought he was an assassin out to kill her.

Once the needle was removed he let her go and the girl walked dizzily away towards the door, and after a few metres fell. Dorren caught her before she hit the ground. He was a bad person, but not bad enough to let that happen. She had to be kept in good condition anyway, otherwise Lord Nerida would come back to his home with a vengeance. Right, time to get her out of here, he thought, looking around the room. There had to be a means of getting her out.

He retrieved a sack that was big enough for her and put her in, then quickly grabbed some rope from the weapons rack and put that in as well before heading for the exit. She wasn't too heavy to carry but if the guards found out who he was then he would not be able to run with her for long.

He reached the unconscious guard and stepped over him once again. The guy must have been her bodyguard. What a dreadful bodyguard, as he could not handle Dorren for more than a second. He must be new.

Dorren continued back the way he came and towards the exit, but as he neared he saw another man blocking his way and looking right at him. He was around his early thirties with short black hair and a black shirt and trousers, and he was very big. He must have been about 6' 4" with broad shoulders and arms, but with an agile look about him. It was a good thing that Dorren wasn't going to fight him with his disguise on. But then, why was this man glaring at him? Dorren looked down and cursed. He had been so preoccupied with Sileena that he had completely forgotten about the disguise. Well, he was going to have to fight him. Just what he needed.

He put the sack down gently, and at the same time picked up a stone as the man stood silently waiting for Dorren to make the first move. Why was he not calling for aid? The black attire he wore might mean that he was also not where he was supposed to be. But considering that he had clear intentions to harm Dorren, and a very confident expression, Dorren suspected that the man held a sense of confident victory about him. This angered Dorren. He thought he was going to win this fight without backup. I'm just going to have to show the man otherwise, he thought.

He braced himself and lobbed the stone down the corridor, aiming straight for the larger man's head. However, the man caught it in his hand with a sneer on his face. He threw it back with such ferocity that Dorren only just managed to duck in time as the stone shattered on the wall behind him.

Dorren stood up again and drew his katana for the first time today. The man drew his own broadsword, except unlike Sileena, this man wielded a sword that actually looked like it suited him and he wasn't waving it about stupidly. Apparently he was not going to be as easy as Sileena.

Dorren charged and made a stab at the man, but it was parried at an angle so that the man could stab back quickly. However, Dorren saw this coming and took a step to the side. The man adapted the stab into a swing, and Dorren had to quickly block it with his sword. The force sent him back two steps to avoid falling to the ground. The broadsword swung again, and the katana parried it at an angle so it would bounce off and the man would take that much longer to recover. Dorren was about to make another stabbing attack when the man punched him in the face, realising that the sword wouldn't come round in time. Both Dorren and the man took a step back, readying themselves again, and attacked. An exchange of blows occurred as one tried to get the advantage over the other. It seemed to be an even match and it became clear that the loser would be the one who made the first mistake.

The man made another jab, but went too far and stumbled forward. Dorren seized the opportunity and made a downward sweep with his katana, cutting the man's sword arm clean off. The arm fell to the ground with the sword hitting the stone, making a clattering noise.

The mutilated man did not show pain, but rather shock and despair as Dorren then turned his sword sideways and jammed it into his heart. The man slumped to the ground and was still.

Dorren did not hesitate and quickly grabbed the sack containing Sileena before racing outside again and back through the city. Maintaining the same tactic of going in one direction, he kept going until he eventually found the real wall and not another keep. It would have been really bad luck to come across two keeps, Dorren mused himself as he made his way to the wall and could see no guards nearby.

There were steps further along, and he moved across and up the stairs to the top of the wall. Dorren then dipped into the sack and pulled out the rope. Luckily Sileena was still unconscious. She should be out for a while, as the knockout potion was supposed to knock out fully-grown men for at least a day. Hopefully Sileena would be out cold for long enough to allow Dorren get all the way back safely. Dorren tied the rope round the sack and lowered it to the ground below. Once it had reached the bottom he let the rope fall, and at that point he heard a yell from behind.

Sighing, Dorren knew what that meant. It was a miracle that he had made it this far without being caught, but it was still annoying that he was so close, only to be seen once more. He turned round and saw another guard, this one knocking an arrow and readying it to fire. Quickly Dorren disappeared over the side and started to climb down as the arrow flew over the wall where he had been standing. The man was obviously a good shot, considering that when Dorren last checked, the archer was a distance away.

He raced down as fast as he could and almost slipped as one of the hand holds did not support his weight and broke off the wall. Luckily he managed to catch another one in time and kept moving. At a reasonable height he dropped and hit the ground below with a thud, bending his knees as he braced against the impact. At that point the archer appeared at the top of the wall and released the arrow. Luckily it hit the ground beside Dorren as the man was obviously in too much of a hurry to aim correctly. If he had taken his time, Dorren knew he would have been dead.

Without hesitation he picked up the sack and made a run for it. Another arrow flew overhead and hit the ground ahead of him. Keep missing, Dorren desperately thought to himself – safety was just a short distance away and he would be out of range for the archer. By the time the soldiers made it round to where he was now he would be long gone. But when the second arrow flew he knew it was futile.

They were too close. The man was a good shot. There was no escape.

But then something strange happened. He felt a sensation hit him. It was so unusual, like everything seemed to slow down. He could sense the land; he could sense his surroundings and feel them move. He even knew that a few metres away there was a single ant that seemed to have lost its colony a few metres to its right. He could feel the arrow flying through the air, and knew that at its current velocity and angle it would hit his head directly.

He turned as fast as he could, and with all his might swung his arm round, catching the arrow with an inch between the point and his forehead.

For a second everything stood motionless and still as the sensation slowly disappeared and Dorren was back to his normal self. The archer on the wall was as stunned as he was. But after a second it was Dorren that came to his senses first, and he quickly gave the archer a finger gesture before turning and running again. The archer still just remained there, stunned, as Dorren kept running out of range of the bow and to safety.

# 2

# OUTCASTS

"What do you mean, escaped?!" Lord Nerida was in another one of his rages again, Nok thought to himself. This happened frequently and everyone always wondered when the next one would take place. One time he'd started yelling that his food was not cooked. But when he found out that it was supposed to be served cold, he started raging about nothing. The angry episode would eventually increase as he would usually start hitting his servants who did the littlest thing wrong.

Sileena would often receive most of the yelling. Whenever Nok was there he would make sure she was escorted away to her chambers before she was actually hit herself. But those were the times when he was there to put a stop to it. What about the times when Nok was not there? The thought made him uncomfortable. However, he usually didn't care when his father was in one of his rages. He stopped caring a long time ago. But this one did bother him. Not because food was stolen, not because a guard was dead but because his younger sister was missing. This had him feeling agitated. How did this happen? More guards should have been stationed to guard her. His little sister had been taken by a bandit and dragged to some unknown place where she could be going through hell. That didn't seem to bother Lord Nerida, though. He was in a rage because the thief had escaped, not because of what he had escaped with.

"I'm sorry my lord, I tried to stop him but he caught my arrow in mid-fligh—"

"I don't care!" yelled Lord Nerida, his face glowing several shades of red. Nok was standing in the hall where meetings with the lord took place within the keep. The hall was large, with pillars dotted down the left and right sides and was constructed entirely from highly detailed marble. At one side of the great room was a massive wooden door. The wood was probably oak, but Nok had never bothered to find out. It just didn't seem that important, and he was usually too busy. However, the door was highly furnished. Two of Lord Nerida's personal bodyguards were standing at either side of it. They were heavily armoured and very big men. To Nerida, the bigger the better. They could be used for intimidation as well as brutality when circumstances required.

At the other side of the hall was a set of stairs that led up to the most highly detailed chair in all of Sarden. It was where Nerida was sitting before he stood up and started bellowing at the two men kneeling and scared out of their minds at the bottom of the stairs. Two guards, just as big as the two at the door, were standing behind the lord's chair.

"Where the hell is Radikador anyway? I need him here!"

Nok was hearing every word ringing through his ears, though he didn't think this was going to last much longer. He was standing at his father and lord's side and, because of the yelling, Nok could swear that the ear closest to his father was going numb. He had to suppress a sigh.

"But sir, he was too quick, there was nothing we could do." One of the two men kneeling gave a very strange tale of how he'd tried to shoot the thief down, but his story of how the thief caught his arrow in mid-flight was hard to believe. Even if his story was true, the archer had tried to shoot down the thief while he was carrying Sileena. The arrow might have hit her, and then he would be facing an even graver sentence.

The other man kneeling was the soldier who had been guarding Sileena before being knocked out just before she was taken. They had both failed to do their jobs. The guard failed to protect Sileena and the archer on the wall let the thief escape. Had the decision been Nok's, he would have had them repurposed until they realised the importance of their jobs and understood to what extent their failure has cost them.

"There is always something you could do! Where's Radikador?!"

Nok's ear was now ringing in a manner that he knew was not going to go away for hours, but he was not going to move. If he did, then he would be disrespecting his lord and that was something that he would not do.

There was a loud banging on the massive wooden door at the other side of the hall and a soldier came rushing into the room.

"My lord," he said, panting, "Radikador is dead."

"What! How?" Nerida replied.

"My lord, it looks like he fought the thief and lost. His arm was cut clean off and he was stabbed through the heart."

Nerida went pale. Radikador was the best hunter and swordsman ever, and he was killed in a fight with a simple thief? The thought was unnerving.

"You see," one of the kneeling men said, "there was nothing we could do if Radikador was killed."

"Quiet!" Nerida had enough. "You disrespectful scum!"

The man faced the floor again and fell silent.

"Sir," the man who came in the door said, "what should we do about getting Sileena back? The thief has no doubt come from the Outcasts' Land and today's events show that he is clearly skilful. Once he reaches his land, and with our current resources, it will be near impossible to get Sileena back."

Nerida actually had a look of concern on his face. He sighed and sat back down, pondering the situation. He then started taking deep breaths and scratching his beard. There was silence in the room. Nok didn't know which of the two was most uncomfortable – the screaming or the deathly quiet. Well, it was not quite as quiet as the ringing seemed happy to continue playing in his ear. Nerida seemed to calm a little as he was deliberating what to do now that Radikador was dead.

"Nok," he said in a calm voice.

"Yes, my lord?"

"I need you to gather several of our best trackers and go after Sileena. I also want you to bring back the thief's head."

"It will be done, my lord." A sense of determination filled Nok. He was going to be able to get his sister back, and get revenge on the man who caused much despair and death in the town. "What about those two?" Nok said, pointing at the two kneeling men.

Nerida didn't hesitate. "Execute them immediately. May they be an example to what happens when someone fails me."

A look of shock crossed both men's faces. Nok thought the sentence was a little harsh. It was not as though they had abandoned their posts. They were just really bad at their tasks. But this man was his lord and his father. He was not going to dispute the order.

As the four broad men and the soldier who came through the door advanced, one of the kneeling men drew his sword and charged at Nerida in a desperate act of defiance. It took another second for the archer to follow suit and get an arrow ready to fire. Nok considered for a moment that they should probably have had their weapons removed before being told they were to be executed. When faced with death, most would try to fight it if they had the means to do so.

Nerida hadn't budged, and didn't seem to take any notice of what was going on. His was a kind of bored look, as if he had seen this whole thing coming. He was a user of magic, and yet he did nothing even though he could probably kill his assailants with a wave of his hand.

Nok quickly went towards the charging man and drew his sword. The guard lunged at Nok, which he easily parried before stabbing his sword through the man's heart. He fell down the steps, dead. The man didn't even put up much of a fight, and yet he'd been assigned to guard Sileena? The thief wouldn't have needed to sneak up on him. He could probably have taken him on with his little finger.

The archer at this point had fired an arrow before the soldier who came through the door plunged his sword through the archer's chest from behind. One of the big soldiers behind Nerida stepped in front of him and the arrow sank into his shoulder. He didn't even flinch. The big guards really did have their uses if they could just stand in front of the target and take the shot. A very loyal man to do that. Or just plain stupid.

"Nok, prepare to leave," Nerida ordered.

Nok nodded and began to turn and walk for the exit as the large soldier pulled the arrow out of his shoulder. Finally, he thought. Time to have some vengeance.

Sileena opened her eyes and looked around. Her vision was a bit blurred and she could not make out anything. She must have slept for too long because the light was bright. It must be sometime in the afternoon. Oh no – her father was going to kill her if he found out. It was under debate in her mind as to whether she meant that last statement literally. Because she was the lord's daughter and not his son, she was treated like a slave and if she screwed up she would likely get beaten. For the moment, though, she didn't care. She was pretty used to the beatings by now, and anyway she was too tired to bother getting up, even though her bed was unbelievably uncomfortable. It was unusually uncomfortable. Had her brother put rocks in her bed for a joke again?

Wait – she remembered getting wine for her lord. She had turned round and a stranger who was clearly not supposed to be in the stores was looking at her with a look of newfound hope. His intentions were clearly malign, so she grabbed the first sword she could reach but it was too heavy for her and so when she lunged forward the sword carried her forward, and the stranger stepped to the side and she felt a quick pain in her neck before…waking up now. She wasn't in her bed at all. The reason she felt like she was sleeping on rocks was because she really was lying on rocks; more like small stones and pebbles really. Sileena could also feel a breeze over her so she must be outside, not in her bedchamber. The situation was bad, and so she had to be careful.

It was a deathly quiet. Only the wind could be heard in the background. Perhaps the man who had taken her had gone off gathering or hunting or whatever these people did. Not likely, though. He was probably close by, and so she had to make no sudden movements just in case she provoked a response.

She slowly rubbed her eyes and moved her head round to get a better view. This time it was easier to see and she could clearly make out the bright blue sky. There were a few clouds hovering overhead but for the most part it was a nice day. She turned her head further to the side in the hope of making out her surroundings. She was lying on the ground next to a river. It was a bit surprising that she hadn't heard it until she actually saw it. Looking around to the side of the river she saw that she was in a forest. The trees were towering but thin, with no branches growing from their trunks until a few metres from the ground. The wind flowing through the branches seemed to make the forest feel alive. It was enchanting. Across the river there were no trees at all – just an open plain of grass. In the distance Sileena could see mountains and the distant clouds that covered the peaks. The place where she was lying was clearly a beautiful place, and she would have happily admired it for a long time and stayed put if not for her circumstances.

She continued to move her head slowly, looking for the kidnapper. There was a massive boulder sitting next to the river about six metres away from her. On top of that boulder was the man who had kidnapped her. He seemed to be doing nothing, just staring out to the mountains. This was a good thing for her though because it meant he was facing away from her. She was going to have to move quickly and quietly to try and get away. She would move deeper into the forest and out of sight. Once that was done and she knew she was clear of this man, she could decide what her next move would be. She slowly sat up and started to crawl away.

"I wouldn't do that if I were you." The voice was very calm and clear. A feeling of dread cascaded through her. Sileena turned to face him. He hadn't budged at all, and was still staring at the mountains with his back to her. She began to move away again in the hope that what she had just heard was all in her head.

"What do you plan to do once you get away from me? The forest is home to the wolves and the giant wolf-beast Vartak." At this point the thief finally turned his head and faced her. "How well do you think you will fare in there? And you couldn't cross the river into the plains because that would be going the wrong way. I'm interested in hearing." His face was very young and pale. He must be somewhere in his twenties. He had short, scruffy brown hair. His face was clean-shaven but a little dirty, probably because he was a bandit and didn't wash. But then why was he clean-shaven? Perhaps he did wash and he only looked dirty from the travelling he had done. He had a medium build and was clearly athletic. There was no way she could outrun him, so she glared at him in the hope that he would find that she was not easy prey.

"I don't know what your intentions are for me so I don't know whether I would be better off with a pack of wolves and their beast leader."

The man gave a gentler smile this time, compared to the one he had given her back in the stores. "Good point. Very well, if you don't prove a hassle and do as I say then you will not be harmed at all. I give you my word." He said it softly, and his face was gentle. She found it hard not to believe him. But there was still a wariness about her and she had to be certain. This person kidnapped her, and had probably killed a few people in his life. How was she to know whether his word was at all trustworthy? The kidnapper didn't seem to care at all about this line of questioning.

"How am I supposed to believe someone who took me against my will?"

"Again, another good point, but then again do you have a choice? Now, we will have to get moving or else we won't get back before dark." He stood up and faced the river, looking out towards the mountains. "I will need to carry you."

"What?!" She was shocked at the statement. "I can walk myself, and to hell if I'm going to make this easy for you. You will have to force me because I'm going back into the forest and there is nothing you can do to change my mind."

At that point the thief took out a syringe and held it so she could see it, but kept facing across the river. She knew that this was now basically futile.

"The reason I carry you is only to get across this river – after all, you do not want to get that pretty blue dress of yours ruined in the water."

Sileena looked down and saw that her dress was already a bit dirty. She knew that if she went through the water the dress would be as good as ruined. But he said that as if she would care. She didn't care if her dress got ruined. There were plenty of others that she could wear.

"Besides," the kidnapper continued, "I will be quite honest with you. If you had tried to run away I would have caught up to you, knocked you out and dragged you back anyway. I've stolen you for the ransom, and frankly that makes you too valuable to us just to let the wolves eat you."

"Us?" Sileena said, stunned. There must be a group of these bandits. They probably realised that they stood a better chance in numbers.

"Not now," replied the kidnapper, still looking across the river. "We must cross this river and keep moving right now or else we will not make it back before nightfall. Unless you want to go hungry, because I only have enough food for the rest of the day." There was a bit more seriousness to his tone compared to before.

Sileena looked up at the sky and could see that the sun was soon going to disappear behind the mountains. She must have been unconscious for the whole day. "How long have I been asleep?"

"For a day and a half." This was a day longer than she thought, and probably why she felt so hungry. Another point she got wrong. Sileena couldn't help but feel powerless. This man was probably lying to her. He might have incredibly unpleasant things planned. Someone who would kidnap a helpless girl was definitely not a good person. The thief seemed to have his mind elsewhere when he was talking to her as he was facing across the river with his back to her. She could run right now and probably be out of sight before he turned around. Then again, he said he would catch her and Sileena did believe him on that point. She weighed her options. If she ran away, Sileena would likely be killed by the wolves. She heard the stories of the wolves of the forest. They were apparently very intelligent for animals, and not at all a friendly bunch. And Vartak was a very big wolf who, if the tales were true, had a paw the size of a man's torso. No man entered those woods.

If the thief caught her, though, she would be injected again and fall unconscious. She would much rather be awake, so she knew where she was going to retrace her steps for when the time was right to get away. Sileena also had an idea that the thief was one of the Outcasts, and she had heard that they were a barbaric group. The forest lay between her town of Sarden and the Outcasts' Land, which meant that was where they were probably going. People used to joke that the wolves of the forest were more intelligent than the Outcasts because the Outcasts kept killing each other for power. This meant that she was better off with the stupid Outcasts as at least with them she might be able to craft an escape plan. So for now she would cooperate, but just for now.

"Fine, I'll go with you."

"Splendid," the kidnapper said as he put the syringe back into his pocket and turned to face her again. He then indicated her to come to him. She did so with a feeling like she was giving in, and had to remind herself that her options were rather limited, and this was the best decision to make in the circumstances. When she reached him he picked her up over his shoulder and took a step into the water. He was ankle-deep, knee-deep and very soon up to his waist in the river. Sileena could feel the thief's hand on the back of her thigh, and thought that was fair enough. He must have a little decency, as it could have been somewhere else. And he was gentle. This was strange to her, as she was not usually handled gently. Her brother stopped holding hands with her at the age of five, as he thought it too much for girls. She had always dressed herself, and had no one to help as far back as she could remember. And the only other person to touch her was her father, and that was only to hit her when he was in the midst of one of his angry episodes.

She was facing the river and could see it flowing downstream. The current was very strong and she could see the water rising a couple inches above the thief's waist. If she had attempted to cross it herself the tide could have easily taken her and she would have been swept away. The combined weight of the two of them must be what was keeping the thief standing instead of him being forced to swim as hard as he could to cross. After they passed the middle of the river the water level began to drop until the thief managed to get out. But a question came to Sileena's mind. She was a curious individual, and she knew it.

"How did you manage to get through the forest and survive? I could imagine that you might fight off one or two of the wolves but no one gets through the forest safely, especially carrying an unconscious person over their shoulder."

They were now out of the water and the thief put Sileena back onto her feet.

"Let's just say I am familiar with the wolves."

They continued walking and followed the river. She could see the river widening a little, and getting deeper. The point where they crossed was probably the only point safe enough to do so without drowning. She was going to have to try and remember it for when she ran back. But then, she was still going to have to find some way to get through the forest without becoming a tasty snack for the wolves. She just needed to find out how the thief did it, because the wolves would not be able to tell one human from the next so there must be a way to be recognised as an Outcast and get through safely.

"That does not fully answer my question."

"What do you think I am, stupid?" He sounded bemused. "You will have to try harder than that to get the information you need to get back."

Fine, she thought to herself, maybe they were not that stupid as to allow her to ask the questions while they gave the answers. But she would find a way.

"By the way, you can't hide the fact that you are taking me to the Outcasts' Land. So there is no point in trying to hide that from me."

The thief glanced at her, and then faced the direction in which they were heading again. "Clever girl. It doesn't matter anyway, considering you were going to figure it out when we actually get there."

"So how are you going to be protecting me as a hostage?"

The thief looked at her with a confused expression on his face. "What do you mean, protect you?"

"You know – if you want your money I will need to still be alive by the time the exchange is made, and still in your hands. What if I get stolen by another one of your kind, or killed? It will have been a complete waste of time to come all this way and get me."

The thief smiled smugly to himself as they continued to follow the river. It had now stopped expanding. "You know, I don't think it will be a problem. As I said before, as long as you behave you will be completely safe."

Sileena was getting frustrated because this man's answers were providing many more questions than before, and she was getting nowhere in formulating an escape plan. "What are you talking about? The Outcasts' Land is a barbaric place with people fighting amongst themselves to gain as much power as possible."

"Wow, you talk about it as though you know of it first-hand." The thief was clearly being sarcastic. "Tell me, when did you last go there to get that perfect description?"

He was annoying her a lot more now.

"We have all heard the stories from other people."

"What? Other people who have been there? What do they say?"

Sileena had a sudden epiphany. It was so obvious from the little hints he was giving her now. She was surprised she had not thought of it ever since he had said 'we'. "It's not as barbaric as people think, is it? You work in groups together. So whichever group you are in could protect me from the others."

The thief said nothing. This as good as acknowledged her suspicions.

"You know that my father will come after you and try and get me without paying first, and he has an agent with spectacular skills. He can track anything and could kill you in a fight without breaking a sweat."

The man seemed intrigued by this possible challenger. "How do you know that?"

"He's bigger, stronger and faster, and has never failed any task." She spoke in admiration of the man. She had never liked him as he was basically her father's right-hand man, and was almost as unpleasant as her father was. But this one time, he could be her greatest hero.

"Does this man have a name? Perhaps I can recognise the man who would teach me a thing or two about combat." Was the thief mocking her? Of course he was. But that was not going to deter her from the hope that at least someone could come and get her away from these bandits.

"He's called the black viper," she said, with more pride than intended.

The man gave a little thought to what she said. "Does he perhaps wear black and have short black hair, and a terrible sneer about him? Oh, and he has a scar across his nose."

She looked at him with surprise and nodded.

"He will not be following us then." His tone was serious then, which was disturbing. He could not have killed him. At least not fairly.

"You backstabbed him?" She felt desperate. How could she be rescued?

"No. It was a fair fight."

Sileena was distraught at first. How this idiot bandit could best the black viper fairly, she did not know. He must be lying. But eventually she regained her confidence. There were others that could rescue her.

"My brother will come, then – he will find me."

"Again, no – he will track us to the woods where a note will be waiting with the ransom notice."

Sileena did not reply. All options for getting away were running out, and the situation was getting worse as every moment she was getting further away. She was going to have to get away from several people instead of one to escape, and she still did not quite know how she was going to get back safely on her own.

"What is the point in this? Why do you need money?"

The thief sighed to himself as he moved forward. "You know, you ask a lot of questions. How about you stop asking?"

Sileena went to open her mouth again, but the man quickly motioned for her to remain silent.

"How about you just stop talking altogether? Just remain silent until we are there. I could do with the peace and quiet."

Sileena glared at him, but remained silent. She didn't think his good mood would last if she continued to question him, and she was still anxious about what he might do to her.

The two of them continued to walk for about another hour. The forest disappeared in the background and all that was around them was an open plain and the river flowing beside them. As they kept walking Sileena saw a strange sight. The grass on the ground was turning green. Not the normal kind of green. The normal grass was darkish with a hint of brown in it. But now the brown was disappearing and the green was getting...well, greener. It was very unusual. As they walked the grass became a bright and strong green, and Sileena felt uncomfortable; even more uncomfortable than before. She had a sudden urge to turn and leave, but she couldn't as the man would end up dragging her back.

"What is this place?" she asked, with a knot still in her stomach.

The thief looked around with a calm expression on his face. "Home," he said simply.

# 3

# HOME

"This place is your home?" Sileena said with disbelief, gazing out at the very unusual colour of the grass.

Dorren wasn't listening. He was looking around his home with a feeling of being safe again. He knew, however, that not all of these feelings were coming from him. When crossing the threshold into his home a magical presence passed through him. This happened when moving out onto the unusually light green grass. There was a magical atmosphere that was placed all over the land of the Outcasts. Those that had been enchanted, which was all the Outcasts, would get a higher feeling of belonging and safety. It was to help them know when they were close to their home. Dorren had once thought that the unusual colour of the ground on which he stood would have been enough, but apparently it was a side effect of the aura. For those who were not enchanted with this magic would start to feel uncomfortable, and feel the need to leave. This way any stragglers that dared to try and enter the Outcasts' Land would decide it was not a good idea and get out. This was not entirely a deterrent. Those who were determined to enter would feel uncomfortable, but that was as far as it went. Anyone willing enough go into Dorren's home would still be able to do so, and a couple of explorers did get close. Luckily other measures were put into place and the secret of the Outcasts remained secret. The aura was the first defensive measure that had been placed.

"Why does it look like this?"

Sileena was probably feeling a great discomfort right now. But she was taken against her will, and would happily leave even without the help of the surrounding magic. Dorren didn't believe that the aura would be enough to get her to run for it. She knew it was futile and it turned out his theory that she wouldn't run was correct. He didn't need to look at her to know she was glaring at him. But he didn't care. To be fair to her, she was being a good hostage. Apart from the constant talking, she was complying with every command given. It may have been out of fear at first, but when Dorren briefly glanced at the girl as she looked at him with annoyance he guessed that the fear was severely lacking.

"Hey, I am talking to you."

What a strange girl, he thought. Why would she stop being scared after little more than an hour with her kidnapper? Did she not think he might beat her if she put a foot out of line? Or even worse? He had said that she would not come to any harm if she obeyed, and apart from the flapping of her mouth she had done just that. Whatever the reason, he didn't care. Whether Sileena didn't run because of fear of what might happen, or because of the simple truth that she would not get away if she tried, didn't matter. Just as long as she remained close.

"Are you listening?"

Dorren sighed. "You know you talk far too much? Can't you be a nice quiet hostage? I'm not answering your questions."

"But—"

"Shush. Do you hear that? It is the sound of the wind and the movement of grass, and *not* your voice."

"I thought you might be a gentleman," she said in a sarcastic tone.

"Have I hurt you?"

"Yes, you've hurt my feelings."

Dorren knew when someone was making a joke and he was not going to oblige her with a reply. The reason she didn't run was certainly not fear if she could make those kinds of comments to him.

"You know, a gentleman—"

"The sound of the wind is being drowned by some kind of whiny noise. I wish it would stop."

Sileena responded with a cold glare, but stopped talking.

37

Dorren knew she had got the message, and kept moving forward. For another hour they continued to walk alongside the river in complete silence. She was clearly thinking of the situation that she was in. This would have been overwhelming for her. She had come from a noble's life in which everything would have been easy, and she in a position of authority. However, now everything had suddenly changed and she was the one being told what to do. It was rather satisfying to know that the nobility could be pushed around despite their power lust. This capture was going to make Dorren very popular. Sileena was probably deciding on a way to escape and to assess her situation, but she would not get far.

Dorren continued alongside the river until he saw a strange purple shimmer. This was only noticeable to those who bore the same enchantment used on the Outcasts. This was an indicator to turn left away from the river and head south to his real home. The other kingdoms did not need this kind of use for magic. All they needed were roads and actual signs. This was just a consequence of the Outcasts trying to keep themselves hidden.

"We turn left here."

"How do you know? I don't see anything that would say that."

"I just know, now let's keep moving."

"Do you even know where you are going? I mean, what if we end up in a lair of monsters, or..."

Dorren sighed to himself as Sileena continued to speak. This meant a lot more questions, and she wasn't going to shut up this time. Why did he have to open his mouth? It was like an invitation for her to start this barrage of questioning. He could always knock her out again, but then he would have to carry her. No rest for the weary.

"There is nothing heading east of the forest, sir. If the Outcast went round that way, then he did a good job of keeping his tracks clear."

Nok was a bit bewildered at the situation. The tracks had led him to the edge of the forest and then completely disappeared. He had sent two very good trackers to either side of the forest in the hope that they would find more footprints, which they could then follow while he searched the area. There would be no way that the kidnapper would go through the forest when the great wolves were an ever-present danger. Nok had heard the stories of those beasts. No one had gone through the forest and got out the other side alive. Well, almost no one that he was aware of. A few still try, but were usually never heard from again. The last story he'd heard dated from before his lifetime, when a straggler barely got back out of the forest with his life. Nok used to enjoy listening to these stories as a child, but now they were causing him problems. He looked to the tracker who had delivered the news.

"Very well, we will wait until our other man is back with a report before moving away."

"Yes, sir."

Nok was not going to give up on his sister. She certainly had intelligence in her. His father, Lord Nerida, had taught Sileena nothing. Nok was the favourite because he was the heir and the eldest. It was he who was taught everything he needed to know. He was educated on how to rule, about his family and many other attributes. And everything he learned he passed down to Sileena in secret so their father would not find out. She was a lot quicker to pick it up than he was, so he knew that she would find a way to escape her kidnapper and get home, or at least stay alive until Nok reached her. Nevertheless, another minute spent looking was another minute in which Sileena's life was in danger.

After another few minutes of waiting his patience was beginning to thin, and he was ready to continue without the tracker. He wanted to keep moving because he was losing ground and was desperate to catch up with Sileena and her abductor before they made it to the Outcasts' Land. If that happened, then getting his sister back would be that much harder. He would go through the forest if he had to cut the thief off. Luckily Nok knew that if the kidnapper managed to get from the Outcasts' Land to the town of Sarden without going through the forest – because surely he knew what would happen were he to do so – then he could not be stupid enough to go through the forest on the way back. So Nok knew his sister would not be eaten by wolves, at least. But time still seemed to drag and Sileena might be gone forever. Nok quickly pushed that thought away and renewed his determination. There was no way this damned kidnapper would get the better of him like he did those guards. Nok was still waiting at the side of the forest with the tracker and two very good soldiers.

Let's see that Outcast fight us alone. I will gladly take his life when we meet, and get my sister back to safety, he thought.

Finally he could see movement coming from the west side as the tracker was making his approach.

"Sir, there are no tracks to follow on the west side," said the tracker as he rushed to meet him.

Nok cursed to himself. What was he going to do now?

"But I did find this. It might be of interest." The tracker took out a piece of paper and handed it to Nok.

"Very good." Nok unravelled the paper to reveal a note. "Where did you find this?"

"It was stuck to a post at the edge of the forest, sir. There was a flag of Eceriden on the post so I thought it would be of interest to us anyway."

Nok looked over the note carefully.

*Nerida,*
*By the time you have found this note I will have made it through the forest and be out of your reach. Your daughter is safe – that is, as long as you keep away. I want 500 gold pieces brought to the post where this letter was found, thirty days after your daughter's capture when the sun is at the highest point in the sky. We will trade and go our separate ways.*

Nok scanned the letter again, hoping to find a way around its demands, but couldn't. He did find it a little strange that the Outcasts would take a chance that he would find the note. A simple letter left on a post just outside the forest?

That was not important, though. How on earth did the kidnapper get through the forest? He was possibly lying and still on his way round. He might know some sort of secret path, but there was no way for Nok to find something like that in time. There were many questions, but Nok knew what he was going to do. The only thing he could do.

"What is our next move, sir?" The trackers and soldiers stood at the ready for what would come next. They were good men to have that kind of motivation.

"We head back and give the note to Lord Nerida. Then we will make the exchange that this kidnapper demands."

The men briefly looked surprised, but their training quickly covered it. Nok knew what he was doing. Sileena was safe, her abductor claimed, and although Nok couldn't really take his word for it there was no other option. He was not going to risk Sileena's life by going after them. And 500 gold pieces was not an overwhelming amount. It was possible. When Sileena was back, however, Nok would go to the king of Eceriden and ask for the use of the army, and destroy all of the Outcasts. Then he would get his money back. No one should get something for stealing, and then trading what they stole with the real owner.

He mounted his horse, and the soldiers did likewise before they all turned around and rode back to Sarden. The Outcasts in general were a tiresome bunch. They were allowed to do whatever they wanted, and to get away with kidnapping was simply not going to happen. It was time to act, and after his sister was back safely, Nok would wipe them out.

Sileena had walked for miles, and she was getting tired and hungry. She had never had to do this kind of thing before, and it was clearly affecting her more than it did the idiot next to her. She had tried to ask the thief many questions, but he was not answering any. The man was unbelievably stubborn. She only got one thing out of him, namely that his name was Drake. It wasn't much but at least she'd managed that. This could mean that he might be persuaded to divulge some information.

She was also a little curious. If the land of the Outcasts was an unusually lush green landscape, then there must have been some sort of magic involved. She knew the vivid colours had not been provided by anyone outside, so these Outcasts must have somehow created this atmosphere, though she didn't understand why the overwhelmingly bright green. She guessed she was going to figure it out soon, because they would end up at the coast if they didn't reach their destination, and the sun was now almost completely gone.

The place was empty. All around them were barren grasslands. Everywhere, from the edge of the forest to the coast, were empty grasslands. It was amazing that they had not passed anything of interest. There were no other bandits or holdings to be seen anywhere. Something about this flat, empty scene was unnerving. The landscape was so barren that Sileena could even notice the smallest dot in the distance. One appeared, but she did not take much interest in it.

Well, that was until it got closer and began to take shape. It started to look like a piece of cut wood, abandoned in a field. Something that had been misplaced and was not where it was supposed to be. Then it appeared more like a shed, but this still seemed out of the ordinary. Why would there be a shed standing alone in this desolate place? When they got close enough Sileena realised that it was in fact a cabin, and they were heading directly for it. This must be where they were going to stay.

When she reached the cabin, Sileena expected a few people to be waiting. A couple of thugs, most likely. She had been beaten by her father before, so thought she could probably handle what they dished out. But here was this small place sitting in the middle of an empty space. It must have only been able to maintain three people at most, and there was nothing around it. No growing food, nor fences. It stuck out, like something that shouldn't be there.

Eventually they managed to reach the building, and instead of knocking Drake just entered. The cabin was not big. It looked worn and rotten. There were a few windows, and two of them were smashed.

When she entered the atmosphere was very similar to that outside. There were just two rooms. There was a bedroom and a combined living space and kitchen, with dirty dishes and a filthy table in the living space. The bedroom had only one single bed and that was in tatters.

The two of them had better not be sleeping in the same bed, she thought to herself. It was true that it would be sensible not to argue, but from what she could tell her captor seemed somewhat different to what she had expected. Granted, they had to keep moving as the sun was gone but apart from carrying her across the river he had not touched her, and he didn't speak like a barbarian. So if he thought that getting them to sleep together in this small bed was a good idea, then she would have something to say.

When she looked around the living room further, she almost jumped as there was a rocking chair in the corner of the room, and an old man sitting in it with some sort of odd-looking pipe. The pipe was in the shape of a strange loop she had not seen before. It was probably crafted by the man himself. His clothes were worn, like Drake's, and he had a cane sitting at the side of the chair. This old man had a bald patch on the top of his head, and grey hair coming out the sides. He looked to be in his eighties, but because he also looked drained and tired he was probably younger.

"Hello, old man," said Drake in a slightly sarcastic tone.

"Call me 'old man' again and I'll shove this cane up your back-side."

The two of them then smiled as the old man stood with an energy he had not hitherto appeared to possess. Drake walked over to the stranger and the two hugged. Sileena was a bit bewildered by the whole thing. They must be close friends; perhaps the old man was Drake's father.

"So how have you been?" Drake asked.

"Wonderful. I sit here all day, with nothing but my imagination to keep me company. But someone has to do the job. When's it your turn, anyway?"

Drake gave him a look that clearly indicated that he was not going to do it, whatever 'it' was. "When I feel like having a day to myself. Could you imagine me alone with my thoughts for a day? I'd go mad. You don't need to keep watch again for at least a year once today is done, anyway."

Sileena was completely confused by what was going on. None of what they said made any sense.

43

The old man then looked at Sileena. His expression became a little more calm and positive. "Well, you actually did it. I never doubted you."

Drake snorted. "Yes you did."

"And she just followed you here without any resistance?"

"Almost none. But she wouldn't shut up."

"Hey!" A frustrated Sileena could not think of a better comeback as the attention was now focused on her.

The old man still looked at her, his calm, reassuring smile never faltering. "She's a pretty young thing. You should keep her. She can steer you away from your thoughts with the chit-chat you speak of."

Sileena crossed her arms in an attempt to demonstrate her annoyance, but the two of them didn't seem to care. Of course they didn't care. They were her kidnappers.

The old man looked at Sileena, and his gaze drifted over her face before looking her dead in the eyes. His expression changed from the calm smile to one of curiosity. "Dorren, did you notice...?"

"Yes, don't worry." Drake had his back to the two of them as he made his way to the bedroom.

"But are you sure it's safe?"

What were they on about?

"The circumstances would be different if it wasn't safe."

"You could have at least knocked her out. You know, so she does not see."

Sileena went to protest. See what? But Drake spoke before she could open her mouth.

"What's the point? She would obviously figure it out and the cabin is not exactly large. It wouldn't take a genius to know where to look."

The old man disappeared into his own thoughts for a few seconds, before losing the curious expression and smiling again. "Be that on your head, Dorren. Well," the old man said with a confident expression, "don't want to spoil the welcome party."

Sileena was just as confused as ever, but now knew one thing. "Your name's Dorren, not Drake. You lied to me." The idiot had only told her one thing, and even that was not true.

"Did you expect anything any different? I'll see you later, Lockarr," Dorren said, with emphasis on the old man's name. He then opened a wardrobe and pulled the back away, revealing a passage of stairs going down.

"Well," the old man said with an amused expression, "that was very spiteful. I say your name by mistake and you use mine."

It was something that Sileena thought would have been bad, but the old man really did not seem to mind. He was a strange one.

Dorren looked at Lockarr and shrugged before turning to Sileena and beckoning her. "Come on, I've been travelling and I'm wanting to get to my bed already. I'm sure you will be as well."

Sileena was relieved to know that she was not going to be sleeping in that bed in the cabin. However, it might be much worse downstairs: a dungeon, perhaps. She might be tied up in chains within a cellar. If that were the case she would happily take the ruined bed. Thinking about it was making her uneasy; even more than she had been before. But she had little choice, and so followed Dorren into the dark passage and down the spiral staircase.

"So, what will happen to me?"

Dorren stopped to look at her with a thoughtful expression, before turning and continuing downstairs. "You will be safe and kept healthy. Once the meeting takes place we will trade you for what we want and then we shall go our separate ways. You should not be worried. That is, as long as you play the part of a good guest and don't try anything stupid."

"I'll behave as long as you play the part of a good host."

Dorren laughed. "You see? We are getting along now after all."

Sileena could only see the back of Dorren's head, but could assume he was smiling. The back of his head was covered in short, light brown hair. It was scruffy, giving him an immature look. That might have been because of the journey, though, as she also felt in desperate need of a wash.

They had finally reached the bottom of the spiral staircase and were now in a narrow tunnel which only stretched for a few metres, with a door at the end.

"So who's the old man then?" Sileena asked.

Dorren turned to look at her. "One of my best friends," he replied. "He is not old though, he's only forty-two – well, somewhere around that."

Sileena looked at him, her mouth open. "What? But he looks eighty!" She pondered for a second before realising. "Oh, let me guess – the work of magic?"

Dorren smiled. "Oh, look who is clever. Perhaps you should be given some sort of award."

Sileena was not amused by the comment. His sarcastic sense of humour was annoying. "I thought you were going to play the part of the good host?"

Dorren turned away again and made for the door. "Yes, but you are still talking."

Sileena closed her mouth again.

Dorren opened the door at the end of the tunnel and a wave of bustling commotion rushed through that caught Sileena off guard.

"What is that?"

"That is the sound of freedom." Dorren's vague answer did not give her any kind of clue. But when she went through the doorway, her eyes opened wider than she'd ever thought possible. Well, this changed a few things.

Leading a kingdom was hard for Kell. You could never make everyone happy, no matter what you did. But when you had absolute authority and control over the grandest armies in all the land, then keeping control was not too difficult. Many people remained unhappy, but they could not put their grievances into action without facing the might of his forces. There had been a couple of rebellions against him, but none that had posed any serious issues. After all, he was the king of Duka and there was no man that was feared more than him. Fear was Kell's greatest tool in his kingdom. It was the only way to keep control over a land in which ritual sacrifice for the great god of the earth was necessary.

Not only did they keep to sacrificial traditions, but had also remained under constant raids from the Grey Forest to the east. The forest got its name from the obvious lack of the green that you would expect to see in a forest. The leaves remained grey through most of the year, hence the title. Within this enormous forest lay at least a hundred tribes of barbarians. Most of the time they fought amongst themselves, but occasionally small groups would leave and commit raids upon Kell's kingdom. But like the rebellions, he managed to crush those who were foolish enough to not return to their home in time.

Kell would have liked to eradicate the barbarian tribes completely, but trying to take the Grey Forest would be suicide. The sheer size of it meant that clearing it of the barbarians would be next to impossible. Besides, he had no idea of the kind of numbers that were held within. It was safer to simply maintain a defensive perimeter to stop anyone from getting out.

There were not only the forests to the east, but also the Eagle Jay Mountains to the west. These mountains peaked higher than any others known, and were said to hold all kinds of monstrous creatures. Oddly enough these creatures tended to keep to themselves, with only one such monster leaving the mountains in Kell's lifetime. But he knew how dangerous they could be, as a few miners who moved too far into the mountain range had met with disastrous fates. It was even rumoured that the mountains might be home to one or more dragons. But Kell believed those rumours were probably superstitious nonsense.

Then there was Duka itself. Most of the land was made up of deserts, with the odd lush oasis dotted around. So what Duka had to trade with its northern comrades was whatever minerals they could mine from the mountains, and the rare fruits which you could only get from an oasis of Duka. These fruits had been useful to trade with the Misty Grove Forest to the north, where they were turned into potions – Kell didn't know exactly what sort of potions. Just as long as Duka was taking in sufficient wealth to stay together, that was enough for him. With this and the threats from all sides, it was no wonder the kingdom was so aggressive, and turned to things like ritual sacrifice.

The country was overpopulated and the kingdom was feeling the weight. As most of the land was desert, the populations were condensed into small areas where they had access to fresh water. Food shortages were regular, but there was not much that could be done unless Kell was able to obtain aid from the land of Eceriden. But there was no chance of that happening. He would rather die than ask for help from those who would happily watch his country burn. The two kingdoms were on the brink of war, and tensions were fierce.

This was the topic of the discussion that was taking place right now between him and his other generals within the meeting chambers. The land of Duka was too big to be run by a single ruler. Although Kell was the undisputed leader, he did require others to govern their own parts of the land to keep everything under control. They consisted of his closest advisers and friends, whom he appointed himself. This was the only way to make sure there were no serious uprisings, and that he would get all the support he needed when he called for it.

"Eceriden must be taken. Duka is far too overpopulated and we need the resources." One of the advisers had put forward a strong case regarding the possible invasion. He seemed to believe that the diminishing resources and dying population were enough to warrant such an attack. Kell, of course, agreed. The tensions between the countries had built up over the years, and this was his opportunity to declare war on the kingdom he hated so much. Kell's brother, Surdan, who held the highest rank in the room after him, was, however, against the invasion, as seeking Eceriden's aid might be beneficial to their relationship. The important thing in these meetings was to allow everyone to have their say, even though Kell made the ultimate decision. Of course, it was his right to do so as king.

The room in which they sat was dark and dreary, very different to the atmosphere of Kell's throne room. The candlelight in the room did not help the situation, but Kell preferred to keep his meetings private and this meant no outside light getting in. The room itself was circular, with a table that was also circular. Around the table were all his closest advisers, all of whom were giving their input into the topic at hand. All but one was for the invasion and giving very similar arguments for it.

The main reason why Eceriden and Duka were not on the best of terms was their religious differences. The two kingdoms worshipped different gods and had bickered over which one was right for centuries. They had warred in the past, and that all ended in an awkward stalemate. But that war had been over one hundred years ago. Now it was being decided that it was time to put an end to all squabbles and prove which kingdom was superior – something that Kell was eager to resolve. His brother, however, seemed to think that this war would be a pointless and suicidal endeavour.

"We must remember what would happen if we were to go to war. The people of the Misty Grove Forest would think that the balance of power would shift. They would not stand to let this invasion pass. They'll no doubt defend Eceriden."

Then there were the allies from the Bryton Mountains, who would fear Duka becoming too powerful. They would run from their mountains to join Duka's opponent's side as well. Against Eceriden the fight would have a clear outcome. Duka would win simply because of their superior numbers. But with Eceriden's allies from the north joining them, Duka would be outmatched. They still outnumbered the combined forces, but the enemy had the equipment and training needed to win.

However, war was inevitable and Kell did not care much for these odds. He was not going to stand by and let his people suffer while Eceriden lived their rich lives in ignorance of what was happening around them. The council was right. Duka needed the resources for an overpopulated land, which just did not have the landscape for making its own.

But there were still two problems to be faced. Leaving his own kingdom unattended could be disastrous. These barbarians might sniff out the weakness and bring Duka crumbling to its knees. And the other issue resided in how to overcome their enemies on the battlefield. These two problems had caused Kell to constantly rethink his intentions to invade. For years he had wanted nothing more than to bring his enemies to heel, but there was no way of doing that without sacrificing his own realm. Kell loved the idea of war and knew that

49

no one could dispute his righteous authority, but he was not stupid. There would always be someone idiotic enough to challenge him. This annoyed Kell, as they had no right or power to challenge him face to face. Ignorant people, he thought to himself.

However, these problems he faced had seemed to be resolved thanks to one individual who appeared to come out of nowhere. Kell had been approached a few months back by a man who kept his face hidden under a cloak. With a wave of his hand he had shown Kell the way to victory. It was true that there were those who challenged him, but at least there were also those with the right kind of obedience. The cloaked man claimed to have manipulated all the barbarian clans to his side and combined them with the Dukan forces to destroy all Kell's enemies. At first Kell did not believe him, but after a demonstration of power he was quickly swayed. This individual had more magical potential than any other Kell had seen before. This was probably due to the staff the man held in his hands – a very rare piece that Kell had only heard of in stories. This kind of instrument was believed to have been created before known history. Its powers were tremendous, and could boost an individual's natural talent multiple times. Well, that was what Kell believed. He considered taking the staff himself, but as a man of no magical potential he would not be able to make much use of it. Besides, this sorcerer was a very loyal servant and deserved the chance to serve his king.

This mysterious figure, who had merely looked for an audience a few months back, was now sitting as one of Kell's honoured guests at the meeting this day. The service this sorcerer provided had earned him the right to stand with them in this council.

Many advisers at first protested at this man they did not know being there, Kell's brother most of all. But as Kell was the one with absolute power, he had the final say. Surdan had obviously not seen his authority yet. If he were any other man Kell would have had him executed for his treasonous behaviour. But this was his brother, and he would never do that to him despite his attitude. Most of the time they got along but these recent events had sparked a number of arguments. Surdan knew to keep these arguments private, but they were tiresome.

Kell remembered better days when they used to play together in the courtyard while their mother and father watched over them. But that time had passed and he now held a responsibility that even his brother could not understand. Maybe once this war was over and Kell maintained absolute power, they could perhaps go back to a happier time.

Kell looked to the mysterious man who had remained quite silent throughout the meeting. He also appeared to keep to the darkest part of the room. The hooded figure certainly liked to remain in the shadows, he thought. The sorcerer was not the kind of person who made his presence clear. If there were a shadow in the room he would probably be standing in it. This kind of thing would normally warrant suspicion, but here was Kell's best opportunity to destroy his enemies while keeping his kingdom.

At the beginning of this council the sorcerer had brought in his second-in-command, a massive man wielding a tremendous axe. He held a red band, signalling his position amongst the barbarians the sorcerer had brought under his control. He had a scar that was barely visible through the hair across his chest. This barbarian also had a dark complexion, and the dark beard sprawled across his face did not help. His appearance at the meeting annoyed Kell, and he was immediately ordered to leave. The mysterious man obeyed immediately of course, and told the man to wait outside. His ignorance could be forgiven as he did not know the rules that were applied to these meetings. So the sorcerer himself was allowed to remain.

He had actually managed to communicate with these savages and take them under his control. This was a very impressive feat, and one that Kell was excited about. With two armies and an all-powerful sorcerer at his command there was nothing that could stop him. It was strange to think that he would be working with those who had previously caused him so much trouble. Now they were slaves to the man who he controlled, and this gave Kell immeasurable pleasure.

The sorcerer was sitting quietly, while all the other generals and nobles argued over the war. They had by now all agreed that a fight was necessary, but whether it was winnable was the topic of discussion.

After another minute of debate, the sorcerer finally decided to speak. "If you are concerned about the numbers then you need not worry. I and my...subjects will aid in the fight against Eceriden. With our combined numbers we will crush the opposition without any difficulty."

Everyone went quiet. Some were still unhappy that this man was even allowed into the council. Others were merely contemplating this stranger's reassurances. Unlike Kell, they did not trust him; Kell's brother least of all. Working with these savages was not something he would have liked. Yet he needed them, and there was little choice on the matter. Besides, it was not so much working, but rather using them to achieve his goals. Any advisers who did have concerns, however, remained silent as Kell had made himself quite clear on the matter. The combined Dukan army amounted to several thousand. Combining it with the barbarians would triple that size, if what this sorcerer told him was true. The odds would be overwhelmingly in their favour.

The silence in the room gradually subsided as the adviser Krator spoke up. "I am happy to work with these barbarians but there would be many of our soldiers who might not be. How do we convince them?"

This statement was true, and this angered Kell. His soldiers should obey his command but there might be a few who would still try to fight those who had given them previous grievances. But Kell knew how to go about this.

"Do not be concerned about that, Krator. I already have a way to avoid this issue."

Kell could tell Krator was expecting him to explain, but after a moment smiled and nodded. Kell just thought that the fewer people who knew the exact plans, the better.

"Then it is decided. All generals here will mobilise their forces. Make the necessary preparations, but I want to maintain secrecy. When we are all ready, we will march north. I want us all to move fast so the enemy has as little time to prepare as possible. Are we clear?"

Those sat around the table gave nods of understanding.

"Good, then this meeting is done."

With that statement, everyone stood up and began exiting the room while talking amongst themselves. Kell walked towards the sorcerer with his brother at his side. When the sorcerer noticed their approach he remained standing until all others had exited the room.

"I want you to keep me updated, and to let me know when you are ready to march north."

"Understood. I will give you something that I can use to communicate with you when the barbarians are ready."

"When we leave I do not want our armies travelling together. We should leave combining our forces until the fight itself because my men will not be pleased about travelling with barbarians. You understand?"

The hooded man looked at him with his expressionless face. "Yes. I understand. I will gather an army and will follow a day behind you, and when the time is right we will join. I will keep contact and wait until your command for my forces to meet with yours."

"Fair enough. We will discuss this soon."

The sorcerer nodded his understanding and waited for Kell to leave the room before exiting himself.

Outside, Kell looked to his brother, who seemed concerned. Surdan did not want this war. That was abundantly clear. But Kell did, and war was necessary anyway. If there was no war, then two problems would occur. The obvious was that Kell's people would starve and die. The other was the rebellion that these same people would bring to him for not providing enough food and other important resources. This rebellion, unlike the others, he might not be able to stop. He might have a divine right to rule them but he could understand them committing to this act if he could not rule well. His brother would just have to accept this.

# 4

# THE RULES OF CONDUCT

Sileena looked around in complete disbelief at what she was seeing. The noises she was hearing were actually voices – lots of them. She was looking down upon a large hall. It had no metal or stone. It was all held up by wood and dirt in a way that seemed like it should not hold. There was probably magic put into that as well, to keep it secure. Where did these Outcasts get their magic from, she wondered? It was just one of many questions that were now thundering through her head.

The circular hall had two floors. The main floor on the ground had scaffolding which led up to a stand in the middle of the room. This must be where a spokesman would go to make some sort of big speech, as often happened in Sarden. At one side of the hall was what appeared to be a food stall. There were wooden seats that looked a little worn away in front of the stall, where people were sitting and eating different kinds of food together.

Staircases moved along the wall, heading up to the second floor where Sileena was standing. The second floor was merely a path circulating around the hall, with rails on the inside. Tunnels went in different directions on both floors. Where they led, she had no idea. It was an entire underground network.

People were coming out of the tunnels into the hall and vice versa, doing all manner of activities. Some were moving crates and other merchandise around. Others were merely in groups talking amongst themselves, and there were those eating at the food stall. It was like they were living completely normal lives. The people here all wore relatively shabby clothing in comparison to that she had seen back at home. Some had various weapons at their sides.

This was not the picture Sileena had in mind. It was not a ragtag group of evil bandits. It was an entire community. There were elderly in groups, and children running around the hall, much to some of the adults' irritation as they were trying to move barrels and crates around.

"Wh-what? I did not expect this."

The so-called Dorren was smiling. "No one would."

Everyone was too preoccupied to notice the two of them as they entered the great circular hall. And of course, why should they? This place must have hosted countless people. They would never be able to notice a stranger entering.

"I don't understand. How is this possible? Why aren't you...you know...killing each other?"

Dorren seemed to ignore the question and instead beckoned her to follow as he started to walk around the path. "Yes, we are all evil people who go around looking out for themselves and killing anyone who gets in our way. Don't you know that all of the people who are banished to this land are those who do not worship your god? This does not mean we are bad people. Those who commit a crime are locked away in your own country. But because we have not committed any real crimes, we're therefore banished."

Sileena did not know this. It sounded like something she should have known. Her brother must have forgotten to mention it.

Dorren then took a turn into one of the tunnels, and Sileena followed beside him. The tunnel went down a straight path with doors occasionally appearing at either side of them. Dorren smiled pleasantly. This was not the usual cocky smile he wore when he was overconfident and clearly felt like he knew something she did not. This was a look of happiness, as if he had just achieved something great. She suspected that it was his taking her against her will. Yes, what an achievement – to kidnap a helpless girl. He must be so proud. These people might claim to be normal but normal people did not kidnap others and hold them for ransom. However, Sileena did feel a lot safer now that she could see the

Outcasts for what they were. These were not ruthless bandits, and that thought gave her a little more comfort.

"Well," Dorren said, "just about no one outside our land is aware that we are not just a group of crazy killers. So congratulations are in order." He was back to his sarcastic humour again. But he seemed less of a hostile, evil man now that she could see the world he lived in. Here he was just a silly boy with a massive ego.

They were now coming to an opening in the tunnel. "So if it is not our god you worship, which one do you bow down to?" Sileena asked. "Not Duka's god of the earth, is it?"

"No!" Dorren looked at her and seemed to take offence at this question. "No one here practises ritual sacrifice." He turned away again and muttered, "Bloody morons" to himself. The man clearly had issues with religious beliefs.

"So then which god is it you worship then?"

"None, why should we? They constrict what we can achieve now and are the cause of so many evil things in the world."

Sileena was shocked. "How could you say that? The teachings of Abodem say that we are to treat each other with charity and kindness. Even those we hate."

Dorren smiled as if he knew better than her, which just irritated her more. "Is that so? Then why have people committed such evil acts because of your religion? So much war and death – and all because of your so-called faith."

"You can't just blame the actions of people on our faith."

"Yes I can. Everyone here has been banished because we didn't believe what you believed. Where is that sense of charity you were speaking of then? If there was no religion, then we would not have been forced into exile."

Sileena could see where Dorren was coming from but she had been taught differently. "Those are the actions of people, not religion. Faith is important and holds good moral teachings that most people follow. There are just a few that manipulate it for themselves. Blame those people. Not our faith."

Dorren frowned and was obviously pondering over what she

had said before replying. "Very clever. Did one of your great religious priests teach you that?" He had obviously conceded.

"No, it was my brother."

Dorren did not reply.

They had now walked out of the tunnel and into another two-floor room which had the same features as the previous one, except that it lacked the stand in the centre and was a little smaller. Wooden poles were dotted around the hall and holding up the ceiling from the ground below. Dorren moved around the path and started walking down the stairs to the floor below.

"You must have something you all work towards," Sileena ventured. "What's the point in kidnapping me when you seem to have everything you need? What would a little money do?" It did seem strange. If this place did work on a currency, then it would not be Eceriden's coinage. Why bother with it? Unless of course she was not being ransomed for money.

"There is a reason why I did this. A goal that our people are working towards. It—"

"Dorren!" came a cheerful yell from across the hall.

Sileena and even Dorren were slightly startled by it. Sileena looked around for the source of the noise. Dorren quickly recovered and smiled as he looked across the room at two figures moving towards them. One was rushing forward through a crowd of people while the other was just moving at a casual walking pace. The rushing man was slightly smaller than Dorren. He had bright blonde hair and blue eyes and seemed slightly younger as well. Probably just turned twenty. He was lightly built and wore light clothing with dual swords sitting at his hips. The man slowly walking towards them was much bigger. He stood taller than any other person in the room. People clearly respected this, as they moved out of the way as he passed. He wore trousers and was topless except for a strap that went round him and was used to hold a huge double-sided axe that was on his back. He had no hair on his head, which seemed to be made up for on his chest, and he had light brown eyes. The man looked about thirty, and had massive, well-defined muscles.

Dorren went over to greet them. The smaller of the two went to embrace him and Dorren was about to do the same, but he quickly diverted and swerved to the side to avoid the hug.

"Ha," the smaller man said. "I always win this game."

Dorren seemed irritated, but an amused kind of irritated. Sileena moved to Dorren's side at the same time as the bigger man.

At this point the smaller man noticed her. "Well, hello beautiful. You seem to be new here. Whatever rumours you hear about me are not true. Perhaps later we could meet up and I give you a tour of the place."

Sileena was too taken aback by the comment to say anything, but Dorren managed to get in.

"She is not to be touched." He turned to Sileena. "And any rumours you hear about him *are* true."

The smaller man looked a bit upset, but it seemed more put-on than real. "Oh I see, you want her. Well, as your friend I will not stand in the way."

Dorren sighed. "Did you not even realise I was gone?"

"Of course we did. So you picked her up along the way?"

Sileena started to feel a little uncomfortable. They were speaking about her as though she was not there.

"No, she is my hostage. We can ransom her for what we need."

The smaller man looked at her questioningly, gazing from her face down to her hands. "Well if she's a hostage, should she not be tied up or something?" He then appeared to lose himself in thought. Sileena was uncomfortable enough without this guy picturing her tied up. She could guess what kind of rumours would have been spread about him.

"Hey Dorren," said the bigger man, who had a fairly deep voice. This was expected. But the smile was not that of an evil criminal. It was actually quite pleasant. Strange that she would be more comfortable with this larger, more dangerous-looking guy than the smaller one who was still silent in thought, and with a more sinister grin on his face.

"Well, introductions should be made," said Dorren. "This is Derain." Dorren pointed to the smaller man, who was coming out of his thoughtful silence, but still had his grin. Sileena decided that she didn't like this man. Dorren then pointed to the bigger man. "And this is Gabe."

Derain turned to Dorren, finally taking the smirk off his face. "Should you be using our names?"

"Well." Dorren smiled. "Lockarr used my name and therefore I am not satisfied until I bring you all down with me. And as for not tying her up, she has behaved – well, except for the talking she does." Sileena gave Dorren a sharp glare as Dorren continued, "So I'm sure that she will not cause any problems."

Derain considered Sileena for a moment and then turned to Dorren. "So who is she?"

"She's Nerida's daughter."

Derain gave a little gasp of surprise. "Oh, well done. Can't believe you went all the way to Sarden and came back with a noble girl."

This was all starting to anger her. The two of them were still talking about her as if she was not there, and didn't seem to care that they had just forced a helpless girl away from her home. But for some reason Gabe did not seem to be saying anything. His smile had vanished, as he too seemed to take notice of Dorren's and Derain's disregard of Sileena.

Derain spoke up again. "You know, Master Pagar is wanting to see you as soon as you got back. The man looked very angry about you leaving."

Dorren grimaced. "This certainly sounds like fun. I bet he finds something I did wrong and uses that against me. I'm getting rather sick of it. Thanks to what I did we can now drive our cause forward by years. He should be thanking me."

There was a pause for a moment as Derain tried to think of something to say. Gabe had just opened his mouth to speak when a knife flew right past Dorren's head and embedded itself into the wall behind them. Everyone in the group, as well as a few others close by, turned to see what had happened.

A man was standing across the room with a smug grin on his face. He had messy ginger hair that seemed to spike up in the centre before flowing down to his shoulders. This man was lightly built, but the two big men standing behind him made up for that. It was very much like her father Nerida to have big men for guards. The two larger men were in great physical condition, but it was still certain that Gabe was the largest and held the most presence in the room. The smaller man was tossing a throwing knife in the air and catching it again.

"Who is that?" Sileena asked in a bit of a gasp, after the shock of the knife whizzing past their heads.

"That's Severa," Dorren muttered, with a dark look Sileena had not seen from him until now. She guessed that the knife was meant to miss, as no one seemed to care that someone could have died. Severa and his men turned and walked away, disappearing into one of the many tunnels. Once they were gone the group seemed to ignore what had just happened and went back to their normal conversation.

"Derain, Gabe – can you two take Sileena to her room? An empty one, preferably."

"Wait, you're dumping her on us?"

"Yes, I did all the work kidnapping her. You can at least take it from here. And once she is in her room, lock it from the outside. If she escapes, I'm blaming you."

Derain didn't like the situation he was being put in, but when he looked at Sileena he obviously changed his mind and gave her a provocative smile. "Well, it looks like I will be getting to give you that tour after all."

Sileena's heart sank, but she was soon relieved to hear Dorren speak again.

"And do not try anything, Derain."

The provocative face disappeared and became glum.

"Gabe, hit Derain if he tries anything. I've got to pay a visit to Master Pagar."

"Pagar? Is that the leader of the Outcasts?" Sileena asked as Dorren was about to leave. Dorren finally smiled for the first time since the knife-throwing incident.

"In a way, yes," he said, and with that he walked away and disappeared into the crowd of people. Some were clearly murmuring about what had just happened. Others were talking and pointing at Sileena, which made her feel out of place. The rest of the crowd were just continuing their daily lives and had not even appeared to notice the event that had just occurred. It was amazing to her that no one had tried to stop this Severa from carrying out what seemed like a dangerous trick. He could have killed someone if the knife had hit a person instead of the wall.

"Come with us," said Gabe, beckoning her to follow.

"We will show you to where you will be staying for the next while," continued Derain.

She followed them out of the room into a corridor. "What is to happen to me while I'm here?"

Derain pondered the question. "That would be up to Master Pagar. He will decide what to do once he finds out what Dorren has done."

So Dorren was obviously acting alone in this endeavour. He might have been trying to prove something, although Sileena did not know what that might be.

She could see down the tunnel quite clearly, despite there being no light source. The whole place was infused with magic. There must be a few users here to keep this presence up or the magic would eventually fade and die.

The place was a little dirty. Being underground clearly did not help keep things overly clean. She might be a little extreme, however, as she was practically raised in a palace that was the very definition of cleanliness. For all she knew the town of Sarden might be similar to this place. A town that she was never allowed to go out and see, despite living in it.

"I love the decoration," Sileena said, with a hint of sarcasm in her tone.

Derain turned his head towards her as they were walking and winked. "I'm glad you like it."

It was good that Gabe was there or else she would have guessed that Derain might have tried something. She then moved her mind to other thoughts and a question popped into her head. She had noticed that there was a greater tension between Dorren and Severa. The eye contact between them was powerful. Everyone else just seemed to be secondary participants.

"So what is the deal between Dorren and this Severa guy?"

Both Derain and Gabe frowned, but it was Derain who answered. "The two of them have been rivals since they were kids. They are considered equal at most things, especially swordsmanship. No one can fight as well as Severa and Dorren." The corridor they were walking down was heading towards a dead end, but before they could reach it Gabe and Derain stopped at one of the doors. "The two of them are getting worse though, as what started as a little rivalry has become complete hatred for each other. Incidents like the one you have just witnessed are the result."

"Oh. Why did no one do something about it?" If someone helped, then perhaps this could be resolved.

"Do what? The only thing that Severa is better than Dorren at is the throwing knife. The guy is a pro. He always gets his target. There would be no way he would hit anyone anyway. If he did hit Dorren then he would truly suffer at the hands of Pagar. If there is one thing that Pagar will not tolerate it's deliberate violence that is not training or a little fun. And this stopped being a little fun a long time ago. Besides, Severa would suffer, especially if it involved Dorren."

Sileena was beginning to get frustrated again. This just gave her more questions than answers. "Why is that?"

Gabe opened the door leading into a room beyond as Derain continued. "That question would be best answered by Dorren. And I think I've told you enough anyway. Now get inside."

Sileena did as she was told.

The room was small. There was a little cabinet with an empty bowl sitting on top of it. The wall around the room seemed to be made of solid mud, so she might be able to dig up and out. Then she could get away. A quarter of the room was taken up by a bed, which was clearly nowhere near as comfortable as the bed in her chamber back at home. She was actually starting to miss her home.

Derain spoke again as she continued to take in the room. "The door is locked from the outside, so you will not be getting out until someone comes and gets you. That person will be Dorren as he was the one that captured you. No one else will, so if it is not Dorren assume you are in danger."

Sileena looked to Derain as he continued. She thought Dorren had said he was done looking after her. Maybe it was just for today. She looked to the walls again, wondering how she might be able to dig her way out, but Derain clearly noticed and guessed what she was thinking.

"Also, trying to dig out would be stupid as there is a magical ward around the room. The consequences of trying that would be severe." Well, so much for that idea. "Other than that, I wish you a very nice stay at our home."

Derain gave her a wink and left. Gabe gave her a polite nod, then closed the door. Sileena heard the lock click, and turned around in the enclosed space that was her new home. This was certainly a lot nicer than that old shack at the surface, and better than the old dungeon or sewer she had pictured. But it still did not match the luxury she used to live in. Sileena had just exchanged one prison for a slightly worse prison. She only needed to put up with it for a little while and then she could go back home. That is, if her father would bother to give the money they demanded to get her back. There was actually the slightest chance that he simply would not care.

She looked into the cabinet to find clothing inside. Again, it was not the brilliant clothing she used to wear but it would have to do. There was a pair of light-coloured long shorts and a shirt of the same colour. It used some sort of elastic so it could accommodate all manner of sizes.

She was going to have get out of her dress soon – she smelled and was eager to wash. But there was nowhere to clean herself here, so that would have to wait. She had realised there was another cabinet behind the door. She looked inside that to find many different undergarments. She guessed the room was meant to be for any individual, male or female. Whether she could wash or not, she had to get out of her dress and put on the new clothing. But she could not guess where else those undergarments had been, so thought it best just to stick with the long shorts and shirt.

Once Sileena had changed, she sat on her new bed. So many questions were still going through her mind. What was going on between Dorren and this Pagar guy? What did Dorren mean when he said that Pagar was 'in a way' a leader amongst the Outcasts? How did these Outcasts become organised and keep it secret from everyone else? And this rivalry between Dorren and Severa…

Her mind then began to wander to her home, and what had happened. She was too much in shock, and eager to know so much that she hadn't realised the main points. These people kidnapped her and so they were the bad people. Her father may not care about her capture but her brother would not let her suffer, so this thought reassured her. But she was missing home.

She lay back and closed her eyes. Sileena's head was buzzing with thought, but after a moment her exhaustion got the better of her and she drifted off to sleep.

Dorren was now in an empty corridor, at the end of which lay a spiral staircase leading up. Dorren walked up the stairs slowly in the hope that he could delay the inevitable until he got to the door at the top, and then paused. What was his master going to make of the past few days, and what was he going pick on that Dorren did wrong? Dorren did not fear Pagar. He just thought of him as an individual who would not leave him be just because of who he was. Dorren sighed. There was certainly no way of making things better by remaining outside. Better to just get it over with. Raising his hand, he gave a couple of light taps on the door.

"Come in," came a voice from inside. Dorren entered and looked around for where the voice came from. The room was split into two sections. The first had shelves filled with various notes, books and potions. There was a table in the centre capable of seating up to six people. A door was in the corner, which went into a small kitchen. This was used for meals on the occasions when Pagar wanted to have dinner here or in a small group rather than at the food stall. The table was used for these meals and occasional meetings. There were a couple of stairs going up to the second section of the room. The walls were covered from floor to ceiling in shelves which were filled with books. Dorren knew that these books ranged from many different kinds of magic, history, literature and stories. It was Pagar's office but basically the official library too. The Outcasts' supply of books was limited and so could all fit into this one office.

In the centre of the room was a desk with different instruments on it. Sitting behind the desk was a man who looked like he was in his late forties. His hair was light brown and long, with a beard to match. He had brown eyes with a very small hint of gold in them. He wore a robe that went right down to his feet, and was pleasantly surprised to see Dorren.

"Dorren, welcome back. So how was your journey?"

"Tiresome," Dorren replied.

The man did not appear to be angry at his disappearance at all, which in itself unnerved him. He was now looking back down at the parchment he was reading. "Yes, apparently so. I'm curious, how is our new guest getting on?"

Dorren took in a breath of surprise. How the hell did he know? It took a moment for him to work it out, but the only logical explanation was that Severa had got here before him and told Pagar what he had seen. Severa would do anything to get Dorren into as much trouble as possible. He had once put rotten fish into the food courts and framed him. Pagar punished Dorren for something Severa did, and it took two weeks to clear his name and pass the blame back to the culprit. Pagar had never apologised for making the mistake.

"Derain and Gabe are taking her to her room."

"I see. Well, it was you who found her and so it's your responsibility to make sure she settles in nicely. You seem to have forgotten your duties these last few days since you left, but you will not forget this one." Pagar's tone was now less cheery. Dorren knew that he would have to keep an eye on Sileena or else it would be his head. "So what did you find out about her before you took her into our home?"

"I know who she is. The girl is Nerida's daughter. I have managed to kidnap her."

Pagar practically choked on his own saliva. "You did what?" He was clearly not happy.

"It was the best thing for us."

"I am actually curious as to how on earth your mind could possibly think that."

Oh, here we go, thought Dorren. This was the thing he had done wrong. "We can hold her for ransom. A noble's daughter held for ransom would make us so much money."

"You haven't even considered the consequences of doing something like this. Well, at least I know where you have been these past few days."

The man should be thanking him. Dorren had achieved so much for his people by doing this.

"Look, I have managed to drive our cause forward by years."

"That is, if they choose to pay. And even so, what then? Do you not think that the girl's father will seek some sort of vengeance afterwards?"

"Nerida will not find us. As far as he is concerned we are just a bunch of ruthless bandits. He could never find us here."

Pagar shook his head in dismay. The man clearly thought he knew something Dorren did not. "Yes, but what if the girl, Sileena, talks? She can give away information that you have been telling her."

"I have not been giving any important information to Sileena."

"That's not what I hear," said Pagar, with a calm anger enveloping him.

Severa will die for this, thought Dorren, whose anger was as great as Pagar's.

"I've heard that she was not even blindfolded."

Dorren had not thought of that. He had screwed up.

"This kind of thing could make things a lot more difficult for us."

"Fine, that was my fault. I had forgotten all that but she is secure and will not be getting out."

Pagar was now losing patience. "Stupid child. That is not the main issue. It is what happens when we deliver her back. The worst possible situation is that when she returns she talks all about the threat we actually pose. This could mean war for us. It would be a war that we just could not win. We are not nearly as big in numbers, supplies or land-mass to win a war with either Duka, Eceriden, or worse, both." Dorren tried to intervene, but Pagar continued. "We have done so much to get this far and no one outside the Outcasts' Land knows anything about our organisation. I will not have my son ruin everything we have achieved."

Dorren was getting angry now. "I am not your real son. Now lis-ten!" Pagar was taken a little aback. "No one would believe anything that Sileena would say. When all this is over it will not go as badly as you say. I did mess up, but it will not mean the end of the Outcasts. Who would believe that this group of ferocious bandits have worked together to build their own society?" There was a pause in the room. The silence was as bad as the arguing.

Pagar calmed down now and spoke more pleasantly. "Yes, you are probably right but as the leader of this Underground I must assume the worst possibilities and outcomes to protect everyone here and at the other Undergrounds. There are rules regarding how things are con-ducted, and they are there for a reason. Any prisoner must always be out of eyesight and earshot of anything that could give away important information about the Outcasts. You have disobeyed this rule, and by doing so you disobeyed me again."

Dorren could not argue with that. But like Pagar he was also too stubborn to apologise, so he stood in silence and listened.

"Another point that you have made is that the girl is secure. But as I have heard, this Sileena is not as secure as you have made out."

Dorren paused and thought for a moment before realising what Pagar was talking about. Her eyes. "What has Severa said?" Dorren asked. Pagar knew that Severa was always out to get him, and so there was no point in disguising the fact that it was he who had told Pagar everything.

"That even from a distance he could make it out. I would like to see it for myself but this is a very serious matter."

Dorren was feeling a little idiotic now. It was true that Pagar irritated him as much as Severa, but unlike Severa Dorren did not want to disappoint Pagar in this way. He had disobeyed him on leav-ing in the first place and then continued to go against his master's wishes by kidnapping the girl in the hope of impressing everyone.

Pagar continued. "Her eyes are more golden than anything ever thought possible, or those were his words."

Dorren thought about it for a moment. Severa was actually not exaggerating. The gold in someone's eyes was a clear indication that they were a powerful magic user. But it was always little tints of gold. Pagar was a powerful sorcerer. He could muster up power that only a handful of people actually possessed. You did not need the gold to be able to use magic, but those who had more power than most could be recognised by the little bits of gold in their eyes. No one had ever been thought to possess more than a hint of gold. When Dorren thought back to Sileena, upon first seeing her he had noted that the colour of her eyes was purely golden. The power that she would have was beyond comprehension. But it could all be a trick, as the gold in her eyes was the only indication of any kind of magic whatsoever. Dorren faced Pagar.

"If she knew what it all meant she would have destroyed us all by now. She never knew that we have things so organised here, so at any point she could have stopped me."

Dorren knew he was getting through to Pagar, as Pagar appeared to comprehend what was said. Dorren knew he was on thin ice. He was making a lot of mistakes. Perhaps he should have thought about the rules before leaving. He was getting everyone he knew in trouble and for what? To get one up on Severa? To prove something to Pagar? To show off to Lockarr, Derain and Gabe? At the end of the day it would all be pointless compared to the problems it might cause. It was strange that his pride upon entering the room had now been quickly extinguished by the man before him. Pagar did have a nasty habit of pointing out where Dorren had gone wrong.

"You are probably right again, Dorren, but I would like to meet her in person. She has seen enough to do the damage. No changing that now. Bring her to the training grounds early tomorrow morning. I wish to talk with her."

"I will," Dorren replied.

Pagar looked back down to the parchment that he had been

reading before Dorren had entered. "You may go now and enjoy your evening."

Dorren turned to leave. It would be nice to just put his feet up for the rest of the day.

"You know," Pagar said as Dorren made for the door, "I will always think of you as my son, whether it be true or not, and I will always treat you as such. I just hope that one day you will see me as your father."

Dorren opened the door, and as he was about to exit he turned around to face Pagar. "I'm sorry for what I said. I have always thought of you as my father."

Pagar smiled at him as Dorren closed the door behind him. He then started walking down the spiral stairs, thinking back to what Pagar had told him once he was old enough to hear it. When Dorren was a very young child, too young to remember, his real father was murdered. He and Pagar were the joint leaders of the Underground, and were the ones who had led the construction of it. Apparently they were the best of friends.

When Dorren's father was murdered Pagar felt the need to raise Dorren himself and adopted him as his own son. Dorren loved Pagar like a father and a role model. He only ever said that Pagar was not his real dad in anger, but he never meant it.

His father's murderer was never found. There was no evidence uncovered to find who was to blame. The investigation was dropped after a time as there were no more murders afterwards. It was as if a ghost had come out of nowhere and killed his father, only to disappear from existence. It angered Dorren that the killer was never caught. When he found out he'd tried to resolve it himself, but there was no evidence whatsoever and was quickly forced to give up.

Dorren was pulled out of his thoughts as he reached the bottom of the staircase to see Derain waiting for him.

"Where is Gabe?"

Derain smiled as he approached. "He is waiting for us at the food court. Once Lockarr has finished his duty he will be joining us there. Your very pretty new friend is safe. So when are you going to tell us about her eyes?"

Dorren looked at him. "I know as much as you do. Well done for not bringing it up in front of her."

"Well what do you think I am, stupid? Now once we get to the food court you must tell us about this wonderful adventure of yours."

"Of course." Well, Dorren thought, at least he had managed to impress his friends. The other people he hoped to impress were a lost cause but this would do.

# 5

# TRAINING GROUNDS

Sileena had next to no sleep during the night. She was spending most of the time thinking about everything that had happened, and what was now going to transpire. Her life had been very uneventful until now. She'd been nothing more than a noble girl who was not allowed beyond the confines of her own home until she was suddenly kidnapped by this Dorren character and dragged to the Outcasts' Land.

Now here she was, locked inside this very small room without a clue as to what is in store for her. Lying on the bed, she stared up at the ceiling as if looking at the blank surface would somehow clear her mind. Unfortunately, this was not the case, as her imagination moved from one scenario to the next, some of which gave her shivers.

And then of course she had met some strange characters, whom she was still trying to understand. Lockarr and Gabe seemed normal, although she wanted a chance to have a proper look at Lockarr. The reason for this was nothing more than curiosity.

But Derain made her feel uncomfortable. The man was unnerving because of the obvious creepy signals he was giving her. Sileena was afraid that he was going to have his way with her, with or without her consent.

Gabe was a huge guy with a rather sweet personality. He was scary to look at, and at first glance seemed like he would be part of a ruthless gang or something similar. But there was something relaxing about being in his company, compared to Derain's.

Dorren was still a blank slate. Sileena did not really understand him, despite having being in his company for longer. She was also curious about the relationship between Dorren and Pagar, whom she had yet to meet. Then there was this Severa character whom she also didn't know anything about, other than the indications of hatred between him and Dorren.

All these thoughts were flowing through her head when a knock came at the door. Abruptly sitting up on her bed, she looked at the door. Sileena did not speak, as she did not know who was on the other side. The door opened slightly and a voice came through the gap. It sounded like Dorren's.

"Are you decent?"

Sileena was confused by the question, before understanding what he meant. "Yes."

The door opened completely now, and Dorren stood in the doorway holding a set of clothes. "I hope you rested well because you have a big day ahead."

"Oh joy," Sileena said sarcastically.

Dorren was obviously pretending to be taken aback by the comment. "You will have fun...I think. But first you need to wash. I can smell you from here."

Sileena glared at him. She was starting to get an idea of Dorren's character. He was a simple-minded man who liked to use sarcasm to mock people. But then, wasn't that something that she was now doing? Sileena knew she couldn't judge him for something that she was doing herself.

Dorren stood to the side and beckoned her to follow. She did, and he starting making his way down the corridor. Sileena followed him and they moved through passageways and rooms until she was completely lost. It must have been early morning because there were not as many people moving around as there had been the day before. But that was all she had to go on as she tried to figure out the time of day.

"So what am I supposed to be doing today?" Sileena asked, even though she knew that the answer would be derivative or non-existent.

"You will find out later," came the reply. Knew it.

They continued through the passageways and rooms until they

came to a stop at the entrance of a rather interesting hall. The room they had just come through had only one entrance and was filled with steam. There was the sound of moving water in this hall, although the source could not yet be made out. Dotted at either side of Dorren and Sileena were cubicles that lined the other side of this massive room. Wooden poles made up the framework of the cubicles, and fabrics completely covered the sides, concealing whatever was inside. Steam was coming out of the top of each one. Outside a couple of them were items of clothing. This place was very strange indeed. It did have a sort of enchanting feeling about it – the steam and flowing water seemed to have that effect on the room. Sileena liked it.

"Right," said Dorren. "This is the place where you will wash. Use one of the baths here and remember to put a piece of clothing just outside unless you want to accidentally receive some unwanted visitors."

Sileena gazed at the room before her, but was listening intently. She figured that Dorren was probably not the kind of person who would enjoy repeating himself. He turned to her and handed her the clothes and a sponge. She looked through the clothes and noticed that they were pretty much identical to the ones she was wearing now. Dorren continued his instructions.

"The water is filled with herbs that cleanse the body. Just wash and put on the other clothes. I will wait at the entrance until you get back."

Sileena did not know what to say, so she just nodded at him and walked to one of the unoccupied cubicles. Holding the fabric wall to the side, she gazed inside to find a pool of water releasing great clouds of steam. It looked much too hot to step in, but when she put a foot into the water she found it pleasantly warm. It must have been heated in the same way as the baths at home, through magic. The herbs used would be contributing to the excess steam.

Over the next few minutes she bathed in the waters, feeling completely at ease. Sileena enjoyed it to the extent that she had completely forgotten that Dorren was waiting outside. Eventually, though, there had to come a time for her to get out. Stepping out of the water Sileena suddenly realised that she did not have anything to dry herself with.

But when she looked down she found that her skin was already dry. It was certainly a very clever system that had been put into place. She wondered where these Outcasts managed to get hold of the materials they used to create this place, but presumed she would never know. Still, they used them with great efficiency. Never before had she been completely dry after stepping out of water. Even at home this was not the case. She put on the undergarments and clothes and stepped out of the cubicle. Looking towards the entrance she could make out Dorren leaning against the wall. When Dorren saw Sileena walking towards him he straightened himself.

"Oh, I need to get my old clothes," she exclaimed.

"Leave them," he replied. "Someone else will take and clean them."

Sileena obliged.

"Your dress will also be taken to be cleaned."

"So what's next?"

Dorren smiled and beckoned her to follow again. She almost had to suppress a sigh. What was the point of asking? The man was so stubborn. There was no point in him not telling her considering she was going to find out anyway. Sileena decided to stop herself from making any comment and followed Dorren, who now led them back through the corridor. She was actually much more comfortable now. Despite Dorren's occasional sarcastic comment she felt a lot more relaxed around him. Possibly because he could make sure she did the right thing; or it could be that he was the only person she knew here, otherwise she would feel out of place.

They made their way through the never-ending maze of passages and halls and Sileena noticed that more people were moving about now. Some were carrying materials, while others were in groups, exchanging, from what Sileena could tell, simple gossip. These Outcasts were feeling less like the barbarians she had been told about by the second.

Eventually they came to a stop outside the largest room she had seen so far. The ceiling was around three floors high. All over the place were arenas of sand, grass, or water with wooden floats bobbing on it. In other sections of the room were dolls placed on poles that lined the walls. They were training dummies. Sileena could see one individual fire an arrow and it embedded itself in the doll's chest.

"Welcome," said Dorren, "to the training grounds."

Sileena looked around with curiosity. She could see a few people dotted about doing their own training. Around the edges were racks that held many different weapons from maces to swords to pikes to bows and crossbows.

"I'm meeting the group here. They should be around shortly," he said, and took in a breath when he saw Derain, Gabe and another individual standing not far from them. "Why are they here so soon?" he muttered.

Dorren started to walk off towards the group and Sileena had to quickly follow. As they went, Sileena gazed curiously at what was going on all around her. She passed an arena where someone was spinning a staff around. The person was clearly skilled, but then he lost his grip and the staff hit the ground. Perhaps he needed a little more practice. He proceeded to pick it up and started spinning again. She could also see a few archers shooting at the dolls that were dotted along the walls. Most of their arrows hit their targets. At the edge of the room in a sand square was a man in a purple robe. He was standing in middle of the square with his arms stretched out and appeared to be focusing on something. After a few seconds there was an explosion around him and sand was blasted all around. The man in purple robes was still standing with his arms out as the sand fell to the ground.

Sileena stopped looking at him as she noticed that in one of the grass squares two people were fighting. One had a cutlass while the other had a pike. At either side of the grassy ring were two people holding out their hands towards the combatants.

"What are they doing?" asked Sileena.

Dorren stopped to see what she was referring to before answering. "Those two at the edge of the arena are sorcerers. They are protecting the two people in the centre as they fight."

Sileena was confused as she watched the continuing fight. The guy with the cutlass dodged the pike and slashed at the person wielding it. The cutlass bounced off his opponent, at which point they stopped fighting. Sileena had a moment of clarity as the realisation hit her. There must be a protective shield around the combatants that was ensuring they did not cause severe injury.

"You see," Dorren continued, "once one of them has dealt a blow that in a combat situation would be critical, they will stop the fight. There has been a training battle organised for me later, which you may watch if you want."

Well, that ought to be interesting, Sileena thought. Dorren was giving her an invitation. He clearly wanted to try and do a bit of showing off. Part of her wanted him to fail spectacularly just so there would be something to mock him for. The man did have a little bit of an ego about him. But a question popped into her head.

"Organised?"

"Well, it is hard to get magical people to do this for you. There are only a few here and it is hard to convince them to do it. They have other things to do, like keeping the baths functioning. This as well as stopping the tunnels from collapsing and maintaining the auras. Then they have their own social time." Dorren started moving again, and now Sileena could see Derain, Gabe and another man standing by one of the arenas. The other man was sitting on top of a massive boulder.

"So you need to organise a time with someone who is willing to do it?" Her questions regarding the use of magic in the maintenance of this Underground and its baths were also answered. Sileena understood now. "So in real battles this is what sorcerers would do? They would protect the men as they fought?"

They had now nearly reached the group, and passed another individual in red robes as they conjured a fireball and threw it at one of the dummies, hitting it directly. The dummy caught fire, at which point the person blasted it with some sort of frost enchantment which put out the flames and left the dummy with icicles on it.

"Not necessarily," replied Dorren. "The magic that it would take to shield someone from a blow that would kill them uses enough power to kill ten people. Logically speaking, it is just not worth it. In battle scenarios you are better off using magic to kill people than to shield someone. We only use it to shield during training."

Sileena didn't like that thought. If there was ever a war, Dorren was saying, then it would be better to kill someone than to protect another. This was why logic was not always the best thing.

"Although," Dorren continued, "it would probably be used to protect the leaders of an army. That is why it can be so hard to kill them."

"Oh." Sileena did not know what else to say. If it were a choice for her, she would protect her friends before taking any life. Her father would obviously choose to take life in order to win a war, but she would not become her father. However, it was not so clear what Nok's decision would be. What would he do? Should she ever see her brother again, she would have to ask.

Dorren and Sileena had finally reached Derain, Gabe and the other character. This man had short brown hair and a matching beard. He was of a medium build and looked to be in his early forties. So this might be Lockarr in his normal form. The man appeared to be lost in thought. Whatever he was pondering, she would never know. Her suspicions were confirmed when Dorren greeted him as Lockarr.

"Hey, Dorren," said Derain in a cheerful tone. "And hello, beautiful," he said, turning to Sileena. She gave him a cold look.

"I don't think she likes you," said Lockarr with a calming smile. He was sat on top of a massive boulder, sharpening a knife on it. Gabe and Derain were standing on the ground below, and all of them were clearly waiting for Dorren.

Sileena ignored the comments, still taking in the differences between Gabe and Derain. Although Derain was only slightly shorter than average, the difference in height between them was incredible.

"Well, most girls like me," reasoned Derain with a frown.

"No they don't," replied Lockarr, who had sheathed his knife and now started sharpening his sword.

Dorren smirked. "Perhaps she should just get to know you better and that would solve the problem."

"I doubt that," Lockarr said quickly. This was greeted by a glare from Derain.

Gabe gave Dorren a polite nod and a gentle smile. Dorren looked to Gabe and offered his own greeting. The way the four men interacted made it clear to Sileena that Dorren was the leader of the group.

"So why did you invite us to the training grounds so early?" asked Derain.

"I am here because I was told to bring Sileena for this time."

It was Derain's turn to speak. "So why are we here? None of us needed to be here right now, did we?"

Dorren sighed. "I said I would be here early. I never told you to be."

"Told you," said Lockarr. "Well, we are here now."

Derain looked disappointed. "Aww. I could have still been in bed now, enjoying my sleep."

Dorren smirked. "You would be enjoying something, but it would not be your sleep."

At that point Gabe, Lockarr and even Sileena smirked. Derain was obviously a little bit of a pervert, and Sileena's original impressions of the man were negative. Yet she could not help but feel a little sorry for him. He was being picked on by all his friends, but he did ask for it with the comments he made.

"Dorren!" came a yell from somewhere in the distance. Everyone in the group turned to see Severa and two of his lackeys approaching them. They appeared ready for a confrontation. "What are you doing here? I thought I had the training grounds at this time."

"We can come here if we like, Severa," came Derain's reply.

Severa looked at Derain. "I'm sorry, I do not believe I was talking to you." Turning his attention back to Dorren, he spoke again. "You get evenings. I get mornings. So you'd better have a good reason for being here." It was at that point he noticed Sileena. "You even brought the Eceriden girl."

This angered her. Severa was even trying to insult her, in his own way.

"It's Sileena, actually," she replied. Even from this brief exchange with Severa, she knew he was bad company. At that point she was glad that Dorren was the one who had kidnapped her and not Severa.

Severa ignored her and continued. "So is it wise to have her moving around and seeing the sites, Dorren? She'll be getting all this information that will ultimately lead to our downfall."

"Well, Pagar asked me to bring her here. If you have any problems with that or why we are here, then I suggest you bring it up with him." Dorren was unleashing his anger on Severa. They truly hated each other.

"That's Master Pagar picking favourites again," came Severa's angry reply.

Sileena was curious as to why they did not hold a battle to see who was the better fighter, although she doubted it would resolve their hatred of each other. Sileena could not see how these two were the best fighters compared to everyone else she had seen. There were people who were of much better build and looked like they could hold their own against either of the two men. Dorren and Severa were obviously very fit, but in comparison to someone like Gabe, they looked like they would really struggle in combat.

"You know," continued Severa, "we have unfinished business. You go off and do this" – he indicated Sileena – "and do not leave me any indication of what you were doing. I feel left out of all the fun."

The three big guys behind Severa were wearing sinister grins, and stood at the ready to help their leader if it was required.

"That is because I knew you couldn't handle something like that yourself. And you would miss me so much if you knew I was gone," replied Dorren with a smirk of his own.

"Oh, I doubt that. But that is not the issue. The training grounds are mine in the morning so I suggest you leave."

"We cannot do that," replied Dorren. "We have been ordered to come here by Pagar so I suggest you deal with it."

"I don't care what you think you have been told. I will keep an eye on the girl and you can leave."

"Oh bugger off, Severa," said Lockarr, who was now poised on the rock like he was ready for a fight. "No one cares about what you have to say. And besides, if you are looking for a fight then you had better find one that you can win."

Sileena had only just noticed that like Lockarr, Derain and Gabe had both adopted battle stances. Dorren, however, seemed to know something the others didn't as he remained quite relaxed and grinning smugly to himself.

"I could take you on, old man," Severa said coldly. If that was the best that he could come up with then he was obviously not the best at insults.

Lockarr seemed completely unfazed by Severa's comment. But he too relaxed his fighting stance and casually replied, "But you can't take us all on, even with your little backup. And I am far from old. Personally, I have wondered how you would react if I stuck my sword through you. Maybe one day we will find out."

At this point Severa reached for his sword, as did the two men behind him, but like Dorren and Lockarr, the rest of their group stopped their fighting stances and just stood, smirking. Severa and his lackeys, however, looked as if they were mere seconds from charging them. Sileena began to panic before she saw the confidence in the faces of her group. They clearly knew something she and Severa didn't.

A hand landed on Severa's shoulder. He turned at the ready, but instantly went pale as he saw a man with long brown hair and beard. The stranger was dressed in a red robe, and was looking intently at Severa.

"Master Pagar," said Severa in a wavering tone. He took a step back from the man and took his hand off the hilt of his sword. Even Severa, who was clearly a nasty individual, was halted by the presence of the man now standing before him. This new man was not much taller than Severa, but he still had the strongest presence in the entire room, greater even than Gabe. So this was Master Pagar. It was strange, Sileena reflected, to be so happy to see someone that she had never met before. Just by being here, Pagar had ensured that the almost inevitable fight was quickly stopped.

"Severa, Dorren," he said in a very sharp and clear voice. "I thought I said that you are not allowed to be anywhere near each other. Now Dorren, I need you here as I asked, but Severa..." There was a pause as the anticipation built. "Might I ask why you have chosen to completely disobey my orders?"

Severa was obviously trying to think of a good reason. "I use the training grounds in the morning. Dorren gets the evenings as was agreed."

"Yes it was agreed, but that does not explain why you have chosen, in this very large hall, to try and pick a fight with the man I told you to stay away from. I want you out of my sight."

Severa had a defeated expression on his face, and looked to the ground. "Yes, Master Pagar." He and his cronies walked away towards the exit.

"Right," Pagar said, and turned his attention to Sileena. His tone changed completely. Within a few seconds Severa's dismissal was like a distant memory. "So this must be Sileena."

"Yes, Pagar," came Dorren's reply.

Sileena noticed that Severa had called him Master Pagar, while Dorren just referred to him by name. The horrible man showed more respect to their leader than Dorren. Things must be more complicated than she first thought. It would take time for her to fully understand the people here.

"Good, good," Pagar said pleasantly. "I am Pagar, leader of this Underground. I am aware that Dorren here has been giving away information about the social protocols here."

Sileena went to protest, remarking on how little she knew, but Pagar, who was still smiling pleasantly, continued.

"It will help you while you remain here."

Sileena did not know what to say to that. She just stood there frowning at the man, who was being incredibly courteous. She was suspicious that there was something going on. This leader might be hiding another motive behind that smile. He had after all appeared to change his personality in a second after dealing with the issues Severa had caused. As her thoughts strayed over the possibilities she quickly realised that her frown had darkened and quickly pulled it back. Now was not the time to be aggressive.

Pagar took her silence as an invitation to keep speaking. "Well, there was a question I had for you. It turns out there was no exaggerating about you."

Sileena, who was still pondering, finally spoke. "What is the question?"

"Well, have you ever looked in a mirror?"

Oh, it was about her eyes and how abnormal they were. She was wondering why they had not brought that up before now. None of the people here had even acknowledged the fact that her eyes were gold.

"Ah, yes I have. You are talking about my eyes, aren't you?"

Pagar's expression betrayed his interest, if only a little. "Well, actually, yes. I was curious if you know anything about it."

Dorren and the rest of the group did not say a word. They stood back, but were listening intently. When Sileena glanced at Dorren he indicated that she should answer.

"Well, it's something I was born with. It's nothing to worry about from what I've been told. It is just an accident of nature."

"I see. So, Dorren, your first idea was right."

Sileena looked at Dorren again. So he had noticed her eye colour, and had even spoken to his leader on the matter. Why did he not ask her about her eyes all through their journey? Perhaps he was trying not to make her even more uncomfortable after putting her through the kidnapping – questions about her deformities in addition to that would have been trying.

Pagar continued to speak. "Sileena, my next question has to be about you. Have you ever practised magic? Before your kidnapping we did know of your family. However, we knew nothing about you other than your name. There may have been more we did not know." Pagar must have been choosing his words carefully and trying not to offend her. She could not help but admire that, as most of her previous company, including before her kidnapping, were not nearly as generous. She was still frowning, and not making as much effort as him in this exchange. It was as if he was sorry for her kidnapping. But the man was still prying for information, and she was still a prisoner. It was something that Sileena had to remind herself of over and over. She could simply refuse to answer. But there was no point in doing something like that other than to spite them.

"No. I have never been taught any kind of magic, and have been explicitly forbidden to read anything. But I do know how to read and write." She felt like there were a few glances exchanged between the group standing behind her. However, Pagar's pleasant expression remained unchanged.

"I see. Well, that is about all I needed to know. Thank you for being very cooperative. We may see each other again between now and when you leave. But for now, Dorren will be your host. There are just a few things I need to sort out. I hope your father is a reasonable man and will make the trade. I do not want any complications in this."

Sileena almost smiled. Her father was far from reasonable. But if her brother were there, he would be the one to sort things out. In the meantime, she had a question of her own. "Why did you send Dorren to kidnap me?"

Dorren coughed as Pagar answered.

"Well, Dorren was not supposed to go. He left on his own accord. But what's done is done and we must accept it. Besides, he succeeded so we don't need to have that discussion, do we, Dorren?"

Dorren looked at the ground in a very similar manner to Severa.

Pagar nodded at him and turned to leave. "Don't do anything stupid, Dorren, and hope the fight goes well," he said, walking away. Dorren smiled.

"So what is it between you two?" Sileena asked as Pagar disappeared out of sight.

"He is my father," Dorren said, watching Pagar leave. Oh, she thought. Now a lot of things make sense. She still had questions but asking them now might be unwise. She could ask later when Dorren was in a more indulgent mood.

Once Pagar was gone, the red-robed individual who had cast the fire and ice at the dolls approached them, pulling the hood over their head. As the figure drew closer Sileena saw that it was a woman who must have been a little older than herself. She had blonde hair that only just reached her shoulders, and bright blue eyes. Sileena noticed her elegant movements and beautiful face; the opposite of her initial impressions of the Outcasts. How fast opinions can change, she mused to herself.

"You always get into trouble, don't you? One of these days, Dorren, Severa will stab you in the back."

"But that would lose him his reputation, and he would never be able to prove that he is the better out of the two of us," came his reply.

"Well hello there, Anna," said Derain in his provocative tone. "So when is it you are going to leave your partner and join me?" At least Sileena now knew that she was not the only target for Derain's lascivious manner. It was quite funny to watch when she wasn't the target.

Anna merely smiled. "Like I've told you before, there is no chance of you getting someone like me."

Derain laughed. Anna then walked over to Gabe, and when she reached him he lifted her gently off the ground with the ease of a man picking up a pebble, until they were face to face. They then kissed passionately in front of them all. At that point Dorren and Lockarr laughed as well. It was all a joke to them. Even Derain was smiling. Perhaps he wasn't actually trying to seduce Anna, but just being himself. Maybe he was not as bad as Sileena thought.

Anna and Gabe were not a couple Sileena would have expected to be together: the man who looked like a brute and the pretty, petite girl. But they looked happy and she was not the kind of person to judge. Gabe put Anna back down and she curled an arm around his and leaned against him.

"I wish you two would sort out your differences," said Anna. "I reckon you would make a very good team."

Dorren laughed again. "I doubt that."

Sileena then quickly came in with a question before Anna could reply. "So why don't you and Severa ever do one of those fights to see who's the best? You know, one of those training fights?"

Dorren grimaced, so it was Derain who jumped in and answered.

"They did. The match was completely even. But when it should have been declared over and a draw, the two of them continued to hack away at each other until Pagar himself forced them apart. They have never been allowed to fight since."

"We were young and got carried away," Dorren reasoned.

"And from what I saw," said Anna sarcastically, "you two have really grown up since."

Dorren continued to protest but was soon defeated by the consensus from the rest of the group. The topic quickly changed when they noticed a group of people holding an archery competition, and moved to watch.

Over the next while the group moved about the training grounds and talked. At first Sileena remained silent. She did not know what to say. Occasionally a question was directed at her and this gradually brought her into the conversation. More people began to arrive, while others who had finished with their tasks left the grounds. Their group had even watched another fight between two people. After what must have been an hour three more people joined them. They were all in robes, which suggested that they were people with magical talents.

"Right then. Are we going to get this started?" one of them said.

Dorren nodded and they moved into one of the grass arenas. Derain and Lockarr followed. Gabe gave Anna another kiss.

"Destroy him," she said. At that Gabe smiled and entered the arena too. Sileena, whose first impressions of the Outcasts seemed to have been completely wrong, was once again proven right by Anna and her commanding presence. This fragile-looking girl clearly had a bit more of a kick to her.

"Don't worry," said Dorren. "I will make sure he comes back to you in one piece."

A few people in the training grounds took an interest and came to watch. At one side of the arena stood the three other magical people, while Anna and Sileena stood at the other. Lockarr, Gabe and Derain moved to the side with the three other magical people, and each took out their weapons. Dorren stood opposite and drew out a katana and a dagger. He then proceeded to stand posed at the ready.

Sileena was a little shocked. "Is this not unfair?"

"Yeah, it is," said Anna. "We need more people to go against Dorren before it would be fair."

That was not what Sileena meant.

"Should you not be supporting your partner instead of Dorren?" bellowed Derain.

"I am," Anna said, smiling. "But you must face up to the result. Ready!"

The other magical people also said 'ready', as did Dorren, Lockarr, Derain and Gabe. There was a brief pause, and silence from all around. Sileena froze in anticipation. She was actually getting excited. She was almost appalled with herself for her interest in this fight. But that thought was quickly thwarted when Anna spoke again.

"Go!"

At that point all party members charged towards the centre of the ring. Dorren ran through the grass towards his opponents while the other three moved in unison towards Dorren. When they got close enough Derain fell to his knees and slid across the ground with both his dual swords at angles to intercept Dorren. Dorren jumped to avoid them, but Gabe had swung his axe effortlessly just above the two dual swords. Dorren must have anticipated this as he moved his katana at an angle and deflected the axe high enough for him to fit through the gap. When he hit the ground he rolled to his feet and turned around quickly to hit Gabe. Instead he was met by Lockarr, who was at the ready and stopped the strike. Dorren quickly kicked Lockarr away, but before he could do anything else Derain had jumped into the air with a kick of his own, hitting Dorren in his chest. Dorren fell back to the ground as the two-sided axe swung effortlessly towards him. Dorren rolled to the side just as the axe hit the earth and pieces of grass and mud shot into the air. It was amazing to Sileena that she could see all this happen and it was all in a couple of seconds.

Derain had already lunged at Dorren, but before he could hit him the katana managed to deflect both weapons and the swords embedded themselves in the ground. Dorren got to his feet in no time and moved his knife down towards Derain. But Lockarr and Gabe were on him again. Lockarr hit the dagger out of Dorren's hand, while Gabe swung the massive axe towards him. Dorren had to jump to the side to stop Gabe scoring a direct strike. Sileena noticed that Dorren for the most part was avoiding the axe blows. While he had managed to deflect the massive weapon, it was only just slightly, so that he could successfully avoid a strike that would have lost him the match. She guessed that

Gabe was just too powerful for Dorren to block his attempted strikes. Sileena also noticed the teamwork between the three others. As long as they continued what they were doing Dorren was never going to hit any of them. Whenever he had an opening against one opponent, another jumped in to save their teammate.

Dorren lunged at them with his katana at his side. The other three stood ready. Derain was spinning his dual swords around and moved in to hit his adversary. Dorren countered and stabbed at Derain, who deflected the shot with his other sword. Lockarr was also stabbing at Dorren, but this attack too was countered. The speed of these strikes and parries were amazing to watch. Sileena had never seen anything like it before. No wonder many people had come to watch. Dorren, armed with one katana, was fighting against three other swords. Gabe was behind the other two and readying himself to swing the axe. A series of blows was initiated between the swords but not a single one landed as they were all deflected to either side. After a couple of seconds both Derain and Lockarr ducked as Gabe's axe swung towards Dorren, who quickly backflipped to avoid the sharp steel. The axe passed just over him, narrowly missing his jaw.

By the time Dorren was on his feet Derain and Lockarr were on him again. He quickly deflected Derain's shots with sufficient force to make Derain take time to recover before attacking again. In that time Dorren also deflected Lockarr's shot to the other side and kicked him away. Dorren turned to strike Lockarr, but even Sileena could tell he was out of range. Lockarr seemed to notice this too, and prepared for his own strike once Dorren had missed. But instead of missing, Dorren let go of his own weapon. The sword flew through the air and Lockarr merely smiled as the blade struck him on the chest. But instead of embedding itself in his flesh the katana deflected off a magical barrier that was protecting Lockarr, and fell to the ground.

"Out!" came a voice from one of the three sorcerers. The axe had at that point swung down on top of Dorren, who quickly jumped to the side to avoid it. Lockarr walked out of the arena with absolutely no sign of disappointment. He clearly didn't care that he had been defeated in the ring. Turning back to the fight, Sileena saw Derain move towards

Dorren's katana. He kicked it out of his hand, and the sword landed behind him next to the knife, which had previously been knocked out of Dorren's grasp. Dorren turned to face his predicament. Gabe and Derain stood between him and his weapons. There was another moment of pause as the two waited for him to make the first move. But Derain was clearly impatient and attacked. Dorren quickly grabbed the hilts of both Derain's swords and the two of them struggled with each other while Gabe came from behind and swung the axe at his opponent. Derain saw it and ducked, while Dorren jumped over the crouching man, again narrowly missing the swinging axe. Dorren finally found an opening and dashed for his weapons. He picked up his katana and knife and turned to see Gabe and Derain lunging at him, clearly desperate to finish him before he could fight back. He moved to the side of the axe and parried one of the swords. Moving past Derain, he swung his sword to hit him from behind, but the other dual sword was positioned behind Derain and it blocked the strike. Dorren then quickly took a step back and kicked Derain, who went face first into the grass.

Gabe moved in to swing the axe again, this time with one hand. Dorren moved to the side, only to be caught by Gabe's other arm. Gabe picked Dorren up and threw him quickly at Derain before Dorren could strike. Derain slashed at Dorren as he neared, but Dorren managed to block both swords with his katana and knife before again hitting the ground. He quickly rolled to his feet, only to be met by the dual swords again. Dorren fought them off and managed to kick Derain away. Derain fell to the ground, stunned, but Dorren focused his attention back to Gabe, who was unnaturally fast with an extraordinarily heavy-looking weapon. Gabe swung the axe in a downwards diagonal direction. Dorren moved to one side and slashed at Gabe's knee with his knife, hitting the invisible barrier once again. Surprisingly no one said 'out', but Sileena remembered that it had to be a critical hit.

Gabe swung the axe in the other direction with one hand while the other clenched fist moved towards Dorren at unnatural speed. Dorren moved away from the axe again, but this time swung his katana and hit Gabe across the chest. The blade met the shield and slid across, not scratching the giant man at all.

Gabe's fist, however, was still swinging and it hit home. Dorren went flying back and hit the ground with a thud. It was just too late to have stopped the strike as Dorren's sword hit its intended target before being knocked back.

"Out!" came a cry from another of the three sorcerers. Gabe turned and left the arena with a disappointed expression on his face.

"Nice try, dear," Anna yelled. The audience were cheering now at the skilled fight that was transpiring before them. Dorren got off the ground and turned to Derain, who was already at a stance, ready to fight. The two of them exchanged looks before charging at each other and trading blows. Derain was spinning the swords about frantically while Dorren made all manners of strikes. Derain was obviously skilled. They fought back and fore but Derain would not make any bold moves because he was clearly too wary of the much better fighter he was now facing alone. He was staying on the defensive and trying to keep Dorren at bay. After a few more blows Dorren was the one to make the bold move as he lunged his full body at his opponent. Derain parried the initial attacks but Dorren adapted the lunge to a spinning attack with his knife and katana as he passed. Derain could not stop all the attacks, and he would not commit to any strikes of his own. The knife and katana bounced off the shield a couple of times before Dorren and Derain were finally back to back.

"Out!" came the final call from one of the sorcerers. Everyone applauded and cheered as the fight was over and Derain left the arena. Sileena could not help but join in as well. It was very impressive. They were brilliant. Derain, Lockarr and Gabe also applauded as Dorren bowed to everyone and gave a separate bow directed at Sileena before exiting the arena. Sileena shook her head. He was such a show-off. He moved around the arena to join the others. All the spectators including the three sorcerers began to leave and return to their own activities.

"We were close that time," said Derain, happily trying to goad Dorren after his defeat. Dorren merely snorted in response. "I'm thinking we will beat Dorren next time, right everyone?"

"Yeah," replied Anna. "In his sleep. So what are we going to do now?"

"Well, let's go get some food," said Dorren. "Me and Sileena have not had any breakfast yet and I'm starving. What about you, Sileena?"

Sileena shyly nodded. She became a little more confident than she'd been first thing that morning, but there was obviously a way to go.

"Brilliant. After that I am to give you the grand tour. Anyone else up for that?"

"Of course," said Derain, and everyone else nodded. "I don't know about all of you but I think I've forgotten where some of the facilities are."

Sileena could see that Derain had some of Dorren's sarcastic humour. Dorren had probably rubbed off on him a bit over the time they'd spent as friends.

Sileena followed them out as Derain started talking about how he had stayed the longest in the arena before getting beaten, but Lockarr pointed out that he'd saved him a couple of times. This started the debate as they left the training grounds.

Nok was back home, sorting out the money that would be needed to pay Sileena's ransom. He had been spending most of his time pretending that nothing had happened, merely continuing with his duties as the son of a lord. This bothered him greatly; wishing he could do something but was instead being forced to keep everyone happy.

When he spoke with his father about Sileena, Nerida merely told Nok to prepare the money needed to pay the ransom. At first it surprised him that his father was so willing to pay, but there was obviously a hidden motive. Once Sileena was back Nerida planned to invade the Outcasts and kill those that had dared steal from him – those were his words.

Nok was sitting in his study and deciding where to get the resources. Just as he was finished sorting out the details his father entered the room.

"Have you put the coin together?"

"It is finished, my lord. We are ready for when we make the exchange. It will not cost us anything important."

"Good, good," Nerida replied. "When we make the exchange and Sileena is back to our side then I will deal with all those foolish enough to come and make the exchange. After that, it will be over for them."

Nok thought to himself that he was glad he was not on their team. But once Sileena was safe, Nok would join his father's side and gladly aid in the destruction of those that had bothered them for so long.

"I will unleash everything. Not a single one of them will survive. And then I will make their land my own. They have made a fool of me for long enough."

Nok could see the anger and the slightest hint of gold in his father's eyes. "Very good, my lord."

With that, Nerida left the room. Well, it was good that for a change Nerida was venting his anger at someone who was not here. Nok usually disagreed with his father's aggressive choices and felt that they were too harsh but not this time. He was looking forward to leading a force and cleansing the land of the savage people that stayed there. For once, he completely agreed with his lord.

# 6

# THE MARSHES

Throughout the rest of the day Sileena and her new company conversed on trivial matters. Subjects that came up included what would happen if you shot ice and fire at each other, while another questioned why fruits each had their own colour. This complete ignorance of any kind of serious talk puzzled Sileena at first. But as the day wore on the puzzlement soon turned to genuine joy, and it was not long before she completely forgot about her predicament once more.

The group at first went to the food stall where they each took fruit and meat to eat. Dorren gave strange tokens to the woman running the food stall, which Sileena later found out were ration coupons. Afterwards they went on their tour through the tunnels and caves to many different parts of the Underground. There was the farm that raised animals and grew the food needed to maintain the entire community. There was no access to sun, and water was scarce so the crops were grown through magic and potions. The whole process fascinated Sileena. She had never been to a farm, and seeing the way it functioned was intriguing to watch. She heard about one particular potion that could conjure up the water needed from the ground. Sileena watched as one of the farmers tipped the potion into a hole and water came up where the drop had landed. It filled the hole, and once it reached the top it spilled through a network reaching across the field. The fields stretched further than she could see, and were bustling with people, all contributing towards this effort.

After witnessing the fields, the group headed towards a set of dead ends where some people were digging away at the earth. This was where they were expanding the Underground, making new homes and new halls. If any strangers were to arrive then the rooms would be ready to receive them. Sileena had to acknowledge that from what she saw Pagar knew exactly how to run this sort of community. Everything functioned so smoothly. It didn't look like they were struggling. This puzzled Sileena and brought a question to her mind: why would they need her for ransom then? Their lives were set. Why did they need the money? They don't even use it themselves. This ration system was their personal form of currency. But when she noticed that her company were now making their way to the exit she decided to push those thoughts away, follow and find out what they were going to show her next.

As the group walked through what seemed to be an endless stream of passages they conversed about many things. About Severa and Pagar. A few questions were directed at Sileena about Eceriden and what life was like there. Sileena was glad that she could be the person answering some questions and not the one completely in the dark.

Another topic that came up was something known as 'the Reunion'. From what Sileena could gather it was some sort of big celebration. She got this idea from the mention of dancing and drink. The Outcasts did not seem like the kind of people who would do that kind of thing. But then, on countless occasions she had been surprised by them, and if there was one thing to learn from this experience it was not to be surprised by anything.

The group moved through more tunnels, passing by the people's quarters. Inside they were very similar to Sileena's room, except each room was a bit bigger and more elaborately decorated. They passed by one door that appeared no different from the rest, except for the number thirty-seven carved on it. Dorren commented that the room beyond was Gabe's room. Sileena knew the number but it would take a miracle for her to somehow find this place in the maze of passages. It was a wonder how anyone could find their way here. The Underground seemed to have no structure to its layout. When she asked about it Dorren seemed surprised at the question. There was a structure, apparently, and judging by his confused expression it must have been pretty obvious. However, this was her first tour of the place and so it would take a little more time to see it.

Throughout the tour Dorren kept taking out a shining stone from one of his pockets and looking at it before putting it back. The stone was shining blue and gradually turning red, and then slowly back to blue. It was a beautiful object and the changing colours must represent something. But before Sileena could ask, Derain started speaking about something entirely different so she turned her attention back to the system of tunnels.

As the day moved on Sileena was beginning to understand the network and how the passages intersected. She noticed a couple of patterns here and there. She still didn't have complete understanding, but her confidence grew now that she was starting to understand it a little more.

Sileena guessed that the group were now at the back of the entire underground system. It led to a particularly large hall, with the highest ceiling she had ever seen. It was a massive cave which was shaped like a giant dome. The dome was entirely empty except for a couple of people who moved a few of the boxes around. A single pillar, certainly large enough, held up the centre.

"You have been kidnapped at the right time," said Dorren with a smile.

Sileena looked at Dorren with a questioning expression. "Why?"

"Well, you will be here to witness the Reunion, and it is taking place here this year."

"Uh, no she won't," said Derain. "She will be hidden away from it for safety reasons."

"I'm sure I would be fine," Sileena said, irritated. She could handle herself.

"Not for you. For us. Giving you a tour and showing you vital information about us – well, more than we already have – is not the best solution."

"You sound like Pagar," Dorren said.

"Well, don't you think that he is right, though? He is our leader for a reason."

Dorren muttered something, but then walked back into the cave system and the rest followed.

Throughout the day Sileena saw a theatre room with a giant

wooden stage, and a couple of market rooms selling various ornaments and potions. It was not nearly as good as the market back in Sarden but she guessed that it was all that these Outcasts could have mustered. Despite not actually being able to go to the market back at home she could still see it from her window at the keep. She wondered how many of the items were stolen.

Then, coming across a different food stall, they stopped for something else to eat. Sileena received bread and meat, and a strange cake that she had never tried before. It didn't look very nice but her curiosity got the better of her and after trying a bit she found, yet again, that looks could be deceiving. When she queried about it she found out that it was a delicacy that was found in Duka. It was interesting that the culture of the Outcasts' Land appeared to be a combination of Eceriden's, Duka's and other cultures. The place was a hybrid of many civilisations in one. Those that arrived contributed their own ideas to the culture, and with those ideas the place grew.

After the meal everyone in the group said goodbye and left, leaving Dorren and Sileena walking about the corridors alone.

"So what's happening next?" Sileena said, with a bit too much excitement.

Dorren looked at her, smiling pleasantly. "Now I take you back to your quarters. It is getting late. I am glad you enjoyed yourself despite the knowledge that you are my prisoner."

Sileena was listening to that last part, but more focused on what was said at the beginning. "It is getting late? How can you tell?"

Dorren took out the shining stone, which was no longer red but had now almost completely turned a dark blue. "Because we live underground we cannot see the sun, and therefore cannot have a good idea as to what the time is. This stone does it for us. Blue means it is night while the red means that it is daytime. The colour you see now indicates that it is nearly midnight."

Sileena admired the beauty of the stone. "Does it take magic to make these stones as well?"

"No, not with these. The stones are found in the mountains to the south of here. No one seems to know about them apart from us."

"You risk lives to get stones that merely change colour? Don't the monsters in the mountains pose a threat?"

"Actually these stones are found at the borders between us and the Eagle Jay Mountains. We do not need to venture too far and so there is no risk to our safety from monsters and dragons."

Sileena pondered what Dorren said. She clearly did not know much because her father had restricted her learning so severely. She therefore had no idea what life was like in the nearby lands. She had heard of the people of the northern kingdoms, the forest folk and those of the Bryton Mountains, but then again, who in Eceriden had not heard of them? What if everything she had known was a lie as well? The Outcasts were not a bunch of bloodthirsty savages after all. What if Duka was not filled with ritualistic psychopaths? What if Eceriden was not the land of good after all?

As she was in thought, Dorren had noticed that something was bothering her. "What's the matter?"

"Oh. It's...well, I have so many questions and they can go on and on."

For once, Dorren was the person wearing a questioning expression. "I am happy to answer any questions – well, any questions that do not require me to betray vital information. I think I've told you enough of that," he mused. "But it is not a bother to me. It's good to be able to answer. Most questions that have been put to me before now received the answer, 'But it wasn't me!'"

Sileena smiled at this.

"But for now you only get one more question, so choose it well because we need to get you back to your quarters and I want to get to my bed."

Sileena thought for a moment before deciding on one that was not for the vital information Dorren spoke of. "Can I get one of those special stones for telling the time? I think I might need one for the rest of my time here."

Dorren considered for a moment before answering. "I will ask to see if you are allowed, and if so I will get one from the vault and give it to you tomorrow."

"Vault?"

Dorren instantly closed his mouth with a look of shock on his face. He had clearly given too much information away. "Are you coming?" he said, pretending that Sileena never asked about the vault.

She followed him back through the tunnels and once they had reached a certain point she began to understand where she was, and before she knew it they were back at the corridor where her room was.

Dorren opened the door to reveal a new set of clothes sitting on her bed, as well as a sponge. "You will need those tomorrow after the bath. Obviously people do not need to wash as often as we do, but because we are underground it is dirty, I think, so we wash every day and get into a new set of clothes."

Sileena looked at him and nodded politely. "Goodnight," she said, and Dorren said the same thing back before closing the door and locking it. Sileena could hear Dorren cursing to himself, most likely about the vault he spoke of, and she smiled to herself. She was not going to leak any of this information. Certainly not to her father as he would not believe her, so Dorren shouldn't worry.

She put the clothes on the cabinet and lay on her bed. Dorren was a peculiar one. He had some intelligence, but little common sense. She couldn't help but smile at some of the silly things he was doing. How the hell did he sneak into Sarden and kidnap her? One of life's great mysteries, she mused to herself. But he did have a degree of determination that few possessed, and she had to acknowledge that he was certainly smarter than her. Her time at home, though, was the reason for her lack of knowledge. After pondering this it was not long before she realised how tired she was. She let her thoughts go through all that she had learned, and then to all that she wanted to find out. After a little while exhaustion overwhelmed her and she was in a deep sleep throughout the night, happily dreaming about a dragon flying over her head and landing in front of her before greeting her with a polite nod.

Sileena awoke to a knock on the door. When she said to enter, she was happy to see Dorren come in to greet her.

"Sleep well?"

"Very well." She was still a bit tired from just waking up, but it was the best sleep she'd had in a long time, and that included the time before her kidnapping.

"Here," he said, and handed her a stone that was shining with a bright red glow. "I talked with Master Pagar and he said that it would be fine to give you one of these stones."

It was a bit smaller than Dorren's, but she guessed that the stones were mined from the mountains in many different forms and sizes.

"What does this colour mean?" she asked, indicating the stone's bright red glow.

"Red means midday, and when faded it means the colour is soon going to change. This colour means that it is early afternoon."

"Early afternoon?!" She must have slept for half a day. Perhaps she was more tired than she'd first thought.

"Yeah, sorry about coming here so late. Have you been up long?"

"I just got up."

"Oh, great. So you really have had a good night's sleep." Strange – it should have sounded like a sarcastic comment, but for once Dorren didn't give that impression, and his smile was genuine. "Right let's get you to the bathroom and washed. I've already bathed. Then something to eat, and you can go back to wherever it is you want to go. Within reason of course."

Sileena followed Dorren out and back to the baths. The day seemed to pass in a similar manner to the previous one. The only difference was that Dorren basically gave Sileena a personal tour of the place. Better him than the perverted Derain, she thought. He would have probably been something similar to 'These are my quarters, tour done – want to come in?' At least this way she was getting to see everything. Even if it was with her kidnapper. With him she was really getting the feel for the Underground.

Dorren explained that everyone contributed towards the running of the Outcasts' home. That was why Derain, Gabe, Anna and Lockarr were not with the group this day as they were all doing their jobs. When Sileena asked why he was not doing any work he explained that he was, by keeping an eye on her, as she was important for the ransom. This reminder dampened her spirits for a little while but soon the questions returned and she was oblivious to her situation. Dorren proceeded to tell her about the mountains to the south, and about Duka and its supposedly brutal traditions. Ritual sacrifice was important as it helped keep the people of Duka safe from evil spirits. Only the great god of the earth could keep the spirits away, and it needed to be appeased. It was considered a great honour to be the person who was sacrificed. Only one was chosen out of the whole of Duka each year. Only those who worshipped the god by doing the great pilgrimage were able to join the list of candidates allowed to do it. Sileena also found out about the barbarians that lived in the eastern forests of Duka. They were the only people that Dorren believed to be savages and crazy. But he acknowledged his ignorance on the matter as he had never been there, nor witnessed these people. He'd only heard rumours, apparently the same rumours as Sileena, but they both knew that rumours could be false.

The conversation moved from the barbarians of the Grey Forest to the dragons of the southern mountains. It then drifted to the wolves of the forest that Dorren had originally taken Sileena through.

Dorren did not speak of these animals in the same manner as he discussed people. His attitude certainly showed that he preferred animals. However, he did say that the great wolf Vartak was a bad one, according to the stories. Whether these dragons and the great Vartak existed remained a mystery. But it was always fun to speculate.

Sileena wanted to know more about the mountains to the south where there was apparently a wealth of minerals to be had, but no one ever mined them. Dorren clarified that some tried but didn't get far as the beasts of the mountains usually killed them. Sileena was also curious about the vault that Dorren had mentioned and the Reunion, but she did not want to put pressure on him. He seemed willing to answer any questions regarding their everyday lifestyle and anything outside the Outcasts' Land. But he might not be willing to answer personal questions. If she did ask, then she might cause Dorren to stop replying and anger him. So she asked why the Outcasts made all this effort to go underground, and why not live on the surface, even though the answer was obvious. Dorren explained that it was for safety reasons, so they could never be found should anyone try and invade. It was important to keep their civilisation hidden so they were never found out as actually being civilised and deemed a threat. But Sileena didn't perceive them as a threat. They seemed like normal people going about their lives. If this was all an illusion, then it was a brilliant illusion. No one originally knew of her kidnapping. It was all Dorren's scheme. Yet despite knowing this Sileena couldn't help but enjoy the conversation with him. Without the silly sarcasm at her expense it became one of the best companionships she had experienced in her life. Even more so than that with her brother.

During the tour Sileena was shown a new room that she had not seen yet. It seemed to be a massive games room where people played different sports. These games didn't seem to involve people attacking each other, as they did in the training grounds. There were some unusual, fascinating instruments she had never seen before being used for different sports. Sileena tried to focus on one game at a time, and to decipher the rules. Some were easier than others.

Dorren didn't speak much, except to answer any questions she asked. But Sileena was too interested in the games being played. When she glanced in his direction she noticed that he was watching her. Possibly to stop her from making any kind of escape attempt. Whatever the reason, she didn't care. The games were fascinating to watch. Part of her wanted to join in, but she was not dressed the part so decided against asking.

"It's time to head back."

Sileena was a little taken aback, and glanced at her new stone. She was surprised to find out that it was the end of the day already. Despite it feeling so short she felt as if she had learned more than ever. Not just about the Outcasts, but about the other kingdoms. Her brother had taught her how to read and write, but very little about the outside world. There was only time to teach her the essentials without being found out. After today, though, she felt like she knew a lot more about the world which she was part of. She had better not tell her father, though, or else she would end up regretting it. Hostage or not, it was still a good day.

It was not long before the two of them were standing outside her room again.

"Goodnight, Sileena. I will see you again, perhaps at some point over the next few days."

Sileena frowned. "What?"

"I have other commitments around here. I can't just leave the jobs I am supposed to do."

"I thought I was your job?" she said.

"You were, but the jobs change so people get to do different things. I was to make sure that you knew where everything was so from now on you will be able to handle yourself."

She was taking this slight change more harshly than she would have expected. Why should she care if she got someone else to look after her? "Yes, but—"

"But now that is done you are now free to move about as you please – with some exceptions, like Pagar's office, other people's rooms and of course the front door. At some point in the morning someone will come and unlock the door for you. There will be someone stand-ing outside and they will watch you and follow just to make sure you don't do anything stupid. The guard will have your ration coupons so they will be able to pay for your food."

"Who is it?"

"I don't know. Sorry. But I wouldn't worry about it," he said with the warm smile he'd seemed to recently acquire.

Sileena was shocked. "What am I supposed to do?"

"That's up to you. Go back to the games hall if you like. You certainly seemed to enjoy it."

Sileena was about to try and argue, but thought against it. The two of them said goodnight and she slumped back to bed.

Over the next ten days Sileena started to get much more comfortable. Despite being a prisoner she was able to move about more freely than back at home. It was rather ironic, after giving it some thought. Back in Sarden she was never allowed to be around for certain guests and never allowed to leave the castle grounds. Yet here she was able to move almost anywhere, provided she was accompanied by the guard. The Underground was a lot bigger than the castle.

At first she was a little confused about what to do now that Dorren was not around to guide her. So he *did* actually do other work, she mused to herself. From what she could tell he was a bit of a rebel so actually helping with the Underground seemed a little unusual for him.

When she exited her room she found a man she did not recognise standing outside, and when she started moving down the tunnel the man followed a few paces behind. She did what she had done for the past two days and went for the baths first. Once changed, she then moved to the eatery for something to eat.

When Sileena had got the food she needed she turned to see many people all sitting down and eating their own breakfasts. Most were huddled in groups discussing daily topics. She looked around for a bench to sit on and found an empty one at the back of the room. As she moved towards it the man following her moved to the counter to pay the rations and get something for himself. She sat in a spot alone and ate. She did not know what she was supposed to do. Perhaps go to the games hall and just sit and watch.

After eating awkwardly for a few minutes she heard her name being yelled. When she looked to see who had made the noise she could see Anna sitting with a group of girls. Sileena moved across to them and was quickly and cheerfully greeted by the girls. The group was made up of different ages and sizes and arguably the largest crowd in the eatery, and certainly the loudest. She started talking to them and got to know each of them one by one through the wonderful introductions Anna gave. She got a few questions directed at her and started asking them questions back, many of which she had been pondering the night before.

"So what job is Dorren doing?"

"Well," one of the girls replied, "he would be working on the farms today. Isn't he?"

"Yeah, he is," replied another.

"Is he any good at it?" Sileena said jokingly.

"We don't know. We don't usually work alongside him."

As the conversation developed she noticed that Anna didn't say much. She just sat there and smiled at Sileena. The smiled widened as the questions kept going, which made Sileena a little uncomfortable.

After everyone had finished their meal the group invited Sileena to come along, and she happily agreed. Together they moved through the endless tunnels. Sileena could still not figure out where they were heading or where they were. But she didn't have long to think about it as one of the girls noticed that they were being followed. Sileena told them that it was the man who was guarding her. The group started talking in angry whispers, and then one of them spoke up.

"Oi! Girls only!"

The man stepped forward and spoke in a deep, authoritative voice. "I have a duty to perform. I have to guard her." He pointed at Sileena.

Anna stepped in front of him and levelly faced him. "We can keep an eye and guard her. You can run along now."

"I am afraid I cannot do that, Anna."

"Listen," Anna continued. "Unless you want to be embedded in the wall behind you I suggest you turn around and walk away."

The man hesitated, looking from Anna to Sileena. After briefly pondering what to do he decided to oblige, then turned and moved away, disappearing around the corner.

Sileena felt surprised by what had happened as Anna turned around to face her.

"No one messes with us. Not even Severa's group. There is only one man who would try anything stupid against this group of girls."

Sileena smiled as she only had one person in mind who would be that foolish. "Derain?"

At that name some of the girls started giggling, which earned a cold look from Anna. There were some girls that actually liked Derain?

"He is not a very nice person."

"Says who?" said Anna. "He is actually a nice guy. He may look like he is trying but he would not make a move on a girl who did not want it." Anna glanced at the giggling girls, who lowered their heads in shame.

After that Sileena enjoyed their company throughout the day and the other days ahead. On some occasions she met up with Dorren, Derain and Gabe. On others she met up with the girl group. One morning Sileena moved to the bathroom with her guard behind her. After that day with Anna he would keep an eye until she joined either of the two groups and then he would disappear. He waited at the entrance while Sileena went towards one of the bath cubicles that did not have clothes outside it. When she opened the cubicle she was completely shocked to see Derain and a young woman sitting in the bath side by side. Derain had one arm around her and even with the steam Sileena could guess that they were both completely naked. They noticed her and Derain gave her a pleasant smile.

"Hi, Sileena. There's room for one more."

Sileena quickly closed the cubicle flap and walked away. She smiled as she headed towards another cubicle without a piece of clothing outside it, and when she looked in she found that it was empty. With a sigh of relief, she went in to wash. Apart from that she had no more problems in the bathroom.

She went to the training grounds to watch a few fights, but she spent most of the time in the games room and witnessed a few rounds of whatever strange sport they were playing. At one point she was invited to join in, and it was fun, despite her being awful at it. The others did not seem to mind how bad she was, though. It was fast-paced and tiring. Dorren also joined in and he helped her get to grips with the rules, teaming up with her where he could. But despite working together the two of them and their team ended up losing.

Dorren merely smiled and gave her a gentle pat on the back. "Next time."

As the days wore on Sileena felt a little useless. When she asked Dorren if she was supposed to do any work he told her that she was not allowed to work as a prisoner. She tried to reason but it was fruitless.

There was the odd occasion when she would walk past Severa, but he usually left her alone. Only if Dorren was there would he say anything. At one point Sileena convinced the girls who were not working on that day to go to the farms to annoy Dorren and to mock him as he was working. Dorren, however, just laughed at them for wasting their time.

After a few weeks of living in the Underground she felt a lot more comfortable at being able to move around freely and even make plans with her friends. She was starting to feel bad about the prospect of leaving them and returning to Sarden. The guard every morning was a gentle reminder that she was a prisoner. A lot of time had passed and it would not be long before she would be able to go through with the trade and return home. Back to being nothing more than a slave, learning nothing except for whatever her brother could find the time to teach her. Back to being confined in the dreary castle where her father was waiting; a man who might hit her for something that had nothing to do with her. This was entirely unfair. She did not want to leave.

Dorren stared at his half-filled glass and sat in the eatery with his thoughts, surrounded by his friends. It was getting late and Sileena had just left to get some sleep. She was adapting well, he thought to himself. The girl had gone from being a shy and helpless victim to what would seem to be an official Outcast, in all but name anyway.

Derain and Lockarr soon followed Sileena's lead and gave their farewells before leaving the eatery for their beds. The numbers of their group were dwindling as time passed, leaving only Gabe, Dorren and Anna.

"Goodnight, dear," said Anna to Gabe as he rose from his chair. Gabe gave her a kiss and walked away to his quarters. Anna turned to Dorren and sat next to him, giving him a penetrating look that would have unnerved him if not for the fact that it was Anna. It was just the sort of thing that she would do.

"So, you going off to bed yet?" she asked, still with her piercing gaze. She obviously wanted to tell him something.

"I will once I have finished this drink."

There was a silence for a moment before Anna spoke again. "You know, she likes you."

"Huh?" Dorren was confused about what Anna meant before realising her implication. "Oh, you mean Sileena. Well, that's kind of strange considering I was the one who kidnapped her," he said in his normal sarcastic tone.

Anna seemed annoyed by his comment. "No. I mean she is interested in you. Not the friendly kind."

"What? No, that's not right." Sileena was friendly but she never gave any indication that she was into him in that way.

"Are you serious? When she asks questions they are all about you. She was the one who wanted to mock you while you worked. I think she just wanted to see you."

Dorren considered the statement for a moment which just angered Anna more. He did not understand why Anna was getting irritated with him until she spoke again.

"Well, if you are going to be that ignorant then I will just leave you to it. You should talk to her about it. Not directly though. That would be stupid. Just hint at the subject and see how she responds."

When Dorren didn't reply she shrugged before getting up and leaving. Dorren was a bit surprised by the conversation that had just transpired.

He was never good when it came to girls. His first crush had come to nothing as he was still very young and couldn't find the courage to say a word to her. The next girl he did find the courage to speak to, but the words didn't form properly in his mouth and that just made things worse. After that came Tania, someone with whom things seemed to go really well. But through their immaturity the relationship ultimately failed.

It had been a long time since his last relationship had ended. He might be a bit more mature about it now, although he knew there was still a way to go. His thoughts shifted from whether he was ready or not to the idea of him and Sileena. He did sometimes think of her as being a bit more than a friend. He considered the possibility for a moment before quickly shrugging it off. Whether she liked him or he had feelings for her, the relationship would not work. Ultimately Sileena would go home and they would probably never see each other again. For that reason, there was no point in trying to think about the subject, despite Anna's claims. Nevertheless, there was one thing he wanted to show Sileena before she left.

Dorren woke up knowing how much time had passed since Sileena had been captured. In five days they would take her back for the meeting with Sileena's father. Pagar himself had said that he would be there to make this important exchange. Today, however, Dorren had got a day off from his duties and so he was going to show Sileena the reason for the ransom, and why it was so important to the Outcasts. He had barely slept throughout the night, mostly because of what Anna had said the evening before. It was still early but he thought that he might as well get up. It was not like he was ever going to get back to sleep.

He went to the baths, washed and moved to the eatery to get food and pack it away for the journey ahead. He then went to Sileena's room. It was still a little early, he thought. Perhaps it might be best to wait a while, just in case she was sleeping. But he decided to unlock the door, and knocked on it gently to see if an answer came. From the other side he heard a voice which seemed quite alert say, "Come in."

When he opened the door he was greeted by a smile from Sileena, who was sitting up in her bed. Her hair was a bit of a mess but that would change once she was ready. Even when she was a little scruffy, she still looked pretty. Oh crap, he thought to himself as the realisation hit him. He did like her. Why were these thoughts going through his head now? Was Anna right? Was Sileena actually interested in him? Oh no – of all the people it had to be one who came from nobility. It had to be a member of the enemy side. It had to be his own hostage. It had to be the one person he could not end up with.

"Yes?" Sileena was sitting expectantly, still smiling. Dorren hadn't realised that he was just standing staring at her.

"Sorry. You seem quite awake."

"Yes, I woke up a few minutes ago and couldn't sleep again."

"Oh good, 'cause you will need to be awake for the trip."

"Trip?"

"Yeah. I shouldn't be showing you this but I won't tell if you won't." That was awful. The kind of crap he was coming up with. He was actually surprised that Sileena didn't just slam the door on his face.

She giggled a little at what he had just said. Probably at how bad it was.

She got up out of bed and took the clean set of clothes, and the two walked side by side to the baths. After Sileena was ready Dorren led her through some tunnels and then in a direction that she had never been before. She seemed a bit confused but didn't say a word about it. She wasn't as talkative this morning as she had been before. The wave of questions had diminished. Perhaps it was because she knew that there was no point asking as she was going to find out simply by waiting.

They eventually emerged from the tunnel into another cave. This cave was littered with hay, and wooden stables stretched across either side. The sounds of hooves and neighing could be heard all around them as about a hundred horses at either side of them stood grazing away. One man was walking around the stables and gave Dorren a nod as they passed. It was his job to make sure all the horses stayed healthy and were accounted for.

"So let's take these two," Dorren said, and he picked up two saddles and put them on two tame horses. Both were brown and looked ready for the ride. Once that was done Dorren helped Sileena onto one of the horses and then jumped onto the other. He couldn't get the same read on Sileena as before. She was usually filled with wonder and curiosity at seeing something she did not expect. Now her manner was more like 'Oh, that's new.' She still seemed interested, but no longer surprised. After all that she had been through in the last few weeks he was not shocked by her reaction. Nothing should surprise her now.

As they rode to the other side of the stables there was a ramp that led right up to the ceiling. The stableman pulled a lever and the ceiling opened to reveal the outside world, and the horses rode up the ramp and outside. The sudden brightness made Dorren cringe, but he was expecting it. He heard Sileena curse, politely though. He should probably have warned her about it.

"You feeling well?"

"Huh? Oh, yeah, yeah. I just need a moment to see if my blindness is permanent."

Dorren laughed and steered his horse to the west. When Sileena showed signs of regaining her sight she looked in his direction. Noticing where he was facing, she looked west too.

"I must warn you," she said, "I have only ridden a horse twice. I may struggle with it."

"We will go at a pace that you are comfortable with."

They started riding slowly at first, but Sileena got the hang of it quickly and they were soon racing towards their destination. Horses were certainly a much faster way of travel. They would be at their destination in a fraction of the time it would have taken to walk.

Sileena did not say much throughout their journey. They did talk a little and exchange the odd joke, but other than that she remained quite distant. Something was on her mind. It might have been worry about where they were headed, or perhaps something else. But something was definitely bothering her. It may have simply been the overwhelming light. The bright blue sky and the incredibly bright green grass did make the eyes a bit uncomfortable over time.

As they rode the sun was rising higher and higher, and by the end of the morning was nearing the centre of the bright blue sky. By that point Dorren could just make out their destination ahead. The ground suddenly stopped, leaving a cliff going down about a hundred metres to the ground below.

"Slow down," he said, and they pulled on the reins and were soon trotting towards the cliff edge. Dorren stopped and got off a few metres from the drop; then helped Sileena dismount. The two of them proceeded to move as close to the drop as possible without being in any danger. They looked down at what lay before them. It was a marshland that stretched as far as the eye could see.

"That's it?" she said mockingly. "It's a bog. I was expecting a spring, waterfall, mountain – something beautiful."

"I could show you something like that any time. This is what the Outcasts have been fighting for. This is what we want. This is why we have kidnapped you."

Sileena wore her frown again. It had been a while since Dorren had seen that. The fact that he was thinking about how pretty that look made her was beginning to annoy him as well. Stop thinking about that and focus. Just think about the fact that she was leaving and there could be nothing between them.

"Does this have magical properties?"

"No."

"Does it have a special mineral in it?"

"No."

"So then what is it that's so special about this?"

"It is just a plain, old, boring marshland."

Sileena gave him a look telling him to get to the point.

Dorren took a moment before explaining. Part of him was enjoying this too much.

"The Outcasts' Land, in comparison to Eceriden and Duka, and, as a matter of fact, every other place, is tiny. More and more people are going against their kingdoms' beliefs and are being forced to the Outcasts Land. We will need to expand and become known as a kingdom. We hope to make it a kingdom of freedom that is tolerant of everyone's beliefs."

"Oh, so you want to make this marshland habitable?"

"Exactly. We want to raise this marshland and double the territory we have. The next step is to make ourselves known to the two other major kingdoms and try to get them to see us as our own independent community. They will no longer have a place that they can freely throw people into like rubbish."

"How do you plan to raise the land?"

"With magic, of course. We need money to hire anyone magically capable. It will take many of the most powerful magic users to raise it all. There are many people out there for hire and they are willing to be bought by anyone for the right price. Even the Outcasts."

"What about your own people of magic, like your master?"

"We do not have enough people to do it all at once. Something like that requires a magnitude of power we don't have."

"So do it piece at a time until you are finished," Sileena said.

"Not possible. We tried it but every time we tried to raise the marshland it just sank back down. It must all be done at once and dried out to make sure that it is steady and firm enough not to sink back down."

She looked out across the place with a sceptical expression. He understood her doubts, as he himself felt the same way. The project felt like a long dream that did not seem possible.

"Are you sure that it would work? Sounds like something that would simply be impossible."

"We don't know. But everyone has to have a dream. Something they want, even if they might not be able to have it."

"Oh." There was silence for a moment before Sileena spoke again. "So how far does it go?"

"It goes as far as the western ocean."

Sileena was about to reply when they heard a sound in the distance, and turned to see what it was. The sound was that of galloping hooves, and they could see three figures not far from them. Dorren quickly noticed who they were and cursed to himself.

"Hello, Dorren, and look, he even has his girlfriend with him. The girl that should not see this."

Dorren glared at Severa and his two bigger friends, who had just jumped off their horses. The two groups were only a couple of metres apart.

"She is not allowed to be here. Wait until Pagar hears of this."

"You're all talk, Severa," replied Dorren. "You have your thugs there to back you up. Without them you are nothing." Dorren looked briefly at Sileena. She was glaring at Severa. Dorren had also noticed that she had not uttered any protest when Severa referred to her as his girlfriend. No, stop thinking that. She will be gone. It is impossible.

When he turned to Severa he could see him drawing his throwing knife and his sword. His face was red with anger. "I could take you myself. You are the one who should be worried. And my "talk" will make its way to Pagar. Let's see what he makes of it."

"You're a waste of space. Here you are spending your time trying to make others miserable because that's what you do."

"Speak for yourself. It is you that breaks the rules. You are the one who can't grow up."

"What?! You break as many rules as I do when it suits you, and you're the one who is throwing knives around people, so tell me exactly who the one that needs to grow up is."

There was a deafening silence between them. The argument was pointless and they both knew it. They were merely insulting one another; no reason nor logic in their arguments. But Severa eventually spoke up.

"You were an idiot for leaving alone."

"Not alone!" shouted Sileena.

Dorren was a bit taken aback. He could not help but notice that she disliked Severa just as much as he did.

"Oh yes," replied Severa. "Like you can do anything."

Dorren was now drawing his weapons ready for a fight, as were the two men behind Severa.

"If you can take me yourself then why don't you prove it?"

"How stupid and gullible do you think I am?" Severa moved slowly towards Dorren, and the two men followed.

Incredibly, Dorren realised that their hatred for each other had really gone up a level. It was more than just a rivalry. He knew Severa would not dare kill him. But it had still gone too far. Dorren was not going to allow this idiot to beat him. He moved forward and prepared for the fight. This was going to be the fight that Dorren and Severa had been waiting for. And it had just begun.

Severa quickly threw the knife at him. Dorren was ready to deflect it, but the blade just halted in mid-air before him and hovered briefly before falling to the ground. Dorren noticed, but Severa continued his attack so Dorren was forced to ignore the strange occurrence.

Their swords were about to collide when a sudden force hit him. It was something invisible that threw him through the air. He hit the ground with a thud and was quickly back up again at the ready, while looking around for what it might have been. He could see Severa and the two men also getting up. They had been blasted back too. Sileena was still standing where she was with her hands over her mouth. Both Severa and Dorren looked around and saw the figure floating towards them just a few inches from the ground. It was Pagar. Dorren stood straight, as did Severa. They really were in for it now.

Pagar landed on the ground and stood between them, his face contorted with rage.

"I will not tolerate this! You are both Outcasts and you will adhere to the rules I have instated!"

Dorren remained silent. Severa, however, did not.

"But Master Pagar, Dorren—"

"Enough!" The ground began to vibrate as Pagar's anger forced cracks around his feet. Pagar was the most powerful user of magic Dorren had ever seen. Severa stopped and looked at the ground, as did his two thugs.

"This is the final warning for both of you, and as for you two…" Pagar looked at Severa's friends. "Get out of my sight. Now!"

The two men quickly obliged, jumping onto their horses and riding away.

"There is no other way to solve this. The day after tomorrow both of you are allowed one more arena challenge. This will be the only one you are permitted to find out which one of you is the best. Then once it is over you will show each other, and me, respect. You will not disobey my rules and if either of you ever break them again I will have you thrown out of my Underground, and you will not be welcome back. Is that clear?"

Dorren and Severa nodded and replied, "Yes."

"Leave now, Severa."

Severa nodded, climbed onto his horse and left. Once he was out of sight Pagar turned to Dorren.

"Dorren, I am disappointed in you." Pagar was no longer yelling but his tone was still very angry.

"I was forced to defend myself."

"That was not what I meant. I meant what you are doing here with Sileena. It's like you go out of your way to break my rules, like they do not apply to you. Now I want you to prepare for Sileena's departure in a few days."

"Sir," said Sileena, but Pagar just continued, not hearing her.

"She will be leaving soon and I want this to go as smoothly as possible."

"Yes, Pagar," said Dorren glumly. He should really start obeying the rules, he thought to himself. Well, at least he could start preparing for Sileena's departure, and that might be enough to give him a kick and stop him thinking of her as something more than a friend.

"Erm, Mr Pagar?"

Pagar turned to Sileena and his expression softened. "Yes, Sileena, what is it?"

There was a pause before Sileena replied. "I want to stay."

There was a look of shock on Pagar's face at what had just been said. This was nothing compared to the expression on Dorren's face. Once the surprise had ebbed sufficiently for him to think, there was only one thought that was going through his head. Oh bugger, I have absolutely no excuse now. Anna is going to have a field day with this.

# 7

# RIVALRY

"Wait...what?" said Pagar, still bewildered at what was just said.

"I want to stay...please."

"Uh, you will have to forgive me. Not many people who are kidnapped end up wanting to stay with their kidnappers."

Sileena looked disheartened by Pagar's response, and almost pleaded.

"I'm sorry if it's a problem. But I really don't want to go back. Even held hostage here I have more freedom than back at home. My father restricted me to certain parts of the castle and I had to do everything he said or risk getting hit."

"Well," said Pagar. His anger had completely gone now and the surprise was quickly ebbing away. "Anyone is welcome to the Outcasts' Land. You would be the first who was not cast away by their original kingdom. But if you really want to stay then there would be little that could stop you. Everyone is welcome."

"I am sorry if it would stop you from getting this ransom."

Dorren couldn't say anything.

"Money's money. I'm sure the Outcasts will manage. Now let's head back. There will be people who'll want to discuss this, and you need to be prepared for criticism."

"Um, yeah." Sileena was smiling broadly. Dorren guessed that she had not been expecting to be able to stay, and Pagar saying that anyone was welcome raised her spirits. She turned to face Dorren, who was still in complete shock.

"You don't mind about this, do you?"

"No, not at all," he replied too quickly, and stuttering.

Sileena's smile widened and she turned to the two horses. Pagar walked towards his own horse further away before rejoining them. Dorren forced himself to straighten and gather his wits. He again helped Sileena onto her horse before getting onto his own, and they both rode towards the Underground.

Sileena could see the sun shining brightly at the highest point of the sky. It must be midday then, and because they were already nearly back, they did not have to worry about it getting too dark.

Her head was buzzing. She could not believe it. She thought she would have to plead and still be refused, as the money was meant to be more important for their cause. Well, it was very possible. She would have to be ready for these people to argue for her to leave but she just hoped that it would not be enough.

She was also curious about Dorren's opinion. Was he happy that she might not be going back? Or was he annoyed? All the effort required to get her, and the money that would have been gained. That is, if her father was going to play fair, which he probably would not.

When she glanced at Dorren she could see him frowning. This was not a good sign. Her excitement faded and she felt a little hollow inside. She had hoped that he would have been happier. Maybe he was angry with her for ruining the Outcasts' dream.

They rode back without a word. Despite the bright day, the silence made everything feel dull. This dampened their spirits through the trip back to the Underground.

By the time they returned the ramp into the stables was already down waiting for them, and Sileena was stopped by Pagar at the bottom.

"Right, Sileena, I am sorry but I must ask you to go to your room early while Dorren, I and a few others discuss what we just talked about."

Sileena nodded in reply.

"Now," he continued, "are you sure about staying, because if you have reconsidered now is the time to say. There will be no going back after this."

Sileena nodded again firmly.

"Alright. Nella!" Pagar called, and a lady walked towards them. She had short grey hair and looked like she must have been around sixty.

"Yes, Master Pagar?" she said, standing straight and ready for orders.

"I want you to escort Sileena to her quarters and lock the door."

Nella nodded and beckoned Sileena to follow her. As they walked back Sileena pondered what would be discussed regarding her, and what sort of arguments could be made against her.

Once the two women were gone Pagar turned to face Dorren.

"Let's get this meeting over and done with."

Dorren looked at Pagar questioningly as they walked to the quarters. "You didn't seem taken aback by what Sileena said. I thought you would have been just as surprised as me."

"I was, but I'm just better at hiding it. You must remain calm and confident in all situations. Otherwise, how good a leader can I be? Imagine if I was quivering in the corner," he said jokingly. "People would end up losing respect."

Dorren understood what he meant. To lead would require a lot of patience from Pagar, and readiness for the unexpected. Especially when it came to those who would go against his wishes regularly. People like Dorren.

"So what about the money? Because if this passes we will not get a thing, and all this work will be for nothing."

Pagar thought for a moment before answering. "Unfortunately that's true, we will not get the money if she is allowed to stay, but we will just have to wait until another opportunity arises and keep doing the smaller trades and thefts. Eventually we will succeed."

Dorren didn't reply, so Pagar continued. "It will just take a little longer. Besides, she is a nice girl and would probably make a fine addition to the community."

Dorren felt a little ashamed as he realised that he had been implying that the money was more important than Sileena. Pagar didn't say it directly, but did bring attention to what Dorren was saying and how it sounded. On the contrary, he was far from unhappy. But for some reason his stomach was turning.

Dorren remained silent as they walked through the corridors and knocked on the doors of random quarters. Some were answered, at which point the occupants nodded their understanding at what was expected and made their way towards the meeting place. This process was in place to discuss any new people who were to be integrated into the Underground. Pagar would go through doors at random until he got twenty people including himself to discuss whether the newcomer should be allowed to stay. If a person was not in their quarters, or if they answered and said they can't take part in the discussion then it was just left alone and Pagar would keep going until he had twenty people who were willing.

Unfortunately for Dorren one of the doors that were answered was Severa's. He must have gone to his quarters when he got back to stay low long enough for the incident to blow over. Unlucky for both of them that his door was chosen. Severa probably felt like he should take part in the discussion to get back into Pagar's favour, and so headed to the meeting place. Eventually the two managed to get eighteen people, and Dorren and Pagar would make it up to twenty. They then headed to the small, empty room that was usually used for these debates. Often they were quick and easy. Usually the people under discussion were just new Outcasts who wanted to find a new life. Sileena, however, was taken against her will and now wanted to stay. It seemed odd, and would probably be the topic of a much longer debate. When Dorren and Pagar arrived the discussion was initiated. The room was small, and dimly lit by magic. The only furniture was a large round table that had twenty-one chairs around it; twenty for the people who made the decision and one is for the person who wanted to stay.

At first everyone was chatting amongst themselves before Pagar spoke.

"Right then," said Pagar, which got everyone's attention, and the room quietened as chatter stopped. "This is a different situation than normal but we must act appropriately. Sileena has just asked to stay, and her case is clearly different to the others who have come here. Is anyone unaware of who Sileena is, or unfamiliar with anything to do with this situation?"

There was silence, and a few of the people around the table shook their heads.

"I have decided Sileena will not be brought before us for this assessment. Everyone here will argue any point they wish to put forward and in the end we will have a vote."

Further silence.

"So does anyone have anything they want to put forward?"

Again there was a pause before anyone answered. Dorren was still unaware of what to say to this. He was thinking about an answer. It was another who spoke first.

"Why does she want to stay?"

"Does that really matter?" said another.

"Well yes, it does actually because if she has an ulterior motive then it could mean disaster for us."

"What other motive could she possibly have?" said Dorren. "She was kidnapped – there was no way to plan this."

"That may be so," said Severa, "but we must also be aware of her magical potential."

There was no look of surprise on anyone's face. Word had clearly spread about Sileena's eyes, and some of the people present at the meeting would have seen it for themselves. Others soon joined the argument.

"It would be taking a lot of risk for someone with that much potential power. The outcome could be catastrophic."

"But we always take a risk when taking someone on board, and we have always operated under the belief that we should not make snap judgements of others."

The arguments continued as one by one they all joined in. At first it was just to put points across, but gradually the tone changed to people taking sides and arguing why they believed Sileena should be allowed to stay or made to leave. Even though Severa and Dorren had

119

recently been threatened by Pagar, it was the two of them that took the front stages of both sides. Severa was constantly arguing to get Sileena sent away.

"What of the money that will be lost because of this? It took a lot of effort and resources to keep her here and it will all have been a waste of time. Our goal will have been set back for goodness knows how long."

"Our goal will remain the same and we will get there eventually," replied Dorren. "It's not right to achieve it at someone else's expense. Our ideas are meant to help those who come to our land. Not to cast them out for a little profit."

The argument continued but there was no clear winning side. It was a good thing that Pagar had decided to allow the fight between the two of them to happen because now they would be able to find out who was the better fighter, and in controlled circumstances. So this reduced the tension between them, and granted them cooler heads for the debate.

Eventually the argument came to a stage no new points were made. It was just the same ones being spurted out by different people, only phrased differently. Pagar noticed this and decided to speak.

"Well, I think it is fair to say that this argument can be drawn to a close. The cases for Sileena staying are that it is our policy to let anyone stay if they want to, and she definitely wants to. Also, she has made friends here and I believe that she would integrate well. The arguments against focus on her magical potential, and the threat it could pose to everyone. But she has shown no signs of being aware of this, or shown any kind of ability to use magic. The other reason is that we would lose the ransom money, which it would slow down our progress in raising the swamps. Now we will take it in turns to write down on a piece of parchment what your verdict is, and what will be decided here is what will happen so choose carefully."

With that Pagar took a long piece of parchment and handed it to Dorren with a piece of charcoal to write with. Dorren did not need to think about it. He voted for Sileena to stay. Then he folded the parchment over what he had written and handed it to the next person, who wrote down their answer and passed the parchment on. Dorren was feeling very nervous. What would the answer be, and what would happen afterwards? The debate was not nearly as clear as he thought it would be. What if the group voted against her and made her go back? The thought unnerved him. The piece of parchment had now reached Severa, and Dorren knew how he would vote, and that it was just to spite him. Severa would do almost anything to get at him, even if it meant casting Sileena away.

Was Dorren any better, though? If the roles were reversed would he act any differently? He liked to think so, but was not sure. At some point he would have to grow up and behave more maturely, but for now, who cared. Their rivalry was never really going to disappear, but at least the upcoming fight would be helpful for getting rid of some of the stress.

The parchment had been folded many times and finally made it back to Pagar, who without a word began to unfold it and silently read everyone's answers. His face was expressionless, which just agitated Dorren more. He wanted to find out what the result was and Pagar was unreadable.

"Twelve to eight in Sileena's favour," said Pagar without any pause. A huge wave of relief washed over Dorren. Sileena was going to be allowed to stay. Thank goodness Pagar was not one to spend time building up tension.

Dorren could not help but glance in Severa's direction. He was frowning, but other than that was not really showing any signs of annoyance. Perhaps he really did not care whether Sileena stayed or not, and just wanted to annoy Dorren. Or it could be that Severa was just looking forward to what he believed would be his opportunity to take revenge against him in the fight to come. Dorren didn't care. Sileena could stay, and he could feel his face getting warmer. He hoped no one would notice and realise his feelings for her.

This was actually happening. At first he did not know whether to be upset or happy because of the discomfort in his stomach, which had been turning constantly since Sileena said that she wanted to stay. But the way he'd fought for it to happen made him realise how much he wanted her to stay.

"I will bring Sileena and tell her the news," said Pagar, as everyone made gestures of acknowledgement. "She will be made aware of what is required to be a member of our community, and that will be the end of this matter."

Everyone stood up and moved for the door. Pagar and Dorren stayed in the room until the last individual was gone before speaking.

"Well, that was one of the more interesting debates I've taken part in," said Dorren.

"Indeed, it's nice when you can enjoy a little bit of what you do once in a while, although I suspect you may have been a little nervous."

Dorren was taken aback. "Why would I be nervous?"

Pagar smiled ominously. "Well, she may have a lot of power in her." Pagar was obviously on to Dorren. Sileena's power was just a cover for him, knowing how Dorren felt about her. And Anna too – why did everyone know Dorren better than he knew himself?

"Well, we don't know yet if there is power in Sileena."

Pagar's strange smile disappeared as he pondered the statement. "Yes. I won't give up my hopes but I do see an opportunity in this. I was curious about her magical potential but did not dare try and find out myself just encase it endangered the Underground, but if she is with us and willing to give it a try I would love to see whether she is as powerful as we believe."

Dorren and Pagar headed out of the room and towards Sileena's quarters.

"By the way, Dorren, I hope you are right about this. I would like to believe you on this matter. If she does intend to harm us there could be severe consequences."

What? Did Pagar disagree with her staying? "But we risk this with every single person. Why is she so different?"

Pagar looked at Dorren curiously for a moment before answering. "Well, for one thing she is the daughter of a noble from Eceriden – we have had no others like her. Also, she was originally brought here against her will, and her potential could be more dangerous than that of a normal person."

Dorren looked shocked. Pagar was right: what if he was letting his feelings control his actions? Pagar clearly noticed his expression, for he quickly spoke again.

"I think you have made the right choice to do what you did for her. I would have made the same choice and voted for her stay too. I was just pointing out the possible problems and consequences to help you understand why others would want to choose the alternative."

The two of them had now made their way to Sileena's room, and knocked on the door.

"Come in."

They entered the room and found Sileena sitting up in her bed, smiling nervously. Dorren did not know what to say, so he just smiled back.

"Well then," said Pagar. "The Underground has come to a conclusion and decided that it would be fair to let you stay if that is what you wish."

Sileena kept smiling and nodded, so it was clear she had not reconsidered. Dorren did not understand. She was leaving behind all that wealth and status just to live in a filthy Underground with people she had only known for a few weeks. But then, he was not really the brightest person and there was a lot he could not explain.

"There will be a ceremony to make you an Outcast. You must be aware that now you are a member of our group and no longer a hostage. This means that you need to follow our rules and take part in the necessary jobs."

Sileena nodded again. "Yes, I understand and will be ready for any work."

"Good. The ceremony will be the day after Dorren and Severa have brought their ridiculous rivalry to a close. You can no longer change your mind. So in a way, you are already a member of the Outcasts. Welcome." Pagar was about to turn and leave, but quickly stopped and turned to face Sileena. "Oh, and could you stop by the training grounds, Sileena, as soon as you get up? I will meet you there."

"Of course."

Pagar smiled and walked out, leaving Dorren and Sileena alone. Dorren thought it would have been hilarious if Sileena replied with a 'no'. How would Pagar react to that sort of statement? To be fair, it was more of an order, but he'd made it sound like he was asking out of courtesy. Nevertheless, it would have been funny to see the unexpected reply.

There was a moment of awkward silence between Sileena and Dorren before he spoke.

"You have got a few big days ahead of you."

"As do you," she replied. There was a pause before Dorren spoke again.

"Sooo...what made you change your mind and want to stay?"

Sileena looked away. She seemed a little sad. He'd crossed a line, and quickly tried to fix it.

"You don't have to answer."

Sileena looked at him with a smile, but there was still a little sadness in her expression. Whatever the cause, she obviously didn't want to talk about it. He guessed she just wanted to be left alone for now.

"I will let you be and see you tomorrow."

Her energy seemed to have been drained, and he couldn't tell if it was because of what he'd asked. Saying final farewells, Dorren left the room, leaving Sileena to her thoughts. He guessed there was probably much more on her mind than his. And sometimes just sitting with your thoughts to help clear your mind was a good thing.

So what was the Underground going to be like now? Probably the same as it always was. No real changes except for her and him. This petty little crush had better go, he thought to himself, because this was not like him at all. His usual confident self was being replaced by a stuttering and unsure fool. So he transferred his thoughts to the upcoming fight, and then his mood changed. Sometimes sitting with your thoughts was a good thing, but sometimes doing something was better. So he marched his way to the training grounds to prepare for the fight that was to come. He must not lose.

After Sileena had managed to get herself ready she moved to the training grounds. As usual there was someone following her, making sure that she did not try anything. It was rather annoying that she still had

124

to be followed. She guessed it was because she was still not technically an Outcast, and she knew of Pagar's strong belief in the rules. She saw that yesterday during the encounter between Dorren and Severa.

When she reached the training grounds she could see Pagar and one of his friends or associates, she did not know which. Dorren, Gabe and Anna were also there. She was greeted warmly by all of them and Pagar, as usual, went straight to business.

"Great to see you look well and awake."

"Thank you, I am," she replied in anticipation for what was to come.

"Excellent," he said, beaming. "Just before we begin I would like to know how much you know about magic."

"Well," she replied, "I know it exists."

"Hmm. Well, to sum up the reason why we are here, is because of your eyes."

"What?"

"Not to worry. So you know that they are an unusual colour?"

"Yes. Why do you ask?"

"Well, to best explain I would like you to look into my eyes."

Pagar's eyes looked normal from her distance. But there had to be a reason for his instruction, so she took a step closer and looked into his eyes. As she guessed, there was nothing overly special. They were brown in colour and looked perfectly fine in shape.

But as she was about to answer, she noticed there was a small glint of gold in them as well.

"They have a bit of gold in them. Like my father. He has the same."

"Yes, we know of that. Well, people who have these small hints of gold in their eyes have magical potential beyond that of normal people."

Sileena could quickly see what he was getting at, and suddenly her head was filled with questions.

"Magic is a huge and complex work. Many people can use magic but very few have these hints of gold. It is believed that those who have great magical power have it bursting out of them in a physical form.

This physical form is in the gold in their eyes. It is believed to be the colour of magic in its dormant form, before it is transformed."

Sileena had to ask a question. "But my father would have known of this power, right?"

"Yes, he would have. You are a very unique case. I have never heard or seen anyone like you. If a hint of gold can make someone that powerful, then imagine what it would be like for someone whose eyes are entirely gold."

Suddenly it all made so much sense. Her father was all about power. No one could be more powerful or strong-willed than him, as far as she was aware. So the thought of his own daughter holding more potential than him would have infuriated and scared him. That was why he kept her away from most people, and why he treated her the way he did. It was because he was desperate not to allow her to read and find out the truth. Why he didn't just kill her, then? But that was another question, and one she was probably never going to find out the answer to.

"But," continued Pagar, "this could all be wrong. For all we know this is your natural eye colour and there is no magical power there."

Sileena looked around and could see everyone around her waiting for the part that would fascinate them, but for now they looked relatively bored, waiting until Pagar got to the part they were waiting for. What Pagar was telling her was basic knowledge. Everyone knew it except her. She felt so stupid, and irritated that she was being told information that was obviously meant to be taught to kids in school. Why did you do this, Father? Why keep me away from this truth?

Pagar seemed calm about the whole thing as well. While everyone else was looking bored he was explaining matters in a manner that did not sound like he was telling someone something they should already know. She appreciated this. The other person who was not looking at her in that way was Dorren, but this could be because he was still in thought and not really paying attention. What the hell was he thinking about?

She was roused from her thoughts by Pagar.

"Very well, you are willing to try this, then?"

"Yes."

"Excellent. The first thing we are going to do is allow you to use magic. Then we will train you to use smaller spells, and finally see how far you can go."

Pagar reached into his pocket and drew out a stone. The stone was small and could easily sit in the palm of his hand. It was purple, smooth and even shone a little. "This is a power stone. These stones are what people use to unlock their power and enable them to use it freely. Thankfully they are very common as it is one of the major products mined and sold by the men of the Bryton Mountains."

"So how does it work?"

"Touch it."

"Is that it? Sounds a bit easy." It would explain why her father went to such extreme measures to keep her away from the world around her.

"Yes, that's it. There is nothing more to it. But just before we do that you should probably know a bit more about magic and controlling it, just in case you accidentally bring down the cavern."

"Does everyone have to go through this before using magic?"

"Many people are taught a little beforehand, but most aren't. The only reason why we are doing this is because of the risk. As far as I am aware, golden eyes like yours have never been seen before. Now, I want you to look at your hand and think about moving it, but don't move it."

Sileena was a bit bewildered but did as she was asked.

"Now I want you to move your hand."

She did that too.

"Magic works in the very same way. With mental control over movement you can control magic, but it just takes practice, as if you were crawling."

Sileena continued to listen intently.

"Eventually you will be able to unconsciously control it and cast spells without even thinking."

"Why doesn't everyone use magic then?"

"Because most people don't have enough magical talent to cast even a small and basic spell. It is hard to come by people with great magical talent, especially in the Outcasts' Land. Now, are you ready?"

Sileena nodded in reply. Pagar indicated that she should hold out her hand and Sileena did so, whereupon he dropped the small stone into her palm.

What happened over the next couple of seconds was unexpected.

The stone just sat there in her palm. Sileena half-expected there to be some kind of reaction, but there was nothing. Did this mean that she had no magical power, that her golden eyes were nothing more than an abnormality? She could not help but feel disappointed. It would have been nice if she were able to use magic. She had no idea what could be done with it except what she saw her father accomplish, as well as what she had seen done in this place. It was a lot but she could guess there was a lot more to it than that. The potential for magic seemed limitless from the displays of the Outcasts.

"Fantastic, the place is not a complete wreck and we are still alive," said Pagar's associate. His voice was very deep and croaky. Pagar merely smiled and gestured for her to hand back the stone, and he put it back into his pocket.

"Well," he said happily, "it's good to know that at the very least you can control the power you have if you have any."

Sileena was taken aback by the statement. "But does this mean that I have no magical potential?"

"What?" replied Pagar. "We still don't know – oh, sorry, did you expect something to happen? Oh no, this is what happens with everyone, although I did have the displeasure of coming across someone who had no mental control over their power at first, and the moment they touched the stone the place caught fire around us. Thankfully he was not that powerful and I managed to put the flames out quickly enough before they caused too much damage."

"So what happens now?"

"Now comes the moment everyone has been waiting for, which is to see if you have the capabilities that we're curious about."

A couple more people who had entered the grounds had noticed what was going on, and some had come closer to watch.

"There are different kinds of magic that you must be aware of. Which ones are you familiar with? I might be able to associate each with an attribute."

Sileena went with the most obvious answer she could think of. "Making fire."

"Ah, it is rather unfortunate but that is one of the most dangerous types of magic, and yet it is one of the easiest to do. Fire is, as everyone knows, an element, and those people who focus on elemental magic are known as mages."

"Oh yeah, I know that. I know that there are druids, mages and sorcerers. My father is a sorcerer."

"Ah yes, we know this. We conducted research on your family before Dorren decided to…well, kidnap you," said Pagar with a smile. "But there are some professions that you have missed out, such as clerics, who perform healing magic, necromancers, auras and shamans. Then there are the craftsmanships within magic, such as making magical runes and crafting staffs."

"Can you learn more than one kind of magic?" asked Sileena.

"Of course. Many people do, but for the most part individuals tend to focus on one and become really good at it."

Sileena could not help but continue to think that she had no magical potential, and that this whole thing was just a waste of time.

Pagar seemed to notice her discomfort. "Well, we should probably just get this done. Now we will go with the most basic of mage powers, which is wind. You can control the movements of wind by thinking 'move the wind' to yourself. Try and make it a nice gentle breeze."

Sileena concentrated hard and tried to move the air around them. She even closed her eyes trying to focus her senses into the magic, but nothing happened. There was no wind or any kind of breeze; it was just quiet. Pagar started to speak again.

"Remember, it's like moving the hand. Are you thinking, 'move the hand' but not actually moving it, or are you moving your hand?" It was an interesting analogy to make, but Sileena concentrated again and this time she did not focus on thinking 'move the wind'; she just relaxed and told herself she was moving it slowly past herself and the people around her. With that she felt a tingling sensation, which she thought was just a shiver down her spine.

But it wasn't. It was a very soft gust of wind that moved past her, and, annoyingly, made her feel a little cold.

"Well done, I certainly felt that," said Pagar.

"And again it pleases me to know that a hurricane was not created, bringing the place down," came a reply from Pagar's accomplice. Sileena did not like this person. He was mocking her and she was getting irritated. Everyone else was just ignoring him except for Dorren, who gave him a dark look.

"Well done, Sileena. Now I want you to practise the control of the wind. I want you to direct its course. Make it as unpredictable and complex as you like, and take your time."

Sileena did as she was asked, and again it took her a little time to gain the understanding of how to actually use and create the air, but once she got past that the rest came easily. At first she made it move around her, and could feel and see her clothes move with it. Her mind moved to Dorren, and she thought it would be fun to direct the wind towards him. She moved it like a snake and let it flow towards his feet, turned it into a spiral and moved it upwards. She saw the movement of Dorren's clothes, and at first he got a bit of a surprise, before smiling at the realisation of what was happening.

After that Sileena extended the flow of wind so that it could circle around everyone. It was easy, way too easy. She could make it go faster, and so she sped up and kept it spinning. Yet it was still too easy. It could go faster, but as she was bringing the speed up she felt a sudden difficulty at her concentration. Something was pulling at the wind, and in shock she relinquished control and stopped what she was doing, looking around in confusion. Everyone was still standing there fascinated, and Pagar was smiling again.

"That was very well done. If you were wondering what happened, I could feel the air beginning to pick up the pace and so I slowed it back down again."

So that was what she felt. It was Pagar using his own magic to pull the wind back.

"Sorry but I thought you were going to really pick up speed and I don't think a hurricane in here is the best solution to see how far you can go. It took a lot of time to set up these grounds. Now, for the next step I would like to go outside where we can test the limits of your powers, and we shall use a different element for this as the wind, although is quite a nice kind of magic, lacks beauty to the eyes."

"Where are we going?"

"To the ocean. It should not take as long as it did for you and Dorren to reach the marshes, but nevertheless I would like to leave as soon as possible."

"I'm ready to go now if you like."

Pagar raised an eyebrow at that statement; then glanced to his assistant, who nodded.

"Very well, we shall head off now. Dorren, would you like to come?"

"Certainly," he replied.

They headed for the stables and the ramp lowered, allowing Pagar, his assistant, Dorren and Sileena to ride out into the light once again, this time heading in a south-westerly direction. The journey allowed Sileena to think a bit more about magic, and she even tried to continue practising while they were riding. She moved the wind from place to place, and even at one point moved it around Dorren again. He acquired an odd expression when it happened and then glanced at Sileena, who could not help but start giggling. Dorren smiled, shaking his head. Pagar glanced back at the two of them curiously before turning to face the direction in which they were headed.

As the day wore on they eventually came to a different cliff edge. This time when they looked out beyond Sileena did not see a marshland that seemed to go on endlessly. Below them was the sea, and she could see its deep blue colour that stretched out into the horizon.

"The next element we will be working with today is water. This place is perfect as there is no one but us for many miles, which makes it a good place to test the extent of your power. Now observe." Pagar then moved to the cliff edge and pointed his arms out towards the ocean. With a small motion he moved his arms back and forth. Sileena looked out to sea and could see the water moving back and forth. Waves crashed against the cliff edge and continued to get higher and higher. Then, with one swift hand movement Pagar raised the water up the cliff and even got it to go higher, creating what looked like a fountain. The water continued to rise and once it reached a certain height it poured outwards, falling back into the ocean. Pagar repeated this for a few seconds before letting his arms collapse by his side. The water fell back into the ocean and gradually returned to its normal state. It was an incredible sight.

"Right, I want you to try and do that, but start small. Make the water flow at your will. Move it in waves and then try and raise it."

Sileena moved into a standing position at the cliff edge and stood ready.

"Now do the same thing that you did with the air, except think, 'water' instead. It sounds quite simple when put into words, but it's easier said than done."

Sileena concentrated and felt herself move the wind again, just to get a feel for it, then focused on the water below. This came faster to her than the wind magic had, as she began to push the sea out and then back in. Looking down, she could see the waves getting higher. This was easy. It was too easy.

"I used gestures, if you noticed," said Pagar. "They helped me concentrate on the water. They might help you in a similar way." But Sileena did not care about that; she did not need gestures. She could feel the movement of water below her, and she concentrated now on raising it.

At first she made the water rise slowly, and began to extend it so she could move more of the ocean at the same time. One metre, two metres and she kept going. Everyone peered over the edge of the cliff but the water had not lifted enough to take much notice. Sileena extended her control outwards, raising the water to meet the same level to what she already had power over.

Ten metres, eleven metres, twelve metres.

The process was going a bit slowly but she wanted to make sure she had control over it. Twenty metres, twenty-five metres. It was still no struggle. She could not feel any pressure against her. But was she taking more than she was meant to? Would she try and raise it and find that nothing happened because she was wrong to think she could handle it?

"Umm, Mr Pagar, do you feel it when you take on more than you are capable of?"

"Yes, it is as though you are out of breath. Why, do you feel the strain?"

One hundred metres, beyond a hundred. She thought that would be enough to take.

"No." And with one movement of her mind and arms in an upward motion, she pulled the water up, up into the air. Dorren and Pagar's assistant jumped back, falling on the ground in complete shock as the water passed the cliff top, while Pagar just stood and smiled. Once the water reached a certain height it began to spill back down creating a fountain effect. This made Pagar's trick look like child's play. It was a wall of water that went over fifty metres to either side of the group, and after a few seconds she let her mind release and the water came crashing down back into the ocean. Then there was nothing but the sound of the wind passing past their ears, wind that Sileena was not controlling.

"Well," said Pagar, smiling again and breaking the silence, "I think we can put our theories to rest now. So how did you feel when doing that?"

Sileena was in too much shock over what had happened to reply immediately. It took her a few seconds to come round and answer.

"W-well, I felt the same sensation I had when controlling the air, but that was it."

"Did you reckon you could have done more than that, then?"

"Yes, if what you say about feeling tired is right."

Pagar frowned for a moment and then smiled before speaking again. "Well I guess that can conclude the lesson for today. I would ask, however, that you do not use anything more than small spells and only with the two elements that you know until I can teach you more, is that fair?"

133

"It is," she replied.

The journey back was a quiet one; not as lively as the journey to the ocean. Pagar, Dorren and Pagar's associate were frowning and deep in thought. She knew that they were all thinking about what just happened, and judging by their expressions they did not seem overjoyed by it. Sileena was a little bothered by that. For the first time in her life something good had happened to her. She should be very happy, but no one seemed to be happy for her. It was something she should be used to but now that she was part of a different crowd she expected different reactions. This thought stuck with her throughout the remaining ride.

Dorren finished his work for the day, then moved to the training grounds. During that evening he committed to one of the most extreme training sessions he could put himself through before heading to bed. There were two things that bothered him, and if one thing left his head the other emerged like a nagging pain. He liked it much more when things were simpler.

The first problem was Severa, and what was going to happen tomorrow. The fight he had been waiting for was coming up, and what if he failed? He had not thought about what would happen if he lost. He merely assumed that he could win through sheer determination. Perhaps it was because there'd been a constant belief that the match was never going to happen. Now that it was just around the corner Dorren could feel his stomach sink. If he were to lose he would no longer be seen as one of the best to the Outcasts, and fighting was one of the only things he was good at. He was certainly not wise or intelligent. He would have to just come to terms with the result.

The other issue that had his stomach in knots was Sileena. She was a lovely girl; one that he was growing fonder of by the day. Maybe he should take Anna's advice and speak to her. But how would he go about doing that? And then there was the new development regarding Sileena's power. It was true that her eyes absolutely reflected her power. He had never seen its like before. Not even Pagar could muster up something like that. She was such an innocent girl and yet she held more power than anyone in all the lands. How far did it go? These thoughts were not helping him sleep.

But who else was, at the moment, still awake and staring at the ceiling, lost in their thoughts? Sileena was very likely still up. Pagar was good at hiding his feelings but with this new development, he was probably still awake too. And was Severa also nervous, the night before their fight? Yes, times were certainly simpler before.

Dorren let his thoughts take over, and for a time they remained on his mind until his exhaustion overcame him and he fell asleep.

Dorren stood in the grass arena, face to face with Severa, who had a determined expression on his face. He could guess that his own expression was pretty much the same. Neither was willing to lose.

The biggest crowd ever seen in the training grounds surrounded the combat ring, watching intently. Why shouldn't they? This was the fight everyone was waiting for.

Dorren knew he could win. He just had to make sure that he never let his guard down. Part of him didn't know what Pagar was thinking by allowing this match. They certainly hated each other more now than they had at their previous encounter. If it were not for the fact that Severa would have been five at the time, Dorren would have ended up accusing him of being responsible for the death of his father. That was just how much he hated him. As he let his mind wonder he realised his focus was waning and he had to take his attention back to the arena and the fight of his life.

Pagar stood at Dorren's side and protected him with a shield, while at Severa's side stood Anna, forming a barrier around him.

"Now remember, as soon as this contest is over you will both stop immediately."

Dorren was listening intently to what was being said. There was no way he was going to let himself lose this fight. He had waited a long time to be allowed another shot. But he gave a quick nod to show Pagar that he was listening.

"Begin!" shouted Pagar, and at once both Severa and Dorren kicked off the ground in a running motion, heading for each other.

It was barely a second before their swords collided and the fight had commenced.

Dorren was the first on the offensive, striking faster than his opponent, and so Severa put himself on the defensive, parrying every blow and biding his time for an opening. Dorren gave it to him when he swung his katana low, at which Severa jumped and swung his own sword down, but Dorren had seen this coming and took his knife out its holster, blocking the sword. The block came just in time, as the opposing sword came within an inch of his head. With another swing of his katana Severa was forced to step back, losing ground.

Dorren seized the opportunity and pressed on with the continued strikes, and Severa kept stepping back, blocking while drawing out his own knife to keep up with the number of blows delivered. It was not long before Severa had backed right up against the edge of the arena. When Dorren used a stabbing motion Severa stepped to the side and counterattacked. It was quickly parried, but Severa pushed his whole body weight towards Dorren and attacked again, forcing Dorren to block and step back before Severa could knock him over. Severa kicked Dorren square in the chest, sending him back through the air to hit the ground. Dorren rolled back and quickly parried a knife that Severa had thrown. The motion had knocked Dorren off balance, and by the time he recovered Severa had charged and was swinging his sword frantically at him. Dorren spent most of the next few minutes dodging the strikes and countering the ones that he could not avoid. He did have the advantage of having two weapons though, as Severa had thrown his knife earlier. Dorren attacked with knife and katana simultaneously, and Severa was finding it difficult to keep them both at bay. Desperately, he used his free hand to punch Dorren again, stunning him for long enough to allow Severa to hit the knife out of Dorren's hands and began the attack anew. Dorren spun round, Severa avoiding the attack, and the two of them were back on an even face-off, exchanging blows.

The sequence of attacks was enough to show Dorren that even after all this time since their previous fight they were still relatively evenly matched. They were just going to have to wait until one of them slipped up first.

The duel lasted a long time as they both desperately focused, trying not to make the first slip. Dorren was the first to lose patience and lunged forward. Severa stepped to the side, causing Dorren to move right past him. Dorren's instincts took over and he swung his sword, ignoring his impulse to block the next attack, if it would come. But Severa had the exact same idea as both swords went round and, in what seemed to be slow motion, hit their marks right on the neck of their opponent. But instead of decapitating the combatants, the steel bounced off invisible barriers.

"Out!" came the cry from both Pagar and Anna. Dorren and Severa stood motionless and silent. The crowd around them had also fallen silent.

So what now? Dorren and Severa were just staring at each other, but there was no rage in their expressions; just questions. Who had won? Who had hit the barrier first? Pagar walked up to them. The crowd were now bustling.

"Are you both sufficiently satisfied with the result to allow you to stop this bickering?"

They both looked at him questioningly.

"So who hit the barrier first?" asked Dorren.

"You both did it at almost exactly the same time. There was no way of telling which of you hit it first, but does that really matter? From the speed of the swing you would have killed each other no matter who made contact first. Now that is the end of it." And with that, Pagar turned and left.

The two of them faced each other without expression. Dorren did not have it in him to be angry anymore. For a moment they stared at each other before Severa turned and left.

Anna had to hurry to catch up with Pagar, but eventually saw him making his way to his room through the corridors.

"Sir!"

Pagar turned around and smiled as he saw Anna rushing towards him. "What can I do for you, Anna?"

"I just had a question. How did you know they would just stop fighting after that? How did you know that they wouldn't just keep going at each other, like they did last time?"

"It was not a case of knowing, but rather guessing," replied Pagar, who continued to smile. When Anna gave Pagar a bewildered look he continued. "I was relying on the fact that no matter who the victor was, both would lose interest. It was a way for them to get all their rage and frustration out."

"But last time they just kept going at each other and had to be pulled apart."

Pagar still smiled as if he had just achieved something great. "Yes, but you are missing the most crucial part of the difference between then and now. They are older and have grown up from being completely immature to being...well...slightly more mature," he finished.

"A risky move, then. You could have had them trying to kill each other again."

"Indeed, but sometimes risks are worth taking. The same thing could be said for taking in the very powerful Sileena."

"Do you think she will be able to control her power? Or do you think she might accidentally blow up the place?" Anna said in a tone that indicated she was exaggerating.

"I stand by what I said: it is a risk, but some risks are worth taking. If it reassures you I'm very positive that she will not blow up the place."

Satisfied with his answer, Anna nodded. "Thank you, sir." She turned around to walk away.

"Nice speaking with you, Anna."

Sileena lay in bed, looking at the ceiling and away in her thoughts. What was to become of her now? She certainly liked this place but what was she supposed to do? Up until now she had not been doing anything other than hanging around with Anna and her friends or Dorren and his friends, or merely lying in her room as she was doing now.

Obviously she was going to be put to work like everyone else, but what kind of work? Perhaps she'd be made to work the farms. The thought was not a pleasant one. It was not the kind of labour she wanted to do. What if she was sent out on what the Outcasts called 'missions'? Outcasts...she was going to have to stop referring to them as a separate people. She was soon going to be one of them now. Besides, a lot of the people were not originally Outcasts and had been banished to this place.

And what about her newfound magic? It was strange that she didn't feel any different. She could control wind and other elements at will. She wondered what was to happen with this too, because she'd surprised herself with the sudden feats she'd accomplished. No longer a helpless girl, she was now a very powerful magic user. She remembered what Pagar had done when Dorren and Severa went at each other outside the Underground. The power he emanated had scared her. He might look like nothing more than another man, but she reckoned no one in the Underground could take him on in a straight fight. Sileena reckoned even she could not take him. Her understanding of magic was limited. It was all new to her. Pagar, on the other hand, had been practising it for a long time. But being able to lift water to the extent she had caused her to both wonder and fear. Her own power suddenly scared her, and now she understood everyone's apprehension. Who wouldn't be apprehensive about someone being brought in who held enough raw power to do something like that? Power she didn't know she had until now. With this elemental power you could do so much.

How was steel supposed to beat magic? The thought seemed absurd. Dorren was one of the best swordsmen, but how could he contend with a jet of flames, or some other kind of magical blast? Perhaps the ground beneath his feet could be moved. Sileena did not like this kind of thinking, and so tried to dwell on other subjects such as what the Reunion would be like. But she didn't get to dwell on it for long before a knock came at her door.

"Come in."

Anna opened the door and beckoned to her. "It is time to go to the induction."

"The induction?" Sileena asked.

"Yes, it is where you will be told what happens next. You will have to swear an oath to the Underground."

Sileena frowned. "Swear an oath? This sounds similar to how things are done in Eceriden."

"Yes, we do not disagree with everything they do. To disagree with everything they do just because of dislike breeds ignorance."

It took a moment for Sileena to understand what Anna was talking about.

They continued through the tunnels until they reached an unfamiliar spiral staircase leading up. Reaching the top, they entered a room in which Pagar was sitting behind a desk and quietly reading a book. This must be where he works and manages the Underground, she thought. It was a very nice-looking room, with books lined along the shelves. It felt like ages since she'd last been able to read anything, and part of her longed just to look at one of the parchments or novels filling the shelves.

Anna moved towards Pagar, and when he noticed them coming he put the book down and stood up.

"Welcome, Sileena. Has Anna told you what you are doing here?"

"Kind of," she replied.

Pagar moved round his desk and faced Sileena. "We are here to induct you into the life of an Outcast. The first thing to cover will be your work."

Sileena gave a nod to this.

"Your use here will be in your magical potential. We don't want you taking part in manual work as there are other uses for your gifts. You will be using magic all around the Underground, adding to what is already there."

Part of Sileena was relieved at the prospect of not working on the farms, or in other manual work. Perhaps it was simply not knowing what to do that made her anxious. But no manual work meant she would have to find other means of exercise to keep healthy. She loved the games hall and would probably be there for a lot of her free time. And there would no longer be a guard. Sileena's excitement got the better of her and she had to quickly drag her attention back to Pagar, who was still speaking.

"Other magic users you may have already met, such as your friend Anna, do this job. She can help you understand how to do it."

Working with Anna certainly sounded like fun, although her friend was a rather competitive person. She looked in Anna's direction to find her standing back and flicking at some papers like a bored child. Anna seemed like the impatient type so working with her should certainly make things very interesting.

"What would I be putting magic into?" She already knew of a few places that obviously required it.

"Everything. The foundations of the Underground are of vital importance, but other areas include the aura we have placed above the ground, the baths, the light, the potions and the infirmary."

There were doctors here? What a silly question, of course there would be a place to treat the sick or injured. It surprised her that she hadn't thought about a place like that until now.

"Do you accept this work?"

Sileena looked at Pagar and nodded. "I do." She couldn't help but beam. Her excitement was getting the better of her. There was the issue of how to do these tasks. Anna could show her, but Sileena knew nothing beyond a little elemental magic, which was apparently the easiest to manipulate. "But I don't know how use magic in that way. How will I do these tasks?"

"That brings me to the next step. I will teach you how to control your magic and use it."

Sileena smiled and nodded, reassured that she was being taught by the Underground's best.

"However, I will not always be around as I have many other responsibilities within this place, so a lot of the time I will be unable help with your progress. When this is the case, Anna here will teach you what you will need to know."

Sileena again nodded.

"Once the basic lessons are complete you will be allowed to start your work. Anna will direct you to what tasks you should do. Anyway, if you agree to all this then we can get to the final stage of these proceedings."

"I agree."

Pagar smiled pleasantly; then picked up a piece of paper from his desk. He walked to stand just in front of her. "Kneel."

Sileena did as she was asked and kneeled.

"Now repeat after me. I, Sileena, vow never to betray the land of Outcasts."

Sileena repeated this statement.

"I vow to respect everyone of every Underground and work towards the cause which has been acknowledged as a free and independent kingdom of our own."

Again Sileena repeated this.

With that, Pagar beckoned her to stand. "Well, that's it. You are now an Outcast, welcome to our society."

Sileena smiled. "Is that it? I thought there was more to this induction."

Pagar give a small smile as he returned to his desk. "Of course not. I have to manage a great deal, including getting new people to settle, which happens fairly regularly. Managing between five and six hundred people is harder than you think. Small, quick, efficient ceremonies are good enough."

There was a pause as Sileena took this in. To be honest what she repeated did not sound very eccentric and doubted the vow had been rehearsed. She expected something a little more official.

"Anna can escort you out and get you ready. There is a party coming up and you might want to be there."

Anna took Sileena's hand and led her out of the office. The two of them worked their way through their corridors. Anna who was buzzing with excitement now that the boring ceremony was over talked about all the things they could do now, and her speech moved at such a pace that Sileena lost track of what Anna was talking about. But now she could find out what this Reunion thing was all about.

# 8

# THE REUNION

Sileena was back in her bed clearing her mind, which seemed to have become a routine. Bed and the baths were definitely the best places to be with your thoughts. Perhaps it was because you could be alone, or maybe it had something to do with comfort.

As she pondered her new magical talent she wondered how to manipulate the elemental power into helping with the everyday running of the Underground. Most of the magic needed for the Underground was natural auras, which she did not have any clue about but was relieved to know that Pagar or Anna would be teaching her what she needed to know. Before she could think any further there was tap on the door.

"Come in," she called.

The door opened to reveal Anna, who walked into the room. "I think it's time we got you ready for tonight, don't you think?" she said, smiling.

"Ready?"

"Yeah, we had a talk with Pagar and he said that now you are a member you can come to the Reunion. It will be great fun. Now come on before you're too late, 'cause I want to choose my outfit as well."

Sileena stood up and followed Anna out the door and through the tunnels. "Anna, what's the Reunion?"

"Ah, well, we are not the only Underground in the Outcasts' Land. We're one of many and the Reunion is the best time of year for us. It is when we all go to one place and celebrate. This year it is taking place here."

"Celebrate what?"

Anna took a moment to find the right answer. "Showing that we work together. Right, we are nearly there." It sounded like, for Anna, the Reunion was less about the reason they were celebrating and more about having a little fun.

They turned around a couple of corners and then entered a room Sileena had never been in before. This room was fairly large and was filled to the brim with clothes that varied in shape, size and texture. They were all hung neatly around the room, making it easy to choose garments.

There were already several girls in there choosing their outfits, but not a male in sight. When Sileena asked about it she was told they had a separate outfit room. Sileena could also see some of Anna's friends dotted around picking their attire. In the back of the room there were several cubicles with sheets in front of them where those that had chosen their outfit could try them on.

"Now I want you to choose something and see how it looks. Make sure you have the right size and we shall see if it is the right one for tonight."

Sileena began looking through the endless stream of clothes. Moving to the dresses section, she had a fair idea of what she was looking for. She just hoped that what she had in mind was here amongst the dresses. Anna was away looking through a different section.

After a few minutes of going through the dresses Sileena thought she had found the perfect one. It was elegant, flowing and seemed very nice. It was made from gold-coloured silk, and had white streaks going down it with silver decorations. It was long and without any creases. She wondered how many rations it would cost to get something like this. It couldn't be cheap.

She went up to Anna and asked how much clothes generally cost. Anna, who was still looking through the endless stream of outfits, told her it was a one-off free piece. Everyone received one free set of clothes and that was the one you would wear tonight. Sileena nodded and went back to the dress and was relieved to find that it had not been taken.

Her dresses were always chosen for her back in Sarden. But that did not take away from how magnificent they looked. She had to look the part as a noble daughter, despite only being allowed out on certain occasions. These dresses were somewhat less glamorous in comparison but that did not take much away from the joy of being able to choose one for herself.

As Sileena went to claim it she caught sight of another dress out of the corner of her eye. It seemed familiar, and unbelievably, was the one she was hoping to find. It was the dress she had been wearing during her kidnap. The Outcasts had taken and cleaned it on her first day in the Underground. It was incredibly fortunate that she was able to find it, and even more so that no one had taken it. The dress was more magnificent than any of the others in the whole room. What a strange thing that no one had chosen it yet, but that didn't matter now. She took the dress and went into a cubicle to change. Well, it was her dress to begin with. The Outcasts had sort of taken it as their own and assumed it was not hers anymore. At least it was back in her hands and it would be nice to stand out.

After a minute she was finished and looked in the mirror within the cubicle, smiling as the dress matched her perfectly. It may have been chosen for her but whoever decided what clothes she wore had impeccable taste. She smiled and went out the cubicle to find Anna, happy with her choice.

"What do you think?" She heard a few giggles in the background.

"Oh my," replied Anna, looking at Sileena up and down. To Sileena's surprise Anna was shaking her head. How could this dress be wrong?

"What? Does it not suit me?"

"It suits you very well. You have great taste but I don't think that is what we are looking for in a party like this. Here, I think I should help choose you something. Something that will work for the Reunion."

Sileena, still surprised by Anna's reply, went back into the changing rooms and got out of the dress and into her normal clothes. It was a bit sad as she put the dress back where she found it. She guessed it would not be back in her hands for the time being. Sileena then found a couple of girls with Anna, choosing their clothes away from the dress section. Were dresses the wrong choice?

"Stand straight," said Anna, and Sileena obeyed. She was curious as to what Anna would see as appropriate attire for this occasion. Anna held something against Sileena's waist; then held something else up to her chest. "Yes, I think this will do. Now go and put this on." Anna handed her the two pieces of material Anna held against her, and some boots of the same colour. Sileena just stood there, waiting for the rest of it. "Well, go get changed," said Anna, smiling.

"But it doesn't seem like much," she replied.

Anna frowned and again indicated towards the changing area. Perhaps there was some sort of magical properties to them, hence why the non-magical dress was wrong.

There was no point in trying to argue with Anna, so she entered the changing room and unfolded the clothes. They looked like a top and a skirt meant for a child. But she did as she was told and put on the outfit before looking in the mirror and frowning. This was not right. The only thing that actually fitted her were the boots. The top was sleeveless and only covered her breasts, leaving her belly completely exposed. Her skirt was also way too short, leaving her legs completely bare. Her boots went just above her ankles but fitted perfectly.

"Are you done in there yet?" called Anna.

"This doesn't fit. We need to find something else."

"What? Let's see you."

"No. I'm far too exposed."

She could hear a sigh from outside. "Are you in the outfit, though?"

"Yes but—"

The curtains swung open and Anna stepped in. Sileena gasped and quickly tried to cover herself with her hands. To her astonishment Anna had also changed, but she was wearing even less than Sileena. Anna was wearing similar shoes, but red, and what looked like undergarments. A top and pants, in thick red leather that matched her shoes. It did make

Sileena seem less bare in comparison, but that didn't make her feel any better. Anna walked up to her.

"Stop being such a baby. Now stand straight and let's see you."

Sileena did not comply, and so Anna grabbed her hands and forced them to her sides. Sileena looked away, embarrassed by the exposure.

"Fits you perfectly. I knew you had a perfect, slender body underneath all those clothes."

Sileena blushed, but still looked away.

Anna released her hands and walked out of the changing room. "You will take that set for tonight. Now let's get something to eat and then we will sort out the rest before it's time to get to the party. We don't want to be late."

"But what about my clothes? I need to get changed back."

Anna frowned and went into the changing rooms, took out Sileena's clothes and put them on a pile of others that seemed to be the dirty ones people were leaving behind to be cleaned.

"There, now follow me. The girls are all waiting."

Sileena reluctantly began to follow Anna out of the room into the corridor where the group of girls were standing. It was a bit of a relief to see that they were all wearing similar outfits to Anna and herself. Some were wearing as little as Anna, while others were a bit more decent. Some had their bellies covered while a couple of others were wearing a very thin material over their legs. It annoyed Sileena that they got to wear that while she had to wear the outfit Anna had selected. When they greeted her she looked away, reluctantly saying "hello" back.

"She is a little shy about wearing very little," said Anna.

"What for?" said one of the girls. "You look wonderful. The guys will be all over you."

Sileena gave a forced smile at the compliment. "So what kind of party is this?" she asked.

"Well," said one of the girls, "it's not one of your ballroom parties." Unfortunately that did not answer her question. But it was the only one she was going to get.

"But why must we wear so little? It just feels so innapropriate." Anna gave Sileena a warm smile.

"Honestly don't worry. The Reunion involves countless people all together in one place. It gets very very warm so you will be glad of your attire when the time comes. And most people will be in similar outfits. Trust me."

The group went to the eatery for something to eat. When they got their food and sat down the girl spoke again. "Did you see the man who was serving you, Sileena? He was looking at you. I told you they were going to be all over you."

The thought was not making her feel very comfortable at all.

"Oh, stop it, Liz," said Anna. "Some girls have standards you know, and don't like it when guys see them as objects to be used, unlike you."

"Hey, I was just saying, there is nothing wrong with liking to be looked at."

Anna glared at her, but said nothing more on the subject.

Once the group had finished what they were eating they went to one of Anna's friends' rooms, which had a selection of perfumes and makeup, which the girls individually selected.

"How did you get all of these?" asked Sileena.

"Well," replied the girl, "it's just a selection that I have been gathering for years. They just slowly built up and here is the result."

"She is a collector of perfumes," said Anna.

While some of the girls were applying perfume and makeup, Anna was getting others to sit down and magically styling their hair according to their wishes. Some wanted straight hair, others wavy hair; some styles like those of the woodland folk, but Anna was unsure of how they styled their hair and so made something exotic up. When Sileena sat down, though, Anna did not ask what she wanted.

"Seeing as you are not accustomed to this kind of gathering I will decide what style you get."

Sileena was uncertain, but nodded. She had let Anna decide everything else so might as well let her do this too. It was not like she was going to shave her head. Although she might. Would she? She was putting all her trust in Anna and hoping that she was not just being set up to be humiliated. But Anna was her friend and she was using similar things so she was sure it was going to be fine.

Sileena felt something strange, like a sort of tugging at her hair. Looking in the mirror in front of her she could see where her hair had started smoothing out, and lengthening as a result. Then chunks of her hair fell to the ground, and kept doing so until her hair was neatly cut to just below her shoulders. The hair then slowly curled slightly until it became wavy. It was not as extravagant as some of the others, but certainly looked nice.

"Done." Anna clearly had experience with this sort of thing. After her makeup was applied she looked in the mirror and saw a very different person. Her skin was not quite as pale as it usually was. Her eyes seemed to be darkened but still had the glowing shine of gold there. Her hair was the biggest change, though; now wavy and much shorter than it usually was. It was very different, but she did look pretty. However, when she stood up and saw her whole self in the mirror she again saw the small top that only covered her chest, and the short skirt, and she began to feel awkward again. She did notice though that her hair matched the clothes.

The rest of the girls were also done sorting themselves and they were all looking very pretty, giving her a little more confidence. They seemed to know what they were doing.

Once everyone was finished they began to walk towards the giant cave where the Reunion was to be held. The last time Sileena was there it was practically empty, except for a few boxes. It must look very different now. What sort of changes had they made?

Sileena lost that thought when Liz dragged her back into the conversation. Liz was a rather odd girl. She seemed to be enjoying the idea of attention, even if it demeaned her. Luckily Anna was not that kind of person.

Some time passed and they reached the giant cave and entered. There were tables all along one side of the cavern which had food completely covering many of them, and more constantly being added. Further along were more empty tables that Sileena presumed were going to be covered in more food and beverages. At the very back was a giant wooden block with stairs going up to it. It seemed to be for someone giving a speech. This at least gave her some idea of what to expect. There were smaller blocks dotted around this great room, which were stands she suspected for people who wanted a vantage point. The giant pillar in the centre had small fire lights spiralling up it. This was strange, as she knew they used magic to keep the place lit. Why did they need lights? When she asked she was told it was to make the place look nice.

The massive hall had a lot of people in it already; by her estimate nearly two hundred, but that was still nowhere near enough to fill the place. Most were hanging around at the tables while groups seemed to be huddled in conversations.

"There," said Anna, and started walking towards the tables, and the rest followed suit. Once they neared Sileena could see Gabe and Lockarr standing talking to two other people. They were both dressed up in slightly better quality clothes than normal. Gabe was wearing trousers and shoes and went topless, while Lockarr was wearing the same except with a sleeveless open shirt. When Lockarr saw them he gave a casual smile.

"Hello ladies, welcome to the party. I thought you would have been the first ones here."

"No," said one of the girls, "we were busy getting ready. So what have we missed?"

"Oh, nothing really. The party hasn't really begun yet. The people from one of the other Undergrounds have arrived and their food is currently being added to the tables. Pagar and Drak, the leader of the Zorku Underground that has just arrived, have just been talking." He pointed and in the distance Sileena could see Pagar talking to a slightly older man. "We are still waiting for the rest, and once they have arrived we will hear Pagar's speech, and then the music will start and we can have some fun. You're all looking very pretty though."

The two men they were talking to had left to speak to others.

"Thank you," said Anna, who was now leaning against Gabe with his arms around her. "So where is the rest of the group?"

"Well, we thought we would have some fun and meet up here. This way there is the challenge of trying to find each other. Me and

Gabe here were lucky to come early and cross paths. Poor Derain and Dorren might have more difficulty because they are too slow and lazy to get their butts out of bed," he said, smiling.

"Typical," said Anna.

"How did this Reunion end up like this?" asked Sileena. This all seemed so strange. The way people dressed suggested a rather peculiar event yet it sounded like a normal party.

"Well, it began with just one Underground," said Lockarr. "But as time went on more people began to alter their perspective due to the changes in the laws of some of the lands. Not following the same religion does not count as a capital offence now, so instead they're thrown out of the kingdom."

She already knew this, but everyone was silent, allowing Lockarr to continue the story. Sileena made sure to listen intently.

"But this change led to a rapid increase in the population of these lands, and it was not long before another Underground came into existence. The two at first fought each other but later a truce was made and each year they met to honour this peace. Initially it was just the leaders who had to meet but eventually more and more people got involved, and as more Undergrounds came into existence it became a massed gathering to celebrate the peace."

Sileena thought for a moment before Lockarr spoke again.

"You will be taught all this because Pagar is particular about everyone understanding how we came to be. It's just been a very busy time."

"But why has this gathering turned into some kind of party?"

Lockarr thought for a moment; then laughed. "Because when the leaders began to formally meet and give speeches about maintaining the peace between the Undergrounds it...well...got very boring. So drink was added, and then more drink, and food and music. It eventually became like this and now each Underground takes it in turn to host."

Sileena nodded, satisfied with the answer. She thought about how the Reunion first came about, and had changed over time to become something more. However, she knew what drink did and wondered whether fights would break out, and if that might not lead to further conflict. But these people were not idiots and if fights were to break happen then they would not let something as small as that start a war.

She let these thoughts slide and returned to reality, where Anna was bickering lightheartedly with Lockarr over how much drink he could handle. Lockarr was predictably claiming to be able to drink more than most men could handle. Anna was laughing and saying, "We shall see." Some of the other girls then changed the subject when Sileena noticed a large crowd enter the room. It must have been from another one of the Undergrounds, because she didn't recognise anyone. As the people entered she saw Pagar and the older man he was with greet the woman who led the newcomers. She also looked older than Pagar, probably in her sixties.

"Dran!" Lockarr shouted, and moved towards the new crowd. The group approached him and he greeted them in kind. The talks continued as questions were exchanged about how the other Undergrounds were, and a little debate came up as to which one was doing better. They were very competitive. As time went by more Undergrounds appeared and it was not long until the entire room was packed with people and the tables were completely covered in food. Sileena decided to focus on the group she was with so she could not lose them in the crowd. This was a very strange experience. She had never been in such an overpopulated place before, with so many people. Having been kept away from others throughout her life, she now felt very much exposed in what she was wearing, despite so many wearing something similar.

Anna came up to her again, smiling and holding two cups, handing one across to Sileena. "Here, you seem a bit uncomfortable."

"I'm sorry, I'm just not used to this kind of situation."

Anna gave a small chuckle. "Yeah, on my first time at one of these events I also felt out of place."

Sileena looked at the drink, which did not look like water. She took a sniff of it and suddenly felt dizzy. "What is this?"

"That is something to help you feel more comfortable. I think one should do the trick with you. It's a strong drink but you'll like the effects."

"Is it alcohol?"

"It's a combination of two alcoholic drinks, mixed with a hypnotic potion. Just drink it."

Sileena eyed her friend suspiciously but gave in and drank.

Dorren entered the great hall and laughed. Bloody hell, the place was packed. How the hell was he going to find his friends in this? Usually if there was a gathering of this size it would be a battle.

First he would head into the crowd and search for his friends. Dorren was wearing the nicest trousers he had, and a shirt which was unbuttoned, leaving his chest exposed.

After a couple of minutes of weaving through the crowd he found a friend. It was Derain, who was chatting up a girl Dorren had never seen before. Derain was wearing similar clothing to him, although Derain himself was not as physically broad as he was. The girl was probably from one of the other Undergrounds. Dorren moved up and grabbed Derain by the shoulder, dragging him away from her. He at first protested, but quickly stopped.

"Where are the others?" Dorren asked.

"I don't know," Derain replied. "I only arrived a couple of minutes ago. Don't worry, I'm sure we will find them. Seriously though, why does it matter? Look around at all these new people we are supposed to meet."

"You mean new girls you haven't tried to sleep with yet."

Derain just maintained his expression and repeated, "New people."

Dorren looked around and then back to Derain. "Give me a hoist."

Derain sighed, put his hands together and picked Dorren up to look over the crowd. He peered around at the clusters of heads until he saw the one head he was looking for.

"Over there!" He could see Gabe, who was over in one corner of the hall about fifty metres away. Thank goodness for his massive size. No one else compared. Dorren then headed in that direction and Derain followed, apparently feeling that this was more important than continuing his conversation with the girl. As Dorren moved through the crowd he could see that a few people were already out of their minds (or getting there) from the drinks and potions. Dorren sighed; the music had not even started yet. He glanced over to a higher platform on which stood the musicians, who were happily talking to each other.

Dorren felt a hand on his shoulder, and turned to see who had stopped him. He cursed to himself when he saw Severa standing before him and clearly drunk. There was a girl who looked just as drunk standing next to his old adversary. Damn, he was not in the mood to fight. Severa looked at him for a few seconds before speaking.

"You...you are such a dick, you know that?"

"Is that all you have to say because I really should—"

"No, I'm not done. I have disliked you for a long time and it's because you're a dick. But you are good fighter and I...respect you. We are connected, like family."

Dorren was a bit taken aback by this and so hesitated before replying. "Thanks, I think. You are a good fighter too."

"I know that. Now go away before you ask me for a kiss. I don't want to kiss you. I want to kiss her." He put an arm around the drunken girl next to him and the two of them disappeared into the crowd.

"Well, that was strange," stated Dorren.

"How come he gets to leave with a girl and I don't?" Derain complained.

"I didn't say you had to follow me."

Derain just moaned in reply and they continued through the crowd. Ignoring Derain was something that Dorren had managed to get used to.

After moving a little further they found Anna, Sileena, the group of girls, Gabe, Lockarr and Dran. As they approached it was Sileena who saw them first.

"Dorren!" she exclaimed, and ran up to him and embraced him warmly. Dorren stood limp with surprise at this change in personality.

"Umm, hello, Sileena, you seem in a different mood today." He could not help but notice what she was wearing, and blushed. She was very attractive. When she let go and stepped back he noticed her eyes. "You look very pretty."

Sileena's smile widened. She really did. Her eyes matched her outfit very well.

"Hey, what about my hug?" Derain complained.

"Oh yeah, here you go, my little pervert." She embraced him as well. The line earned a few laughs in the background and a disgruntled look from Derain. He was obviously still upset about being dragged away from the girl earlier.

"Hey, Anna?" Dorren muttered so that only Anna could hear. Anna looked at him in acknowledgement. "What's going on with Sileena? Didn't you make sure she did not take the wrong drink?"

Anna merely smiled. "Well actually, I gave her a little something to ease her up. The poor thing was so uncomfortable that everyone in the vicinity could tell. She is all yours now."

"I'm not going to take advantage of someone in this kind of situation."

Anna gave him an irritated look. "Seriously? You should stop being so goody-goody. You break the rules all the time, pretty much drive Pagar crazy. If you must then wait a while, the effects of the drink will eventually wear off."

Anna then moved over and leaned on Gabe, who gently put an arm around her. Dorren shook his head. What was wrong with him? He was never good with love. The group talked for a little while before a booming sound resonated through the hall.

"*Quiet!*"

The room fell silent as they all turned to the main stand of blocks, on top of which stood Pagar. His voice was being amplified by magic. There were four other people standing behind him: two much older men, a younger man and an older woman. These were the leaders of their respective Undergrounds. Whoever hosted the gathering was to give a speech, as was tradition.

"This is our one 109th gathering, in which we celebrate one of the longest periods of peace in any nation."

This statement got a cheer from the crowd that shook the room.

"We have been working towards creating ourselves as an acknowledged kingdom with our own rights for all, and have come closer and closer with each passing year. We will raise the marshes and we will maintain ourselves as equal to the rest of the world, and one of the greatest communities that has ever existed."

Another booming cheer.

"You have done us all proud by maintaining the peace. Now is the time to celebrate."

With that came the loudest roar and then a booming coming from the drum. Another couple of booms sounded from the drum and then the music kicked off. Many people moved to the floor and start dancing. Dorren and the others picked a few drinks from the table and after a while they felt completely free. Gabe was the only one able to keep his cool, although the fact that he rarely spoke did not help show everyone whether he was in the same state as the others.

"Dorren, let's go dance," Sileena giggled.

"Of course." He beamed and the two moved onto the dance floor and let themselves go. Anna and the girls followed along with Derain and Gabe. Dran had gone off to find his own friends and Lockarr merely remained at the side watching the development of the party. He was never the dancing type.

As the night wore on the musicians kept going, occasionally switching with others to get a break. There were glimpses of people Dorren knew who were all moving, some in more ridiculous ways than others, on the dance floor. Even Pagar and the other leaders were up and dancing or having a laugh. This was the one time a year where all problems disappeared. When everyone was free. The aftermath the next day was also a free day but was seen as a recovery day. For now, however, it was simple freedom.

The dancing, drinking, eating and discussions went on for hours and a few people began to retire. Accommodations were made for those from the other Undergrounds and some moved in that direction. The music began to slow into a more melodic tune. Gabe and Anna were sitting down and holding each other. It was nice to see, thought Dorren. Two people just being together. Sometimes there was the passion but occasionally the simple things like just sitting in each other's company was nice too. Dorren and Sileena moved back onto the dance floor and began to do a slower dance along with many others. Sileena appeared to feel more relaxed.

"Ugh, I don't know how to do this kind of dance," she said.

"Here," he said, and pulled her closer to him and put his arms around her. They then moved back and forth in a slow dance. "There, you have it. Not so difficult."

Sileena chuckled then fell silent as they continued back and forth on the dance floor. Time continued as more and more people left. Lockarr left, saying goodbye to the group, and not long after Derain turned up with a girl at either side of him.

"Hey Dorren, have you met Jenifer and Rain? Jenifer is from the Nordu Underground and Rain is from the Migra one."

"Umm yeah, very nice to meet you."

The girls looked fairly drunk and were cuddling into Derain. Derain turned to Anna and Gabe. "Well, I will see you all tomorrow I suspect. Have fun."

"Bye, Derain," replied Anna. Gabe gave a simple nod. Derain then turned and led the two girls to the exit. Dorren could hear Derain speak as he left.

"So have you two girls ever considered experimentation between Undergrounds? I call it the Underground three-way."

Dorren shook his head and turned back to the group to see Gabe and Anna get up.

"Well, I think Gabe and myself are also heading back where I can show him who is in charge."

Gabe gave a small smile to those words, shaking his head slightly.

"Yeah, sure. I will see the two of you tomorrow," replied Dorren. With that two more people left. Dorren turned back to see that it was just the two of them. Everyone else had either gone their separate ways or turned in. Dorren looked to Sileena, who was beaming.

"Do you want to turn in too?"

"Yes, I think another hour and the party was going to be over anyway, and I think the effects of my drink are wearing off."

Dorren smiled. "I will take you to your room."

The two of them made their way to the exit. There were still a few people on the floor dancing and a couple of groups huddled. The music was also still playing, but appeared to be soon coming to a close. He could also make out Pagar, who was happily chatting to a few other people, still full of energy. The man had a surprising amount of stamina. The two exited the hall and made their way through the tunnels to Sileena's room, and then Dorren would make his way to his own. He was done celebrating for the night. It was a lot of fun but with all his friends gone there would be no point in returning.

As they were walking, they passed a few people in the halls. Some were just standing, some were passionately kissing, and some were walking back to their rooms. There were even a couple of people who had either passed out or fallen asleep on the ground, failing in their task of getting back to their room. Dorren and Sileena had a giggle at them. But soon the conversation changed as they made their way through the tunnels. They mostly spoke about the night and what Sileena thought of it. They eventually came to Sileena's door, but continued to talk outside.

"I have never been anywhere with so many people."

"But," Dorren replied, "you were part of the nobility. I'm sure you have been to a party before."

"No, I was always kept away from events. My father did it so that I could never meet anyone new. I think it was because of my eyes. He probably thought that it would be brought up. Maybe I would be taken away or experimented on."

Dorren frowned. That did not sound right. Even in Eceriden they would not take a child away just because of her eye colour, even if it suggested she might hold power.

"So your father kept you away from everyone else?"

"Well, except for certain subjects and my brother. He looked after me and taught me everything. Whenever my father hit me he would be there to give me comfort afterwards."

Dorren was shocked. The lord sounded bad. Really bad. He wasn't scared that Sileena would be taken away from him. He was scared that she would be a threat. Dorren was going to have a talk with him when it came down to the meeting. But instead of bringing that up he changed the topic.

"Your brother sounds very nice."

"He is. So what about your family?"

Dorren was in thought. What about his family? His father was banished from Eceriden along with Pagar, and the two of them founded this very Underground together. Dorren was raised for a couple of years in the Underground before the incident.

"I don't have much family. Pagar is my adopted father. My real father was murdered many years ago. No one found out who did it. But when nothing else happened they stopped the investigation."

Yes, because that was certainly a much cheerier subject. Sileena looked sad as she listened to the story.

"Pagar took full control of the Underground and adopted me as his own."

"Do you not wonder if the murderer is still around?"

"I do sometimes, but there is nothing I can do really. I was so young and there is no evidence anywhere. The most likely thing is that it was an assassin that came in, killed him then left."

"What about your mother?" Sileena asked.

"She died before we were banished to the Outcasts' Land." There was silence for a moment before Dorren spoke again. "It seems neither of us have the best of pasts. The right thing to do is to not let them destroy our futures."

Sileena smiled. "Yeah."

"Well, I should let you get some rest. I think you were on the dance floor for longer than anyone else."

He turned to walk away but a hand grabbed him by the shirt and pulled him in. Sileena grabbed his collar and to his surprise their lips met. Time seemed to slow as he tried to take in what was happening. His heart raced as their lips remained locked. They were kissing. This thought had to go through his head a few times before he grasped it. Dorren's shock quickly subsided and he let himself go. After a moment had passed Sileena pulled away from him with that beautiful smile and her hands still on his collar. Her smile became a little more playful and radiant as she dragged him into her room, closing the door behind her. He didn't know what to say. But nothing needed to be said as

Sileena took over and pulled him to sit next to her on her bed. Dorren gently slid his hand over her cheek as she leaned in and they kissed passionately. Dorren's heart fluttered in a way he had not experienced before as his hand moved down from her cheek past her shoulders, over her arms to her hips. Sileena pulled away and removed her top.

With a gentle push Dorren laid Sileena back onto her bed as he continued to kiss her. His hands gently moved from her belly to her bare chest, her own hands around his waist. With a few simple touches he listened to her reactions for the best effect.

Within a few minutes the two of them had taken off what clothes they had left in preparation for the passion that was to follow that night.

# 9

# MEETING

Dorren was standing on the edge of the forest where he'd left the message for Sileena's father, telling him where they were to meet.

Some time had passed since that night but Dorren could not stop smiling. Sileena had also seemed to be in a very good mood and that just made his day feel brighter. That was, until it was time to leave. The journey was much faster than before but that was because he did not need to carry Sileena most of the way. This allowed them to reach their destination faster than he first anticipated and now they were waiting for the others to arrive for the exchange to take place.

However, no trade was going happen. Instead this meeting was out of courtesy to tell Sileena's father, or whoever showed up, that she would not be going back. That would hopefully stop any rescue attempts.

Dorren never would have thought that this situation could occur when he first managed to kidnap Sileena. He was bemused about how the last few weeks developed. Despite the concerns he and Pagar had, Dorren was still feeling good; happy and at peace. The first concern about this trip was why they should leave at all. Perhaps if they did not turn up, that would be a message for Sileena's father. He did not seem the type to look out for his daughter's wellbeing. It would surprise Dorren if he turned up at all, considering the things Sileena had told him. However, she did want to go because although her father might have no interest in paying for her, her brother was a different matter. So Sileena and Dorren departed together, despite Pagar's concerns about the matter. It could have been a trap, and Pagar was insistent that others accompany them. However, Dorren knew the forest and how to avoid the great wolves that dwelled within. The people of Eceriden did not and as such would never enter the forest themselves. So if something were to go wrong then they would quickly retreat into the dense woodlands. After a rather persuasive argument Pagar was convinced and the two of them set off.

When they had reached the forest Sileena was reluctant to enter, but Dorren merely stated that there was nothing to worry about and his confidence helped quell her fear. Moving about one hundred yards or so into the trees they came across a rope hanging from a branch of one of the stronger trees. When Sileena looked up she could see wooden planks that appeared to extend between the branches. It was a walkway. She smiled and shook her head.

"I thought you said you made it through the forest because you know the wolves?"

Dorren giggled, with a gleam in his eyes. "You remembered that, did you? Well you're right, I do know the wolves. I know they cannot climb trees."

Sileena sighed but smiled. She put her arms around Dorren as he climbed up the rope. She was not too heavy but it was a lot of work to pull them both up. He had to supress a gasp once he reached the top and Sileena let go. He really hoped she didn't notice, and if she did that she would not take offence. But there was no indication of either in her expression, which relieved him.

The walkway was not the best construction but it fulfilled its purpose well. It was not going to break any time soon. As they were moving Sileena peered down at the dark ground below.

"Have you ever seen any wolves?" Despite the simplicity of the question it was hard to answer.

"I don't know. I think I have, but they are only shapes moving along the ground. Never seen one up close. Probably for the best, though."

Sileena was still looking down to the ground below. It was hard to make it out because it was so dark under the branches, and they were pretty high up.

"What about the great wolf Vartak? I've heard stories but they are only rumours."

"No, I don't believe I have seen the great wolf. It is just a story. Of course in a group of animals there are always rumours about one who is bigger than the rest. It spices things up. So I don't think it exists."

"It?"

"Yes, I sort of have to use the term 'it' because no one has any idea whether the wolf is male or female."

Sileena realised the silliness of the question and pretended she never asked it. So Dorren obliged and changed the topic.

Once they had made it to the other side they came across something different. It was not just a hanging rope but what appeared to be some sort of elevator. Wooden boards were tied to a thick rope that connected to a pulley system. When Dorren and Sileena got onto the board he took the rope and let it slowly slip through his fingers. As he did this the board lowered smoothly. Reaching ground level seemed to please Sileena. She was apparently not very fond of heights. Heights had never really bothered him for some reason but he rarely pondered why. There were usually better things to think about.

Dorren led her outside the forest and followed the treeline until he found a large post standing on its own just outside the forest. The note that he'd posted there was now gone. Either the elements had taken it or someone had found it.

"We are here. We will wait until midday for the others."

Sileena nodded and sat next to him on the grass, waiting for someone to arrive.

And now here they remained alone, waiting for someone who might not actually turn up. Time wore on and Dorren could not help but notice the sun passing the point of midday. Perhaps Nerida really didn't want to get his daughter back?

Dorren did not have time to take the thought further as he could make out distant figures approaching. Once they got closer he could see about ten of them, most of them much bigger than Dorren, riding towards them. So now he was severely outnumbered, which was not an appealing thought. Dorren and Sileena preferred to avoid a fight so if it appeared that one was about to begin they would simply retreat into the forest. Usually in such situations his pride would take over, but with people he did not even know he was happy to run away, especially if it kept Sileena out of danger.

All Dorren could think was that this was a bad idea. Something about this meeting might give Eceriden the idea that perhaps the Outcasts' Land was not as barbaric as everyone had thought. This might ruin the secret that everyone had spent so much time to keep. But it was important to Sileena that she made her feelings clear, to make sure there were no attempts to rescue her. The risks of an attempted rescue were probably more severe than her family finding out the truth in this way.

The horses had now stopped and everyone got off, slowly moving towards them. Judging by the age and noble appearance of the man taking the lead Dorren thought he was probably Nerida. Riding next to him was a younger man about the same age as himself. The two of them were surrounded by massive men who probably spent more time trying to get bigger than practising combat. One of the bigger ones was carrying a bag. So they were actually keeping their word? If that bag was the money Dorren had demanded, then his respect for these people would grow. It would be very honourable for them to pay to get someone important back to them. Perhaps they were not as bad as he thought.

Dorren and Sileena stood side by side and waited for them to make the first signal.

"Here's your money," said Nerida as he indicated to the man carrying the bag. "Now I want you to hand over my daughter first. I will not have a savage backstabbing me the moment I hand this over."

Dorren looked to Sileena, who looked a bit nervous so he decided to speak. "I'm sorry but there has been a change of plan. You can keep your money but Si...the girl stays with me."

Nok and his men quickly moved their hands to their weapons ready to attack. Dorren wanted to keep up the idea that he was a savage, so calling Sileena 'the girl' seemed like one small step of maintaining this pretence. But he was not good with words, and this was made abundantly clear here. He'd only said one thing and the others were already about to take up arms against him.

The only other man in the group who was not massive spoke. "You think that we will let you get away with that? Where is your sense of honour? You kidnap a girl, hold her for ransom and still don't stick to your agreement? You didn't even have to come here. Are you here to gloat?" This younger man must be Nok, Sileena's brother.

"What? I would have been happy to kidnap you but you were hiding somewhere else at the time." Nok's statement was actually a little true. He had kidnapped a girl and held her for ransom. Did this mean he didn't have honour? He was going to have to question this later, but now he would deal with the task at hand. Nok was quick to reply.

"At least I have my honour. I will gladly fight you right here and now. One on one, and the winner gets Sileena and the money."

That statement did surprise Dorren. Judging from Nok's stern expression he wanted this fight to the death. Dorren did not fear fighting this nobleman as he believed he could win, but he was not going to kill Sileena's brother in front of her. Perhaps if he just beat him without killing him then he could have the money as well.

"Careful, Nok," said Nerida, looking intently at Dorren. "This is the man who beat Radikador. He is more than capable of beating you."

"I don't care, he probably backstabbed him. He is not the type to fight fair."

Seriously, this man sounded like he had a personal vendetta against him. Dorren guessed he did; after all, he'd kidnapped his sister. Nok went for the hilt of his sword and was about to draw it.

"Stop!" cried Sileena. Nice of her to join in, thought Dorren in relief. She had finally overcome her nerves and he could see determination in her face. Thank goodness, as he was simply making things worse. "Stop, Nok. I want to stay. He is not dishonourable. I asked to stay and he agreed."

Nok, Nerida and his men exchanged glances of shock. But Nok moved from surprise to distrust.

"Sileena, is he forcing you to say this? Don't worry, we will get you back."

How could he not trust him, Dorren jokingly mused to himself. But then, Pagar rarely trusted him. In fact, no one trusted him. It was a sudden realisation, and one that he would have to rectify.

"Nok, I want to stay. I am not lying and he is not forcing me to say this. Please just let me stay. I am here to say goodbye."

Nok didn't know how to reply. He was clearly confused and trying to piece it together. Why would she want to leave her noble life and live with a savage?

Nerida took over. "This is not how this happens. Sileena, you are not staying with this savage. You will come back with me, now!"

"Sileena, I can't be sure you are telling the truth. I bet the moment you try to leave with us he will kill you," said Nok.

Sileena looked to Nok, with more determination now, and started walking forward. Dorren saw what she was doing and instinctively went with it. He took one step back and sat down to show that he did not pose a threat. But he made sure he was seated in a position from which he could quickly react should it be needed.

Sileena stopped halfway between her family and Dorren; then repeated, "I want to stay."

Nok was speechless, looking from Dorren to Sileena and back. Sileena looked at Dorren, who smiled and waved. Sileena sighed and shook her head; then turned back to Nok, smiling.

The expression on Sileena's face seemed to give Nok the message. "I see," said Nok, beginning to understand the situation.

But Nerida was by this point fuming. "Sileena, you are not staying. You're coming back home. Your mother did not sacrifice herself for your life to be spent with barbarians."

"No, Father, I will not go back with you. I am happy with Dorren and I will remain with him. You will not command me anymore."

Nerida was about to retort, but stopped when he saw Nok move towards Sileena and draw his sword. Dorren quickly stood up, ready to act, but stopped when he saw Nok drop his sword on the ground and come to a halt just in front of Sileena.

"Can I speak to him?"

Sileena nodded, and Nok moved towards Dorren. Once he was close enough he spoke.

"So, Dorren," Nok said in a serious tone. Dorren faced him, unflinching. He was quick to catch his name. "Do I have your word that no physical or mental harm will befall her if she goes with you?" Nok seemed to go from a very hostile standpoint to one of more understanding. He was a very intelligent man. Certainly more intelligent than Dorren. Dare he say that Nok and Pagar would probably get along splendidly?

"You do."

Nok stared calmly at Dorren for a moment, but seemed satisfied by the answer. However, he was not finished. "You know you killed men, men with families?"

Dorren looked at him blankly. "So have you. At least I have only killed those who tried to kill me. I have no plans to do any more kidnapping or killing from now on, if that's what you want to hear."

"What are you going to do, then?"

"I'm going home."

Nok nodded, then turned and walked back.

"What did he say?" shouted Nerida.

"Sileena is safe. She is happy. Let's just go home, my lord," replied Nok.

Nok saw the game change and reacted accordingly. A wise man, despite his age. Nerida, on the other hand, was not.

"No! I won't allow this to stand! This Dorren takes my daughter, convinces Sileena to betray us, kills my best soldier and we are just going to let them go?"

Sileena was determined and angry too. "Father, I will not go with you anymore! You have yelled and hit me enough! Here is my chance to be happy and I will not let you stop me!"

Nok was now at Sileena's side. He smiled at her warmly, ignoring their father. She reacted in kind. Nok moved in and embraced before moving back to the group of larger men. Sileena smiled too and turned before walking back to Dorren.

"This will not happen! I did not lose the woman I love giving you life so you can walk away!" cried Nerida.

A sudden force moved in the atmosphere as Nerida conjured up a magical blast and fired it directly at Dorren. The next second seemed to move in slow motion. Dorren could sense it; it was the same sensation as the one he'd experienced when he caught the arrow. He could sense the magical blast moving towards him. The force held more than enough power to destroy him. He might have been able to avoid it but Sileena, who had noticed what was happening, moved between Dorren and the magical force. But Sileena's efforts were to sacrifice herself. She did not know how to shield with her own ability. She was going to die. Dorren couldn't stop it. He could not get to her in time. His senses of his surroundings were not enough to help her. He was being forced to bear witness.

In terror he moved towards her but his senses picked up another movement. In that very second Nok jumped in front of Sileena. In the space of three seconds Nerida fired a magical blast at Dorren, Sileena jumped in front of Dorren to save him and Nok jumped in front of her. The blast collided with a blinding light. Dorren couldn't see, but he could still sense the area around him. Using this time to his advantage he reached and grabbed Sileena by the hand, pulling her towards the forest. The light emitting from the blast gave them the cover they needed to get into the darkness and disappear from sight.

"What happened?" said Sileena, who had just come to her senses. Dorren quickly got them onto the hidden board and pulled on the rope to get up to the tree tops above. Once safely back on the walkway he stopped after he realised he was holding his breath. Sileena repeated the question but all he could do was give her an anguished look. He knew what had happened but could not find the words. Sileena took in the expression questioningly, but soon heard the cries from a couple of hundred metres away.

"No! Nok! Why did you do it?"

The yelling from outside the forest brought Sileena to a realisation. She looked back but they couldn't see through the trees. A look of complete despair was on her face. Breathing heavily and more rapidly, tears very quickly swelled.

"Dorren! I will find you! I will kill you! You have my word! Nok, my son, I'm sorry!"

Dorren looked in the direction of the cries. Everything had gone completely wrong. This was not supposed to happen.

Sileena broke down. She was trying in vain not to cry out loud. She dropped to her knees, and Dorren quickly followed and put his arms around her. He spoke as her teary face was pressed into his chest.

"I'm sorry, I'm so sorry."

# 10

# THE SANCTUARY

The journey back started with Dorren taking the blame for not getting out of the way, but Sileena quickly corrected him and wished aloud that she had never gone, that somehow she should have known what was going to happen.

"I didn't think he would do that, go that far. Why?"

Dorren didn't know how to reply. He wished he could find some way of comforting her. She knew she couldn't go back to the Underground, as much as she wanted to. He could see it in her expression. A very brave girl. Despite having experienced that kind of torment she was still handling the situation well. He couldn't help but respect her more because he knew if he had been in that situation he would have dealt with it very poorly. He might consider trying to answer her question as to why, but he still couldn't come up with an answer. However, it looked as if he didn't have to answer as it was clear that her question was rhetorical.

Once they had reached the other side of the forest Sileena moved to the banks of the river. Dorren followed a couple of steps. Looking in Sileena's direction he saw her sit down, looking out to the open plains that lay at the other side of the flowing water. She seemed to have calmed a little but it was obvious it was going to take a long time for her to move forward. From the conversations the two of them had, her brother was the only person she was close to in Eceriden. The only good thing in her old life.

Dorren slowly moved next to her and sat down. He could see the tears in her golden eyes. As he got close, she leaned in. Dorren was trying to think of something to say that might help. But instead he put his arm around her. Perhaps words were not the best thing right now.

Together they remained seated, merely staring out at the peaceful landscape before them. The sun moved through the sky and yet they remained seated together on the bank of the river. Despite what had happened, this was nice. A time to be silent with just your thoughts and the person you care for.

But as the day wore on it was Sileena who broke the silence.

"Can we not go back just yet? Move away from everything?"

Dorren smiled. He knew this was just the situation talking but it certainly was a nice thought. The two of them had only just become a couple.

"What, just us two? You would get sick of me pretty quickly."

"I doubt that." Her voice was calm but sad. She just needed a bit of time away, he thought. Perhaps it would do her some good. But if they never returned then Pagar would be sure to send out a search party. He was just stubborn like that. Despite Dorren being an absolute nuisance, Pagar constantly insisted on looking after him. He knew he didn't deserve a father figure like that. The least he could do was go back and not leave him worrying. But for now he still had a little time before the worrying would begin. Despite it being silly to simply disappear, an idea suddenly struck him. Just a little further into the forest was a sanctuary with a few provisions. It was kept safe from the prowling wolves and was meant for when an Outcast couldn't reach their destination before nightfall. Any Outcast passing by could use it when needed. They should not remain away for too long, but it was certainly ideal for a couple of days away.

Dorren put forward the idea to Sileena, who smiled and jumped at the thought. Together they moved back into the forest towards the sanctuary he had mentioned.

It was a nice-looking spot not that far into the forest. The light filtered through the trees, creating a pleasant, tranquil effect. The ground was covered in different kinds of flowers and shrubbery. Dorren did not remember the place being like this. Perhaps the plants were just left to grow as time went on. Within all the shrubbery was a mound that hid some steps leading down to a very well-sealed door. After opening the door he looked inside, it was a little dusty and dark but once a few candles had been lit it did not seem so bad. All the supplies they needed were sitting in a small cupboard at the side.

"I need to head back out for five minutes. Can you keep the door closed until I get back?"

"Where are you going?" Sileena had adopted that very pretty, confused expression again.

"There is a post at either side of the forest for messages. If a search party comes looking for us, then they will know where to find us. I will be back shortly."

He could hear the locks click as he moved away from the mound. Good. Although it was unlikely that something bad would happen, they could never be too careful. Especially in these woods.

Surdan stood on the balcony looking out upon the capital of Duka. The city was in decay, with poverty and crime taking a foothold because of the desperation of the kingdom. Despite this, on an evening as the sun was setting, the place seemed peaceful and dare he say, beautiful. He could make out the walls that surrounded the city, and the sandy desert that lay beyond them. A large river flowed through the centre of the city, stretching for many miles down to the southern sea.

Duka used to be a very rich kingdom thanks to mining and trade, but with the discovery of better minerals to the north they had to turn to other methods. The mountains to the west might have provided useful resources, but they were dangerous; the region filled with all kinds of monsters. Some said even dragons live there.

So perhaps another place, then. The forests to the east might have provided new partners in trade. But they were occupied by the forest folk, who would not give access to any of their resources. A very stubborn people, considering they barely touched these resources themselves. It was not the Dukan people's right to force their way into their homes to gain these materials but apparently they can invade Eceriden for their resources. So why not invade the Grey Forest? The notion was actually considered, but these people, despite lacking any discipline, were vast.

Trying to fight them on their home turf would have been suicide. And then there was Eceriden.

"So, do you feel powerful when standing over a city?"

Surdan turned to see his brother, the king, moving onto the balcony next to him.

"Oh, yes, I can feel myself getting power-hungry right now." Kell smiled. The two of them were quite different people, but they were brothers and they respected each other enough to get along at the best of times.

"Tomorrow, word will go out commanding the armies to gather as quickly as possible, and then we head out. It's not likely but perhaps we can get to Eceriden before word reaches them of our movements."

Surdan frowned at this statement. They had already spoken about this but he still wasn't sure why they couldn't just try and ask Eceriden for help instead of invading them. That would have been a more peaceful solution, but Kell stated that it was futile because they would want something in return and Duka had nothing to offer. The thought of countless deaths when an alternative existed was something that regularly passed through Surdan's head. It was a little ironic coming from someone who was part of a nation that believed in human sacrifice. It wasn't something he particularly liked, but their god demanded such offerings and without them they might risk its wrath. Besides, the people who were sacrificed were volunteers. Hundreds lined up and it was a great honour to be the vessel for the great god of the earth. But this war was different. Many good men were not going to come back.

Surdan sighed. So far this had been confined to the generals. No one else knew of what was happening. This was to ensure that word would not reach Eceriden before they even made a move, but still. Many people were going to die in the next few days. They did not even know they were about to be forced to go to war.

He turned to Kell. The man always put on a strong face but as a brother he could tell that it was just a front.

"So we will look out for each other on the battlefield, fight together as we have done in the practice arena."

Kell frowned for a moment before turning to look at him. "You will not be going."

Surdan went to protest, but before he could speak Kell intervened. "Look, the thing is, while I'm gone conducting my war I need someone to rule in my place. You are the only person I can trust. I need it to be you who will cover the duties of the crown until I return."

Surdan went to speak out in objection, but yet again, he was cut off. "That's an order."

Damn. You could not disobey the king's orders. Even if he was your brother. They both turned to face out of the balcony again. For a second there was silence. Things were about to get very complicated so they enjoyed this simple moment; a nice view with peace and quiet. Right, moment was up.

"You'd better make it back. I really don't want to be ruling indefinitely."

Kell smiled again. "Oh, you can count on it. On our own it doesn't look like we could prevail, but with the help of that sorcerer and the forest folk, victory is all but assured."

And then there was that. The sorcerer was a very shady character, coming out of the blue with this strategy as things went from bad to worse for the kingdom. He'd turned up like a miracle-worker giving them the option of fighting Eceriden. How did he get hold of the most powerful staff known, and how was he controlling the barbarians? The mysterious figure rarely spoke, and kept his face hidden under a hood the entire time. This so-called miracle-worker had not even made any kind of requests for his service. This was all from the goodness of his heart to help the people of Duka. How could Kell, who went on about how people never do anything for nothing, agree to this? This sorcerer was very good at manipulation and Surdan couldn't help but feel that Kell had fallen sway. He'd already made his protests to his brother but his arguments were pushed aside and he was told that this was a wizard who was used by the gods as a vessel through which they could communicate to the Dukan people. Surdan remained unconvinced but for now the war remained the top priority. Tomorrow it was going to begin and Kell and the armies of the capital would leave and meet up with the

174

other forces around the land. Tonight was the last night Surdan and his brother would be able to speak, just the two of them, until after the war. He had pestered Kell with complaints the whole time but this time, for once, he was just going to enjoy the moment. Tomorrow they would ride out for war and he would be left to rule a decaying kingdom.

It was very warm inside the sanctuary. Dorren could tell that it was a glorious day from the small rays of light that came inside through the small gaps around the sanctuary. But the real warmth came not from the fire that was starting to die, but the sleeping girl next to him.

The night before they had lain side by side and Sileena spoke of her brother and the experiences they'd shared. The way he tried to protect her and secretly teach her whenever no one else was around. He had been the one truly good thing in her previous life. Dorren listened and asked the occasional question as she spoke. Eventually Sileena fell asleep while Dorren stared at the ceiling until dreams embraced him as well.

Both awoke in the early morning, whereupon Dorren started a fire and made something to eat. But instead of heading home they decided to go back to bed. It was just not the time yet. One night was not enough to stay away from everything. Sileena fell asleep again and Dorren was just enjoying the peace. At first he could stay like this forever. But give it some time, however, and it might drive him nuts to not be part of the action, to miss the arena, the events and his friends. But for now this was exactly what he needed. And it was what she should have as well: just a little retreat to clear their minds and return home fresh. Sileena needed this more than him. If his life was chaotic then there was not a word to describe hers. Dorren would explain the situation to Pagar and he was sure he would allow them this time away. Frankly, he was sure Pagar would actually like the idea of keeping Dorren out of trouble. A funny concept, he thought.

Dorren lay there reflecting on this before he heard a light banging on the door. He turned to Sileena, who had not stirred. She was a deep sleeper, that one. He got out of bed and peered through the spyhole in the door. Outside stood three figures, and judging from their statures he knew who they were. He opened the door to find Lockarr, Derain and Gabe standing with bewildered expressions on their faces.

"Seriously, what the hell—" Derain started to say, before Dorren cut in.

"Shh, Sileena's asleep. Why are you here?" Dorren moved outside and closed the door behind him.

"Because," Derain continued, lowering his voice, "you had not arrived on schedule so we came looking. How were we supposed to know you'd decided to spend a little time alone with Sileena? Well done, by the way."

"This is not what it looks like. The meeting did not go well and we just needed some time away."

"What?" Derain appeared to be speaking for the group. "What happened? And why could you not just head back, then go on your little vacation?"

Dorren sighed, looking to Lockarr, who was frowning too, and Gabe who looked, well, calm, and had the slightest twinge of a smile. It wouldn't be surprising to Dorren if he'd gone with them because they asked. He was always calm when faced with any situation. Dorren often wondered how he would react if anything was to happen to Anna.

"Look, it's not my place to talk about it. I didn't think you guys would be here today."

"How could you not think a search party would go looking for you?"

"I didn't think a search party would look for me in less than a day beyond schedule. I didn't think Pagar would send a party that fast."

The others looked at each other.

"He didn't send you, did he?"

It was Lockarr who spoke this time. "We were worried that the meeting would go wrong and you might be captured or dead, so we went looking when you didn't return last night. And we were right. You said yourself it did not go well."

"Look, you obviously found the note otherwise you wouldn't have known we were here, and even that said we were fine. As much as I appreciate your concern, we will be well."

"Well, it's not just that," Lockarr continued. "You are with Sileena, a possible ticking time bomb with enough power to disintegrate men with her mind. And she might have done it to you – accidentally, of course."

Oh yeah, Dorren had completely forgotten about how Sileena's immense power unnerved some people. You would think that her golden eyes would remind him but he just didn't see her eyes that way.

However, she hadn't lost control of her power. She could not have been put in a worse emotional position and she didn't accidentally blow a hole in the earth or harm anyone. This proved that all the concerns were for nothing. Dorren believed Sileena had control and would never do something unintentional. How could his best friends not trust her?

Dorren quickly confirmed to them that Sileena had complete control and there would be no men disintegrating, after which any opposition from the others soon ceased.

"Dorren?" came a voice from inside the refuge. The door opened and Sileena looked outside at the group and smiled. "Hello everyone, what are you doing here?" she said sleepily, clearly having just woken up and heard the voices outside. She was curious. Dorren liked that about her. She had a personality that was a little like his.

"Hey Sileena," replied Lockarr. "We were just checking up on you guys when you didn't return."

"You know you can come inside, right?" she said, sounding more upbeat.

Derain laughed. "We didn't want to disturb, seeing as you were asleep."

"Oh, I didn't think that would usually bother you," she said sarcastically. Her confidence since her first appearance at their home had improved drastically. So much so that now that she was willing to go toe-to-toe with Derain. Gabe had sat down on a stump while the conversation continued, which brought his head level with theirs. His expression was calm and bright. Derain and Lockarr were talking with Sileena. Things seemed to become a nice relaxing day and everyone eventually brought their conversation into the sanctuary.

After a little time had passed Dorren had an idea. "Sileena? Would you like to remain here a little longer before heading back?"

Sileena smiled and gave an expression that signalled she did.

"Derain, when you get back tell Pagar we will be staying here a little longer and will return once we're ready."

Derain nodded, and after farewells were said the group headed off. Sileena and Dorren went for a wander along the edge of the forest, talking about the different experiences they'd had in their lives, and sharing funny stories about the interesting characters found within the Outcasts' community. It was a nice conversation that could have gone on and on, but after a time they agreed to turn back and reached the retreat before they could finish.

They got something else to eat and Sileena went to sleep, while Dorren remained with his thoughts a little longer.

He went back to question the encounter between him, Sileena, Nok and Nerida. Why had Sileena not done anything with her immense power to stop that situation from happening? The question came and left in less than a second. Of course she couldn't do anything. She was still new to the concept of using magic. She did not know how to manipulate shields because that kind of magic was more complicated than using the elements, and took time to develop. Even he knew that and Sileena only had basic, although powerful, control over the elements; real, physical things. It often led to people assuming they could control other people or animals, but for some reason that could not be done. It had been argued that this was because the spirit inside the body is so powerful that not even the strongest magic could do that. That thought was a reassuring one. He didn't like the idea of someone controlling him.

But this all led back to the question as to why Sileena did not use elemental magic to stop Nerida's attack, which again was quickly discarded. In its basic level she could only use the magic for offence and she would not do that to her own family. Even her father was not shooting at her. It was Dorren that was his original target. Sileena and Nok just jumped in the way. None of them had time to think. In any case, he was not going to think about this anymore. There truly was nothing they could have done in the circumstances. Nothing that could have been predicted. No one knew what was going to happen and it was over too quickly for anyone to react differently. Even with whatever it was Dorren has been experiencing. That was something that he would have to dwell on a little longer.

More than once now his life had been in danger, and his awareness of the world had changed. He could sense more than any normal person could sense. This was something that he had no answers for, and he probably would not have any until after he had spoken to Pagar. It could have had something to do with the danger he was in; some sort of reaction to imminent death. Then again, in both cases Sileena had been there. Perhaps it was something to do with her. But she was unconscious when he caught the arrow. Arguably it was impossible for her to stop the arrow while unconscious. However, her powers progressed beyond normal people's capabilities so it might have been her all along. It was funny how things could get very complicated very quickly. But Sileena, she was much less of a question and certainly not a fear anymore. She was a lovely girl whom he was falling for, and who appeared to return his affections. With that last appealing thought he closed his eyes and fell asleep.

# 11

# RETURNING HOME

A couple of days passed on this peaceful retreat from everything. They would eat, sleep and go for walks to different places around where they stayed. Following round the edge of the forest, making sure they do not move too far from the treeline. They could not venture inside because of the threat posed by the wolves. But they were so close to the edge that they didn't even hear them, let alone see one. The days remained bright with little rain or clouds. Dorren would occasionally leave to practise his swordsmanship, just as a form of exercise and to stop himself from getting off balance. He also went hunting for food when the supplies started to run low. Sileena occasionally meddled in magic for practice, but nothing on the scale of what she'd achieved by the sea. He doubted it was because of her capabilities but rather just being careful not to do anything she could not control. She would not try to expand her power without a trainer. Or so he thought, until one day he returned from a hunting trip to find a very unusual sight.

Sileena was sitting on a tree trunk and happily petting a rabbit sitting next to her. Instead of running away it had willingly approached her and was now sitting next to her and quite content. That kind of thing was rare, but what made it stranger was the other woodland animals gathered around her. Some little birds perched on her shoulders and other little animals lay down at her feet.

He gazed silently at the strange behaviours of these animals for a while before Sileena noticed him. She gave a simple nod to the rabbit on her lap. It leapt off and alarmed Dorren when it dashed at him and snuggled next to his feet. It didn't seem to take notice of its dead cousin over his shoulder.

"What are you doing?"

Sileena was smiling as she petted another creature that had now jumped to settle in the spot where the rabbit had been. "I am playing with the animals."

Dorren had put the dead rabbit to the side and gently picked up the one snuggling into him. "Yeah, but how are you doing it?"

"I don't know. I'm using magic and somehow I'm able to get into their heads."

Well, that's not creepy at all, thought Dorren.

"I sort of sent signals to let them know it's safe."

He sat near her with the rabbit cradled in his arms. "How did you learn this? I've never seen this kind of magic before."

She frowned. "I really don't know. It just happened earlier."

It just happened? No one can magically move into the mind of someone else and manipulate it. Perhaps it was unfair to call it manipulation but it was still a little unnerving to see this newfound power.

"Can you manipulate me?"

"I would never do that." Of course she wouldn't, unless he asked her. "Can you try now?"

Sileena's frown deepened. "No. I'm not going to."

"Please, just try. I would like to know what it feels like."

Sileena seemed unconvinced, but nodded.

For a moment she seemed to be concentrating. He couldn't tell if she was trying yet as he remained seated next to her. He couldn't feel any strange sensations, nor the need to do anything. Sileena's concentration deepened for a moment but then quickly subsided.

"Well?"

"I can't." She was smiling broadly. "For some reason I can't do anything to your mind. And I'm pretty sure that is the same for all people."

He couldn't help but feel relieved. She was incredibly powerful but to go that far would have been much more of a burden. He turned to the critter in his arms and smiled.

"Well, this makes hunting a lot easier."

Sileena gasped. "Don't you dare! They have given me their trust and I will not let you use that trust to kill them." Oh, when she put it like that he sounded like a monster.

"Of course I won't."

Sileena relaxed at his assurances. The animals around them jumped from their perches and disappeared into the shrubbery and trees, leaving him and Sileena to get the food he had caught and head inside.

As the days passed they enjoyed each other's company, but it was just that. Sileena needed someone to be her shoulder, especially after the events that transpired. She needed time to recover and a friend to be there for her. They both still held affection for each other.

But on the last night as Dorren was putting his belt, sword and harness in the trunk at the foot of the bed, he turned to see Sileena move up and take hold of his hands. She stood on her toes and kissed him. He didn't even take a moment to think about it. He kissed her back, allowing them to become intertwined. When they separated Sileena gently pushed him onto the bed and followed him, whereupon they let all thought go and became one. This was not the passion that took place at the Reunion. It was love, and they both knew it.

The next day when they awoke they remained next to each other for a while in silence, just enjoying each other's presence. It was Sileena who broke the silence, saying that she was now ready to head back.

They packed their things and made their way back home.

Dorren wondered how much trouble he was in this time. Leaving his duties back at the Underground may have caused some hassle. He was sure Pagar would be able to handle that and set someone else to the task. But he knew he had a responsibility to his people to not just leave these things unattended again. However, this was just more important. Especially to Sileena, and if Pagar could not see that then that was his problem.

It was not long before they made it to the green and crossed the threshold. He turned to Sileena, who was not as uneasy as when she first arrived. It might have something to do with the fact that she was a hostage the first time. Funny how things change. The other factor was the aura that was no longer affecting her now that she was part of the Outcasts. It was like a wave of comfort washing over you as your troubles seemed to lessen. This effect wore down over time as you remain, but after being away for a while you would get to feel the full effect.

Reaching the cabin seemed to take less time than normal. It was probably because Dorren and Sileena spent the whole time talking so they didn't notice the time pass.

When they entered they found, as expected, a guard waiting inside. It was an elderly woman in about her late fifties. She sat on an old rocking chair. At first she was alarmed by someone entering without knowing who it was, but quickly relaxed when she recognised Dorren.

He caught his breath when he recognised her. Even in her older guise he could make out the complexion of his old girlfriend Tania. They had been together during a time a few years back when he was more immature than now, and she was even more so. It was less romantic and more about passion. But both of them mistook passion for love, and as the passion slowly ebbed they parted ways. It was not a good ending to the relationship, as he recalled her yelling at him. But over time things got better and they had to put up with each other passing through the Underground. Anger turned to simply ignoring each other, and then to the odd comment. Then one day her personality seemed to change and she seemed to hold no ill feelings against him. He never felt angry towards her, even at the breakup. He was the one to initiate it and he knew how crap it can feel to be the end of that. So her temper was something he thought he should bear. But her reaction to him on that odd day was the same as now as he entered the cabin with Sileena, with an open and smiling welcome. Something had suddenly changed her on that day. Perhaps it was personal growth, likely an epiphany. She went from being an immature girl to a pleasant and wiser grown-up. Despite a lot of Dorren's little behaviours he liked to think he too was getting a little wiser; becoming a better person. Thinking about it, he knew Sileena played a large role in his personal growth. He strived to be wiser, especially when she was around. She made him a better person. Besides, Tania now had her own man who was great for her, and she was happy. And now he was too.

"Dorren! Welcome back," she said, smiling. "Some people were wondering if you were actually going to return."

"What about Pagar? Was he wondering this too?" He couldn't help but ask out of curiosity.

"I can't say, I have not spoken to him recently. But I think you should go see him as soon as possible, a couple of important events have transpired that you might be interested in hearing about."

Well, this couldn't be good. Something had distracted Pagar from Dorren not arriving back home on time. This would be fascinating to hear. He tried pestering Tania for details but she insisted that he speak to Pagar. Tania then turned to Sileena.

"Glad you're back too. We need someone other than Pagar to knock Anna off her pedestal as the second most powerful magic user here."

This made Sileena and Dorren smile. Sileena was not really the type to do that, even with her immense power. She was getting more confident but even Dorren knew that Anna would always be the one in charge.

After bidding their farewells Dorren and Sileena headed down the staircase to the Underground, finding it still alive with people as they entered the main halls. Nothing seemed amiss from what Dorren could tell, so what the hell was this event Tania spoke of?

"What now?" Sileena asked, looking around.

"Well, I am heading for Pagar's office to find out what's happening. You can go to your room, the canteen, or find your friends."

"I want to go with you. I think he would want to hear about everything that happened from both of us."

It was a relief to Dorren to have her accompany him. Her presence should lessen Pagar's possible anger.

So they made their way to Pagar's room. A few people greeted them, others gave them blank looks, but most just ignored them and continued about their own business. After a couple of corridors and stairwells going up and down they reached the door to Pagar's personal quarters and gave a knock.

They heard him call, "Enter"; so moved into the room to find Pagar looking through some letters at his desk. Or that's what he appeared to be doing.

He gave a polite smile when he looked up and saw who it was. "Welcome back, Dorren, Sileena. You must have had an interesting time away."

"Master Pagar," both Sileena and Dorren replied, with nods of their heads.

"Well, I believe we have a bit to discuss about the past few days. A bit of catching up."

"Yes," Dorren replied. "I've been hearing that something has happened while we've been gone. What's been going on?"

"We will get to that in a minute. First, what happened to the two of you while you were away? Lockarr said the meeting did not go well and that you decided to remain at one of the refuges for a time before returning. Care to elaborate?"

"Did you know we would return?" Dorren asked.

"I presumed you would. Lockarr did say that you told him you would be coming back. You are unbelievably annoying but you haven't really been one to go against your word. Now, elaboration please?"

It was Sileena who stepped forward and described the events of the meeting. Pagar remained serious and focused through the entire story, not making any comments or asking questions until after she had reached the part where they had decided to remain at the refuge. He disregarded it immediately as a fair thing to do, and said that they could take as much time as they needed. He reaffirmed that there was nothing she or Dorren could have done any better. The time at the refuge was quickly summarised before they made the journey home. Obvious little details that didn't need mentioning were missed. Dorren merely sat at the sidelines, ready to give support if she needed it. But she didn't, managing to get through the entire story on her own.

When she was done Pagar leaned back in his chair. "Thank you for letting me know of the situation. Is your father likely to take this as a reason to go on a crusade against us?"

"I honestly don't know. I would have said no but I didn't think he

185

would do what he did back there, so he might. Maybe I should return if it stops him."

"No one is saying that, my dear," Pagar quickly put in before that thought took much more of a hold. "Certain precautions may need to be put into effect. But for now we have time as your father's attentions will be elsewhere."

"What?" Dorren said with a quick, curious tone in his voice. "What has been happening?"

"Well, while you have been gone it appears Duka has declared war on Eceriden. Their army is marching north as we speak." Pagar seemed to be speaking of this as though it was not that big a deal.

"What?!" both Dorren and Sileena exclaimed. This was a huge thing that could possibly affect everyone. Duka and Eceriden covered nearly half the known world.

"What have we done about this?" was Dorren's first question.

"We are doing nothing but observing the situation to see how it progresses."

"Seriously? But if Duka claims Eceriden they will have enough power to face the entire world. Why are we letting this happen? We need to stop them before they succeed."

"What about my father?" Sileena added before Pagar had time to answer. "He might die in that battle. He is a horrible man but my last blood relative."

"Do not worry, the two of you. First of all, this appears to be the desperate act of a crumbling kingdom. Their poverty is much worse than our own. They will not be able to beat Eceriden."

"But everyone knows that Duka hold the largest known army in the world. Eceriden is severely outnumbered, even if this fight is taken to their own grounds. We should go and do something."

"Do what exactly? We do not have an active military. Most of this Underground is populated by non-fighters and children. And we have even fewer magic users. The other Undergrounds are not going to do anything either."

Dorren almost pointed out that they had Sileena, the most powerful magic user they have ever met. How could anyone possibly compete with that? It appeared that Pagar was expecting him to say it too, but Dorren stopped himself. This was not fair to her. He was not going to make her fight and kill. Killing was just not something she could do. When Pagar saw Dorren stop himself he gave a brief look of surprise, with a little respect. Dorren was becoming more mature.

"Besides, Eceriden is the likely victor. The people of the mountains and forests to the north have rallied their armies to fight for Eceriden. Apparently you are not the only one addressing these concerns. Together their army is bigger than Duka's. On top of that, they are better equipped and trained. Without help Duka can't win and things will return to normal. Eceriden would not dare attempt what Duka has done unless they wish to lose their allies."

Pagar had clearly given this some thought. He probably guessed Dorren would be opposed to what they were doing, but he had time to think this through.

"As for your father, Sileena, he will have been called by the king of Eceriden and will be forced to join the war, giving us time to think about how to keep ourselves safe just in case. But your father will very likely not be participating in the battle. As a lord he will command his men and have his own guards to make sure he is safe. He is also on the winning side of this conflict so I wouldn't worry," Pagar concluded with a calm, reassuring smile. Sileena returned a smile of acknowledgement, but Dorren was still not convinced.

"Those are a lot of theories, but what if Duka wins? What if they successfully take over Eceriden and become too powerful for anyone?"

Pagar calmly looked towards Dorren, never moving from his desk. "I am aware of the possible ramifications. But if it reassures you, I am keeping a close eye on the situation. If events unfold differently then we will deal with it appropriately. Otherwise there is nothing more I can do."

Dorren frowned, but this did appear to be the best solution for now. They were just going to have to wait and see what happened.

A few more comments were made and Pagar told them to get settled back in and then return to work. Vacation time was over. They made for the door and Sileena went to go and look for her friends, who would want to catch up. However, Dorren remained in the room. When Pagar saw him still standing there he motioned for him to come forward.

"Was there something else you wanted to speak about?"

Dorren was not sure how to begin. He guessed he just had to explain it as best he could. He talked about his strange moments of awareness of the world around him, and the power that took hold. He then gave accounts of the time when he caught the arrow, and then when Sileena's father attempted to kill him. Pagar listened intently. Whether he believed Dorren or not did not show on his face. He remained calm, with his hand lightly resting on his chin.

When Dorren was done there was a silence in the room for a few seconds as Pagar sat and processed what Dorren had told him.

"I've heard about different kinds of magic and their manipulation, but never something like that. It's entirely possible for this to happen but I really can't give you any kind of explanation. You are as much in the know here as I am."

Dorren had thought so, but was a little disappointed. He was hoping that Pagar would have the answer.

"It would appear to be a defence mechanism for when you are in immediate danger. Useful, but I would not rely on it. If Sileena and her brother did not jump in the way you would have died. But keep me informed if it happens again."

"Thank you, I will."

The two of them then proceeded to exchange a few pleasantries before Dorren let himself out of the room.

It was not long before Dorren found his friends. They stood with Anna and Sileena in the food court where a small reunion party took hold. It was amazing how being away for a few days could warrant that kind of reaction. Even a few people Sileena didn't know had turned up. Anna's parents appeared for a time, greeting Sileena and talking about how they worked as part of the healing room of the Underground. They briefly talked about how life was like there, which Sileena took a particular interest in. They joked about how during the Reunion the medical area became particularly busy, with more intoxicated people than could be handled. After a time, they took their leave and more of Anna's group turned up, and soon there were around ten of them conversing about subjects that did not even involve Dorren and Sileena. It didn't bother him of course. It had been a while since the last time the whole group got together.

Derain had his arms around one of the girls. Lockarr sat next to Gabe, who had Anna sitting on his lap. Across from them was Sileena, who was leaning on Dorren. It was clear to everyone what was going on, but they already knew so no one mentioned it. The rest of the girls were conversing amongst themselves.

While Sileena was engaged in conversation with Lockarr, Dorren took a moment to take in the situation. This was nice. He never really gave it much thought but he had a good life. Everything was right. And now he had someone to share it with. It was a bit melodramatic for him to think about, but for the moment he could just be a little cheesy. What would be next for him? What was the next adventure? Perhaps there would not be one. This going out and stealing and rivalry and causing mischief was no longer the thing to do. He never knew this growing-up thing would ever happen to him. Certainly not so quickly. Was Sileena having that big an effect on him? He wouldn't just stop doing things like going to the training grounds or going on little endeavours with his friends. But Sileena would be the next adventure. The longest and biggest one. Strangely, this thought gave him a warm feeling. So he sat back and happily watched the conversation unfold before him while losing himself in a dream. It was time to become a better man.

A sensation started to course through him. A sensation that he had felt before. He could see his surroundings again. Without looking, he knew that there was a couple at the back of the room. He could feel the bustling crowd around him and knew exactly where everyone was and was moving to, without thinking about it. This sensation was the same but different. It only lasted a couple of seconds before quickly subsiding. What the hell was this? He looked up and could see that no one had taken any notice; they were all still talking away. This feeling could be very useful if he knew how to control it. But this left him with more questions than answers.

Well, we can rule out Pagar's theory.

He looked around and could not see any danger. If there was danger then he was not aware of it so how and why was this happening? Was it dangerous? It didn't appear to be. Quite frankly he was grateful for this power because without it he would be dead with an arrow through him. But it would be great if he could understand how and why this was happening. Was it something his father had? Perhaps he had done something to Dorren that gave him this gift or maybe he had somehow inherited it. But why wouldn't he tell Pagar about it? Pagar had stated that he had absolutely no idea what it was. What if he was not telling the truth? Would Pagar lie to him? This sort of conspiracy had not been his kind of thing for a long time since his father had died and he'd started accusing everyone of being responsible for it. He even accused Pagar once. But Pagar had put so much effort into the investigation that once Dorren had come to his senses he stopped with all that nonsense. Whatever this power was he was sure that Pagar must have been honest with him. He truly had no idea what it was, and if his father had anything to with it then he did not tell Pagar about it.

"Oi! Dorren. Have you been paying any attention?" said Anna. Lockarr, Gabe and Sileena were looking at him questioningly.

"Sorry, I was away in a world of my own. What were we talking about?"

Sileena smiled and Anna sighed.

"We were trying to come up with a new game. Something involving magic. Once we have taught Sileena everything she needs to know, maybe we can do something fun with it?"

Dorren looked at Sileena, who seemed excited by the idea. To be honest the thought intrigued him too. He guessed he was not as grown-up as he thought. But why couldn't a grown-up have fun?

"OK, so what have you got?"

Dorren listened to their insane idea of making and holding a series of invisible barriers or shields. These were basically normal shields, but more complex because what they wanted to try was to make an invisible maze and the first to get to the other side would be the winner. To be honest the idea sounded like a lot of fun, and certainly entertaining to watch. Everyone running face first into invisible barriers as they tried to navigate would be such a laugh. But holding such barriers, and in a large, complicated pattern, was impossible for a magic user. Maybe Sileena could do it, though? They did not understand how powerful she was yet. Certainly with Anna's help. It was a funny idea to think that with not even a movement she could disintegrate him. But that didn't bother him, he still felt completely safe. And so the game became more and more developed, with rules and other possibilities coming into place before the subject moved to their daily lives; to plans for the future and the possibility of the Outcasts becoming an official kingdom, and then moving to the war taking place. By this point most of the group had left, leaving the two couples enjoying one last refreshment before concluding the evening.

"Well, we had best be going," Anna said as she stood up, stretching. "Me and my man here have to head to our room where I intend to do things that should not be talked about in a public place."

Dorren, Sileena and Gabe all stood, getting ready to make their own ways.

"I am going to destroy you," continued Anna, addressing Gabe. Gabe rolled his eyes and gave a farewell nod to Dorren and Sileena before picking Anna up and lifting her over his shoulder. "Hey!" yelled Anna, laughing. "What are you doing? Not here. If you bang my head on the ceiling I am going to kill you."

Gabe just ignored her as he made for the exit and their private room. "I will see you guys tomorrow!" were Anna's last words before they disappeared round the corner and out of sight. Dorren was laughing the whole time.

"What was that?" asked Sileena, a little confused by what had just happened.

"Oh, Anna is one of the strongest people here. No one would walk over her, but when it comes to the bedroom everyone knows that Gabe commands."

"Is what he did OK?" she asked.

"Trust me, if it wasn't then Anna would do something about it. It's the way she likes it."

Sileena seemed a little surprised by the concept. She was in thought, trying to process what happened, but Dorren was not going to let her finish.

"So what about you?" he said, taking Sileena's hand and slowly pulling her closer. Sileena started blushing.

"If you pick me up I will scream," she said, still blushing but smiling. Dorren stood inches from her face, looking into her eyes. She couldn't help but notice how handsome he looked.

"I'm not going to pick you up," he said calmly. Moving even closer, he lifted his head and gently kissed her on the forehead. She leaned in with Dorren's arm around her and together they walked out the room to her personal quarters. Dorren was not the smartest man, and a little immature at times but those were qualities that she came to love in time. He was there for her, and she was happier in his company.

With one last kiss at Sileena's room he bade her farewell. She invited him in but they were both exhausted and agreed it was best to sleep. She turned in, with Dorren heading to his own quarters, still smiling.

# 12

# A POETIC BATTLE

Kell sat in his personal tent looking over the charts and maps, feeling angry and stressed. The first battle had not even started and things were already falling apart. It was true that he had managed to gather the bulk of his armies without too much hassle and march them into Eceriden with absolutely no resistance, as the guards at the gate ran as soon as they saw the marching banners. So much for the defences at the border. But it was a rabble of what must have been no more than fifty men who would not stand the smallest chance against an army of thousands. But now that they were in Eceriden and marching towards the capital he had been receiving reports that the opposing armies had already gathered and were barely a day's march from them. Apparently word had got to them faster than anticipated and even the neighbouring kingdoms had convened their forces with Eceriden's army. He was outnumbered and outclassed. To make matters worse, the so-called wizard in whom he had for some reason put his faith had not been spotted yet. If he didn't arrive with his army, then Kell would lose the war before it began.

He could not help wondering, now that he was on the brink of the climactic battle, why he who would not trust his closest advisers would even consider trusting this wizard in such an important role. His kingdom, his army and possibly his life were on the line. What could possibly have overcome him that he would commit to such a foolhardy act? Whatever the reason there was no turning back now. After convening with his generals they all moved out to prepare their men. However, even with the best strategies the odds were slim. Perhaps if he could get part of the opposing army to desert then it might start a chain reaction.

As he dwelled on this prospect he could hear a voice somewhere nearby. But there was no one in the room. He looked around and realised it came from a corner of the tent. Moving across, he picked up a reflective metal plate that had sat quite neatly on a wooden box. This was the plate the sorcerer had given to him before he had left as a means of communication. Finally, he was going to get results.

"My lord, can you hear me?" asked the voice, as a blurry image of a face started to appear on the dish. Too blurry to see any detail, but Kell could tell it was him.

"Yes, I'm here. I was beginning to worry. Where are you?"

"I am leading the army as we speak, and we are not far behind you. What is the situation?"

"The situation is that the enemy are at our throats. They have moved quicker than expected and the battle will be fought before the day is over. I need you and your men here now!"

"My lord, you do not need to worry," the sorcerer said in a very calm voice. "The enemy are moving as I predicted and I have made all the preparations on my end to make sure we have a decisive victory."

The sorcerer was very confident. This annoyed Kell. He was always so damned calm. That smile of a man with a bigger ego than even the wealthiest of people. With all that power, he was not surprised. When this was over he would have to do something about that staff. It was useful for now but letting the sorcerer roam free with that kind of power was risky. He knew that with a simple wave of the staff he could be turned to dust. He'd only once seen the kind of power it could wield. By channelling his own already powerful magic it came out multiple times the strength. With his own eyes he'd seen the sorcerer singlehandedly destroy a mountain, leaving nothing but rubble everywhere. That was the point where he knew he needed this sorcerer. The idea was that he would use him until he didn't need him and then find a way to get rid of the staff. But for some reason he had ended up trusting the hooded figure with his life. This would not happen again. Once he had the power over the world and the sorcerer's staff destroyed he would have control. Then he would distribute the wealth evenly across all nations. There would no longer be any famine. He would go down in history as the man who created world peace. However, there was this first hurdle to clear: he must defeat the other kingdoms that would oppose him, and he needed the sorcerer and his army of woodland barbarians to help. And here the hooded man was talking about how everything was working out fine and he wasn't even here.

"Well, how are things working out fine for you when you are not here with your army?"

"Patience, my lord. I will be, but can't appear yet. Your men have little idea that an army of the men they hate is coming to help. It would cause grievances amongst the ranks. If I appear now our armies may end up attacking each other instead of the real enemy and then we would lose for sure. Even my power can't beat such tremendous odds. The enemy will have hundreds of magic users, and combined they would certainly prove a challenge."

"Then what are you proposing we do? How are we supposed to fight against the enemy? I swear, if you do not intend to join the fighting, I will turn this army around and—"

"There is no need for that, my lord. You must put your best strategies into place. Fight the enemy yourself first. Have them diminished and weakened. They will taste victory, but at that point my army will have flanked them and in the face of new, refreshed forces the enemy will lose heart and flee. This will work."

It was actually a good plan. One that would most likely work. And the two armies did not even need to get close enough to start fighting amongst themselves. Yes, it was a good plan...except for one thing.

"Why the hell can't you march against the enemy and we will flank them? That way we will not lose so many men in the process. Waste the barbarians instead. It's not like they will be missed."

But without even flinching, the sorcerer spoke. Kell really hated his smugness, and it was taking all his will to not start screaming bloody murder at him.

"I did try to think of scenarios in which this would work. But my forces are not wearing your banners, so the enemy will know that there are in fact two armies and prepare accordingly. They must be unaware of us until it is too late. You do not have the resources to have the barbarians fitted with the same attire. I am sorry but there is no other way. I can assure you that at the moment of victory this army of forest marauders will march back home."

Why did Kell feel like he was going to be double-crossed at the end of the battle? His own men would be heavily diminished, and in no way able to fight against the barbarians who had already outnumbered his forces even before the battle. Again, the whole situation of putting his life in the sorcerer's hands bothered him. But for now there was no choice in the matter as he was making valid points. He was barely able to feed his own population, never mind equip another army for battle.

"However, if you would like to remove the threat I could have them march north and proceed to take out the next kingdom. Without an army the forest folk to the north would not be able to compete. They will fall, and these barbarians will be so far north they will no longer pose any threat."

Now that was actually a good idea. This was probably why Kell chose to trust this man: because of his devotion to his king, and the fact that he was proposing brilliant ideas that greatly benefited Kell without being asked. Nevertheless, the staff would have to go when the time called for it, even if the man was loyal.

"Very well," he replied, feeling that he had just made a pact with a monster. "March your army round and flank the enemy quickly. Once you hear the sounds of battle you attack. I want to lose as few men as possible for this fight. I want them to return home."

"A very noble gesture, my lord. I will do as you command and try to make sure that most of your men return home. I shall bid farewell and give the commands now."

"Very good, and once the battle is over march your army north and take the Bryton Mountains."

"As you wish, my lord. With one decisive act you will create harmony." And with that the image on the dish disappeared and fell silent.

A little hope at last. Kell could taste the victory. But now he must put in the tactics for drawing out the battle to make sure there was as little loss as possible. Time to quickly reconvene his generals and prepare.

Kradorin stood at the head of the forces looking out at the opposing army ahead. They had chosen their ground well, standing at the top of a small hill where they had placed wooden spikes and spears at the front to slow down any charge. But even with this, the enemy were on the wrong soil. What kind of morons do this sort of thing, he wondered? They must have known they were outmatched.

He looked to his own forces, with the cavalry standing at the front. Foot soldiers were behind them, with the archers behind the foot soldiers. A standard formation, but there was a reason why it was so common. Despite what was about to happen, Kradorin could not help but admire what he was seeing. The shining armour gleamed in the sunlight as the formations stood perfectly calm and aligned. It was certainly impressive what the human race could do. Then again, he was always a man who could appreciate art and there was nothing more artistic than a battle. Before the fight, when the formations and men were in perfect unison. And then there was a different kind of art in the battle itself, where it instils chaos rather than alignment, and that too was a wonderful kind of art. It was probably a strange thing to think when many soldiers were about to die too young but he was one of those people who would look at the good of everything. Even war. Most would disagree with him but he didn't care. It was not like he was a king. He was a general and he was made for war. Art was merely his hobby, and it was nice to see the hobby in your job.

However, his loving wife, who had tried so hard to keep him away from the fighting, was usually quite fond of his art. She was often intrigued by his perspective on the world, which was one of the reasons for them being so compatible. She shared his interests, and that too maintained his affection for her, despite her past life as one of the common folk. That in itself was artistic, as the rich man fell for the common girl. He positively loved the idea of his own life being poetic. But this had changed somewhat as she was strongly opposed to his march to war. Her fear of him not returning offended him, but as the duty-bound lord he must obey his king. And besides, he wanted to ride out to indulge his poetic interests.

There was silence in the air, except for the little grunts of horses or whispers here and there. In the distance he could vividly make out the opposing king at the front, along with a few others riding towards the centre of the field. He turned to his king, who happened to be two places to his left. When his king started to ride towards the centre, which was his cue to follow along with the highest-ranking lords and generals. It was a great honour to ride out with his king; one that he, above all others, appreciated. Looking to his king riding in front, Kradorin thought that he was certainly a man of art. The armour he wore was more spectacular than any other he had seen before. It held inscriptions of duty and honour as well as the crest of his house, which was a white tiger. Of course they had no white on the armour but instead they used clear jewels to represent the tiger. The pauldrons also held the same crest, and were edged with gold like the rest of the armour; the cuirass, faulds and gauntlets. The helmet was simpler, merely edged with gold. It used to have plumes of hair that came out of it but they had been removed for the sake of this battle as they might have been more of a hindrance as they would annoyingly wave about, sometimes in front of their face. A shame really, but it did make sense. What made the armour really special were the magical properties it possessed. So much had gone into making it as strong as possible. No sword was going to go through it, despite it being incredibly thin. Also, any kind of magical attack would not work. Well, not for a while anyway, as eventually the magic would wear off under constant use. By then he would be left vulnerable. That's when magic users would protect him with their own shields, making sure no one could harm him. But if they started to weaken or die then his personal guard would be his next line of defence, making sure no one got near their king. Once they were gone then the king would be in danger. It was a rather funny thought. The king would probably be the main target in the battle as killing him would destroy an army's morale, but he was still likely be the last one to die as people kept jumping to block any missiles aimed at him.

Kradorin looked to his own armour, and despite it being beautiful it did not compare to his king's. He was a little disappointed by this, but he would be an idiot if he chose to try and one-up his king. No one's armour came close to comparing with that of the man riding in front of him. The only armour that would be considered a close second was worn by the man who was riding towards them. His armour was bronze and silver, with beads of gems and gold dotted in patterns across it. Certainly a very close comparison. He was probably as well protected as the man riding in front of him.

They had reached the centre of the field, where the opposing lords were waiting for them. Kradorin wondered, despite the honour of riding out with his king, why they were supposed to do that. The kings were to speak, but the lords were merely there to stand and watch. Perhaps it was to intimidate the others, or perhaps to protect their king should something happen. It was a curious thought but it didn't bother him. He liked being able to observe the talk in front of him, as it was his way of documenting what was happening. Should he survive this encounter, he would write poetry and paint pictures depicting this great moment.

"I, King Kell, greet the great king of Eceriden. I am here to offer terms if you surrender."

"Speak your terms." Kradorin's lord spoke with a calm but distasteful tone. He had been a bit surprised when he had first heard about Duka's invasion, but now his expression had changed to one of anger. Kradorin was not surprised. This war could have been avoided if they had just convened and negotiated on the matter.

"Relinquish your control over Eceriden to Duka's authority and acknowledge me as your overlord. In return you can all go about your lives peacefully and no one will be hurt. If you refuse these terms, then we will be forced to take action."

Kradorin almost burst out laughing. What kind of terms were they? Give us everything of yours or we will kill you. It was like a bully holding a knife to another person. The only thing was, this bully was picking on a person who was bigger, and he was holding a bigger knife.

"Under those terms we will not accept. You come walking into our kingdom, taking whatever you want, and expect us not to do something about it? Then you are sadly mistaken. Here are my terms. You have taken provisions from towns as you came here. You will turn back now and head home, where you will compensate those towns for what you have stolen."

Now those were reasonable terms, thought Kradorin. This was why he followed this king and not the other. That and the fact that he was a general of Eceriden. But even if he were given the choice, he would still choose Eceriden.

Kradorin looked across at the other generals that opposed them, sizing them up. So who was it going to be? He glanced from one to the other, as did his fellow lords and the enemy. As he moved from one to the next he caught the eye of one in particular; a big one riding a massive warhorse. He could see the artistry of this man. A dark beard, and a scar crossing his face. This man was meant to be a nasty one. Kradorin gave the man a cheeky smile. The man just stared at him darkly, clearly not amused by the massive grin. Yep, that was the one. He would seek him out on the field where they would meet in single combat. Oh, how poetic it would be. One would be left standing as the chaos unfolds around them. No one would interfere with the fight. They each had a personal bodyguard who would fight each other as their lord's fought, and none would interfere as it would dishonour their lord. The thought was an exciting one. The odds of finding his opponent on the field amongst thousands of soldiers were slim, but certainly worth a try.

As the two kings had their little spat Kradorin and this opposing general had their own little staring contest. Kradorin was smiling and the other man kept glaring as if they were trying to get the other to flinch. Kradorin took his thumb and gestured that he was going to slice the man's throat. The opposing man gave an amused grunt.

What?! The man thought that Kradorin killing him was an amusing thing? Well, I will show him, Kradorin thought. This man was going to regret laughing at him.

"What are you doing?" asked Kradorin's king. "You are going to commit yourself to an unwinnable battle and for what? Religious differences? To take what we have? Most of your men will die. The rest will be scattered to the winds. Turn back now. Send your army home to their families. Then after that we can negotiate. We can help each other."

Compared to the previous king of Eceriden, this man was a saint. Most would never give that kind of offer. Kell sat on his horse, which remained standing still, and more calm than any of the others, which were stepping to the sides occasionally, or whinnying. This one obeyed his master's every command and remained still and silent. A very loyal horse. A pat on the back for whomever had managed to train that horse so well. Yet this king of Duka remained silent for a moment, frowning at the king of Eceriden before replying.

"You think I would disgrace myself by marching home? If you do not agree to our terms then a battle it will be, and I would think again before considering this battle unwinnable. I will keep my honour."

Ah, indeed; very poetic. Kradorin was enjoying this too much. This king was dooming himself and thousands of men because of honour. A complete fool, but certainly very artistic, and if there was anyone who could appreciate that it was Kradorin.

The king of Eceriden was now completely fed up. By this point even Kradorin could see this was a futile effort. The king of Duka was very confident, despite the odds. Either he knew something they didn't or the man was an imbecile.

"Very well. A battle it shall be." And with that he turned his horse around and galloped away.

Kradorin took that as his cue and followed suit, heading back to his men. Truthfully he would have been disappointed if the battle was to never happen. But apparently over-confidence and pride overtook sense. Yes, if he survived this he would definitely be writing a poem, and completing at least one painting of this dramatic part of history. It was just too artistic, and it would be a crying shame if he didn't do something to represent it.

He looked to his men standing in formation with their blank expressions as they looked at the opposing army. Whether they were daunted by what was to come or excited he could not tell. It was probably a mix of both, as well as other feelings. Nervousness would have been one, as their lives would be put on the line.

Once he had reached his men he turned his horse around to face the enemy. He could hear the shout of the enemy king as he spoke to his men. He could not hear what it was that the Dukan king was saying but it must have been something inspiring as his men gave a deafening cheer at the end of it. As the enemy were cheering and yelling Kradorin's king turned to face his own troops.

"Soldiers! Across this field are the men who wish to take what is rightfully yours! They have entered your kingdom thinking that we will stand by and let them do as they please! We outnumber the enemy, are better equipped and have better soldiers. Now let's show them what happens to invaders! What say you?"

And with that came an even stronger, deafening cheer from the soldiers behind Kradorin. It was not a bad speech. Personally he was hoping for something longer and more dramatic. But to each their own.

He could hear the jeers from both sides. It appeared though that the Dukan army were happy to remain where they were, and were taunting the Eceriden troops. A smart move. They were going to have to go over there and drive them out. And his king knew that too.

"Right, I want cavalry to take both flanks as the main body marches forward in formation! Let's move!"

"You heard him, men! Into formation! Forward march!" shouted Kradorin to his men, as did the generals to their own formations. The soldiers took their shields into a box formation and started the slow march towards the enemy. The men had trained for this for most of their lives, but training and the real thing were very different things. However, as long as they stuck to their training and followed orders they should be fine. The responsibility would be on the generals to make sure that they were not giving the wrong orders.

As the men marched forward Kradorin could hear what sounded like thunder. This was strange as it was a sunny day, and so he looked around to find the source. The Eceriden cavalry forces were racing forward to the sides of the Dukan army, in hopes of doing as much damage as possible before they could recover. This truly was a sight to behold. Never before had he seen that many. He would have loved to join them as he was still on his horse. But he was not part of the cavalry; he was commanding his own forces on foot and he could not command them from amongst the cavalry.

Looking forward, he could see the Dukan forces moving about, and as soon as the Eceriden cavalry were in range a volley of arrows appeared, fired over the Dukan forward troops and disappearing into the cavalry. The first blood was being spilled as many horses and riders fell to the ground. He could make out some of them getting back to their feet, while others remained still. If this was just the Eceriden forces against Duka then he would have been concerned about these losses, but in reserve further back were the armies of the two other kingdoms, ready to fight when called upon. They just had to wait for the enemy forces to be fully committed to the fight, to make sure that they could surround the enemy. But who knows, perhaps this first strike would be enough to cause the enemy to scatter.

Another volley of arrows flew into the rushing cavalry. However, this time they were too far away for Kradorin to be able to make out what kinds of losses there were.

That was it, though. There was not enough time for another volley before the cavalry would be upon them. But his hope turned to dread when he saw the Dukan cavalry thunder from behind the enemy lines to protect their flanks. The two lines clashed as both sides rushed through each other. The Dukan cavalry greatly outnumbered Eceriden's, and they would not be able to hold out for long without reinforcements. Kradorin turned to look at the fallen men on the ground, pierced by the volleys of arrows. Some of them were getting back on their feet, finding a horse and riding back to the fight. No one could doubt their courage. Others were quickly moving between those who were not getting back up, looking for signs of life. They must be the healers.

"Volley!" He heard the cry, and turned to see arrows heading directly for them. But this was unlike hitting the cavalry, as most were deflected off shields from the box formations. Only the occasional shot hit someone. Nevertheless, this was slowing the formations down and many more than two waves of arrows were coming. Kradorin, on the other hand, being on horseback was not as safe from the arrows and had to remain with his guard at the back unless he wanted to risk dying before the battle really picked up. Yes, he was protected by a combination of armour and magic but one good shot could still end things for him.

He turned his attention quickly back to the cavalry to see a mesh of bodies. Despite the chaos he could see how things were turning out on both flanks. They were marching too slowly. They needed to pick up the pace before their friends were slaughtered. Yet again a volley of arrows bounced off their shields. There was nothing they could do. A poorly timed charge that was repelled by the enemy. Not a good start to the battle. It was not long before the men started to turn and retreat; some on foot, while others managed to remain on their horses.

"Let's go, men! Let's show these people how it is done!" Kradorin yelled to his soldiers marching in front. He knew that it was definitely a blow to their morale to see their allies running, but he would be damned if this would change the tide. Other generals were giving similar orders as they continued the march. They had to get into the fight before the enemy cavalry flanked them. They were close now. Now it was going to be their turn to do the damage. As he got ready to give the order a stray arrow flew directly towards his face, hitting him dead on target. But instead of creating a hole it shattered into twigs and fell to the ground in front of him. He laughed out loud at how close he had come to death before he could even get into the thick of fighting. However, he did trust his personal bodyguard to protect him. One was a magic user who was holding a shield around him. So thank goodness for him, or else he would have been dead.

"Fire!" came the roar from his king behind him.

Kradorin looked forward to see that the formations were now close enough to finally do some real damage, and the front line of the enemy were using much smaller shields and pikes. He yelled out the same order to his men, and with that the shields at the front rose and the troops started throwing spears into the enemy, to great effect. Most of the front line of the troops fell to the first volley, and the rest to the second. The enemy started to back away.

Yes! was all he thought. Now we're starting to get the advantage.

Magic users started appearing at the front lines as a shooting contest was initiated. All manner of magical blasts and spears and arrows were being exchanged between the two forces. The magical blasts seemed to vary between the different magic users, dependant on their strength. Some were small explosions, with men flying across the field.

What started as a desperate firing contest soon became more structured and the Eceriden forces were winning this battle.

Apparently the Dukan army had noticed this as the bellowing cries of "Charge!" could be heard across the enemy lines. The Dukan forces charged forward with shields raised and weapons in hand.

"Shields!" Kradorin quickly yelled as his men prepared to receive the oncoming charge. Luckily he was just in time as his men had their shields in position to counter the enemy. Unfortunately, some other parts of the line were not so lucky and the enemy were starting to mingle with the Eceriden forces where they could inflict the most damage.

Now was the time. Kradorin got off his horse and his personal guard did the same. He walked towards the front lines. A man who leads should lead by example.

As he reached the front he yelled, "Kill them! Kill them all!" and greeted his first opponent with a sword through the chest. His men all proceeded to follow his example and the shield wall was dropped, and the clash of swords and screams could be heard all around him.

The fighting quickly became fierce as the armies mixed with each other and formations started to crumble. Kradorin could not focus on that, however, as he was too busy facing down one opponent after another, cutting each of them down. His superior armour and training gave him the greater edge and any who tried to backstab him were countered by his guard. Kradorin started to fall into the routine of using his shield to counter the blow of the enemy before striking in turn with his own sword. He knew the vital points of the human body and where to strike to kill them quickly. It was his job to know these things. The fighting seemed to be unending as there were always people on both sides. At first he could not tell who was pushing the other back as he remained where he could see both his friends and enemies. As much as he would love to he knew he shouldn't move too far forward unless there was a death wish. And he would love to return to the love of his life waiting for him back at home, and all those blank canvases in his workshop.

It was not long, however, before he turned after striking down yet another opponent to see a wave of about twenty enemies charging at him, and very few of his own men to come to the rescue. He quickly moved sideways as two of his bodyguards stepped in front to accept the oncoming charge. At that point he stopped and together they received the assault with shields raised. One down, three down, six down. They fought desperately, against two to three men each at the same time. The magic user stepped in, blasting two of the opponents with earth and fire, killing them with the impact. As Kradorin stabbed his last opponent he turned to see one of his own guard getting cut down by two enemies.

You scum! Kradorin stepped forward, and in his anger slaughtered them with ease. Looking to the motionless man on the ground, he knew there was nothing to be done. After this he looked around to see that he was down to only one guard and his personal magic user. The rest had been slain in the chaos and he was starting to fall behind enemy lines.

"We need to pull back and regroup with the rest of our men."

The other two nodded, with relieved expressions on their faces. He could understand them not wanting to be there.

"If either or both of you survive this, then remind me to fill your pockets with gold."

That certainly picked up their expressions, and their determination. He couldn't help but sigh. It was amazing what money could do to people.

They turned back to where they could see most of their allies fighting, and moved back to join them.

"Men to me!" Kradorin yelled as he joined the line where most of his troops were fighting. Hearing his voice, most of the men in earshot rushed to his aid as another wave of enemies rushed towards them. "Into formation!" he yelled, and they quickly rearranged themselves into a line in front of him and raised their shields. The men quickly cut through their opponents with minimal loss as the formation held. But they did not have time to breathe, as the next wave proceeded to hit them.

It was not going to hold, as his men had to fall back further. The Dukan forces outnumbered them.

"Pull back!" he screamed, and then he started to step backwards, as did his men, moving towards the main forces behind them. But one after another they kept receiving enemy waves. All around him was chaos. Ah, the beauty and artistry of chaos. He would have loved to admire it but was fully aware of the horrible predicament he was in. As he pulled back he got a glimpse of a body on the ground. It stood out as the armour was much more beautiful than that of any of the other soldiers. The armour was clearly of Eceriden manufacture, and as he looked at the corpse's face he recognised it as an old friend, Stroud. This man was another noble, and a long time ago they had spoken many times, and even became friends. Now his body lay lifeless on the ground along with many others, whose names Kradorin did not even know. He did not take much time to dwell on the subject, and instead chose to focus on the task at hand. He could celebrate them when the battle was over, and honour their memory.

As he and what was left of his troops slowly pulled back he heard a cheer start to emanate across the battlefield, but he could not tell what had prompted it. An enemy made a move against him before he could think, and he sloppily countered the blow before killing his opponent. He took a step back and breathed heavily, utterly exhausted from the prolonged fighting. Looking around, he could see that his men were not in any better shape. He made out one soldier who was riding a horse across the field, and about to pass him before he jumped in front of it.

"Soldier. I need your horse," he commanded, and the man quickly and obediently obliged. This allowed Kradorin to sit on the horse, from which vantage point he could get a much better view of the battlefield. To say that it was chaotic would have been an understatement, as he could barely tell where the battle lines were drawn. Both armies seemed to have almost completely mixed together as far as the eye could see. However, it was not long before he could see what was causing all the cheering, and gave an exclamation of relief. It was the reinforcements from the other two kingdoms encircling the battle and rushing in to relieve the Eceriden forces. This was great. Now all he had to do was survive the rest and victory was assured. Despite this, he was not satisfied. He was not going to back away from the battle as it hit its climax.

Kradorin got back off the horse and gathered as many soldiers as possible.

"Men! Reinforcements have arrived, but we will not let them have all the glory! We will push forward and drive them back! To me!"

His men gave a cheer, and together they ended up being the ones charging into the next wave of enemies, rather than the other way around. As if they were an unstoppable wave, they pushed through the enemy, killing anyone who stood in their way. Now this was poetic, Kradorin thought. The glorious race through enemy lines. That thought, however, was soon cut off as he was knocked back by a blast of energy. Kradorin sat up to locate the source and saw an enemy magic user firing all manner of powerful blasts, killing men by the dozen. Kradorin would be dead too if not for his personal magical guard, who had now engaged the opponent along with a few other magic users who had also started firing magical blasts at this robed figure. He was a powerful one, sending blast after blast at the three Eceriden magic users. He was wearing leather gear and a brown cape that had shredded in the face of all the magical energy. The exchange of blasts quickly deteriorated as this man proceeded to kill one soldier and then another, leaving only Kradorin's personal magic user to face this futile fight. A couple of Eceriden soldiers charged at the man, but were quickly blasted apart by the sorcerer.

Kradorin stood just a few feet away from this man. If anyone had any opportunity to kill him it was Kradorin, and with that he quickly stood and lunged at his adversary. His opponent noticed him and turned to face this new threat. But before he could raise his hands and fire any magical power at him, Kradorin lunged his magical sword forward and crashed into an invisible shield. He was close enough that he could see into the man's eyes, and make out a slight glint of gold mixed in with the grey. This man was powerful. He grunted at the impact and went to blast Kradorin to pieces. But luckily Kradorin's personal magic user had already stepped in and was blasting him with everything he had. Then another magic user appeared and he too started blasting him with fire, and for a moment the shield began to waver. The man was beginning to weaken.

Quickly bringing his sword down in a swinging motion, Kradorin brought it down as hard as he could and with a crunching sound the sword embedded into the man's skull and he fell to the ground. A cheer erupted from the men around him for this small victory. All Kradorin could do was smile before falling, hitting the ground with a thud. But for some reason he could not feel the impact. He was just too tired to care. His two remaining personal guards rushed to him and lifted him to his feet.

"Sir, I think we should pull back," stated the magic user, as around them the Eceriden forces were pushing forward with reinforced vigour.

"What, and miss the end of the battle? I still have something left in me. We keep moving forward." He couldn't help what he was doing. He just had to be there for the conclusion. To see how this fight was going to end.

"But my energy is severely depleted. I can't protect you, my lord," replied the magic user. When Kradorin looked at him he could see that his magical guard looked even worse than he felt. But Kradorin could not pull back now.

"I will be fine. We move forward." And with that he stood on his own and started walking forward with his guard following behind to rejoin the fighting.

As they moved into the battle again Kradorin was shocked by the sight before him. He had done it. He had found him. The one that he had been seeking since the beginning of the fight. No one could mimic that nasty look, or that scar across his face. And there he was before Kradorin. In a twist of unbelievable odds, he had actually found his opponent. The one that he would seek for single combat.

And he was dead; lying on the ground, lifeless, with his personal guard dead around him.

Kradorin could not hide his disappointment. He knew he could beat that nasty-looking man and now he was never going to get the chance to prove it. What was he supposed to do now? Find another equal opponent to face? But he couldn't remember any of the other faces that were there. Like a kid having a tantrum, Kradorin stomped forward in anger, continuing to cut down any opponent who tried to fight him, although this was now becoming increasingly rare as most were trying to flee. He even got glimpses of other generals who were still alive and fighting as he pushed forward.

But then his anger waned somewhat when he came across the most poetic scene yet. It was where the fighting remained thickest, and in the centre were two opponents facing off in a duel of masters. On one side stood Slade, one of the generals who had accompanied the king to the centre of the field before the fighting had begun. On the other stood the king of Duka himself as the two of them exchanged one blow after another. The skills of both combatants were the best Kradorin had seen throughout the entire fight. He rushed forward through the fighting that was happening around them. Where was the king of Eceriden, he wondered? Perhaps in another part of the battlefield. The odds of meeting in a fight of thousands were slim. Kradorin would never join the fight, as it would dishonour Slade to intervene, hence why those around them fought each other and avoided the two masters in the centre. But he had to get closer to see this dramatic duel unfold.

As he moved forward he was again taken aback as he saw Kell manage to deflect Slade's blow. With a quick manoeuvre he succeeded in getting his sword through the man's armour and pierce his heart. Slade fell to the ground and went limp as the Dukan forces cheered at this victory. A man in one of the most beautiful outfits Kradorin had ever seen stood over his adversary in celebration. Kradorin had never spoken with Slade before, and as sad as his death was it did not hit him as hard as seeing his friend as a corpse. For a moment he stood waiting as the fighting continued around them. Where was his next opponent? Looking around, Kradorin could see that no one was stepping up. Could this be his opportunity?

Kradorin moved forward and faced the man that stood before him in his greatest and possibly last moment of his life. The Dukan king looked at him with an anger he had not often seen before. But this anger seemed to go through him. He seemed to hate the situation he was in, not the opponent in front of him. Ignoring this, Kradorin stood with his sword and shield raised, ready to meet his adversary.

When Kell met his gesture in kind he lunged forward and the two of them exchanged blows. It was not long however before Kell's sword met its mark and made a small cut on Kradorin's arm. There were no magical shields protecting him. This was a matter of honour. Those that were not engaged in the battle around them were watching. They could in no way help unless they wished to completely dishonour those participating, so this meant no personal shields. Looking at Kell's armour, Kradorin could see that the magical properties it held were greatly diminished. This was a fight with no handicaps. Both sides could seize victory in a second and Kradorin was losing. His own exhaustion was against him. With a right-handed swipe of his sword Kell tried to cut off Kradorin's arm, prompting Kradorin to quickly sidestep before proceeding to strike back, only to be blocked by the shield. It became like rhythm between them, but as the fight progressed it got more and more sloppy. The two of them were tired and Kell appeared desperate. Why didn't he surrender? What was going through his head? It had to be more than honour because this was stupid.

The fight continued; Kradorin made a strike attempt and Kell quickly countered before going for the kill in the same way he killed Slade. But Kradorin saw this coming and used his shield as a weapon, hitting Kell in the face with it. Kell staggered back with his nose gushing blood, and Kradorin took advantage. With his sword he stabbed Kell in the chest, and the blade came out the other side. There were no shields to protect him as all his magical properties were completely gone, leaving him attired in only a beautiful but impractical piece of armour. The fighting around them started to ebb and soon ceased, with only the fighting in the distance still audible.

Kradorin pulled his sword from Kell's body and stepped back.

For a moment things seemed to slow as Kradorin started to take in what had just happened.

Kell fell to his knees, blood gushing from his nose and mouth. "Bastard," croaked the dying man.

"In the end you call me bastard? I would have chosen something different."

The king of Duka gave a weak laugh while choking on the blood in his throat and trying to remain conscious. "Not you. I realise I have been deceived, and now everything will die."

Kradorin gave the man a confused look. What the hell was he going on about? "Who are you calling a bastard?" he quickly asked, before the man before him was lost forever.

"He will be coming for you now that we are weakened. The world will be his." And with that he fell to the floor and was gone.

Well, that couldn't be good. Might have just been a ruse of sorts, but Kradorin was not going to leave anything to chance.

Looking around, he saw the battle ending. Those who saw the death of their king had immediately dropped their weapons in surrender. Further to the edges, others were trying to make a break for it. Pockets of resistance could still be heard, but victory was assured. He could see groups of men, some of them his own, standing in formation in front of him as a sign of respect. This would be the greatest achievement of Kradorin's life. Some would see it as a bit strange that his greatest achievement was killing a man. But he didn't think like that. In his eyes he had ended the war, casting the final stroke. His name would go down in history.

However, it was at that point that he began to relax and realised just how exhausted he was, and collapsed on the ground.

Oh, how nice it is to see you, ground. So very comfortable. I think I will just close my eyes and rest for a while. The poems can wait until tomorrow.

Alas, his sleep was going to have to wait as his men rushed to him and helped him to his feet. This was not fair, he thought.

Time passed and he was given water and a place to sit while others were either treating the wounded or moving the bodies after the battle. The once green, lush field had now become a muddy wasteland. But in time it would return to its original state.

Two men kneeled before him. One was his bodyguard and the other his personal magic user. Both had survived the battle and he called them back to his side.

"Stand. Both of you stuck to my side throughout the battle, despite me pressing onwards into where it was at its worst. You had my back and saved my life."

"You saved mine, my lord."

Yes, he remembered stopping the other magic user from killing the man.

"Yes, I did save you once. But you saved me many times today. Would you like a list? Never let it be said that I am not a man of my word. You will get what you were promised. And for the others under my command that have perished, they will have their names remembered and their families looked after. I will see to that too." How many lords would do that for their people? But he was one of the richest, and he suspected that many others would if they could afford it. The king would probably help in those cases.

"Thank you, my lord," said the two men before him.

"Very good. Now go and get yourselves sorted. You must be weary."

And with that, they bowed and walked away. As they moved away three men approached him. Two were of the highest ranking in the entire army. In the centre, however, was the one man that had him quickly down to his knees in respect.

Oh wow, the ground again. Oh please, oh please don't tell me to rise.

"Rise."

Damn. "My king," he said awkwardly, getting back up again on very sore legs.

"You are the man who slew the king of Duka?"

"Yes."

"I must congratulate you on bringing this fight to a quicker end. I would have liked to face the man myself, but he was not where

I predicted. However, you found him and finished it. For that you have my gratitude."

"Thank you, my lord." He meant it. The king was praising him. How could this get any better?

"For this deed you may ask anything of me, and if it is within my power I will grant it."

Your throne, Kradorin thought, amused. It was funny but he actually did not want it. It was way too much serious work for him. How would he have any kind of fun?

"Of course you may have time to think about it."

Kradorin actually had something in mind. The king noticed it in his expression and gestured for him to say.

"I am a very rich noble and am able to commit to this act, but some are not so lucky."

The king stood listening intently not even flinching, yet Kradorin could tell the king knew what was about to come. Well, Eceriden was a very rich nation and Kradorin knew the king could do this without too much of an impact on their economy.

"Can I ask that all our soldiers that fell on the field today have their names written down in remembrance, and that their families are given compensation for their loss?"

The king smiled. "Done. I will make sure that any noble that can't afford to do so will be helped in the endeavour. This was a horrible time and let's at least end it on something good."

For this Kradorin was going to be seen as a hero. The king too, of course. He gave a bow to his king in respect and gratitude.

"Thank you, my king."

The king before him nodded; then turned to the man on his left, continuing with the business they clearly initiated before seeing Kradorin.

"So tell me how many nobles?"

The man looked down at the parchment before him with his ink quill in hand. "Eight are dead and twenty-two have returned. The rest, we are still trying to find."

"Any of them make any attempts to flee the battle?"

214

"All those who pulled back, such as the cavalry, did not flee the battle entirely. There are none that we are aware of yet who deserted. But there is one who did not turn up when commanded to."

"And which one is that?"

"Lord Nerida from the West Craton never turned up with his men for the fight."

"I want this man summoned to the capital where he will stand trial for betraying his country," said the king without any hesitation.

"Complete fool, thought Kradorin. This man had better have a good reason for not appearing when summoned, or he was going to be in a lot of trouble. It was one thing to not turn up for council meetings; they could be quite easily forgiven, but not appearing in times of war was another thing entirely.

The king and his men walked away, still in conversation. Hmm, definitely not the job for Kradorin. Just leave him to his art and his wife waiting for him back home and he was happy. Well, time to gather what was left of his men, settle anything remaining that needed to be done here, and then go home to reassure the woman he loved that he was not dead. She knew what he would be like, going head first into where the fighting was thickest. Such was his nature. But that didn't stop her fears.

Kradorin sighed to himself. He was going to get a worse beating when he got home than the one he suffered here.

# 13

# EVERYTHING TO HELL

Surdan sat on the very comfortable chair in the great hall. There were at least some perks of being in the king's chair, but the same could not be said for his schedule. A lot of the day had been taken up by people making requests, many of which he simply could not grant. Most of them involved food. This war needed to come to an end, fast. He was only just realising how bad things were. Yet despite the poverty here he was sitting in one of the wealthiest rooms in the entire land. All manner of jewels and fabrics could be seen in this hall. They could practically buy an entire city. And then there were people coming in rags, asking for something. This whole business was incredibly unpleasant.

But as Eceriden was the only adjacent nation willing to do any kind of trade this wealth meant nothing. Eceriden had all the jewels they needed, and the materials they used to be able to trade were no longer in use. So despite this room being one of the richest in all the lands it counted for nothing, as it could not feed the country. Surdan still felt that they should have tried to negotiate with their neighbour rather than invade them. But there was no changing things now.

It felt like an eternity but eventually all duties were done for the day. Silence rang in the hall and he saw that as his cue to leave. But as he was about to stand up he saw a strange movement at the hall's main door.

The doors were not moving, though. They were melting. These giant doors were disintegrating; falling apart and crumbling into dust. What was going on? He was not the only one to notice, as the guards in the hall quickly stepped between Surdan and the door.

Through where the great doors had stood came three figures. On the far left was a giant of a man, rugged with a massive beard and incredibly built, wielding a giant axe. He was the barbarian the sorcerer had brought to the meetings. On the other side was another big man, but not nearly as well built, nor as tall. He was not as rugged, and held dual swords in his hands. Both had red bands tied around their heads. This was the way in which the forest barbarians could tell who the highest ranked of their people were. In the middle stood the smaller but most dangerous man in the entire land. The sorcerer calmly walked forward towards the throne, not breaking his stride as the door crumbled around him.

"What is this? Why are you here? You are supposed to be leading the barbarian army with my brother!"

Without breaking his stride, the sorcerer opened his mouth to speak. "I am here to take what's mine." His voice had changed. He was no longer calm and seductive in his way of communicating. He was ferocious and unrelenting. As the words fell from that despicable man's mouth the guards charged at him, swords raised as the sorcerer's motives became clear. There was nothing Surdan could do. Without even a gesture, simply by wielding that staff in his hand, the sorcerer turned the guards to dust.

"My brother will not stand for this! When he finds out what you have done there will be a reckoning!"

By this point the sorcerer had reached the steps leading to the throne. The two men stopped there, but he marched up the steps without losing his stride, before coming to a halt before Surdan.

"Oh, didn't you hear? Your brother fought valiantly and died in the field of battle. Without the barbarian army he couldn't beat the allied forces. Now if you don't mind, get off my throne or shall I take you off myself."

The shock hit him like nothing before in his life. This was not true. This sickening sorcerer was lying. This was it. But the reality of what had obviously transpired soon sunk in. He was going to die today. He could see into this man's eyes. A madness had taken over. Here was a man with ultimate power, and he had clearly flipped off the edge for some reason.

"What did you do? Where is the barbarian army?"

"I let your brother decide his own fate. But thanks to him, the allied forces are diminished to the point of nothing. It will be easy now to march the barbarian army north and take everything. As for the barbarians, they are here just outside the city, except for a small force I have sent elsewhere. Now get off my seat."

Surdan did not move, glaring into the eyes of this sadistic man. He hated him. He had killed someone close to him and destroyed everything for the sake of what? Power?

Well, to hell with this. If he was going to die then he would do it facing this monster. But a sudden force hit him and he went flying forward down the staircase. Yet for some reason he was still breathing.

"What's the point of this? So you can have absolute power? People will rise against you."

"And they will all fall. They are nothing to me. This world will either follow me or burn. These barbarians understand it. They see me as a god. Then these people will too, or they will die."

"Then kill me and be done with it." Surdan had had enough. This man was nothing. His madness had clearly overtaken any sense.

"Lock this vermin in the dungeons," came the command, and the two men hoisted Surdan to his feet. "You will die, but in front of your people after I have claimed total rule. You will provide an example to any who disobey. Even royalty can't win."

What happened to him? Had his own power driven him crazy? Was it the staff? Or was it something else? With that the men dragged Surdan out of the halls, as the sorcerer added, "Now if you don't mind, I have a war to win."

What could Surdan do? He had no magical power. There was no way of removing the staff, and even if he somehow succeeded, what then? Should he have gone down fighting? He couldn't think. His anger and grief were too great. The two men dragged him down the steps towards the dungeon. As they moved he could see the dead bodies of the people within this great castle, and more barbarians that had clearly sneaked in somehow; probably through the sorcerer's power. They threw him into his cell, where he lay slumped in his grief. It was over. Duka had fallen and it would not be long before Eceriden and the other countries were next. Who could stand to that sorcerer? Who the hell cared? He had just lost everything and now it was sinking in. Closing his eyes, he wept. His last remaining family was gone.

It was nice when the horses were not whinnying away, but remained relaxed, thought Nella. It gave the job a sort of relaxing feel. Looking after the stables could be quite a difficult job. The horses occasionally got a bit restless and it took effort to keep them calm. There was no blaming them, though, given that they were kept in an underground stable. All she needed to do was lower the ramp and they could have the freedom of roaming around the open fields outside. They had to be well trained so they did not just run away. That meant any new horses had to remain inside until they were ready. Many had been lost by people thinking that they were trained, only to see them bolt at the first sign of freedom. This was why they needed a training master like her. No one could tame these animals the way she could.

But it was a little after midnight and there was no letting the horses out for now. However they seemed content so all she had to do was wander around the stables occasionally. A rather nice shift. Looking around, everything seemed fine so she sat down in her chair to relax her muscles. At a little past sixty she was getting tired more easily than she used to, so being able to sit down every so often really helped her on the job.

Looking to the empty seat next to her, she could see her assistant's hat on the chair. Where was that boy? He disappeared and had not reappeared in a long time.

"Tommy?" she quietly called, so as not to startle the animals. There was nothing but silence in return. Sighing, she got back out of her chair and went for a wander round the stables, searching for him.

I swear, if he has run off I am going to extend his hours. This is not fair, leaving me alone to keep an eye on the animals.

"Tommy?"

Turning the corner, she looked down the centre of the room, and alarmed, could see that the ramp had been opened. What was Tommy doing? Moving quickly to the ramp before any of the horses could get out, she quickly took notice of something at the foot of the slope. A shape; a person on the ground. It was Tommy lying motionless. Was he asleep?

Moving closer, she saw with horror the pool of blood around his body. He was dead. Something had happened. She needed to call for help, but a sudden change of temperature could be felt in the room. She felt cold. Standing there for a second, she looked down and saw that something sharp had appeared from her chest. The point of a sword. What a strange feeling. Someone had stabbed her in the back. Who would be so cowardly as to stab someone over sixty years old in the back? But there was no time to think. She didn't need to think anymore. It was a bit of a relief not to care anymore. Closing her eyes for the last time, she fell and was gone before she hit the floor.

Sileena awoke, hearing some sort of scratching noise. Damned rodents, was the assumption. It was an Underground and she was amazed enough as it was that she hadn't heard any before now. But she was too tired to care, and made attempts to get back to sleep. Perhaps the scratching would stop. A couple seconds later, it did. Thank goodness, now she could get back to sleep. The Underground should probably do something about rodents. Surely it would be one of the first problems they would tackle? They could have an aura, like the one already in place, to keep them away. She was surprised they had not already done something like that. In fact, she had not seen nor heard anything that even resembled a rodent. The scratching noise disappeared, and in the silence that followed she thought she heard something else. Was something in the room with her? She turned and dreamily opened her eyes to see a dark figure over her bed. Before she could even act surprised the figure jabbed something into her neck, and within a second everything went dark.

Dorren awoke to a scratching noise coming from the door. Someone was trying to pick the lock. Apparently not very well, as it was supposed to be done silently. Perhaps someone had lost their keys and was breaking into the wrong room by mistake. Well, he was not going to take any chances and grabbed his weapons, standing behind the door as it unlocked and opened. Someone he did not recognise entered, bearing weapons, and moved for the bed. Quickly grabbing the man from behind, Dorren put his knife to his throat before the man could react.

"Who are you and what are you doing here?"

This man was in tattered clothes, and very unclean. This was not an Outcast. Whoever he was, he was clearly not going to answer as he tried desperately to stab Dorren. Kicking the man forward, Dorren adopted a fighting stance. The man quickly turned round and lunged at him. How the hell did he get in? Was he here to kill Dorren? The answer to that last question was obvious as his opponent bore down on him.

Easily deflecting his blow, Dorren cut the man on the leg to slow him down. He was going to find out answers, and to do that he was going to need him alive. Perhaps Pagar could assist with that.

But before he could do anything he heard screams coming from outside the room. Running outside, he looked down the corridor to find more of these intruders entering rooms and killing people. There were many more, and they were clearly laying siege. How did they get in? Why were no alarms sounded?

He had no time to think about it as the man in his room charged out and attacked him, at which Dorren countered and sank his sword into the man's chest.

I don't need you alive anymore.

Turning as the dead man fell, he rushed to the room from where he knew the screaming had come. Once he entered, he saw a dead girl on the bed and the man who killed her turning to exit. But he didn't expect to be met by a sword embedded into his skull. That girl was twelve, you bastard.

Dorren couldn't help but close his eyes to the motionless girl. There was nothing he could do as she was already gone. But there was still commotion outside. He walked out the room to find three more intruders either leaving rooms or walking down to the next ones, heading towards Dorren. Moving forward with his sword raised, he cut through them all, moving out of the corridor and into one of the larger rooms. To his horror, he found utter chaos as there must have been about twenty more of the brutes moving about. A fire was lit in the centre of the room and the dead bodies of the Outcasts were being thrown into it. Others were still alive and being dragged to where an executioner was preparing his weapon.

This was not happening. It was a dream. How could this happen? Dorren's anger rose as he ran round the balcony and leapt off to the floor below, and swept his sword, cutting off the executioner's head before he had time to react. Others had noticed, and raised their weapons to fight Dorren. Heading for the survivors first, he killed the first intruder who was dragging one of the Outcasts to the execution line. Using his knife for speed and his sword as a parry weapon, he made short work of three more of the men, giving him time to free the rest of the Outcasts. As the other intruders were noticing the sudden change, the Outcasts grabbed the weapons from the dead men on the ground and stood at Dorren's side.

We will show them why attacking us is a bad idea.

Together they started fighting the barbarians, killing two, four, seven of them. But more started appearing, and two of the Outcasts had already fallen in the struggle. Other sounds could be heard throughout the Underground: shouts, and what sounded like explosions and steel striking steel. This was happening everywhere.

"We need to get out of here!" yelled Dorren to the remaining Outcast." But before he could help him an intruder stabbed the prisoner in the back, killing him. In despair Dorren turned to the nearest corridor and ran for it. Two men stood in his way and were dead within seconds. He was not going to hold back like he did in the town of Sarden in Eceriden. They attack his home and kill his family, then they die. Running into the next tunnel, he moved down to where the central hall was. Along the corridor he passed various bodies; some of them were small children, others were elderly. These intruders were killing everyone with absolutely no remorse. But first he had to find Sileena, he had to get to her room, and she had to be OK. Nothing else mattered at the moment.

Reaching the hall, he saw utter chaos unfolding as fights were breaking out all over. The element of surprise had passed. Most of the Outcasts must know by now what was happening. He could not stay and fight though. He ran through most of the fighting, killing any who stood in his way or helping out the occasional Outcast in their endeavour.

It was not long before he reached the next tunnel, where Sileena's room was located. This was the same as the last, with bodies littered across the floor. Reaching her room, he found that her door had already been opened. His heart crumbled at the thought of what he might find inside, but amazingly he sighed in relief as he looked in and found it empty. She might be alive somewhere. She did have the power to fight anything she came across, provided she was willing to.

Looking around, there did not seem to have been much of a struggle. Still, staying there was not going to help anyone and so he rushed out and ran back, hoping to find some sort of clue as to where to go next. Looking down the tunnel, he could see what appeared to be flickering lights around the corner. Perhaps something was happening there.

Running to see, he turned to find a charred, burning mess as fires were dotted down the entire passage. Part of the way down was a massive figure towering over another who was kneeling on the ground. Rushing to the unsuspecting person's aid, Dorren stopped to find that the man was in fact Gabe.

"Gabe!"

The massive man turned and gave a sad smile at Dorren's approach.

"What happened here?"

Gabe gestured towards the kneeling individual. Looking down, Dorren saw Anna, who appeared to be cradling someone, and with horror realised that it was Anna's mother. Anna must have turned all the intruders to ashes after finding her mother gone. She was mourning and obviously needed some time. But this was not the right moment as the Underground was in chaos.

"Anna," Dorren said quietly. "Anna, we need your help."

Anna did not turn. She just sat there holding her mother's corpse, with tears running down her cheeks.

"Anna, I'm really sorry. But we can mourn them later. Right now we need to help the people still alive."

"We should go, Anna," said Gabe, who was looking down the tunnel for any intruders.

Anna released her mum and stood slowly. "I am going to kill them all," she said in utter agony and rage. This really was not the time. She would not be able to help anyone if she rushed in blindly and got herself killed.

"Anna, where is your father?"

Anna looked at Dorren, her face tear-stained. "I don't know. He was working when this happened."

Dorren took her shoulders and looked her dead in the eye. "Then focus on finding him. He might be OK."

Anna seemed to come out of her depression at this realisation. But Dorren had been here too long. He had to find Sileena.

"I am heading down this way. If the two of you could head back to the central hall, there are still Outcasts there that need your help. It is also the way to the doctors, and you might find your father there."

Anna gathered her wits and turned towards the central hall. "Why are you going that way?" yelled Anna as Dorren ran in the opposite direction.

"I need to find Sileena!" And he disappeared around the corner and out of sight.

Silence seemed to gather as he started to sneak through the tunnels, avoiding any large groups of intruders. This was horrible. The Outcasts were outnumbered. Most of them were not even fighters. They were a community, and those that couldn't fight were all dying. Those that could were completely outnumbered and outmatched. It was clear that they could not defend their home. They had to get out and find safety. But he would not leave without first finding those he cared about.

He had to stop at the corner as another group of intruders made their way past. But just as he thought the way was clear, he saw Pagar walk past, following the group from behind. Then a sudden realisation hit him. That's how they got in without anyone noticing. It was not through the cabin because that was too narrow, and would take too long for this kind of force to enter. It was through the stables. The ramp was certainly big enough for scores of people to make their way into the Underground. But the ramp could only be opened from the inside, and one had to know exactly where the entrance was. There was a traitor within this place, someone who allowed these people in to take over the Underground. And here he saw Pagar casually follow-ing a group of them down the corridor. It couldn't be? His heart sank at the possibility that it actually might be his own adoptive father. But it didn't make any sense. Pagar had control over the Underground. Why would he want it destroyed? He would have to answer those questions later as he had to keep moving in the hope of finding Sileena. But a feeling of dread came over him as he moved further underground and found no sign of where to look. Despite trying to fathom what was happening, all he could think was: why? Why did this happen? It just didn't make sense. But maybe he saw things wrong. Maybe it was not Pagar, but rather a double agent. If this was the case, then how long had they been inside the Underground? He couldn't think about it anymore as he heard whispers and turned to see a couple of Outcasts gesturing to him. It was a family that he knew, as the father worked on the farm with him. They must have been hiding while the ransacking had been taking place. But they had not moved from where they were.

"What are you doing?" whispered Dorren. "You need to get out of here."

"We are waiting for help. Who are these men?" asked the farmer.

"I don't know. But they are killing everyone. You can't wait. No one is coming. We have lost and we need to get out of here."

The family agreed, and together they started making their way to the entrance that led to the cabin. This place was well hidden, but if someone was to find the two entrances then they were in trouble. The cabin was very defendable but in this kind of situation they had their backs to the corner. If both entrances were blocked then there would be no way of getting out. He had no choice but to hope the intruders were not holding the cabin entrance. Moving around the bodies within the halls and corridors, they made their way back to the central hall. The adults looked around in horror at the motionless bodies all around them, and kept their children's eyes covered. As a community of a few hundred, most people knew each other and there were many faces Dorren recognised. But there was no choice but to keep moving, avoiding larger groups of intruders and making short work of those stupid enough to wander alone.

"Dorren!" called a familiar voice.

He turned to find Pagar rushing towards him with a few Outcasts following behind. Dorren had no time to react before Pagar was right in front him, but to his surprise his adopted father embraced him in a hug. Relinquishing the hold, they took a step back.

"I feared the worst when I couldn't find you. Are you OK?"

"I'm fine, thank you. What happened to you?"

"Well once I realised what was happening I tried to help where I could. We need to leave. The Underground has fallen. We need to get as many survivors out as possible. That includes you, Dorren."

He wouldn't leave without finding Sileena. But he didn't know where she was. And besides, he was still not sure if he could trust the man whom he saw casually following a group of the intruders.

"We head to my room."

"What? Why?" Pagar's room was another dead end.

"There is a secret exit I had installed when this place was built. We can leave that way safely."

Reluctantly Dorren and the rest of the Outcasts followed their leader towards his chambers. A secret entrance was smart. This way, if this kind of situation arose then there was another way out to safety.

"So what do you know?" Dorren asked, hoping to get some answers.

Pagar maintained his serious expression as they moved silently but quickly through the tunnels. "When I found out what had happened I followed a few of the invaders, trying to find some answers, but once I realised it was a dead end and that the Underground was lost I had to get as many of my people out safely as possible. So

I torched every enemy I found and have been leading groups out ever since. What have you been doing?"

Dorren felt his heart sink. "I was looking for Sileena. I couldn't find her. Did you see her?"

"I'm sorry but I didn't. Things are not over yet. We can find her in time," Pagar said, giving Dorren a confident smile. But this did nothing for Dorren's mood, given the thoughts going through his head. He had actually thought Pagar had betrayed them. The man who took Dorren as his son. The man who had led them through the past few years, asking little in return. The man who picked up the pieces after his father's death. He felt sick that he had actually thought it, and he knew Pagar was just trying to bolster his spirits. The barbarians were killing everyone in sight. Why would Sileena be any different?

"Pagar, you know that they must have got in through the stables. The ramp has been opened from the inside, and the only way they could have known where to go is if there is a traitor here."

Pagar gave the slightest indication of anger in his expression. "I am aware of how this must have happened. And trust me, once we have managed to get everyone we can out then we'll find out who did this." There was no mercy in his tone. If they ever got hold of the individual, then they would die. Something Dorren was happy to oblige in doing himself.

As they made their way through the maze of tunnels, in the distance Dorren spotted a figure moving in the other direction, with someone over their shoulder. It was quite far away but he thought he saw Sileena being carried away.

When Pagar noticed Dorren making his way back, he called out. "Dorren! What are you doing?"

"I thought I saw Sileena being carried off. You lead the others to safety. I will catch up."

Pagar knew there was no point or time to try and argue with this, so agreed and kept moving.

Racing after the figures, Dorren could see a few of the intruders making their way to the central hall.

"Hey!" Dorren yelled, running down the tunnel towards his

opponents, and realised that it actually was Sileena who was over the intruder's shoulder. The individual kept moving while the rest turned to face him. You are all going to die, he thought as he swung his sword at his first opponent, cutting his head off. The rest were dispatched as quickly as possible. No fancy manoeuvres, nor paying attention to be sure of victory. He just had to get to Sileena. She was in reach but these people were in his way. His rage was only trumped by his need to get to her. He was not going to lose her here and now.

After dealing with the last one, he kept going. His eyes caught something that he recognised, and he stopped. Looking to the side, he saw another body lying there, as lifeless as the rest, and he recognised the girl he had once completely fallen for. Tania. It was yet another name to add to the list of people close to him that had died today.

There was nothing he could do. She was gone, but Sileena might be OK. And so he continued round the corner and emerged at the central hall. The fighting here was over as the room was almost empty, aside from the bodies that littered the ground. In the centre were a couple of intruders and the one carrying Sileena, who was now laying her on the ground in front of him. She was not moving. Was she dead? Dorren was not going to entertain the thought. But they had killed everyone they encountered, so she must be dead. His fury and fear mounted and he ran to the intruders, yelling out as he charged.

Racing forward to meet his enemy, he literally had to skid to a halt when he saw what lay before him. There was no way this could have got worse except for finding out Sileena was dead, but this was certainly a close second. The man he had called a friend for his entire life turned and saw him, an eager smile spread across his face.

"Lockarr?" What was this? The intruders stood beside this man as if he were ally. It was him? Lockarr opened the doors to the enemy? It was him who had everyone killed, and it was him who now stood between Dorren and Sileena?

"Oh, hello Dorren, it was nice of you to show up here. Could you give me a hand and help me deal with these ruffians next to me?"

The intruders advanced, also blocking his path to Sileena. With minimal effort he cleared them and kept up the slow walk towards Lockarr.

"Why did you do this? What the hell is going on?"

"An excellent question," replied Lockarr, with his normal, cheerful expression. Was this man sadistic or something, to be able to be exactly the same person as before? "Well unfortunately I was ordered by someone to let this force into the Underground, and to kill everyone. Especially you apparently, but unfortunately these stupid barbarians reached your room before I could, so you were already gone when I arrived. It's lucky that you are standing here now. I might never have found you, despite knowing this place so well."

Dorren's shock seemed to subside sufficiently for him to take note of the situation. A couple more of these barbarians, as Lockarr called them, had entered the room and kept their distance from the discussion taking place in the centre.

"What have you done to Sileena?" he asked, dreading the answer.

Lockarr looked to the body lying behind him. "Oh, I drugged her. She is quite well. Unbelievably, she had to be kept alive."

"Why her, and why kill everyone else?"

Lockarr's expression became slightly confused, as though the answer was obvious. "Because I was ordered to. I just told you. You would have to ask the man giving the orders to find out why."

"And who is giving the orders?" Dorren's senses had by now almost recovered, and he was now playing for information. He needed to find out who would be controlling Lockarr and what they wanted. Then he would get Sileena back and kill the one who had singlehandedly killed almost everyone he knew and loved.

"Who? Come now, Dorren, it was obviously her father who gave the order. A father wants his daughter alive. Personally I don't get it, but everyone else does so perhaps it's just something I have to resolve."

The damned idiot could not get her himself. Leaving Lockarr and some petty barbarians to do this job was a mistake. Dorren was going to kill them all, and get Sileena back.

"Why could he not get her himself? He is a powerful magic user."

"The man is too busy fighting a war. I believe he has already taken over Duka and is now on the march to Eceriden."

What? How had Duka fallen? Wait – it was because the army had marched north. They would have fought Eceriden, and the winner would be weakened enough to be easily walked over. This was bad. But where did he get these men? Dorren asked Lockarr.

"These are the barbarians of the forest to the far east. He somehow managed to unite the clans for his own and has accumulated the biggest army in the land. With that special staff he somehow got hold of, the world is now his to take."

This was the reason why Duka had declared war on Eceriden. Nerida somehow manipulated this whole thing to happen. Dorren was only now just understanding. It must have taken years. All so that he could have power over the world? Dorren never understood those who wanted power. From what he understood it was nothing but hard work.

"But you have been here for as long as anyone. Why would you betray us all?"

"Because I was ordered to. I thought we had been over this." It would seem Lockarr was stalling for time as the barbarians were gradually increasing in number.

"Yes, you were ordered, but didn't you care for the people here? You didn't mind that you were betraying them?"

"I never betrayed them. I was never part of them in the first place. I was sent here to keep an eye until this order came through. Sounded like a bit of fun, and it was. But I don't really understand your question about caring. They were here and now they are gone. Personally I enjoyed the thrill, but it doesn't bother me that these people are gone." He said that so casually, as if it was nothing. This man was a complete lunatic. It didn't make sense, but as he tried to process everything Dorren thought back to his interactions with the man he'd called friend. It seemed so obvious in hindsight. Lockarr's disinterest in making a life here, and his general mannerisms when mixing with the group.

"Wait, if you said you were against us from the beginning, does that mean that it was you who killed my father?"

Lockarr seemed to be thinking for a brief moment before coming to his senses. "Oh, that. Yes, I did. He caught on to what I was doing and had to go. No other way I'm afraid."

This was not happening. This whole time, and this bastard did it. Dorren's anger almost blinded him. Screaming, he charged Lockarr, thrusting his sword forward with speed, not caring about any sort of tactics. Lockarr caught this in time by unsheathing his sword and deflecting the shot to the side. Dorren stumbled forward and Lockarr took a step back. The other barbarians made their move to advance, but Lockarr gave the motion for them to stop.

"Stay where you are. Dorren, I believe you have some sort of grudge against me. I may not have the same for you but I was given orders to kill you specifically, and it's fair we do this one on one. It's a good coincidence that you are here. Let's see which one of us comes out on top, shall we?"

Big mistake, Dorren thought. He was miles better than Lockarr. This fight was going to be over before it started, and he was not going to lose himself to his rage and lose the fight. Quickly preparing himself in a fighting stance, he advanced towards Lockarr, sword at the ready. With one of the fastest movements of his arm he swiped his sword at Lockarr. Seeing this, Lockarr quickly parried the blow and countered with his own, which Dorren quickly blocked. The force was unexpected and he had to take a step to the side to avoid falling. Lockarr, faster than before, spun the sword around to attack the other side, but Dorren was prepared for this power strike and blocked appropriately.

The exchange of blows could be heard around the room as the two opponents fought in one of the fastest and most aggressive duels Dorren had ever been in. But this fight was not expected. Dorren was actually on equal footing with his opponent. What was happening? How did Lockarr get this good? Had he been concealing his skill this entire time?

Quickly trying to counter a blow from Lockarr, Dorren missed and had to step back as the blow cut him across the arm. He was losing ground. He was losing this fight. Looking behind Lockarr, he could see Sileena's unconscious form on the ground. He had to get her out, and to safety. Turning back to Lockarr, he took a step to the side and tried to deliver a series of blows that would allow him to get passed his opponent. But it was a futile effort as he was blocked and had to stop the attempt, unless he wanted to lose his head.

Taking another step back, he realised that he was almost up against the wall. What could he do? Looking desperately around, there was no way for him to get out of this, not without beating the man who stood before him. But he had never before faced someone who could outclass him. The man that betrayed them all, killed his father and destroyed his home, while taking the woman he loved, was standing right in front of him and he couldn't kill him.

With his back to the wall he prepared for this next wave of blows, and as Lockarr prepared to strike they both stopped when they heard a yelling noise, and looked to find the source. Out from the tunnels came a few more Outcasts, who were quickly engaging the barbarians. The fight was not over, and Dorren seized his initiative and rushed forward, swiping his sword at Lockarr's throat. Lockarr took a step back to avoid the blow and prepared for what was happening around them. Dorren moved forward, ready to fight as he saw who was leading the group of Outcasts. It was Severa who had cut through two barbarians, and turned to see Lockarr and Dorren face each other before stopping in confusion.

"Severa!" Lockarr quickly jumped in before Dorren could speak. "Dorren has betrayed us. He let them in. We need to take him. He has destroyed everything." His voice was filled with pain over the betrayal of his friend. This traitor was a very good liar.

Dorren didn't know what to do as Severa looked to Dorren questioningly. The only other fighter in this Underground who equalled Dorren stood next to him, and the two of them were the bitterest enemies. How could he convince the man he had hated all these past years that he was the innocent one? Especially when the real traitor spoke so well. In a last desperate plea, Dorren looked to Severa.

"It was not me, it was Lockarr. He betrayed us. It was he who killed my father."

Looking from one to the other, Severa gave a brief pause before making a decision rather quickly, stepping towards Dorren. Dorren could not blame him. The two of them were the worst enemies and Lockarr was a deranged psychopath who was well-practised at lying. But Severa stopped a couple of steps from Dorren and faced Lockarr before putting himself into a fighting stance.

"Lockarr, you scum! You will die for what you did today."

Even Lockarr was surprised by this sudden action. Within a second Severa had decided to believe Dorren? With hopes rising, Dorren also raised his sword ready as the fighting around the room amplified. Lockarr gave a soft sigh as he unsheathed his other sword.

"Well, it was worth a try. Guess I'm just going to have to do this the fun way. Do you ever wonder if anyone can have too much fun?"

Dorren and Severa did not pause to listen to the question as they both attacked in a quick succession of blows. The old rivals fought in unison against their opponent. Lockarr quickly reacted and the three came to a showdown in the centre of the room. Severa gave an exclamation at the skill Lockarr suddenly seemed to possess. But as the barbarians were falling, more seemed to enter the room to engage the Outcasts around them. The Outcasts were starting to thin in numbers and lose ground.

Dorren and Severa stepped to either side of Lockarr and attacked together. Lockarr spun round and stepped back to get out of the situation, striking at Dorren's legs, cutting one across the thigh. Dorren staggered back and Lockarr seized the opportunity for a killing blow, but was quickly countered by Severa who forced him back, thus forcing the fight to continue. Occasionally one of the combatants would receive a blow but none too severe, and it was apparent that Lockarr was still winning. This could not have been humanly possible. How did this man possess the ability to fight both Severa and Dorren?

The Outcasts were really beginning to dwindle in number around them at the realisation that this fight was lost.

"I need to get Sileena out of here. We need to get out. We can't win."

Severa cursed as he had noticed this too. "Go and get her." Severa attacked Lockarr as Dorren quickly ran round to Sileena, and a barbarian that blocked his path. He swiftly killed this opponent and picked Sileena up.

"Right, let's get out of here," called Dorren, and made his way for the tunnel leading to Pagar's room. Severa followed up the steps to the edge of the hall. But he stopped at the tunnel's entrance and turned around to face the enemy. Dorren noticed what happened and stopped. The other Outcasts were now all dead, leaving just the two of them with Sileena over Dorren's shoulder.

"What are you doing? Let's leave!"

"Go, Dorren, they will catch us if they're not stopped here. Get out with Sileena and be safe."

Dorren went to protest, but Severa quickly stopped him. "Tell my family I love them. Now go!"

Turning, Dorren quickly moved down the corridor, and heard the clash of swords as Lockarr engaged Severa at the tunnel entrance. At the end of the tunnel Dorren turned, and to his horror saw Severa being stabbed through the chest in his refusal to budge from the spot. But he did not drop to the ground, and instead he kicked Lockarr straight in the chest, back down the stairs. The other barbarians rushed to attack the already dying Severa. With no hope of saving him, Dorren turned and made his way down the corridor. The last words he could hear came from Lockarr as he shouted "Dorren! You can't get out! Both entrances are blocked! We are coming!"

Ignoring it, he kept moving until he reached Pagar's office and entered to see his adopted father standing at the back of the room. Next to him, the bookcase had opened out to reveal a tunnel that disappeared into darkness.

"Dorren! I feared the worst. We need to get going."

Making his way to Pagar, Dorren stopped at the entrance to the tunnel. "We need to close this off. No one else is coming. The place is overrun and the barbarians are making their way here."

"OK," replied Pagar, and they entered the tunnel, closing the secret door behind them. Severa, Tania and goodness knows how many others were lost. What could they do now? But despite everything Dorren was relieved as Sileena was alive and in his arms. Pagar would decide the next step for them to take.

"Is she OK?" asked Pagar. This tunnel, unlike the rest, was not magically lit so Pagar had to keep a constant fire burning in his hand as they moved.

"She is alive." But things were still not OK. "It was Lockarr. He was the one who betrayed us. What do we do now?"

"It is OK, Dorren. We will figure something out."

Dorren thought back to the conversation with Lockarr, and did not think they had been sufficiently prepared.

"But it's not just here. I know what's been happening. Duka has fallen and Eceriden will soon be next. This has been happening everywhere."

Pagar looked at Dorren calmly, but with the slightest twinges of confusion. He did not know what was happening. Lockarr was a fool to tell Dorren this information. He was overly confident and didn't know Dorren would get out to tell everyone.

"Dorren, I need you to tell me everything you know so we can do something."

He understood, and began to fill Pagar in on everything that had happened and everything that was discussed. However, all Dorren could think about was his relief that Sileena was alive and Pagar was here. Without them he didn't know if he would be able to go on. No more immaturity or not following orders. He was going to do exactly as Pagar said. This was no longer the time for silly actions.

# 14

# PICKING UP THE PIECES

Moving through the darkness in silence, Dorren had a little time to come to terms with everything that had happened. The shock of it all had settled and a miserable bitterness was left in its wake. How many people got out, he wondered? As far as he was aware the group that were with Pagar were the only ones to get out, other than themselves. And what about Anna and Gabe? What about Derain? Were they OK, or did they fall in the fight?

The tunnel seemed to go on endlessly. When Dorren questioned Pagar about it, he replied that the tunnel was meant to exit much further away to safety. This single, straight tunnel seemed to be going towards the sea, but Dorren stopped guessing after a while.

Eventually he could see in the distance a small ray of light. As it slowly became clearer he was relieved to see it was an exit. It felt like they had spent an age in this dark place.

Walking out, Dorren saw that he was right. They had come out on the cliff side, and he could see a small path slowly making its way up to the top. This was certainly a very nice option for an escape route. Once he reached the top, he turned and saw the endless grassy plains heading inland. Looking further along the shore, in the distance he could make out the marshes that took up most of the land that the Outcasts had control over. The most uplifting sight of all was the large group of people that sat waiting at the top of the cliff. Despite the relief, it was still a mess.

And taking a closer look, he realised just how few had made it out. There must have been barely fifty people here. So few survived. At least it was more than Dorren had feared. From the slaughter that he had witnessed back home, he was surprised that twenty people made it out, let alone this many.

"Dorren!" called someone within the crowd. It was a voice he recognised, and he relaxed.

Anna rushed towards him as Dorren slowly placed the unconscious Sileena on the ground. She was not a heavy girl, but carrying her for however long they were down in the tunnel had taken its toll. Anna caught him in an embrace as three others also approached.

"You're OK. I thought you were a goner when you disappeared," she said, looking in much better condition than she had been earlier. Having a little time to come to terms with things had helped a little. Another factor that seemed to come into play was that one of the three approaching was Anna's father. She had found him, and they had got out together. That was a relief to know. And the bigger relief still was the other two people next to him. Gabe and Derain stood in front of Dorren, both giving weak smiles.

"Hey, how are you feeling?" was all Dorren could ask. Really, he did not know what to say. He was just happy they were out. Everyone looked worse for wear, though. Anna's and Gabe's clothes were charred from the burning. Derain had a cut across his face and cuts and bruises on his arms and torso. Looking around, Dorren could see the same wounds on others. Some were injured – a couple more severely than others – but they looked like they had been attended to. Luckily some had made it out without a scratch, but not nearly as many as there should have been. Looking around, there were others that appeared to be missing, including Derain's family.

"Derain? Where are your family?"

Derain merely shook his head. Really? None of them made it out?

Dorren dropped his head at the thought. He had uncles and cousins and all were gone? The Underground was usually full of commotion as people roamed and children kept running around the place. His stomach turned at the thought of them all. So many gone. Derain had lost his whole family. Anna was down to her father. The groups around them seemed to be huddled, with a few stragglers that had lost everything. Yet no one was crying. All just looked distraught. All the tears must have been shed before Dorren and Pagar arrived.

"Lockarr didn't get out?" Derain asked, looking around for his former friend.

Lockarr. The name instilled a cold anger that Dorren had never felt before. He didn't speak. He knew he should tell them here and now, but Pagar would cover the subject when he spoke to what remained of his people.

Two other girls ended up joining the group. They were what remained of Anna and Sileena's friends. But in comparison to others, they got off lightly. The group conversed for a while as Pagar moved through the ground, speaking to everyone in turn, partly to hear what they had to say and partly to keep everyone as calm as possible.

Dorren heard a sigh as he looked to see Sileena opening her eyes.

"Sileena. How are you feeling?"

Sileena put her hand to her head in mild pain and tried to adjust her eyes to the sunlight. "I have a sore head. What is going on? Wait, did you drug me?"

Dorren smiled. She was going to be fine. "No, I did not drug you. What do you remember?"

"Someone came into my room and did something. That's all I remember." Oh, she was unconscious during the whole event and needed to be caught up. But he didn't know how to tell her about what had just happened. Her own father had just ordered the destruction of her new home and declared war on the world. But at that point Pagar had noticed Sileena awaken and approached the group. Looking around, completely bewildered by the scenery that she was waking to, she turned back to Dorren.

"What happened?"

However, Pagar was the one to speak. "Sileena. Can I talk to you privately?"

Sileena, still confused, carefully picked herself back up and nodded at Pagar, and the two of them moved off to the side. Dorren couldn't hear what was being said, but judging from Sileena's changing expressions he appeared to be telling her everything. Dorren was glad it was not him telling her, because he would have been far from adequate at it. He was never good at helping people come to terms with bad news. He had been completely lost when Sileena's brother had died. This was a hard time for everyone, but she must be feeling awful.

As Dorren observed the conversation someone came up to the group. It was Severa's brother, Ray.

"Hey, I know we don't exactly get along but maybe you can help me? Did any of you see my brother down there? No one seems to have seen him."

The others gave each other glances, as none of them had seen Severa except for Dorren.

"Yes, I saw him. He was leading a group against the barbarians that attacked." There was a pause as Dorren tried to think of a good way to phrase it, but there was no good way of telling this young man that his brother was dead. "I'm sorry, but he didn't make it. I was too late to do anything."

Ray's eyes widened in sorrow, but he quickly regained his composure. "I see. Thank you for telling me." And he turned and walked away, back to what remained of his family and friends. It was a poor situation, and Dorren was right. He would never have been able to go back and help Severa before his sacrifice. If it were not for Sileena, he would have stayed to fight by his side and would ultimately die as well.

By this point Pagar and Sileena were back after their talk. She kept her eyes on the floor. It wasn't her fault her father did what he did, but she still appeared to feel guilty.

"Sileena? Are you OK?"

Sileena's eyes swelled with tears. "No."

Dorren rushed forward to comfort her. The poor girl had been through too much. They all had.

Pagar moved away from the group and turned to address the Underground. "Can I have your attention?" Pagar spoke out, and in quick succession everyone turned to hear what their leader was going to say. "As we all know, we were attacked and driven out by a group

239

of barbarians from the eastern forests. We are all that remains."

A few glances and lowered heads at this point.

"We had defences in place for this sort of event, but what we did not know was that one of our own would betray us and let the enemy in undetected."

Some glanced in Sileena's direction. This angered Dorren, but it had to be expected. She was the newest addition to the group and she was of nobility, and taken against her will. It was no surprise that they would think of her as the culprit. But some quickly dropped their gazes when they saw her the state of her in Dorren's arms. It was clearly not her.

"Lockarr is this traitor, for those who know him."

"What?!" came the shout from Anna and Derain. Others were also in commotion at this statement. The whole Underground knew him, as he had been there pretty much since its founding. It was certainly very surprising that he would be the one to do it.

"Dorren, did you know this?" asked Derain.

"I was the one who found out. He had us all fooled."

"But how? How had he managed to fool us for that long?"

Dorren shrugged, but he knew. The guy was a lunatic. Lying was as natural to him as breathing. Pagar gave it a second before speaking again.

"We cannot return—" he started, but was quickly interrupted by another Outcast.

"Is the traitor dead?"

"No, the traitor lives and is there right now. But we cannot return, and anyone who wishes to do so would be going to a death sentence. He was commanded by a sorcerer to take the Underground using an army of barbarians. This sorcerer has created an army larger than any we have seen!"

More commotion from the Outcasts, but Pagar continued.

"Duka has already fallen to him, and the armies will soon march north to Eceriden."

At this point a lot of the Outcasts didn't care. Most of them were here because Eceriden cast them out, so why should they feel anything if Eceriden fell? Some, however, were wiser and knew the consequences should this happen, and held their expression of concern.

"What will we do now?" cried a voice from the crowd.

"We cannot return and we cannot leave this land, so we will make our way to the Zorku Underground that is not too far from here. We will seek shelter from them, and there we decide what our next move shall be. Let's move now before it gets too dark!"

Pagar then walked back into the crowd as the commotion and movement started to pick up the pace. Those that were injured were helped to their feet, and others remained in their groups. They had to get to shelter quickly. Because of the suddenness of the situation none had brought any sort of provisions, and the Outcasts' energy was severely depleted.

Sileena remained close to Dorren, with her eyes to the ground the whole time. No one blamed her, especially since Pagar had obviously chosen not to name Sileena's father as the cause of this. But she appeared to blame herself, and that was something that he could not help with, except to reassure her that it really was not her fault.

It was nearly nightfall when they finally reached the other Underground. The difference was that instead of a hut there was a damaged windmill. The guard stood at the top, and could be seen racing down in a panic when he saw over fifty people making their way to him.

Pagar entered alone, asking to see the leader of this particular Underground. After the leader was called and a brief discussion had been held, the Outcasts were allowed in. A few of those who worked there were asked to take in those that were injured and look after them. The remaining survivors were allowed in to be given some sort of accommodation. After a couple of hours everyone had been seen to and settled into one of the halls. The hall did not look so different to their own. In fact, the whole Underground seemed to bear a striking resemblance to their home. Granted, the layout was different but otherwise it looked almost exactly the same.

Dorren and Sileena remained huddled in a corner, as did most of the others that survived. The others from this Underground remained supportive but confused. They had no idea what had just happened to them. They did not know that their lives might be in danger, nor anything about the war in Duka and Eceriden. Lockarr knew where the other Undergrounds were. He could lead further invasions against them. However, this time they would be prepared. He could not open the doors from the inside, and any invaders would have to make their way through the narrow passages, allowing for better odds in cases of attack. The same mistake was not going to be made.

As Dorren seemed to drift away in his thoughts, Pagar approached them.

"Dorren, Sileena, I would like both of you to join the council meeting with the other leaders. They are all assembling tomorrow and I would like you to be there."

Guess Pagar is running out of people to include into this important meeting.

But Dorren was not going to disappoint anyone now, and agreed to go, as did Sileena. Pagar, happy at their acceptance, walked away.

After a little while beds were set up in the hall and everyone managed to get a comfortable place to rest. Despite being weary, Dorren suspected that most of them were unable to get to sleep. Whatever was going to happen next was to be decided at the meeting the next day, once all the other Underground leaders arrived. Until then Dorren needed to rest, despite his worries and his loss. It proved very difficult after the events that had transpired. But his mind slowly began to drift, and the warmth of Sileena beside him gradually relaxed his mind until he fell asleep.

Dorren awoke to Pagar calling his name. Opening his eyes, he could see that most of the Outcasts were already up, and Sileena was out of bed, waiting next to Pagar.

"Dorren, the leaders are all here and the meeting is about to start."

Dorren took a breath and got out of bed quickly. He must have overslept. Washing and changing could come later. First must be the talks on what to do now. With Anna and one other Outcast joining them, they made their way through the tunnels towards a large room. This room was of simple design, with a massive circular table in the middle.

The leaders all began taking seats. There were only enough for them, and anyone they brought with them had to remain standing behind their respective leader. Most of those brought to the meeting were elderly. Pagar would have probably done something similar by choosing the wisest of the group, but his pickings were slim and Sileena's and Dorren's experience with Sileena's father were needed.

Silence fell as the leader of the Underground they were in gestured for quiet.

"You have all been called here to discuss the wars between Duka and Eceriden, and now this attack on us."

A couple of others looked a bit puzzled. One of them spoke up.

"I thought the war was over. Duka lost and the balance has remained intact."

Wow, thought Dorren. This man is a little bit behind. But judging by the expressions on the faces of the rest of them, they all seemed to be in the same position. He probably would not have known the situation himself if Lockarr had not filled him in. Lockarr was an idiot and overconfident to do that. He thought the exits were all secured and Dorren would not get away. A mistake that he had better pay dearly for.

"That war is over but it would appear that this has all been a ruse. The forest barbarians to the east have all been united by some dark sorcerer, who has already taken Duka and is now on the march north to Eceriden. Their army, from what I have been told," the leader added, turning to Pagar, "is even larger than the one Duka used against Eceriden."

The other leaders all took in the shock of what they had heard. They did appear smart enough to realise what this would mean for the rest of the world. The leader of this Underground continued to explain the events of the wars and the attack on Pagar's Underground, or the Nectus Underground as they called it. But goodness knows why they called it that, thought Dorren. He always just referred to it as home.

The other leaders all remained silent and listened as the events of the last two days were told. Dorren could not help but wonder what these people were going to do. He was glad he was not in their position because the odds seemed to be completely against them.

Once the story was finished the other leaders began their arguments one by one.

"We should fight. Raise an army and use it against these barbarians."

"But we don't have an army. We might be able to raise a couple of thousand soldiers but what can that do to help?"

It was a fair question, thought Dorren. And where would they march? Would they try to retake their home, or would they march against the forces of this sorcerer? As Dorren tried to come up with a solution he realised that he had had a sudden change of attitude. Previously, in any situation, he would have said, 'fight'. Frankly he would have packed a bag and gone off himself. Well, that was certainly growth. But perhaps to fight was the best option. It was the only option. An army was going to singlehandedly take on the world, and it was going to win. They had to fight with what they had. There was nothing more they could do than that, even if it was a losing battle.

The other leaders seemed to be in agreement with what Dorren was thinking. Most concurred that they had to do something. Taking back the Underground was a very doable task, but what did this accomplish in the long run? They had to march against Sileena's father Nerida, and stop him before he could do any more damage.

The talks also progressed this way.

"We must cut the head off the snake. If we can kill this sorcerer, then the barbarians should quickly disband. Without a ruler they would break off into groups again and fight amongst each other."

Now that was a plan. The best anyone could think of. But Dorren knew what this meant, and looked at the girl standing next to him. The one with a father who everyone was talking about killing, and how best to do it.

"Sileena?" Dorren quietly said.

Sileena, who had her face to the ground, raised her head to look at him. She was sad but not crying, nor showing any signs of holding back tears. It just showed that these events had made her stronger. She gave a weak smile in an effort to hide her pain, but Dorren knew this was not easy for her. Her brother had been killed by her father in an attempt to kill him. The same father who destroyed her home and killed so many people, just to possibly get to her and him. Was there any way to avoid this? Dorren didn't know. Maybe this whole thing could have been avoided if he had never gone to that town and never kidnapped Sileena. Then things would have never changed. But then he would not have fallen in love. Was it worth it?

"Sileena? Is it because of what I did? Because I took you? Did it drive the man to do this?"

Sileena had little time to say anything as Pagar had clearly been listening. He quickly turned on his chair while the others were in deep conversation, and kicked Dorren in the leg.

"Oi!" exclaimed Dorren, looking at Pagar with befuddlement.

"It was not either of your faults. You need to pay attention to the circumstances. Just think about it. Lockarr was in the Underground following Nerida's instructions long before your little interference. This plan was in the making for a long time. I also did a little more digging into the man once I found out what he was doing."

Dorren was intrigued, as was Sileena.

"What did you find?"

"Well, it turns out he was actually proven to be good leader, which was why he was given the title of a noble. He set reasonable taxes and built many things for the community. But his wife died in childbirth with you, Sileena. It was not your fault, remember that. But after that incident nothing was heard from Nerida for a long time, and by the time he resurfaced he had changed. Higher taxes, and no more mentions of anything he did for his people. It was also a little later that Lockarr arrived to help with the creation of our Underground."

Dorren took time to consider this. It made complete sense. Nerida was a man obsessed. He treated his son well, but not his daughter. It was nothing to do with gender but rather that he blamed Sileena for the death of the woman he loved. A woman he was so close to that her death drove him over the edge of sanity. So he filled the void by taking the world. It was certainly a big goal.

"You understand now?" Pagar asked.

Dorren nodded, as did Sileena, who still looked sad.

"Sileena, what happened to your mother was not your fault. Did you intentionally do anything, or did you even know what was happening?"

Sileena shook her head.

"Right, so I will hear no more of blaming yourself. The people under my control are only a fraction of what they were because of this man and Lockarr. I blame them, and certainly not you. If I can see that then you bloody well can too."

And that was Dorren's father. There was a man to admire. It only took him nearly twenty years to see that. A proud moment. Pagar went to turn around, but quickly faced Sileena again.

"Sileena. You understand what is being discussed here. Are you fine with what is being planned?"

Sileena gave him a pained look that said it all. "I'm not OK with it but I understand that it must be done." The poor girl. Nerida may have been one of the worst scum, but he was still her father. Her last blood relative. There was no other way to stop this. Both Sileena and Dorren saw that there was no reasoning with the man. He was over the edge and there could be no coming back. It was either him or the world. But as far as Lockarr was concerned, no one was going to be in any sort of disagreement about killing that man. Pagar nodded in acknowledgement at what Sileena said.

"Also, I believe we are about to go to war." Pagar paused for a moment as he considered how to word his next statement. "You hold so much power, but I'm not sure if you are the sort of person who could take a life. Would you like to keep people shielded from harm, and heal those that are injured? Anna's father can teach you how," he said, turning to Anna, who was standing at the other side of Dorren. The girl had not said a word. That surprised him. He would have thought she'd have something to say, but she, like him, was deep in thought.

"Thank you," Sileena said shyly. She was still speaking to Pagar as if he were her father; someone she had to obey without question. It would take a little while for this to change. She was still concerned. How could she not be? The council meeting here was discussing the best ways to kill her father while asking her for help. But Dorren would not discuss the matter until he and Sileena were alone and they could talk about it properly. The council meeting was not the right place to do it. Pagar seemed satisfied with Sileena's reply and turned back to the discussion.

Time progressed, and it soon became clear that all matters were closed. Every leader was to return and recruit as many soldiers as were willing to fight. They would converge at the borders of the Outcasts Land and together they would march to the aid of Eceriden and their allies. But by the end of the meeting, everyone looked grim. They knew this fight was going to be difficult at best. They would number no more than a couple of thousand, plus whatever was left of Eceriden's forces. They would be up against the largest army in all the lands. Victory seemed slim at best, and everyone knew it. The leaders that were able would lead their own troops. But they knew that they were asking for their lives. Most, if not all, would not return.

The council had left, with Sileena and Dorren managing to get out of the hall and into one of the passages. Now he had his chance to speak.

"Sileena, what is it that you want?"

Sileena seemed a little taken aback by the question. "I...I..." Her surprise turned to puzzlement. Perhaps he should have been a little more specific.

"What do you wish to do between now and what's to come? Do you wish to join the battle? Or would you prefer to remain here?"

Sileena now seemed to regain her senses, and looked to the floor. "I...I don't want this. This is not fair."

Dorren was in complete agreement. This was not fair. It was far from fair. The whole world was going to hell because one man could not deal with grief. So everyone else had to suffer too. Dorren did not know what to say. So he did what his senses told him to do and took her hands in his. Why would Nerida be driven to do this to the world?

247

Why did people have to suffer for something that had nothing to do with them? But Dorren changed his perspective. As Pagar said, they could not change this. They did not know how things would play out, and they believed they were making the right choices. People could not change what had happened. So the next question was, what now?

"This is not fair, but what has passed cannot be changed. What is important is what we do now."

Sileena held him close at this statement. A statement that Dorren was shocked he had uttered. Did he just let out a little bit of wisdom? Pagar was really beginning to rub off on him. Oh great, was he going to be one of those overbearing sods who preach the rules? This had better not happen.

"Sileena," called Anna, who was moving in between people to get to them. Dorren and Sileena parted as they greeted their new arrival. "Sileena, we need to get you to my dad right away to learn healing magic. This usually takes years of practice but you have to learn the basics in a little more than a day."

Sileena was never going to learn healing magic in a day, and she and Anna seemed to know this. She was going to have to learn throughout the journey as well. And what about the question Dorren asked? Sileena seemed to know this too, as she looked to Dorren and then turned back to Anna.

"Actually, I don't want to learn healing magic. But could you teach me how to use shield magic?"

Shield magic? Was she going to fight? That would certainly be amazing, as her power could vaporise many men. Pagar knew this but would not ask, as he knew it was not fair to ask this of Sileena.

Anna also looked a little confused. Sileena was not the kind of person who could take a life. "Wait, are you wanting to fight?"

Sileena turned to Dorren. "Dorren, are you going into the battle?" It was a pretty obvious answer, but he guessed she just needed to hear him say it.

"Yes, I will be joining the fight." He was one of their best fighters, and would be cowardly and selfish if he didn't step up now of all times. Sileena nodded; then turned back to Anna.

"No, I don't want to kill. But I don't want to learn healing magic. I want to stay with Dorren. I will be the one who shields as many soldiers at the front as possible, along with Dorren."

This was what Sileena wanted? She would be in amongst the fighting, shielding himself and his allies from harm. To be shielded from the most powerful magic user known was certainly a nice thought. But being shielded throughout the biggest fight of his life by someone who had only learned shielding magic a day or so earlier was not so appealing. It was a little more complicated than elemental control. Shields were created out of nothing, while the elements were right there to manipulate – two slightly different kinds of magic. Then again, healing was by far more difficult and so if Pagar thought she could learn that then she should certainly be able to learn shielding magic. Her talents should allow her to pick it up quite quickly. She picked up elemental control incredibly fast. She pretty much got it right away, and summoned a massive wave that would have been beyond even Pagar's ability.

Anna took a moment for it to sink in. "OK, I will teach you. Let's go now." She took Sileena's hand and started pulling her down one hall, then the next, to the new Underground's own training grounds. It was not as grand as their own but seemed to serve its purpose well enough.

Dorren sat at the side while Anna tried to explain how to use the mind to manipulate barriers from nothing. It took a little time for Sileena to grasp the concept. Nobody got it straight away. Dorren observed for a time but was approached by a few others who pulled him in to join their own training. He made short work of them in the ring, managing to floor each of the men in turn. As Dorren beat each of his opponents he thought back his encounter with Lockarr. Despite his skill, Lockarr had still managed to keep him desperately at the ropes. Dorren was going to lose his next fight with Lockarr. He had not been able to compete against the man he usually managed to thwart in the training grounds. Lockarr had cunningly kept his skill to himself. However, how he did this was unknown to Dorren. Why even bother to hide it? It was not out of fear of getting caught, as his fighting skills had nothing to do with his disguise. It might have been because he was having fun with the role he played. No point in thinking about it now. Better to focus on the training at hand.

"No, no, you're not doing it right," said Anna as she continued to verse Sileena in the ways of shielding magic. Sileena was still trying and had progressed unbelievably far over the past few hours. But Anna was not really a teacher. Her patience was not ideal for that line of work. If it had been anyone else she would have given up by now. However, Sileena was definitely excelling. Despite this Anna was still losing patience with her. Poor girl, thought Dorren, but he was too busy delivering his own lessons, trying to explain positions and sword movements in battle. The problem was, it came down to body memory. Keep at it and your body acted faster than your mind. Hence those that were the best did not need to think about what movements they were doing most of the time. That being said, most would not reach that level so these men should not have to worry about that too much.

After a while Dorren began to lose concentration. They had been on the field for hours. Even he was losing the will to remain. Yet as he turned he saw Anna and Sileena still going at it. They probably would have stopped but this was of great importance for the coming fight, so even Anna was determined to make sure Sileena was going to get it right. But by this point Sileena had managed to create the barriers and Anna was firing all manner of magic that hit the invisible shield. The blasts gradually increased in size and power, as everyone in the arena stepped back and watched what was happening.

"Just say for me to stop the moment you feel yourself start to weaken!" yelled Anna as her power gradually increased. The girl stopped firing elemental blasts and switched to pure energy ones that were a lot more powerful, as they used focused magic rather than manipulation of elements. But each strike hit the barrier and disappeared, merely doing a little damage to the ground on Anna's side of the barrier.

"I will let you know!" yelled Sileena in reply as she remained focused on the task at hand. Anna's power progressed further than that of most magic users. It eventually exceeded anything that Dorren had ever seen. Even Pagar had never displayed such power before. Pagar was more powerful, but he never really pushed himself as Anna was doing right now. The girl was second only to him in their Underground. The other Undergrounds also knew of Anna by name as one of the most powerful magic users in the whole of the Outcasts' Land. And here she was unleashing, from what Dorren could tell, her full force. The ground on Anna's side had caught fire and cracks formed as the floor began to crumble. Each strike created a shockwave that could be felt through the whole training grounds. But Sileena's barrier did not waver. A few more seconds passed and it was clear Anna had reached her limits, firing the last remnants of energy before stopping and putting her hand on her thighs, trying to regain her breath.

"Can I stop?" shouted Sileena, remaining quite still.

"Yes, you can stop!" replied Anna, still breathing heavily and straightening herself out. "I think we are done for the day. You seem to have it down, although you should keep practising until the fight."

"OK," said Sileena, who was walking quite calmly towards Anna. Dorren still struggled to grasp the situation. Sileena was not even fazed by Anna's full power. No gasping for air or even the slightest bead of sweat.

An individual's energy slowly depleted depending on the amount of power they had. The more magical potential, the slower your energy drained when you use power. And shielding magic took more energy out of the user than the attacker. So Sileena used more power than Anna did while holding out against her magical blasts and was still unfazed by it. Yes, Dorren's safety in the fight was very much secured. He would just have to make sure he did the same for Sileena. She would have her own personal barrier but he was not going to let anyone get near her. He would make sure of that.

Once Anna caught her breath she gave Sileena a pat on the back and decided to turn in, unsurprisingly. She had used power beyond any-thing Dorren had seen in his life. It was her full potential and any more would have caused her to collapse. Dorren approached Sileena, who was standing alone in the middle of the training grounds. She appeared deep in thought. Everyone else in the room had stopped observing the situ-ation and decided to continue their business. Dorren could hear one of the conversations. It was hopeful. They were thinking that with people like Sileena and Anna on their side they stood a very good chance. Their ignorance was showing with their hopeful faces, Dorren thought, considering that even with Sileena they were outmatched. But let them feel this hope. What would be the point in setting them straight?

Giving Sileena a touch on her shoulder brought the girl back to the present. Looking at Dorren, she beamed and together they made their way to the food hall. He was hungry and exhausted. Sileena was a little quieter, and this was saying something.

Throughout the time walking and eating Sileena only said a couple of things to Dorren, but the rest of the time she seemed to be in thought. What was going through her mind? Something was bothering her. She appeared to be trying figure something out.

"Sileena, what's the matter? You have been daydreaming all evening."

Sileena looked at Dorren with the same questioning look she had worn since the time in the training grounds.

"Dorren, I have an idea. You have to go with me on this, OK?"

Oh, Sileena was serious. Whatever it was sounded important, and it had clearly been on her mind all day.

"OK." This was Sileena. The girl was clever and not prone to doing anything stupid. He would agree to anything.

He was wrong. This was a bad idea. A very bad idea.

He and Sileena were about to die, and for no good reason.

Even Pagar said it was a bad idea when they spoke to him. It took hours to convince him to let them go. And here they were on the edge of the forest and making their way inside, alone. How the hell did she talk him into doing this? Why did he say it was OK? Whatever the reason was, he would not have to wonder about it for long because even his skill and Sileena's magic were not going to get them out of this one.

Dorren could see the sun rising as they made their way into the forest, continuing onwards and avoiding the sanctuaries and lifts to the walkways above. The trees towered higher and soon the sun disappeared behind the leaves. Dorren had to supress a sigh. I never wanted to die fighting for the world anyway, he thought. I always wanted to go while being eaten by a giant wolf. He kind of hoped Sileena had been joking this entire time and that she was merely making their escape and never coming back. Of course it was spineless but at least then they would not be embarking on this suicidal mission.

Why would Sileena even come up with this idea? She would not kill anyone herself so she had to find a way to use her powers in a different way. But this was suicide.

As they made their way further than any point that Dorren had ever passed before, he could see the forest start to change. It became darker and drearier. The place felt alive as the darkness moved. It was as if something was watching him the entire time. Like a wolf was ready to lunge at them. Was this a figment of his imagination?

Oh come on, get a grip. Here was this girl calmly walking through the trees and he was almost having a fit. If she could do it then he could. Dorren could not see the sun but if he had to make a guess he would have thought that the Outcasts would all be on the march to the assembly at the borders, where they would stay together until they reached the battlefield. Hopefully they could get there in time as it was rumoured that Sileena's father had been on the move for a while. Eceriden might already have fallen. No point in thinking that. You must work with what you had been dealt, and Sileena's idea might have been suicide but it's all they had right now.

By this point the two of them were basically lost. The only option was to keep moving forward. Leaving without saying goodbye to anyone except Pagar may have been a bit harsh but he assumed that the others would have reacted similarly to what Dorren was thinking, and time was important. They could not get everyone and tell them they were leaving, let alone spend the hours convincing them that it was a good idea.

Dorren thought over this for a while before he came to the sudden realisation. No one had seen these wolves. He'd only heard rumours of their size and number, and their leader Vartak. Perhaps this was just a story. Perhaps there were no giant wolves within this forest. Granted, their quest would be fruitless but the thought was a rather appealing one. It would be nice not to be eaten. But then Dorren came to a sudden stop, with Sileena bumping into him from behind. No, of course he was wrong. This little glimmer of hope and they dashed it away immediately.

Appearing from between the trees in front of them came the dark eyes of a massive creature. A great wolf. So they were real. There was just one of them, and right now it was casually smiling at them. Well, it would be classed as a smile if it had been a human making that gesture. Yes, that was definitely an 'I'm about to eat you' look.

A moment passed as they stared at each other. If Dorren moved, then the beast would lunge. If he just stood still, then he would have a few more moments to live before the animal sprang. He could hear it snarling, and make out the outline of fur all over its body.

He made a slow movement, lifting his sword ready for the strike, but at that moment Sileena moved past, slowly approaching the creature. The wolf looked at Sileena and started snarling at her, but the snarl quickly disappeared. The beast then turned around and walked back into the trees. This was a good sign, thought Dorren. It actually worked. He saw Sileena turn and give him a confident look before following the wolf into the trees. This could be accomplished, thought Dorren hopefully, his sense of imminent demise reducing. He started to wonder why he was thinking like a coward, feeling this constant fear of death? He had never been scared to singlehandedly sneak into a town, nor fight to the death with any person. But for some reason this was making him much more uncomfortable. He could feel his fears slowly subside and then quickly rise as he took in his surroundings once again.

Exiting into a clearing, he could make out the silhouettes of many beasts all staring at him and Sileena. This opening was massive but the sunlight could still not be seen. The branches from the trees stretched out and covered them, leaving a dark, haunting feel. And they were now into the den of the great wolves.

There were so many of them appearing. Twenty, fifty, one hundred at least. And those were the ones that were currently within the den. The forest could stretch for miles in either direction. It was big enough to host thousands of them. The thought unsettled him. But he didn't have time to think about it as he followed Sileena into the den. The wolves around them seemed ready to attack, but one by one they stopped and just stood there, watching them with their piercing gaze. Having all those eyes on him was unnerving.

After a moment of taking in their surroundings they eventually came to a stop at the bottom of a small hill with a cave at the top. From within the cave came a growl that would have scared most creatures away. But looking forward, Dorren could see Sileena with her determined expression. She was ready to face whatever came out. He would be too.

At first the giant jaw of the creature emerged from the shadows, followed by the black eyes and the pointed ears. As the rest of the body came into view Dorren was lost for words. It wasn't as though he was speaking anyway, but he couldn't have if he'd tried. Vartak was real. Whatever started the rumours about this creature, they were true. This thing was bigger than a warhorse and completely covered in fur. It looked just like a normal wolf, just a lot bigger. But it was looking directly at Sileena and had its fangs on full display and slowly approaching her. Sileena seemed to be trying to focus. Regaining his wits, Dorren turned to Sileena.

"What's wrong?"

"It's the creature. It was formed by magic. I can feel it. It's making it hard for me to get into its mind."

This was bad. Its fangs remained on display, and it was now certainly within leaping distance. Sileena was the most powerful magic user Dorren had ever known. She could control it. But another second or so and things looked bad. The wolf was still snarling, and crouched as if preparing to attack. Dorren was going to have to try and kill the creature. Getting his sword ready, he stepped past Sileena and raised the blade to strike the beast in whatever futile attempt he could make. The creature noticed however, and made its move towards Dorren with lightning speed.

"Stop!" cried Sileena, and the wolf stopped as fast as it had attacked, causing Dorren to stumble. What? The creature turned to Sileena and slowly stepped next to her, with its teeth no longer on

255

display. Dorren recomposed himself as Sileena stepped forward.

"Are you OK?" she asked, reaching for him. Dorren's fear soon ebbed at the sight of Vartak's calm demeanour.

"Yes, I'm fine," he replied, still getting over what had happened, and looking at the now-calm animal. Sileena pulled Dorren in and kissed him. She had done it.

The great wolf gave a startling howl, which brought the two of them back to the task at hand.

"It worked?"

Sileena beamed. "Yes, it worked. Thank you for believing in me."

Dorren would not have called it believing in her, given that he was scared out his wits the entire time and sure they were about to die. But then again, she didn't know that, although she seemed to notice what he was thinking.

"You came when you could have stopped me. You did believe me."

Dorren gave her a warm smile, but was forced into reality again as the wolf gave another rattling howl.

"What is it doing?"

His answer came to him as he heard other howls in the distance.

"He is calling the rest of them back. They will follow me now. Let's go and meet up with the others."

Dorren nodded in agreement. This had actually succeeded. There was hope now. Sileena had in one day accumulated an army of her own. It may only be a couple of hundred but they were giant wolves.

Let's see what the barbarians have in preparation for that.

# 15

# TO WAR

Dreams could be so nice it was sometimes a shame to wake up. But waking up to something exciting after a relatively average dream was even better. This happened to be one of those days.

Taking a moment to take in his surroundings, Lockarr could make out the tent he was in. He could also see the movement outside as the barbarian soldiers prepared for battle. After finally giving up on trying to get Sileena and Dorren he thought it best to take the barbarians to join the battle ahead. He was certainly not going to miss this. Such slaughter, and if he could not be a part of it then he would be a very disappointed man.

He remained in bed for a moment, staring at the ceiling of the tent, before hearing faint noises coming from a silver dish nearby. He was finally calling. Lockarr had a lot of patience, considering he had played ignorant throughout his time in the Underground. But the difference was, that was fun. Waiting for the call from Nerida was not fun. There was no manipulation and no killing. Just sitting and waiting to be told to join the fight. Taking the dish, he gazed at it and the face of Nerida appeared with that same hot-tempered look about him. It was something Lockarr did not understand. What was the point of all this anger? Like sadness and fear, anger baffled him. However, it was always rather amusing to see it on other people.

"Ah, Lord Nerida. I was beginning to think you were not going to call. So are the forces ready to meet?"

"That is King Nerida to you. And I will meet with what remains of the Eceriden forces later today. Now, have you got my daughter and killed that barbarian scum?"

Lockarr took a moment to think about his excitement at the upcoming battle before realising that the man had asked him a question.

"Oh, I could not find them. A few others also somehow disappeared—"

"What?!" Nerida had no manners, interrupting him like that. "Why have you not done as I commanded?!"

And there he goes again. He has a bad habit of getting angry too quickly.

"They got out somehow. I suspect they had a secret way out that I didn't know about. I can search for them after the battle."

Nerida was losing control of his temper fast. The guy seemed to get angry at anything these days. He was going to blow at some point.

"Well then, go after them! Hunt them! I want her brought back, and this Dorren she was with dead!"

"I'm afraid I can't. I do not have enough men to attack another Underground."

"Another Underground? How many are there?"

"Oh, I'm not quite sure. I think there might be around ten."

"Why did you not tell me this?!"

"You never asked."

Nerida was starting to go red by this point. "You idiot! It is obviously information that I needed to hear! You will take your men and march them back to those Undergrounds, and seize each of them now!"

Lockarr was not going to do that. Besides it being impossible with the numbers available, there was no insider to open the gates like last time. It would be like attacking a fortress, and this time the Undergrounds would be prepared. They were not getting any more. It was just going to have to wait for now. Besides, he was not going to miss this fight. He had forgotten how interesting it was to see something sharp go through people.

"I am not missing this battle. We can get your daughter and kill whoever you like after you have taken the kingdom."

"You dare speak to me like that? You will do as I command! Do you forget that with simple point of my finger I could disintegrate you?!"

No, Lockarr did not forget. He just didn't care. The sorcerer couldn't do anything given the distance between them. Even with his immense power he could not reach what he could not see. Besides, Nerida looked like he was about to explode. Lockarr was curious as to whether he could tip this man over the edge.

"I'm not going back. I will join the fight with what's left of the soldiers."

It was an interesting idea to fight and kill Dorren, whom he had amusingly tricked for many years. Him and the rest of the Underground. But he had already killed most of them. The rest could wait until afterwards.

"I will be the ruler of the world, and you still refuse me! I will execute you if you don't obey me!"

Perhaps just a little more.

"Oh come on, don't be like that. I thought I could be like the son you accidentally killed."

Yeah, that did it.

"I am going to kill you! The moment I see you I am going to turn you into nothing! You will wish you had never existed!"

Well, you're apparently going to turn me into the very thing I want to be. The guy had completely lost it, and was not making any kind of sense. But Nerida was still going on. Something about ripping him apart. Lockarr made his way out of the tent where a man was standing guard.

"Excuse me, could you take this and bury it in the ground somewhere?"

The confused man took the dish. Nerida was still ranting on it, clearly not noticing what Lockarr had done.

"Thank you." Lockarr then went back into his tent and sighed. Well, if he went into battle and was seen by Nerida he would be killed immediately. But he really wanted to join the slaughter and nothing was going to keep him away from it. If he was going to die then perhaps he

259

should leave Nerida with a funny last retort. Maybe something along the lines of 'I'm going to have fun with your wife in the afterlife.' Yes, that should annoy him.

Right then. Time to see if nobles react in the same way normal people do when they are stabbed by my sword, he thought. Never stabbed a noble before. Should be interesting.

The march was a relatively quiet one. It was not a time to be happy. Most of these people were not battle-hardened, and even if the upcoming fight was successful many would not return. Derain looked around at the entire Outcast force. He had wondered what kind of army they could assemble when brought together. It was not nearly as impressive a sight as he was hoping. They were not even dressed for war. Armour was minimal and the Outcasts looked like a mesh of people dotted all over the place, no lines of people marching in unison. And to make matters worse, their trump card and arguably their best fighter had run off on a little errand and not made an appearance, despite the army now being well within Eceriden territory. Well, an errand was all that Master Pagar would tell Derain. It would not surprise him if Pagar had sent them to safety to live out their lives in solitude. But this was Dorren he was thinking about. He would never abandon his friends in this kind of situation. Dorren would be the first one into the thick of the fighting. But when the two of them had not returned Derain couldn't help but feel anxious. Even the scout party had returned and were leading them to where they had spotted the enemy.

When they grouped with the rest of the Outcasts at the borders of their territory, one of the leaders gave a wonderful speech about preventing the end of the world, or something to that effect. Then off they went, ready for whatever faced them. But that was a while ago and now the dread started to sink in. The inspirational speech should have come a little later so that their spirits were at their peak for the fight. He looked to see Gabe and Anna riding horses side by side, with serious expressions on their faces. If only things could have gone back to the way they were; just a group of friends who enjoyed each other's company, and Derain could hit on all the girls he wanted. It was true that in his own Underground he had hit on every girl around his age and a couple that were a little older. But what about adventures in the other Undergrounds? That would be like a whole new world. He only had a brief chance to explore when they found sanctuary and he'd met a girl called Naria. They were both heading for the fight and so decided to look out for one another, spending what could be one last night together.

He turned back to Anna and Gabe, finding their relationship a little strange. They were so committed to each other. Relationships were not his kind of thing but perhaps they could be some day, although not right now. However, Naria needed someone and he was happy to look out for her in the fight. The whole group were planning to stick together. Naria had her own family but all were either too young, too old or just too unfit to fight. So she and a couple of her comrades were on their own, and obviously they were scared.

However, who knew? If they both made it out alive then perhaps there would be some 'we survived the battle' sex afterwards. Yes, he would like that.

Soon the marching noises of the Outcasts mingled with another sound. It was the sound of metal hitting metal. Derain could hear the battle but he could not see where it was taking place. The sounds were coming from over a hill. It must be the Eceriden forces and the barbarians meeting on the battlefield. They were there. Climbing the hill did not take long but it felt like a lifetime.

It must be the calm before the storm; the same kind of feeling as when someone jumps from a high place. Time just feels like it's slowing down.

When they reached the top he could take in the full scope of what they were up against.

They could see a massive battle taking place as the Eceriden forces kept themselves in a tight formation, holding back the onslaught of barbarians with whatever they could. It appeared that their allies were also trying desperately to hold the formation. Whatever they were doing was working for now. They could easily make out who were the enemy and who were their friends. It was obvious that the

Eceriden forces were in tight formation, with more experience and with better equipment. But they were heavily outnumbered and desperately holding out.

One of the Underground leaders stepped in front of the Outcasts and looked back to the crowd. Derain could make out Pagar at the front, listening to what the man was about to say. It was a little strange as Derain was used to Pagar being the one to step forward and take the lead. But that was at their own Underground. When it came to the hierarchy of the Underground leaders, such tasks must fall to whomever they thought best qualified. Apparently this man was the most qualified. "Hear me!" His voice was amplified by magic; probably his own.

How many of the leaders were not actually magic users, wondered Derain. Magic users always got special treatment, he thought.

"The enemy stands before us on the brink of victory. Should they succeed they will singlehandedly take over this land, and it will not be long before we become their target. But we will not let this happen! We will stand strong and protect our world! Protect our home! No one will take this away!"

A cheer came from the crowd. It was not as inspirational as the speech before they left but it was enough to renew everyone's determination.

"Try to remain at a distance from the Eceriden forces. They do not yet know we are on their side! Now ride with me to war!"

Another cheer from the crowd, and the man turned his horse and stampeded towards the enemy. Well, he was certainly one to lead by example as he alone raced towards the enemy. But it worked, as everyone started charging towards the battle. Those that were on horses such as Derain, Anna and Gabe were all ahead, getting ready to smash into the enemy lines. Most of the troops that were on foot were chasing from behind. They were probably relieved not to be the first ones into battle. Those that were on horseback were deemed to be the best fighters and magic users.

In the distance Derain could see the barbarians at the back notice this new force racing towards them. Their confusion was clear as they were all over the place, trying to gather themselves for the oncoming fight. Some seemed to think the Outcasts were friends, while others tried to retreat further into the crowd. The rest desperately tried to prepare themselves for the fight. But it was too late, as the horses galloped too fast for them to react. A couple of spears were thrown, but most of the barbarian archers, if indeed there were any, must have been towards the Eceriden side as they were not expecting a charge from the rear. Magical blasts from the riders in front struck a few of the barbarians that were readying themselves, blasting them back or apart. The cavalry hit the barbarians' line, which could be heard across the battlefield. Then came the sounds of steel against steel, or steel penetrating flesh.

Derain swerved out a bit to strike at his first enemy with his sword. The momentum of the horse and the speed of his arm allowed the sword to move quite easily through the barbarian's skull. Derain managed to cut through two more before his speed was hampered by sheer numbers around him. Swinging his sword left and right, he managed to strike two more out of the way. Whether or not he killed them he did not care, as he was being mobbed and had veered off from the rest of the group. He needed to get back to the main troop. But as he tried to turn back one of the barbarians managed to swing his weapon into Derain's horse, causing it to collapse to the ground. Derain rolled away and quickly regained his composure, drawing his other sword. Two men lunged at him and he quickly used one sword to deflect and the other to strike back, killing them both. But then another five charged, with all manner of weapons. Derain had rapidly adopted a defensive position in preparation for the onslaught, when three of the barbarians were blasted apart one by one. Derain quickly killed another, while a giant axe cleaved the remaining man's head off. Derain turned, and to his joy saw Anna and Gabe, along with a couple of other Outcasts as they joined his side.

"Don't go running off, Derain," exclaimed Anna. "You're going to get yourself killed."

Derain smiled but did not have enough time to deliver a comeback, as more barbarians were on them. The fight was not going to last long as the barbarians were about to overwhelm them. But it was at that point when the Outcasts on foot charged into the enemy lines. After the rest of the Outcasts joined them they were pushing the barbarians back through sheer brutality. It was actually rather admirable that the Outcasts were capable of such ferocity.

A few more barbarians attacked and were made short work of. When working as a team Anna, Gabe and Derain were almost unstoppable. Two more came at Derain. He stabbed one, but before the other reached him a sword stabbed the brute through the chest from behind. As the man fell to the ground, Derain saw Naria walk up to him and she hit him across the face.

"We are supposed to look out for each other!"

"I'm sorry. I was pulled away by unforeseen forces. It won't happen agai—" Derain was silenced as she pulled him in for a passionate kiss. He wasn't complaining but was this really appropriate in the middle of a battle?

"If you two are quite finished," exclaimed Anna, "could you help as my lover seems to be doing all the work?"

Derain pulled away from Naria and turned to see that Anna was not wrong. Gabe was wielding his massive axe like a feather, cleaving though multiple men with unreal speed and picking up others and throwing them into the surrounding battle. Derain took inspiration from Gabe and joined in the action, with Naria coming from behind and Anna defending the rear with multiple elemental blasts against those foolish enough to attack her.

The fight seemed to be going well. The Outcasts were fighting their way through the barbarians with minimal losses as they were looking out for each other; more so than their opponents, who seemed to go with a philosophy of 'every man for himself'. Derain could make out Pagar blasting his way through enemies with ease and precision. A couple of the other Outcasts from their own Underground were with him, such as Severa's brother. But in his admiration of the fight he was witnessing, a couple of barbarians were on top of Derain without him noticing until it was almost too late. Quickly wielding his dual sword, he cut through them, but didn't see the one that swung his sword from behind, striking Derain on the head. The sword shattered and Derain turned quickly, stabbing the man in the chest.

"Derain, would you pay attention?" cried Anna. "Shields drain power quickly so could you please avoid being hit, or so help me, I will remove my shield on you." She was joking of course, but harsh. Even in the midst of battle she was able to slag him off. Typical of her. But no more distractions from now on, as he kept close to the others. The barbarians seemed to be falling further and further back and things were looking good for a while, but it was not long before their adversaries were attacking with renewed effort, and what was a slow push became a deadlock. The cause was a particular barbarian who was yelling out orders. The man was rather large, wielding dual swords like Derain and wearing a red band on his head. There were just a few barbarians between Derain and that man, so if he could take him out then they could go back on the offensive.

"Anna! Gabe! Naria! I need a hand!"

They turned to see Derain charge off into the barbarians, slicing away. Gabe quickly jumped to his side, swinging his axe through multiple men as Anna avoided firing any magical blasts unless they became necessary, but Derain kept moving and was soon upon the barbarian, delivering two fast thrusts with his dual swords, whereupon the barbarian quickly countered and stepped back. For a moment the two of them circled each other. This man was much bigger than Derain, and obviously stronger, but Derain would just have to work that to his advantage. The barbarian quickly ordered his other men around them to attack the Outcasts who were trying to come to Derain's aid. At least the man had some sort of honour to fight Derain one on one. But Derain suspected he was just confident of victory. Both wielding dual swords in a battle stance, they jumped upon each other. One attack followed by counter, followed by another. The swords were spinning between the two and could hardly be seen as they swung them about in expert motion.

The barbarian thrust his sword towards Derain's head and Derain used his speed to his advantage, ducking and cutting the man's leg. The man ignored this and proceeded to kick Derain back and stab him again. Derain regained his composure, leapt to the side and tried to strike the barbarian. But the man countered and started swinging more aggressively. Stepping back for a few strikes and countering those that he could not avoid, Derain could not really see a pattern. The man was going for brute strength over skill. Waiting for his opportunity, he took another point to stab at the barbarian's leg and managed to cut the other one. The barbarian leapt at him, while Derain maintained his speed advantage and dodged, making a few more jabs and managing to stab him in the side. The barbarian, now in a rage, swung his sword sideways. Derain ducked once more, and with a spinning motion cut the barbarian across the chest and throat. The man snarled and spat out blood, but he kept coming. Derain moved further back to avoid the steel in preparation for another assault. But his opponent stopped striking and spat out more blood before falling to the ground, dead. Derain took a moment to regain his composure.

That's right, I'm the master of the dual swords.

The barbarians noticed what had happened and some started to attack Derain, while others fled. But by this point Derain was ready and his friends were by his side once more, and together they quickly cut through those that tried to strike.

Pagar also joined them in their continued assault, but his expression was grim. "There are too many of them. We are making a dent but we are still heavily outnumbered and we are losing too many Outcasts."

Derain's brief sense of victory quickly collapsed at these words. How are we not doing enough? The Outcasts were constantly pushing the barbarians back, but it was like winning every fight and still losing the war. The barbarians completely outnumbered them. For every fifty barbarians that died a couple of Outcasts would be brought down, but by the end the barbarians would still have won. However, before anyone could reply a loud noise could be heard, unlike anything Derain had heard before.

"Was that a howl?" asked Derain. Pagar's grim expression turned to hope as he turned to find the source of the noise. Derain also followed Pagar's gaze, and in the distance he could make out a howling wolf on top of the hill they had just descended. What a strange sight it was. Just a random wolf howling over the battlefield, and Derain was obviously not the only one to think so as many people around them also seemed to take notice. It was incredible that the howl of the wolf in the distance could carry over the noise of battle. After a moment Derain could make out a figure standing next to the beast, and the answer to Derain's question became clear. This wolf was massive. It towered over the figure looking down upon the battlefield. Another figure appeared next to them.

"Wait? Is that Sileena and Dorren? How did they get that thing?" questioned Derain as a smaller wolf, and then another, strutted over the hill and looked upon the battlefield.

Pagar smiled at the sight. "That is our reinforcements."

What?! How did that happen? What the hell did they do to get those wolves to follow them? It was of course a stupid question as the answer was obvious. Sileena and her immense power. She could even manipulate these beasts. Their little saviour had arrived. By now the hill was completely covered in wolves. For a moment they paused, simply gazing at the slaughter before them. But like the sound of thunder, the wolves went from standing quite still to a full-on rush as they charged down the slope towards them. It was like a tidal wave of dark grey as hundreds of the animals thundered across the plains.

Awe turned to hope and then quickly turned to fear. How the hell were these beasts supposed to determine whom they were meant to kill? It was true that the Outcast and Eceriden forces could differentiate themselves from the barbarians quite easily through their attire alone. But could these giant wolves? Derain did not have time to think as the barbarians started their attack anew, and he was forced to defend himself with the aid of his friends. The thunder could still be heard as the wolves were closing the gap faster than any human ever could. The Outcasts turned in self-defence, as did the barbarians, as the wolves crashed into the battle without flinching.

Derain could not see what was happening but he didn't have to guess for long, as in a matter of seconds some of the wolves had already reached him and his group. They were slashing and biting away at the surrounding barbarians. Their claws tore through them with ease and they continued their rampage forward. A couple of them stopped to look at Derain, Pagar and the others before ignoring them and leaping for the closest barbarian. Well, that certainly answered that question.

The Outcasts around them seemed to notice this too and ignored the wolves, which in turn were ignoring them.

Pagar looked around in renewed hope. "Now we have a chance."

And side by side with the wolves, they continued to press forward. The battle felt like continued success as the dead fell behind them, but Derain knew it was not over yet. The sorcerer had to fall and they were still heavily outnumbered. At first the barbarians fell back at the new threat, trying desperately to break through Eceriden's lines in the hope of escaping the wolves. However, it was not long before the barbarians mounted yet another counterattack, overwhelming a few of the Outcasts and wolves, bringing them down through sheer weight of numbers. They must have been getting their inspiration from another commander, but the problem was that Derain could not see who it was. The individual must be another barbarian, leading from behind like a coward. Or it might be the sorcerer. Derain would prefer to avoid him in that case, as he would probably have stood little chance.

There was a standstill as the group tried to push against the barbarians, but their numbers always forced them take another step back. Anna was starting to tire as she blasted apart a few more of the enemy, and occasionally one of their group took a hit. One barbarian made a clear shot at Naria but Derain managed to cut in and counter the attack. The girl was a reasonable fighter but she should not be this far into the battle. She was not equipped to fight this kind of threat. And she was one of the main causes for Anna tiring, as barbarians were getting in an occasional hit against her.

"Naria, I need you to make your way to the back of the fight."

Naria looked confused. "Why? We are supposed to look out for one another."

"I am looking out for you. You need to be safely out of the brunt of the battle. Anna is tiring from protecting you. Don't worry, the three of us are the best fighters and can look out for ourselves."

Naria gave a slightly hot-tempered look but relinquished control.

Pulling him in for another passionate kiss, she then started to make her way to the rear of the battle where it was safer. That girl had a lot of energy. She certainly could keep up with Derain in almost all aspects except the fighting.

Once she was out of sight he rejoined the front, pushing against the onslaught. A couple of wolves were just in front, tearing away at a few enemy soldiers before chasing after some others who tried to make a break for it, leaving a gap that Derain and the others quickly seized, pushing in and managing to cut through a few unsuspecting enemies. Pagar by this point had disappeared elsewhere, leaving the three of them to continue the fight at their end. However, pushing forward seemed to take its toll on Anna as her efforts to fire at any enemies were slowing to a stop. Gabe noticed this and stood very close, cutting through any enemy that got near her. Derain protected their rear from anyone trying to sneak forward. Naria may be safely at a distance but the damage was already done as all the strikes against her shield had caused Anna to weaken considerably.

"I can't fight anymore," she said wearily as a couple of barbarians lunged at her. Gabe stepped in front, blocking the strikes and making quick work of the foes. Derain knew it was time to make their way back. Without Anna's ability to shield them they were in real danger. Especially in their current situation, being too far into the enemy lines. The moment they were surrounded they would be doomed, even with their skill.

Derain was about to turn back when he saw a familiar figure standing behind a couple of barbarians. A figure he had not seen in some time. Lockarr. The man had joined the battle on the barbarians' side. The bastard was even killing his fellow Outcasts without so much as flinching. Derain found it hard to believe that one of his closest friends had betrayed them, but seeing him now just angered him beyond belief.

In quick succession Derain dove through the two barbarians, slicing their throats as he passed. Lockarr was avoiding the lunge of a giant wolf and sinking his sword into its skull, killing the great beast. Derain seized his opportunity and lashed at the man while his back was turned, but Lockarr turned just in time and parried the blows, kicking Derain back.

"Lockarr!"

Lockarr just tipped his head to the side with a calm sense of curiosity. "It is good to see you too, Derain. I didn't think I would see you here on the battlefield. Are you on Eceriden's side?"

Was the man mocking him, or was he genuinely confused at seeing Derain? Derain didn't know and he didn't care.

"You can't win this one. You backstabbed your way through the Underground but now on the open field you will not get away."

"I did not think I was trying to get away, and I only backstabbed one lady in the stables. Everyone else I fought from the front. I only betrayed the Underground because I was asked to. Those were my orders."

"Orders? You have been with us for years. You were our friend. How could you go against us after all this time?"

The man still had a look of confusion about him. "I don't understand. I just gave you the answer. I was ordered to. This is sounding very much like the conversation I had with Dorren." Lockarr was calm, and his usual self. It was as if he didn't think anything had changed.

"But why would you deceive us for so long? Why did you kill the people closest to you?"

"Because it was interesting. It was fun to see how people react to these circumstances. And look at this chaos. It's like living in a fantasy. Did you know that when you stick a sword into a noble they die the same way as common folk?"

The man was without any remorse.

"I would run if I were you. If I don't kill you someone else from the Underground will. And you can't fight all of us." Derain had almost had enough with these pleasantries. He had beaten Lockarr before and would do so again. But he was alone. Gabe had noticed him standing with Lockarr and tried to get to his aid, but his path was blocked by an overwhelming tide of barbarians that were apparently avoiding Derain and Lockarr. The man even scared them.

"Oh, is the whole Underground here? I thought I saw some people from other Undergrounds. Didn't realise everyone was here though. Perhaps I can finish the task I was set. Although I think Nerida might still kill me even if I complete it now." Lockarr was just casually talking as if nothing was wrong. It was as if he was unaware he was in the middle of a battlefield. "Hey, are these wolves from the forest? How have they ended up here?"

"Yes, because I'm going to tell you." Derain was done, and charged at Lockarr, swinging his swords with expert precision. Lockarr countered one blow then the other, as calm as he had been when speaking. Derain's speed was matched and the two of them began to exchange blows, and then it was over.

"Derain!"

He could hear Gabe screaming across the field. That was strange. Gabe very rarely talked, let alone screamed. What could possibly make him yell like that? It wasn't painful anymore, anyway. The sword through his chest only hurt for a second. Besides, he didn't need to think about the fight anymore. It was actually a very nice day. A shame he was not going to have any 'we survived the battle' sex. He knew they were going to win anyway. Dorren and Sileena had joined the battle, and with all the forces combined he just knew they would win. His work was done. Time to enjoy the nice, sunny day and close his eyes. Close his eyes and dream good dreams.

"Derain!" Gabe cried as he tried desperately to get through the barbarians standing between him and Derain who dropped to the ground and was motionless. Anna was following, but was completely out of power. She could not defend anyone anymore. Gabe's anger drove him to smash his way through the barbarians and towards Lockarr. Lockarr noticed and gave him a smile and a wave. The man was going to die. He was going to die.

Charging forward, Gabe was not far from his target, but just as he was closing in for the kill something hit him hard from the side. Something that made even him stagger.

He quickly turned to see a massive axe almost hit him in the chest, but managed to block it just in time. Taking another step back, Gabe took in the new threat. It was another barbarian; wearing a red band, and big. Bigger even than he was. He did not have time to fight this man as he could see Lockarr behind, watching the unfolding fight with interest. The barbarian swung his axe at Gabe with a speed that few could match. But luckily Gabe could, as he countered the blow and began the struggle of strength against strength. The two swung their great battleaxes in unison as they exchanged blows. Anna, who was behind the man, made one last desperate strike, but only had sufficient magic to push one barbarian back a step before falling to the ground unconscious. Gabe desperately forced his opponent back to try and deal with the other men making their way to kill the unconscious girl. He managed to kill two of the attackers but his adversary was back on him before he could counter, and cut Gabe across the shoulder.

Things were deteriorating fast as Gabe stood alone with barbarians behind, his adversary in front, the woman he loved unconscious on the ground and one of his closest friends lying dead with his killer admiring the view. With one desperate strike he forced the bigger man back once again.

Then came a blast from behind, striking at the barbarians to the side as one of the magic users from another Underground joined the fight along with a few giant wolves and other Outcasts. The tides began to turn back as the barbarians were quickly becoming overrun on this part of the battlefield. Seizing his opportunity, Gabe tried again to get at Lockarr, but the larger barbarian was on him again. Gabe could see Lockarr noticing the new threat and calmly cutting his way through a few opponents before jumping onto a horse. Lockarr gave a genuine smile as he turned and rode away. But he was not riding to join the fighting elsewhere. He was leaving the battlefield, heading towards Duka. Whatever reason he had for doing this would have to wait as Gabe was now fully focused on the man currently beating him.

The two began striking blow after blow, with one or the other occasionally receiving a minor wound. Their attacks would knock any other man off his feet. The two matched each other in strength and speed, but Gabe had skill. He learned his techniques from Derain and Dorren. The battle raged around them as the two kept going at it with rigorous effort.

The barbarian made another swing at Gabe's chest, which Gabe took as his opportunity, countering the strike with the blade. Then, using the handle, he smacked the man square on the face and heard a crunching noise coming from his opponent's nose. The barbarian staggered and tried to regain his balance, but Gabe swung his axe round. His opponent tried to counter too late, and his head came clean off. The body followed the head to the ground and went limp. Having sustained injuries in the fight, Gabe had lost any interest in continuing. Looking at his dead friend, he bowed his head in sorrow. One betrayer and another dead. Where was Dorren? He had better not be dead too.

Turning around, he bent over and picked up the unconscious Anna. She had tried her best. She had no power left and could not protect Derain. She could not even muster the strength to do any more damage. Holding her in his arms, he walked away from the fighting, taking her to safety. If there were any healers left they could help with his wounds and protect Anna. The barbarians were being pushed back yet again and now victory seemed possible. All Gabe could do now was hope that Dorren and Sileena were OK, wherever they were.

It was chaos. Wolves were tearing at the enemy, with a couple of Outcasts desperately holding out against the oncoming tide of barbarians. A few were coming at Dorren with determination on their faces. What they did not know was that their choice was going to be their biggest mistake, as Dorren cut through them without breaking a sweat. Sileena followed close behind, maintaining a shield across the allies within the vicinity. Some needed the protection as they would have been killed. But Dorren didn't need it, as not one barbarian was successfully striking him. With Sileena's protection they were winning easily. Barbarians were falling, while all the allies under her protection were not sustaining so much as a scratch.

Casually wading through the barbarians, Dorren cleaved his way through any who tried to get him. At first when they entered the fight Sileena struggled to cope with witnessing the slaughter, but she was determined and was now handling it a little better. Battlefields like this were not nice. They were brutal. Bloody, muddy and cruel. Before the kidnapping Sileena would have never coped, but the girl had been through so much. These bloodthirsty barbarians would destroy everything if not stopped.

Dorren came to a stop alongside the Eceriden army. Bodies were lying everywhere. The wolves also reached the Eceriden forces, and it appeared that they were leaving each other alone. Good thing the soldiers realised the wolves were on their side. Turning, he could see a couple of soldiers fighting within the barbarian lines who were rapidly becoming overwhelmed. Rushing to their aid, he cut through the barbarians that he ran past but was unable to reach the Eceriden's in time, as one man remained alone, desperately holding out against many of these brutes. But as the barbarians delivered blows that would have killed the man, the attacks instead bounced off an invisible barrier. Dorren joined the fight and together they cut their way through the enemy until the two of them stood alone.

"Thank you, my good man."

Sileena joined them.

"Was that you protecting me?" the man asked Sileena.

She nodded.

The man was completely out of breath. He must have been in the fight since the beginning. "Thank you. If you survive this battle, seek me out. I would like to know the people who saved me."

This man was a noble. Perhaps getting on his good side would be helpful to everyone.

"How?" Dorren asked, wondering how he would find the man after the fight was over.

The noble finally caught his breath. "The name's Kradorin. Ask someone and they will take you to me. You don't look like Eceridens."

"We are not."

Kradorin looked intrigued. "I would love to hear your story. Might make a good poem." And with that the man turned and joined his allies against the barbarians. Dorren could see that the Eceridens looked exhausted, and it appeared that their hopes were severely diminished.

Well, most were. That man Kradorin was an odd one. He seemed full of energy, despite the exhaustion.

"Dorren," Sileena called, dragging his attention back to the fight as a couple more barbarians swung their swords at him. It was incredible that she was still able to maintain her influence over all the wolves and keep shielding the people around her. The shields alone would have taken a great deal out of any other magic user.

Fighting through another wave of barbarians, Dorren wondered where everyone else was. He had not recognised anyone on the field. He knew the Outcasts were on the battlefield as he recognised their attire, but they were from other Undergrounds. They must be at another area of the battle. If he found them then Sileena could keep them all protected. Before he could give it any more thought a barbarian with a red band attacked him. This one seemed more skilled than the others he had fought. It took two counters before he could get in a finisher. The barbarians had brutality on their side, but no skill. Dorren kept close to Sileena, making sure no one could lay any kind of dent on her. She was able to protect herself but she would not kill anyone, and any barbarian could just batter away at the barriers until they were through. The two of them were looking out for each other.

A large group of barbarians charged against them, and Dorren relentlessly fought them off but staggered a few steps back to make sure none would lay a hit on him. He cut through each of them in turn before one wave and then another charged in. A few veered off to fight other opponents nearby, but Dorren was forced to fend off foe after foe. There were so many of them. The forests to the east must have sent every fighter possible as an endless stream of warriors attacked him and his allies close by. The fighting here was thick, and it was not long before Dorren could see the reason why.

A massive cluster of Eceriden forces were converging on a lone robed man. Even from this distance and the robes covering the man he could tell it was Sileena's father. The man was blasting all manner of energy at his opponents, killing them in waves. Anyone caught in the blast disintegrated on the spot. The barbarians had the sense to stay clear as the waves of power would have killed them too. Many magic users were firing energy projectiles at the sorcerer, to no avail. The power of his staff was too great, and even with the protection of combined shields they were quickly overcome and killed. His power was immense. These were not energy blasts, but rather waves that matched no other. And the man was obviously holding back.

By the time Dorren cut through the barbarians Sileena was out of sight. Looking around, he could not see her anywhere. The barbarians must have somehow separated them. Desperate, he quickly moved through two more opponents, trying to find her, but with no success. Turning back to the sorcerer, he could see the man making short work of all those who approached. The ground was in chunks and things were looking dire. Sileena's father turned, ready for any new threat, and spotted Dorren. There was no time to move. There was no time to charge. It took only a second for the man to recognise him, and Nerida did not hesitate as a wave of energy unlike any other hurtled towards Dorren.

"Die!" was all he could hear. He couldn't do anything. Could not leap away, could not block it, and he had no barriers to protect him. He was going to die.

Again time seemed to slow down. His senses enhanced and he could feel the world around him. He could sense the barbarians getting out of the way of the blast. He could sense an Eceriden soldier moving to strike down a barbarian a few metres away, and he could sense the wave of pure energy hurtling towards him. But this was no good to him. He couldn't get out of the way. It was too wide, and the senses did not give him the power to stop this pure energy he had never felt before. He could feel the force moving for him, but as he accepted the outcome he could feel something else. Another energy began to form in front of him. It remained completely still, and held a few metres ahead. The wave crashed into it, causing the ground to crack, but nothing came out the other side. He was alive. An invisible barrier was stopping the unbelievable wave of energy.

His senses detected another individual walking up to him from behind, and he turned to see Sileena stopping in front of him with her determined gaze fixed on her father. Her timing couldn't be more perfect. Dorren had been certain that his life was over.

His senses slowly ebbed and he was back to normal. Sileena? This was horrible. He was safe for the moment but his girl was forced to face her father. She could not have the power to stop him. He was on another level, with the staff he wielded. She could not shield, as shielding used so much more power than it took to attack. She would have to strike back. She would have to kill her own father if she wanted to live.

For a second Nerida took in what had just happened, but once it sank in his expression turned to rage, and without even thinking about his surroundings he fired an ongoing typhoon of magic towards Dorren and Sileena. The man had lost his mind. He was even willing to kill his own daughter. As the wave moved towards them the ground shattered into pieces. Anyone nearby was turned to ash by the mere aura of the wave. Sileena remained determined despite the oncoming power, which would blow a hole in a mountain, crashing towards her. The magical blast hit the barrier she had created and the initial blow made her flinch a little. Dorren could see the barbarians around them turning to dust on the wrong side of the barrier. Sileena had the shield covering the allied forces to avoid them coming to any harm. She was pushing herself too hard. The ongoing magical wave was not stopping. There was no way he could help her as any movement might end in his demise. Looking to Sileena, he could see her initial reticence had gone and had been replaced with renewed determination as she kept the power back. The ground beneath the beam was crumbling. At either side it was shattering into pieces, and the magical energy was causing these pieces to float into the air.

Nerida increased the power of his assault, smashing against the invisible barrier Sileena was holding. Sileena had to fight back, thought Dorren. She was using more power by shielding than her father was by attacking. She was not going to kill her own father, though. She couldn't. Dorren could feel vibrations, and the aura emanating from the magical onslaught was creating a sort of humming noise. For a while nothing seemed to happen, as neither shield nor magical force showed any sign of relenting. But then something unexpected happened.

Sileena took a step forward, and then another, and another. Her shield moved forward along with her as she advanced towards Nerida. Nerida noticed this and seemed to increase the force against her. The barrier remained still, with Sileena's expression full of concentration in her efforts to continue ahead.

She stepped onto the ruined ground and continued her steady walk towards her father, who was practically screaming in frustration. By now all bystanders were standing clear of the catastrophic power emanating from the two combatants. The barrier kept moving slowly towards Nerida, whose mood seemed to go from rage to concern. His attacks started to weaken. He was starting to tire. Dorren could not believe what he was seeing. Sileena was winning.

As the shield drew close enough, it twisted into a sphere that surrounded the man in front and began to get smaller. Nerida released one last great force of energy, and within a moment the magical wave stopped and Nerida collapsed to his knees. Sileena stood over the man, holding the shield around him for a moment before seeing that he was beaten. Letting out a slight, tired breath, she stopped holding the shield, allowing it to disappear.

Dorren slowly approached.

"It's over, Father." Sileena bent down and picked up the staff. She looked at it for a moment as Nerida stared in exhausted rage at her and then Dorren. The fighting was over, Dorren thought. They had actually won.

Sileena smiled at Dorren and handed him the staff. Taking it in hand, he took a moment to inspect the instrument. It didn't seem any different to any other staff he had seen. The carvings were mediocre and lacked any imagination. He couldn't even feel anything when touching it. Did Sileena feel anything? Having given the staff a once-over, it was time to get rid of it. Taking his sword, he swung full force at the staff, breaking it in half. No one was going to use that weapon again. He struck the staff a few more times until it was nothing but twigs. Now it was definitely never going to be used. Without the staff Nerida would not have that kind of power.

There were still a few pockets of fighting around them, but the barbarians that had seen what had happened began to flee the battle.

This caused a chain reaction as many others followed their lead and ran from the field. They had won.

Dorren gave a sigh of relief and turned to embrace Sileena. But Nerida seized his opportunity and braced himself with a point-blank magical shot at Dorren. The man really wanted him dead. Sileena did not see it as her head was facing the other way, and within a second Nerida went from kneeling to attack position. But as he was about to make a strike, Dorren saw the point of a sword burst through his chest. Nerida paused at the realisation. Struggling to keep himself upright, he ended up falling back down to his knees. Sileena noticed what had happened and rushed to her father.

Nerida looked surprised, and a little scared. He was no longer angry. He started to fall back, with Sileena beside him, panicking. For a moment he appeared to come to terms with what had happened, and for a moment he was calm. For a moment he was the man he had been before all this started. He turned to Sileena with a struggle and spoke.

"Sileena. I'm sorry." And he was gone.

"Seriously, I'm amazing." The man who had stabbed Nerida was in a world of his own. Dorren recognised Kradorin from when they had met before. But when the man came back from his own thoughts, he looked down to see Sileena holding her father close with tears streaming down her face, and his expression changed. Kradorin looked completely confused, and glanced at Dorren for answers. Dorren just replied with a look that said, 'I will tell you later.'

For a while everything remained still. Dorren then approached Sileena and laid a hand on her shoulder. It took her a moment to acknowledge it, and she released the man who had spent her entire life being cruel to her, only to show her an ounce of kindness in his dying breath. Dorren did not know what to do, but he didn't have to do anything as she turned to hug him. A little time would be required to recover from this catastrophe.

# 16

# CLOSURE

Apart from small pockets of resistance the fight was over. Most of the Eceriden forces and Outcasts were either healing the injured or moving bodies. Others were getting treatment and wandering the field. The once grassy plains had turned to a muddy wasteland. Despite the great victory very few understood the aftermath and the loss.

Dorren was approached by Kradorin, and another who he would soon find out to be the king of Eceriden. Dorren explained to the Eceriden king who he and the Outcasts were and why they were helping. Kradorin seemed more interested than the king when they found out that these were the Outcasts.

"I see."

Dorren knew he was not the right person to speak to.

"You are better off speaking to one of the leaders. They are the ones who do these kinds of talks."

"Can you point to where these leaders are?" asked the king of Eceriden. The man seemed a little uncomfortable speaking to Dorren. Probably due to the fact that he was speaking to someone representing the people his country had kicked out for not having the same faith, and the king held as much faith as the rest of them. But the king was only showing slight discomfort so he was doing really well. Kradorin however seemed completely unfazed, just smiling and very much eager. Whatever it was the man was eager for would have to wait.

"I don't know where they are."

"I do!" A voice came from behind Dorren as another Outcast ran up to join them. Dorren did not recognise him. He must be from one of the other Undergrounds.

The king and Kradorin beckoned to him and he led them away towards where the Underground leaders must be. Behind the king were a few guardsmen keeping a close watch on the situation. Apparently, despite the Outcasts having come to their rescue, the Eceridens still didn't trust them. But they seemed to be open to talks and that was certainly something.

Dorren looked around and spotted Sileena with the great wolf Vartak. She had her hand resting gently on its head, and gave the beast a gentle nod. The great wolf's expression was blank as it stared into her golden eyes. It might have been some sort of psychic communion or just a simple look, but something seemed to pass between the two. The moment passed and the beast gave a howl as loud as any before. Many people around were startled by the sudden noise. The great beast then turned and sprinted away. The other wolves quickly followed as they raced back towards their forest. Dorren stood at Sileena's side as their gaze followed the animals until they disappeared over the hill. Dorren looked on until the last one was gone.

"What happened?" He couldn't help himself. His curiosity was just too great.

"I said thank you." Sileena was also looking towards the now-empty hill where the great animals once stood.

"I wonder what happens now," said Dorren. Duka may still be in the grip of the barbarians. Were any left behind? And what would happen between these kingdoms? Maybe there would be some clever talks instead of another war. The last thing they need was another fight. Eceriden were rich but even they might struggle to come back from this. Sileena also seemed to be thinking the same thing.

"The sanctuary," she said.

Dorren looked to Sileena with an odd expression. Why mention the sanctuary?

"Dorren, let's go back. It doesn't have to be there specifically, but somewhere like that."

Dorren did find that an appealing thought in itself, but what about the people, his friends? They had lost too much to just go back.

"Sileena, I would love to but we should help rebuild. We can't abandon anyone when they need us most."

Sileena gave him an angry look and punched him on the shoulder. "I don't mean now, and it won't be forever. I mean afterwards, and it doesn't have to be far from those close to us. Just think about it."

"OK, I will." But Dorren had already made up his mind. After they had helped rebuild he would go with Sileena back to the sanctuary. Goodness knows it was safe now that the wolves would not attack, or so he presumed. When he was there was one of the times he felt at peace. Perhaps a prolonged time there would do him some good. Sileena gave one of her warm smiles and the two of them continued through the battlefield, looking for anyone they could recognise. It was not long before they spotted, to their great relief, two of their closest friends. Gabe gave a gentle smile, waved at the sight of them and beckoned. Anna was sitting on the ground next to him, which made them look even more ridiculous as far as the height difference between them was concerned. The girl looked completely worn out but alive and well. She must have overextended herself. It was a concern that Dorren had as she was the type to do that, but at least Gabe was there to help.

The group exchanged greetings as though they had not seen each other in over a year. Talks went from 'how are you?' to how the two sides had fared in battle.

"Where is Derain?" asked Dorren, looking to see if he was near. But when he saw the looks on Anna's and Gabe's faces he realised he didn't need to look around. He was gone?

"How?" No, not another. This was not fair. They thought they had lost everything, but the universe took a little more just to prove you wrong.

It was Anna who spoke up. "I couldn't protect him. I lost all my power."

"This isn't the place for blame Anna, you clearly tried," Dorren replied. Judging from her state there really was nothing more she could have done. Dorren gave Gabe a questioning look as if to ask what happened. Gabe seemed to understand.

"Lockarr," he said. Lockarr?! He was in the battle?

"Did someone get him?" He must have died. The battle was won so he should be lying dead somewhere.

"He left the battle. We were surrounded. I couldn't stop it." Even Gabe was being hard on himself.

"Which way did he go?"

Gabe pointed south, back towards Duka. The man was going to get away. The man who destroyed his home. The man who pretended to be their friend for years, claiming his manipulations to be fun. The man who killed Dorren's father, and now the man who had killed one of his best friends. Dorren had thought he would see him when they took back the Underground, but Lockarr would not be there.

Quickly looking around, Dorren saw a horse without a rider, eating away at one of the few patches of grass left after the battle. Running towards it, he jumped on and turned to head south.

"Dorren, what are you doing?!" Sileena cried. Gabe ran after him.

"We need to catch him. I have to stop him."

"I will come with you and keep you protected," said Sileena calmly. Gabe also looked ready to join him, but Anna was in no condition to move. Dorren glanced around but could not see any other horses.

"This horse will not be able to carry two at the speed or distance needed. See if you can find other horses and then follow behind."

Sileena nodded and ran off. Gabe took Anna's hand and kissed it before he too went off looking for a horse.

"I will be fine. Go," Anna said.

Dorren nodded, and with a gentle tap on the horse's side sped south in hopes of catching the bastard. Lockarr was a psychopath who had tormented and destroyed lives. If he was allowed to disappear he would do it to someone else, or he might even return and take more. Dorren followed the road, leaving the battlefield behind. He could make out the tracks, but most were from the army when they marched north. He just had to hope that Lockarr would not leave the road, and that he did not reach Duka before he could catch him. But what then? Lockarr beat him in their last duel. Well, Dorren was not going to lose this time. Hopefully Gabe and Sileena could arrive in time and together they could beat him. Sileena might not have had the will to kill Lockarr but she could keep them protected. Lockarr would not have that same protection. But Dorren could not wait for them. He would just have to catch Lockarr and hold him until his friends arrived. Now it was time to end things properly.

The sight of smoke ahead indicated life. It was a good sign that Dorren was on the right trail. But as he drew nearer he made out a town that was further ahead. His heart sank as he realised he was looking at the aftermath of the community being burnt down. When the barbarians marched north they must have put every town to the torch. Most of the inhabitants would have been killed. It would take a lot of effort for Eceriden to come back from this. Duka was already in a dire situation. The whole world would need to stick together to bring themselves back up. Hopefully those in charge would see that too.

Dorren slowed to a trot as he entered the town. Some of the buildings were still smoking. As he moved through the streets he could see the bodies of people who had been mutilated. Good riddance to the barbarians who committed such atrocities. Some might have escaped. Let's hope they knew their way back to their forests where they could hide. Some might continue to rampage through the country, and become another problem for Eceriden to deal with.

Looking down the main street, Dorren could make out several figures and horses that seemed to be moving. As he drew nearer the men noticed him, and grabbed their weapons. They must have been some of the escaped barbarians.

Dorren stopped and got off his horse, drawing his own weapon. Walking closer, he gradually began to make them out, and amongst them a familiar figure appeared. Lockarr.

"Lockarr!" Dorren didn't really have anything else to say. But at least it grabbed the man's attention.

Lockarr looked in his direction and smiled as he realised who it was. "Dorren? Is that you? I never thought I would see you here. But then again, I didn't expect to see your friends on the field. Tell me, how is good old Derain getting on?"

Dorren almost lost control of himself at those words, but quickly pulled himself back in. The man was taunting him. He would not let him get into his head. He just needed to keep him here until his friends arrived.

"I think you know, Lockarr."

The barbarians were in battle stances in front of Lockarr. He must be their leader. Dorren counted seven of them. None seemed to be hiding anywhere else. They were not smart enough to do anything like that.

"You thought you would run and get away. I didn't think you were a coward!"

Lockarr remained as calm as ever. "You misunderstand. I left because I got what I wanted. The fight was fun but I wanted to do something else. I thought I would go to Duka."

"Why Duka?"

Lockarr seemed perplexed by the question, as though the answer was obvious. "I want to see those blood sacrifices they do. Maybe I could help. They would probably like that."

Dorren knew that was not everything Lockarr had in store. "You will not reach Duka. I will make sure of that."

"Dorren, you could not beat me before. And now you are out-numbered. It is an unfair situation. Did you know that when you stab a noble they die the same as a commoner?"

Had the man completely lost it? But thinking back, Dorren could see the signs, like how nothing seemed to bother him and his disturbing curiosity. Lockarr was always like this. How did he never notice?

"If you think that it's an unfair fight then you won't be so cowardly as to run off again."

Lockarr shook his head. "You still don't understand. And you are my friend. I will not fight you right now. I will be waiting in that building. Once you have killed these men you can come in."

Lockarr then walked into the structure that stood next to the group of men. The man considered Dorren a friend? Or was that another taunt? There was no way of understanding why Lockarr was like that. It would take a madman to understand another madman.

Dorren steadily walked up to the barbarians as they all rushed him with their weapons in the air. He effortlessly killed the first two before the others got close. The following two soon perished as they were not fast enough to land a single blow. The final three managed to get in a couple of strikes which were all parried quickly, and in turn each fell to the ground, dead. Lockarr must have known that these men could not beat Dorren. He just didn't care.

Looking at the building that must be some sort of tavern, Dorren guessed. It looked like it was pretty much untouched by the fires. It had probably not been deliberately avoided, but was just lucky to survive the burning around it.

When he entered his guesses were confirmed as he could see tables and chairs all around the room. It was a place for people to come at night and drink away their problems. Looking around, he made out the figure casually sitting in a chair in the middle of the room.

"Ah, very good. You seem barely scratched. Now it can be a fair fight. I'm curious: are you the type to cower when you realise you are about to die?"

Dorren stared intently at Lockarr, who seemed completely unfazed by it.

"No, I'm pretty sure you're the kind of person to just give up. What if I give you some incentive? If I kill you I promise to not go to Duka. Instead I will go after Sileena and I will find out what kind of person she is as she dies."

Enough. That man had had enough time to speak. Dorren knew he should just keep him talking until his friends arrived but Lockarr had crossed Dorren's threshold. His anger shot through him like fire.

Dorren raised his sword and knife and charged. Lockarr got off his seat without hesitation and drew his own dual swords. The two clashed weapons faster than any other known fighter. Dorren went to strike Lockarr, who countered and proceeded to stab at his torso. Dorren again blocked the oncoming strike and went for a flurry of attacks. For the most part Lockarr remained on the defensive as he dodged and countered. He was only occasionally able to get in an attempted strike, which was usually parried or dodged.

Eventually Lockarr managed to force Dorren back. The fight seemed to mimic the one in the Underground where he was unable to keep up with Lockarr. But he would not let this happen again.

Dorren quickly jumped onto one of the tables to maintain the high ground. However Lockarr was too quick and kicked the table, causing Dorren to roll back towards the stairs to the second level. Taking his first step onto the stairs, Dorren tried to maintain the elevation advantage. But Lockarr continued to make a series of strikes that caused Dorren to take one step back after another. What could he do? Even with the high ground Dorren was being forced up the stairs. Lockarr was a master swordsman wielding dual swords. Dorren's short reach with his knife was hampering him a bit. The only real strikes he could make were with his sword, as any attempts with the knife failed to reach their target. Dorren's rage began to subside and he began to try an organised approach, attempting to read Lockarr's moves.

Lockarr saw Dorren's approach change and reacted in kind, delivering a series of blows against Dorren's torso. Dorren countered them but Lockarr seized his opportunity and stabbed at Dorren's legs, cutting them. Dorren staggered back and, reaching the top of the staircase, moved onto the balcony above the bar.

Locker casually walked forward and the fight began anew as they exchanged one blow after another in a battle equal to none. Not a word was said as they were both focused on the task at hand. Dorren knew that despite Lockarr being more skilled, his opponent had never fought anyone as good as he, and so even Lockarr had to focus. But his focus was paying off as Dorren was unable to land a single blow onto him. The man was untouchable. But Dorren wasn't, as occasionally Lockarr managed to graze him in one spot or cut him in another. He was losing the fight and could not seem to come back. However, this time he was managing to hold his position instead of being pushed back. But this was costing him in the series of cuts on his arms, legs and torso. Desperately, Dorren rolled back in an effort to get away from Lockarr, and as soon as he was on his feet he threw his knife at Lockarr's head.

The knife sped through the air and ended up embedded in the wall further back as Lockarr managed to move his head just in time, and was upon Dorren with a few more blows. But without his knife Dorren was in worse shape than before.

Resorting to punches and kicks as well as stabs, the fight became more of a brawl. Lockarr managed to counter the blows and then used the handles of his blades and succeeded in getting a clear shot at Dorren's face, knocking him sideways into the rail. Dorren went to counter the next blow but didn't realise until it was too late that Lockarr was instead going for a kick, which landed right on target. Dorren was smashed through the railing and fell to the floor, falling through a table. The blow completely dazed him, and he was down. He could feel the blood coming out of his mouth.

Trying to stand, he managed to only get to his knees feebly. He tried to look around, but his vision was blurry. He was beaten. His opponent had tricked him his entire life. The man he was trying to find, who had killed his father. He was right under his nose the entire time, and even when it was all figured out he still couldn't win.

Dorren coughed a little in his attempt to sigh. The man was deranged. He understood that. Lockarr reached the bottom of the stairs and casually walked towards Dorren.

"Dorren, there are none other than myself who can match your skill. But I have trained in this art for a long time. Longer than you. Now tell me. What kind of person are you when you are about to reach death?"

What kind of person was he? He was a man who was at peace. There was no need to worry anymore. The problems of this world were no longer his.

"Just kill me." Yes, release him. He knew Lockarr would not be able to touch Sileena. He knew that everyone would be fine. This world would be fine. So what if Lockarr got away? He was just a sad man who couldn't grasp the concept of life. He lacked any real understanding. And besides, the next world would be nice as well.

Dorren's thoughts went to Sileena. I am sorry I can't be with you. It is not fair but stay strong. I will see you in our next life. And closing his eyes, Dorren felt at peace.

Lockarr stood in front of him and raised his sword. Dorren could feel it. He could sense it. He could sense chairs and tables around him. He could sense the spider moving in the corner of the room. The unusual sensation was coming to him as strongly as ever. Then he understood.

This power was not stopped by danger. It was never that. It was peace. Dorren knew why these strange experiences were happening. Thinking back to the time he felt this strange sensation when he and his friends were talking in the eatery, he felt calm. He felt completely at peace, accepting the world around him. The same way he accepted that his fate was sealed when Nerida shot at him, and the time he managed to catch the arrow. That was the answer. To have a completely clear mind. Time seemed to slow down around him as he felt born anew. As Dorren gently leaned his head to the side, Lockarr's sword narrowly missed its target.

But now Dorren understood it all. He understood this gift and he let it continue as he pulled himself up to block the sword moving slowly towards him. He then proceeded to kick forward while using his sword to block the attempted counter. The blow struck its target, which knocked his adversary back a few steps. Drawing a slow breath in, Dorren opened his eyes.

Things were no longer blurry, but as clear as ever. He could see everything perfectly, including Lockarr, who was charging at him with swords raised. Right then. Time for round three.

Lockarr lunged his sword forward but did not hit home, as Dorren used his one and only sword to block every strike that he could sense coming. The fight shifted, as it was now Lockarr who was trying desperately to hit something. Dorren countered one blow; then the next, and then proceeded to send out a few strikes of his own. Lockarr could not counter them all and one grazed his arm. Then came another series of strikes between the two before Dorren caught Lockarr's leg. Then his arm again. Then his torso. Lockarr seemed utterly perplexed by this sudden change. The man had lost his cool as he tried to grasp the situation.

You will never understand. The fight was over and he still did not understand.

Lockarr used his dual swords into a spinning motion, trying to get one in. But this left him open and Dorren countered a couple of the strikes until the opening cleared and he thrust his sword into Lockarr's leg. The man stopped his strikes and fell to his knees.

For a moment everything was silent. Lockarr was confused as he tried to take in what had happened. Dorren moved in closer as Lockarr made more attempts at besting him. Another couple of strikes later and Dorren managed to get Lockarr to drop his swords by inflicting a couple of cuts to his arms. For a moment everything went silent as Lockarr grasped the situation and frowned at Dorren.

"How? How did you do that?"

Dorren stood over the beaten man. "You will never know."

Lockarr only managed to shout, "Wait!" before the sword connected with his neck and his head was severed from his body. It was not for the sake of revenge. That no longer mattered. It was for closure. It was over. He looked at the motionless body on the floor and let out a breath.

There was nothing more to torment him. Moving outside, he took in the sunlight for a moment as he realised how badly injured he was. His leg got a sudden, sharp pain. The adrenaline in his system was no longer making him immune to the pain, and he quickly sat down. Taking a moment to nurse his leg, he could hear the sounds of horses.

What brilliant timing. Just leave me to do the work and then arrive.

Looking up, he could make out three horses coming round the corner. Sileena was riding at the head of the procession, Gabe behind her and Pagar taking the rear. Anna must be back on the field, recovering from her exhaustion.

But things were not over. He would need time to recover, and then it would be time to fix things. It was time to help fix the world.

# EPILOGUE

Fetching water from the nearby river for the last time, thought Dorren. It was an exciting thought. Being around the flowing water relaxed him, and it helped when he shifted into the state where he could sense the world around him. Once he had figured how to use this gift it had not taken long for him to perfect it. Clearing his mind allowed him to sense the world around him, and he often went into this state just for fun. But today was different. This time he would reflect on the events before rather than his usual practice of his unique power.

It had been a year since Nerida's invasion, and the war. Since then the world had gone through a faster change than had been witnessed in generations. The first thing to happen was that the Eceriden forces, or what was left of them, marched south and liberated Duka from the few barbarians that remained. They released the old king's brother and he became the new king of Duka. This removed any remaining threats but at that point the world was still in a state of loss, and Duka was in the same condition as before the war. Negotiations between the kingdoms lasted a couple of months before terms could be met. Thankfully the new king of Duka was a much more reasonable man. In the meantime, the Eceridens were doing their best, with the help of their allies, to feed other communities. With the new trade routes to Duka, people's lives were gradually improving. Soon Duka would be able to maintain itself again. The Eceriden king was a very forgiving person to let Duka's actions slide so easily. But that was not up to Dorren to decide. Through the Eceriden's king's actions, everything was back to a state of peace.

Kradorin was given all sorts of medals and awards after the battle in recognition of the heroic feats he had accomplished.

The Outcasts also helped with rebuilding homes, and after speaking with the leaders, both kings agreed to allow the Outcasts to name their newly founded nation. The so-called Outcasts' home was no longer seen as a piece of forgotten land void from everything else. It and the Outcasts were now considered part of the world, and free to travel it if they so desired. Dorren, however, was a little disappointed. He would have thought that with Eceriden's riches they might have given some to the Outcasts. But the Eceridens had used all their wealth trying to help with the world's problems, so Dorren understood why they didn't give some riches to them. Besides, they were able to fulfil their longstanding dream in the end.

Eceriden and Duka also sent many magic users to help raise the swamp out of the ground. But it was really through Sileena's power that this endeavour became successful. The land lifted to match the cliff's height and through a force of power never before seen the earth hardened and their country almost doubled in size. It took a few days to accomplish this goal and by the end of it even Sileena had collapsed, exhausted. But it was a worthwhile feat.

Once this was completed the Outcasts proceeded to reclaim their Underground, and a few others joined them as they began anew. Anna and Gabe also returned to their home. Sileena and Dorren remained in the Underground for a little time to make sure things were in order. But once all affairs were settled they told Pagar that they were going to stay at the sanctuary, and for many months Dorren and Sileena lived there. Occasionally Pagar or Anna and Gabe would visit, or Sileena and Dorren would return to the Underground, even if just to say hello. And of course, they did not miss a single important meeting, or the Reunion.

Holding a full bucket at either side of him, Dorren hauled his own weight in water up the bank. He made his way towards the sanctuary where Sileena was sitting and playing with some of the little forest animals. She smiled when she saw him coming back up the path.

"Well, it is about time."

Dorren almost dropped the buckets of water. "Would you like to do this?" he exclaimed, regaining his posture as some of the water spilled out.

Sileena gave him a challenging look. "OK." And with a glance at the buckets, she lifted them out of Dorren's hands and they floated lazily through the air, landing in front of her. "Done."

He should have seen that one coming. There was no challenging the girl. She had acquired a lot of her newer qualities from Anna. Sighing, he sat next to her, taking her hand in his. Now it was just time to wait. They were always late. He had told them countless times and even now they were late. But he didn't have time to go over this again as he could see three figures coming along the path towards them.

Anna waved as she approached. The girl was back to her old self, eager and full of authority. Sileena might have been more powerful but even she would not go against Anna's word. Gabe followed with a gentle smile. Back at the Underground the two of them had made a new group of friends, with Anna at the head as usual. Dorren and Sileena joined them whenever they visited but the four of them were always the closest. Going through life-changing experiences did that to people.

Gabe held a massive pack over his shoulder while Anna carried a couple more items. It was obvious that her lover was holding most of her stuff. Ninety per cent of the items they carried were probably Anna's.

And of course, the man following behind Anna and Gabe. Pagar waved pleasantly as he approached.

"Well, have you actually packed yet?" asked Pagar. It was a genuine question. Pagar was still the father figure. Dorren was in his mid-twenties living an independent life and Pagar was still making sure he'd packed everything. Dorren was certainly proud to call him Father. In his mind of course, because it would be weird to change now after so many years of calling him Pagar.

"Yes, everything is ready. Anyone want a drink before we head off?" asked Dorren, and it was again Pagar who replied.

"Yes, thank you." Pagar was not going to let them get away just yet. And so the group shared fruit and drinks of water as they laughed and talked together, catching up on recent events; remembering the not-so-recent events and speculating over a couple of philosophical issues like whether or not Gabe could fit more than three pieces of fruit in his mouth. They laughed and joked for a time and before long the morning turned to afternoon and it was time to leave. If they did not, they would not reach their first destination in time.

Dorren and Sileena had decided a month before that they wanted to travel, now that they were free to do so. They could explore the world and see the amazing things it had to offer. The first plan was to head into the northern forests. When the two of them told Gabe and Anna they at first tried to stop them. But after a little discussion they jumped at the chance of coming along too Dorren and Sileena happily accepted their company on this adventure. Pagar, however, had to maintain an Underground and so he had only come to say farewell.

"I wish you all the best," said Pagar as he took Dorren into an embrace. It was nice but a little embarrassing. No one else was getting these hugs, and he was sure Anna and Sileena were going to mock him on the first leg of their journey.

"Thank you. You take care too."

The two released each other and took a couple of steps back. There was no point delaying it anymore, and so Dorren moved away to join the others.

"We will return!" shouted Dorren.

Pagar waved from the sanctuary. "I know. See you after your journey! Tell me how it goes."

And with one last wave Dorren turned and looked to the world ahead. Granted, it was still the forest but his senses showed him more of it than ever before, and there was so much more that lay beyond. The mountains of the north, Eceriden and Duka. And here he was with his two closest friends and the girl he loved. He would not want it any other way.

# ACKNOWLEDGEMENTS

*The Outcasts* is something I had been working on for years, starting it while I was still in the academy and finishing it after graduating from uni. Over the years so many people have helped in various ways. I wish I could name everyone but that list would end up being longer than the book. So instead I will simply say thank you to everyone who have helped in small ways over the years. The support I have received from you have been a great inspiration. There are some people I would like to personally thank.

Firstly I'd like to thank Linda Wood. Linda was the first to read through the first couple of chapters and give constructive feedback. It helped me during my first edit and for the first time I could see the story through someone else's perspective.

I would also like to thank Nick Lewis for his moral support over the years. We bounced many ideas off each other. We discussed my book at great lengths countlessly and has been an incredibly supportive friend. Thank you.

Third is Alexandra Allen, who read through the entire novel, giving feedback on story and grammar. She took out so much of her time to go through this novel and I am unbelievably grateful for her support on this project.

Next would like to thank Michal Pietrucin. A friend who is also a talented artist. He is the creator of the wonderful cover illustration for my book and I would recommend him to anyone looking for an artist on his own website, Mewome Imaginative Studio.

I also really want to thank SilverWood Books for their support. Helen, Rowena and their team have been incredibly helpful over the several months' process as we edited and worked over the book and have helped me with publishing it.

Finally I would like to thank my mum. You was there from the beginning and were the first to read through the whole book and give feedback throughout. It is because of you that I am here now and could not have gotten this far without your support.

Lightning Source UK Ltd.
Milton Keynes UK
UKOW01f1134011116

286610UK00004B/139/P